THE RANCHER'S
SECRET SON

BY
SARA ORWIG

MILLS &
BOON

Published in Great Britain 2015
by Mills & Boon, an imprint of Harlequin (UK) Limited,
Eton House, 18-24 Paradise Road, Richmond, Surrey, TW9 1SR

© 2015 Sara Orwig

ISBN: 978-0-263-25290-3

51-1215

Harlequin (UK) Limited's policy is to use papers that are natural, renewable and recyclable products and made from wood grown in sustainable forests. The logging and manufacturing processes conform to the legal environmental regulations of the country of origin.

Printed and bound in Spain
by CPI, Barcelona

Sara Orwig lives in Oklahoma. She has a patient husband who will take her on research trips anywhere, from big cities to old forts. She is an avid collector of Western history books. With a master's degree in English, Sara has written historical romance, mainstream fiction and contemporary romance. Books are beloved treasures that take Sara to magical worlds, and she loves both reading and writing them.

With many thanks to Stacy Boyd,
who made this book possible.

Also thank you to Maureen Walters,
and with love to my family.

One

Nick Milan looked at the small white business card attached to the contract on his desk, and a shock ran through him. Just like last night, when he'd first seen it, he was shaken clear to his core.

"Claire Prentiss."

Just saying the name brought a shadowy image to his mind. An image of a willowy, black-haired, brown-eyed beauty writhing in his arms. The mental picture tortured him, and he pushed the card to the back of his desk. It was almost time to meet his client for what should have been a routine real estate closing. With Claire as the broker, however, it would be far from routine.

The depth of his reaction to the prospect of seeing her again shocked him. It had been four years since he'd held her, four years since he'd been in love with her. Four years since she had rejected his marriage proposal and they'd gone their separate ways. For a long time after the bitter fight that had led to their breakup he'd been hurt and angry with Claire. But that was over. So, why was he still affected by the mere sight of her name?

Claire Prentiss was part of his past now, he tried telling himself. Out of his life for years. She was probably married with kids, helping her grandfather run his real estate agency and still using her maiden name because of business.

Judging by the way his hand shook as he turned his wrist to check his watch, he needed more convincing.

Nick picked up the contract and placed it in his briefcase, snapping it shut the way he wished he could shut out the painful memories of Claire. He had to now. He had work to do.

As he drove to his appointment, he forced himself to focus on the closing, which he wished now he had never agreed to do. But it was for a friend. Paul Smith had called late yesterday afternoon, suddenly deciding he needed his attorney present. Nick had agreed, not knowing Claire would be involved. Why would he? She was a Houston broker. What was she doing closing a deal in Dallas? His friend had sent the contract to Nick's office immediately after the call, but Nick had been too busy to read it until evening which is why he'd taken it home with him. If it hadn't been close to midnight and way too late for his friend to get another attorney, he would have backed out there and then.

He'd spent a sleepless night dreading this meeting and being tormented by memories that would best be forgotten.

In minutes he parked the car and stepped out into a chilly, brisk December wind that whipped through the tall buildings in downtown Dallas. Entering the lobby of one of the office towers, he met up with Paul and shook hands, swallowing the words he longed to say: *Get another lawyer to represent you.* Instead, together they rode the elevator to a commercial real estate office on the twenty-seventh floor.

As they entered through the double glass doors, Bruce Jernigan, the agent who represented the buyer, came forward to meet them.

"If you gentlemen will come this way, we'll get started. As you know, the seller was hospitalized and could not appear, so she has legal representation in her real estate broker." He led them down a long corridor to the conference room, where he opened a door onto a room with dark wood paneling.

Nick's gaze went to Claire instantly. Standing beside the table, she gripped it as her eyes widened and all color left her face. He realized she hadn't known he would attend the meeting until this moment. While he wasn't as shocked as Claire appeared to be, his insides clutched. He felt as if the breath had been punched from his lungs. As he approached and extended his hand, he couldn't drag his eyes from her. At twenty-four she had been beautiful. Now she was breathtaking.

Regaining her poise, she pulled down the jacket of her tailored navy business suit, then shook his hand. "So, we meet again." Her voice hid the tremble he felt in her fingers before she pulled away. "It's nice to see you again, Nick. Mr. Jernigan had just started to tell me that the buyer was bringing an attorney. I had no idea it would be you."

The moment their hands touched, he'd felt an electric current, another reaction that surprised him. Since losing Karen and their unborn baby two years ago, he had been numb around women, his heart shut away, even his physical urges flatlined. Until now. Seeing Claire elicited emotional and physical responses that shook him. He wanted neither of those reactions.

As he moved to a chair beside his client, his gaze roamed over Claire. Tall, with dark brown eyes and raven locks that fell to her shoulders, Claire looked more sophisticated than when he had known her years ago. He didn't have to look at the label to know she wore a designer suit. When her jacket swung open as she sat, her waist looked as tiny as he remembered.

"Let's get down to business." Mr. Jernigan's voice cut into his thoughts.

For the next half hour it was an effort to concentrate on business and not study Claire or let his thoughts drift to the past. He was grateful for a short break while they waited for copies to be made of various documents. He stepped out of the room to check with his office and take calls, then returned, walking to the table where Claire again stood.

When she reached for a glass, he picked up the water pitcher. She glanced up at him and he felt another electrifying tingle as her gaze met his. Smiling at her, he steadied her hand and poured her water, aware of his fingers over her warm, slender hand.

"Thank you," she said.

"So, you're still working at your grandfather's agency," Nick said, recalling how dedicated she had been to her family and assuming she still was. "Is he as active?"

She shook her head. "No, Grandpa's had a heart attack and another little stroke. He had been grooming me to take over the agency for a long time, and I did so a couple of years ago."

"It was a good thing you're loyal and stuck with your family. How's the business going?"

"Fine," she said, smiling slightly. "I'm happy that the business has grown and we have a lot of good listings. I suppose your parents, especially your dad, are pleased with your legal and political career."

"Yes, they are. Especially my dad. So you know I'm in the Texas legislature?"

"Yes. You do make the papers now and then," she said, her cheeks getting slightly more rosy. Was she embarrassed for him to discover she had kept up with his career? He was pleased she had, even though he had always tried to push thoughts of her aside and to avoid knowing much about her.

"You look great," he said, smiling at her, and she smiled in return, a cool smile, yet it sent another wave of longing crashing over him.

"Thank you. I'm sure you enjoy being a Texas State Representative. I know the Texas legislature isn't in session until January, so do you live here in Dallas when you're not in Austin?"

"Yes." He glanced over her head to see everyone returning to the table and he knew soon they would be through and she would be gone.

He didn't know what prompted the feeling, but he didn't want to part. As he glanced back at her, her thickly lashed eyes were gazing at him, making his pulse quicken. Impulsively, he said, "Come to dinner with me tonight and we can catch up."

Her eyes widened. "Do you think that will be of concern to your wife?"

He felt as if he had suffered a blow to his solar plexus. Drawing in a tight breath, he said, "I didn't realize that you didn't know… I'm widowed. My wife was killed in a car wreck two years ago. She was pregnant."

All color drained from Claire's face as her eyes opened wider, looking enormous and panic-stricken, a reaction that shocked him. A visible tremor ran through her and she put a hand on the table to steady herself. He reached out to grab her arm. Odd, he thought. Why would she have such a profound reaction to the news that he was a widower?

"Are you all right?"

Instantly her face flushed and she appeared to pull herself together. She withdrew her arm from his grasp and stood up straight. "Yes. Sorry, it's just…personal. I—" She seemed to think better of what she was about to say and changed her course, giving him a pat response. "I'm sorry for your loss."

He became aware that everyone was getting seated around the table and their time together was over. "Come to dinner with me. It'll be an early evening."

She stared at him so long he wondered whether she heard him, but then she nodded. "Yes. I'll give you my cell phone number after the meeting. We better sit now, because the others are waiting."

While she moved away from him, he saw the color slowly return to her face. He sat down, stacking papers in front of him, but nothing could keep him from wondering about her strong reaction.

What had happened in her life? Had she been in love with someone who was also killed? He couldn't guess why he had gotten such a startling response from her to the news that he had lost Karen and his unborn baby. Tonight he would probably hear why, over dinner.

An hour later, the closing was finalized. As everyone milled around and talked, Nick circled the table to Claire.

She held out a piece of paper. "Here's my cell phone number and the hotel where I'm staying."

"How's seven?"

"That's fine, Nick," she said. "I—"

His cell phone buzzed and he held up his index finger to get her to wait a second. He needed to take the call. In two minutes, when he turned back around, Claire was gone.

Nick finished up with his client, then he returned to the office and was inundated with calls. It was after five before he had a chance to think about the evening and Claire. Now he wondered why he had asked her to dinner in the first place. Their parting four years ago had been so painful, so final. Why was he putting himself in a position to relive those agonizing moments? It still hurt to think back to that time in his life. He'd been so driven to succeed in his career and in politics—was even more so now—and he'd needed a wife who, above all else, supported him in those goals, even if it meant leaving behind her own family obligations. Claire had been deeply involved in her family and their lives had been her priority—and apparently they still were, seeing as how she had taken over the agency from her grandfather.

Nothing had changed.

Tonight he'd make their dinner short. A brief catch-up and then goodbye. It was all he could handle.

Claire ordered flowers for her client and had a congratulatory note attached. It wasn't until she was back in her hotel room and had texted her client that she had a moment to think about the events of the day and her upcoming dinner date.

Instantly, she thought about Nick's news that he was a widower. She could hear his voice. "*I didn't realize that you didn't know... I'm widowed. My wife was killed in a car wreck two years ago. She was pregnant.*"

Nick's wife and unborn baby had been killed. When he announced that, Claire's head had spun and for a moment she'd thought she was going to faint. She wished with her whole heart she had never come to Dallas. Claire ran her hand across her eyes and sighed. She had never dreamed she would encounter Nick.

Why had she agreed to go to dinner with him? Tears stung her eyes. She didn't want to get involved with him again—yet she had no choice. She still hurt over the breakup with him four years ago. Nick hadn't understood her family obligations then. He had simply wanted her to leave them behind to devote her life to him. She'd had to walk away and she didn't want to draw him back into her life now, when she faced life-changing problems far worse than she'd faced before.

She picked up her purse and took out her wallet.

Her heart twisted as she looked at the picture of her son. Nick's son. The child Nick knew nothing about. She looked into the same blue eyes beneath the same dark brown hair as Nick's. She had once loved his father with her whole heart, until their breakup had torn her to pieces. After their breakup she had learned she was carrying Nick's baby.

She hadn't told him right away because she'd needed time to make decisions. Their last time together had been painful, filled with terrible accusations that couldn't be taken back. The memories echoed in her mind even now. He had proposed and she had asked him how they would ever work out being married when she had to take care of her ailing mother and help her grandfather with his business in Houston. Nick had expected her to move to Washington, DC, to be the society wife he had dreamed about—something she could never be.

Nick had accused her of being so wrapped up in her family she couldn't love anyone else. But it wasn't like that at all. Her mother had been diagnosed with Parkinson's and her grandfather had suffered a mild stroke. They needed her the same way Nick needed his father's approval.

She could almost hear herself say those words to him. She accused him of going into law only because of a family tradition. All Milan males had become lawyers. Yet he couldn't see that he was more tied to his family than she was to hers.

Her last night with Nick had been bitter and hurtful, each of them flinging accusations until he had stormed out, slamming the door, and she had let him go, knowing it was over forever between them. Brokenhearted, she had cried most of that night and for days afterward. The memories still hurt and she didn't want to ever go through that pain again.

After their breakup Nick didn't try to call and she didn't want to talk to him. Then she discovered she was pregnant. Hurting, still angry with him, she'd planned to tell him about her pregnancy, but it was easier to keep quiet and avoid another confrontation. Nick would only push harder for marriage. He'd have to, as an out-of-wedlock baby would hurt his political future.

While she was thinking about how to tell him she was pregnant and what she would do about it in the future, time slipped past. From a friend she heard that Nick had gotten engaged. Shocked and angry with him, she was hurt badly that he had rushed into marriage with someone else so soon after breaking up with her. She'd decided to keep quiet about his child. He would marry and have his own family, and he didn't need to know about the baby she carried. Nick had made his choice, so she would go on with her life just as he had gone on with his.

Until now. Now he had lost his wife and their unborn child. For the first time since she had learned of her pregnancy she felt compelled to tell Nick about his son. In spite of the angry words, hurt feelings, the bitterness and heartbreak between them when they parted, she had to let him know he had a child. How they would work out sharing a son, she didn't know. But she knew it wasn't right to keep his son a secret when Nick had already lost one child.

Standing, she retrieved her phone and called home, wanting desperately to talk to Cody. Her grandmother answered and Claire felt like a child again, wanting to blurt out her problem and have her support and her wisdom. But she was grown now and she tried to shelter her grandmother from worries instead of taking them home to her. Grandma would have to know about this soon enough, but she didn't have to hear about it while Claire was halfway across the state of Texas.

She asked to talk to Cody. Just hearing his voice, she wished she could reach through the phone and hug him.

She talked to him about bugs and his fish tank—his two favorite topics. Then she talked briefly to Irene, his nanny, who was there two days a week and whenever Claire left town. She talked again to her grandmother, for almost an hour before she finally told them goodbye. When she ended the call, she burst into tears. The reality of her situation was too much to bear. Nick was so close to his dad, so tied into his own family, that she was certain he would want his son in his life. She would have to share Cody with Nick. But how?

For a long time she had tried to avoid thinking about Nick, but seeing him today, realizing she would have to bring him into her life and her family's lives, she could not keep him out of her thoughts. Staring into space, memories overwhelmed her.

A fellow Texan, Nick was in DC when she met him. She had graduated from college with a business degree and gone to work with her grandfather in his real estate business where she had worked part-time for years. When he sent her to Washington to a sales workshop, she had accepted a friend's invitation to a cocktail party. She remembered holding a martini that she hadn't even sipped when she looked across the room into the blue eyes of a tall, brown-haired man who gazed back. That first moment had been sizzling, a look that caught and held her attention.

As she gazed at him, he raised his glass as if in a toast and she couldn't keep from smiling and raising hers in return.

She had turned back to her new friend from Dallas. "See the brown-haired guy across the room? Do you know who he is?"

"Oh, yes. That's Nick Milan, a lawyer with a prestigious firm here. Rumor has it he'll be entering Texas politics someday. The Milans are a prominent old Texas family. Very wealthy." She sucked in a breath and grabbed her drink. "He's coming this way. I don't think it's to talk to me. I'll see you in a little while."

"Don't go. I don't even know him."

"You're going to," her friend replied, and moved away only seconds before Nick stepped in front of her.

Claire's heartbeat had sped up as she looked into the bluest eyes she'd ever seen.

"I think it's time we make our escape from this party. I'm Nick Milan, single and a lawyer. I live in Georgetown and I want to have dinner with you. And you are…?"

"Claire Prentiss. You use the fewest words and get to the point faster than any lawyer I have ever met," she said. "You don't even know if I have a husband here tonight."

"You don't have a wedding ring on your finger. I looked when I got close. If you had, I would have gone in another direction. May I take you to dinner?"

"That's nice, thank you, but you're a stranger. I usually know the people I go out with."

"You should be cautious, but this is an exception. First, I assure you I'm perfectly safe. Second, you can't deny we have chemistry between us. So go out with me."

She smiled. "Not too bashful, are you?"

He shrugged. "I know what I want." He set his drink down on a high-top table and speared her with his undivided attention. "If you need more information, I can tell you this. I'm from Dallas, where my dad's a judge, but I work in DC for Abrams, Wiesman and Wooten. Excellent client list, I might add." He nodded to where her friend had gone. "I saw you talking to Jen West. She's met me and knows who I am. She can vouch for my character. Or we can go find Lydia and she'll tell you more about me. Then we can tell her goodbye."

His fingers closed lightly on her arm and Claire walked with him to their slender, auburn-haired hostess, who turned to smile at them. "I see you two have met."

"Just met, Lydia," Nick said. "I need a character reference so I can talk Claire into going to dinner with me." He flashed Claire a smile that sent another sizzle through her.

"Now, do I want to give you that character reference or not?" Lydia teased.

"I think you just did," Claire replied. She turned to Nick. "I accept your offer. You can tell me all about yourself over dinner."

"Oh, my," Lydia said. "Now he won't stop talking until midnight."

"I promise, I will," he said to Claire, causing her to laugh again. "Lydia, we have to run. The party was delightful. Thank you so much for inviting me."

Claire also thanked Lydia and in seconds she was in a cab with Nick. She barely saw the elegant private club where he took her to dinner and she tasted only bites of a delicious, perfectly cooked sirloin. It was Nick who captivated her.

Tall, incredibly handsome and charismatic, he charmed her. She learned about his family, which had settled in Texas in the 1800s, mutual friends they had, Nick's political ambitions. She fell in love with Nick Milan that night.

When he asked her to come back to his place for a drink before he took her to her hotel, she agreed. The minute she walked through the entryway into the spacious living area in the suite on the thirty-third floor, she forgot the view and turned as Nick drew her into his embrace.

"This has been the perfect evening," he said. "I knew when I looked across the room and saw you that I wanted to get to know you and wanted to go out with you tonight," he said, his gaze going to her mouth.

She had stood on tiptoe, slipping her arms around his shoulders as he leaned down to kiss her. The moment his mouth touched hers, she was in flames. The chemistry between them had sparked and heated her all evening, but when he kissed her, desire consumed her.

They had made love that night and Nick had talked her into staying two extra days over the weekend.

He had finally called a cab to take her to the airport and, while they waited, he said he would fly to Houston the following weekend and meet her family. On weekends, over the next few months after their meeting in March, Nick had flown to Houston or she flew to DC. In June, on a weekend in Houston, Nick proposed marriage.

It had been a dream come true. She still remembered that night as if it had happened yesterday, not four years ago.

Attempting to shake off the mental picture of that night, Claire stood and walked to the window to gaze at the Dallas skyline. But she saw none of it because she was lost in memories. No matter how many times she thought of Nick's proposal, she always returned to the same answer—she could not leave her family.

When she had rejected his proposal, their fight had been bitter, deep and long-lasting. Nick had flown back to DC that night and they'd had no contact since. Nick had truly broken her heart, but if she had it to do over again she still wouldn't change her answer to him. She had done the only thing she could.

Whatever happened when she let him know about his son, she knew one thing: she'd never fall in love with him again because she never wanted to repeat that pain. And there was so much more to work out now between them, because Nick's political life was on a fast track, while she had her grandfather's business to run and still had her grandparents with her. Plus, the biggest issue of all, now they had a son and had to work out sharing him.

She caught her reflection in the window and saw the concern etched across her face and darkening her eyes. She turned away from the window. What she'd like to do right now was cancel their dinner date and fly home and never see Nick again, because whatever she did tonight, if she told him about his son, she would be hurt.

Nick's November wedding had been months before Cody's birth the following February. Claire had decided he would have his wife and someday, their children, so there was no need to even let him know about Cody.

Tonight, though, she had to tell him. Would he understand why she hadn't let him know? Nick was a successful, billionaire attorney from a family who had influential friends all over Texas. Would he want this son in his life after losing the baby he had expected?

He had been friendly today, but not the sexy guy who had flirted outrageously when he'd first met her and made it clear that he wanted to be with her. She felt he had asked her to dinner tonight on an impulse. Truthfully, if he hadn't been widowed, she would have turned him down. She'd had every intention of refusing his offer until she learned about the death of his wife and his unborn baby.

Glancing in the mirror of her dresser, she studied her business suit. Except for casual slacks and a cotton shirt for travel, this suit was all she had brought to wear and she had worn it all afternoon with Nick. Shedding the jacket, she picked up her purse and went downstairs. The hotel, she remembered, was close to an elegant boutique and she hurried, wanting to find a dress for tonight. If she had to tell Nick about Cody, she wanted to look her best when she did so.

At ten to seven, when she was finally ready, she stood in front of the same mirror to take one last look at herself.

She wore a pearl necklace given to her by her grandfather and a delicate pearl bracelet she had bought herself. She turned slightly to look at her image, smoothing the flawless deep-blue long-sleeved dress with a plunging V neckline. Would Nick even notice her new dress? The Nick she had once known would, but she no longer knew this man.

There was only one way to find out, she told herself. She picked up her flat bag with her phone that held pictures of Cody, locked the door and left her hotel room.

As she rode down in an empty elevator, she couldn't shake the feeling of calamity. She couldn't get rid of her fear about Nick's reaction to the news she was about to tell him. Sure, she was afraid he'd be furious with her for keeping the secret. But far greater was her concern that Nick would want Cody in his life. He was a family man, close to his own father, so she was certain he and his parents would want to bring Cody into their family. The big question was, how much?

When she stepped off the elevator and gazed around the elegant lobby with its marble floor and potted palms, she spotted Nick instantly. In his charcoal suit and matching tie, he was definitely the most handsome man there. Crossing the expanse, he approached her.

Her heartbeat quickened, an unwanted reaction she

couldn't shake. She had a feeling she was in for another terrible fight with Nick and she didn't want to find him appealing at the same time. She wasn't going to let him hurt her again.

Trying to ignore the heat that enveloped her, she smiled at him and gripped her purse even more tightly. She had to get through this evening—without tears, without anger… and without desire. She took a deep breath and faced him. She had to. For Cody.

Two

As Nick watched Claire step off the elevator, desire surged in him. His gaze raked over her, taking in the low-cut blue dress that hugged her slender figure, revealed enticing curves, and ended high enough to display her long, shapely legs. Willowy and tall at five foot ten, she'd always worn clothes well. But there was something about her now…she was downright stunning.

He walked up to her. "Hi. You look great."

"Thank you." She nodded at him, then angled her head toward a corridor off the lobby. "The hotel has a great restaurant. We can eat here and it will be easier."

He smiled at her. "Taking you out to dinner is not a difficult task. C'mon," he said, ushering her toward the door. He'd already called the valet desk and had his car brought around to the front. As they crossed the lobby, he made small talk. "How's your family?"

"Mother passed away a little over a year ago and my

grandfather is in assisted living now. I hope he'll be able to return home before this year is over."

"I'm sorry to hear that. I guess your grandmother is in good health?"

"Yes, but she's older now and not quite the same. What about you? Do you enjoy being a State Representative?"

"Very much. Sometimes it's frustrating and occasionally it's disillusioning, but overall, I like politics and plan to run for a US Senate seat in the next election that will be four years from now."

"You're ambitious, but I knew that before. I'm sure you'd make a good senator, Nick."

"Thanks," he said, aware of her walking close beside him, catching a faint whiff of an exotic perfume he didn't recognize, but liked. He remembered how silky her hair had felt. In spite of their fiery split, he had never been able to forget her, yet there was no point in trying to see her after tonight. They would have the same difficulties, only now much more so, and he wasn't going to get hurt by her again.

When they exited the hotel, the valet opened the car door for her and she slid inside with a flash of her long legs that the valet admired as much as Nick did. He walked around to the driver's side, tipped the valet and thanked him for holding the door.

They drove out of the hotel's circular drive and in seconds were on the freeway. The winter sun had already set behind the tall buildings and the darkness was the perfect backdrop for the bright Christmas lights that gave a festive feeling to the night.

"Where are we going?" she asked, her question breaking the silence that had descended in the car.

"I'm taking you to a private club I belong to. It's quiet enough to talk and they have dancing on certain nights, more often now that it's December and there are more

Christmas parties," Nick said. "We can dance a few times, if I haven't forgotten how. I don't go out except with family or for business."

Her eyes widened as she turned to look at him. "That surprises you," he said.

"Yes. Somehow I pegged you for the type to sort of bounce back, if one ever can from that deep a loss."

"I guess I'm not," he replied abruptly. He didn't want to talk about that loss. His late wife and the child he'd never known were subjects best left for another time. If they had another time. Changing topics, he said, "The deal went smoothly today. Do you do much business in Dallas?"

"Very little," she replied. "We did this as a favor to a long-time client who suddenly went into the hospital and couldn't possibly come."

"Are you running the agency?"

"Yes, I am. They're giving Grandpa physical therapy and he hopes to regain his strength, but he can't ever be in charge again. Still, he can come to the office and be part of it, and that expectation keeps him going. One nice thing that made him happy—the agency has grown since I took over."

"That's what counts," Nick said. He wasn't surprised by her success. He'd always known she would be competent in running the agency and in dealing with people.

Soon he turned into well-tended grounds, winding through trees strung with miniature multicolored lights until they came to a sprawling stone building. Leaving his car with the valet, they entered the lobby where a huge Christmas tree stood in the center, and red ribbon and bows had been artfully strung along a hallway. Nick led her through the clubhouse to the dining room where they were seated at a corner table beside floor-to-ceiling windows that afforded a panoramic view of a golf course. More

Christmas lights lit up the covered veranda and, beyond that, a pond that held two fountains.

In one corner of the dining room a man played a ballad on a piano while two couples danced. The waiter came to take their orders and Nick asked for white wine. When it was poured, he raised his glass. "Here's to a successful deal that closed easily today."

"I'll drink to that, Nick," she said solemnly, her dark eyes filled with unfathomable secrets. He wondered about her life now. For all she'd said so far, she'd told him nothing except that she was head of the family real estate agency.

"Let's see if I've forgotten how to dance," he said, standing, curious if she would dance with him. She was cool, standoffish and seemed preoccupied tonight. He wondered whether she was worried about her grandfather or if something else was disturbing her. Or was it a lasting anger with him over their breakup? She wasn't the light-hearted, fun-filled Claire he had known, but he wasn't the same person anymore, either.

They went to the dance floor where he put his hand on her waist, careful to keep distance between them as they danced to a soft ballad. "You're not out of practice," he said, remembering other times they'd danced together, him holding her close, his heart racing. Even now, he had a sharp awareness of her as she gazed at him intently.

"You're not out of practice either, Nick." He accepted her compliment. "You know, if you're so steeped in politics, I imagine you are out and about plenty."

"Usually at stuffy dinners or fund-raisers. Not much time to find a pretty woman and dance at those events."

He wasn't sure but he thought he saw her cheeks blush before she turned her head. He pulled her slightly closer and gave himself over to the dance. He liked the sensation of having her in his arms. She felt good. Familiar. From out of the blue, one thought kept reverberating in his head. *This woman could have been your wife.*

He still felt heartache thinking about what could have been.

Four years ago when Claire had turned down his marriage proposal and he returned to Washington, he'd turned to Karen. They had dated in college and law school, and known each other since high school, so their relationship seemed only natural once she'd accepted a job in DC working in the office of a friend of her father's.

Nick couldn't work things out with Claire and Karen was there, in DC, wanting to go out, charming him and filling a big void. She was from Dallas, their parents were friends and she would live wherever he wanted. She had wanted marriage. His firm wanted their young attorneys married and so did his parents. He still loved Claire but he knew it was over between them.

Doing what his family, his firm and his career indicated he should, he had proposed to Karen. He could still remember a moment at his wedding when he had been hit by a wall of longing, knowing that it should have been Claire beside him, but he had banked those feelings. Karen had been a good wife, seductive and beautiful, and he had grown to appreciate her more each year. She catered to him, bolstered his career, moved with him, and in return he gave her the social life she wanted. Both sets of parents were happy. Claire was out of his life.

But he had never forgotten her.

Even now, as he danced with her, he had to remind himself that there wasn't any point in trying to see her again after tonight. She was tied to her family and to Houston more than ever, while he had his life in Dallas and DC and he had a political career that held golden promises for the future.

What about the sizzling current he felt as they danced? There was no denying she still had a physical effect on him, but that might simply be because he had been alone for so long now.

As he spun her around and dipped her in time to the music, he was swept away by vivid memories of holding her tightly, kissing her, making love to her. For an instant desire flashed, hot and unwanted, as he looked down at her mouth, wanting to hold her close, feel her softness while he kissed her. He remembered how soft and sweet her lips had been, and more than anything he wanted to taste them again. The desire was undeniable. Lust slammed into him, rising to the surface and surprising him after two long years of total numbness.

But he wouldn't kiss her.

He couldn't.

He swung her up to continue dancing, trying to cool down, to forget the scalding memories. There was no future in seeing Claire and he would not start that again.

Trying to divert his mind from taking her right there on the dance floor, he began questioning her. "Who's the man in your life, Claire?" he asked, certain there had to be one.

She shook her head. "There isn't one. No time. I'm too busy running the office, making sales myself, taking care of my family, visiting Grandpa five days a week. I don't have a social life except through the office, church and family. I keep thinking it will change and things will settle down, but that hasn't happened."

"Maybe you're working too hard. How big is your agency?" He was grateful for the safe path the conversation now took.

"I have three offices and almost seventy salespeople. We deal in commercial and residential properties."

"That's a big business," he said. Studying her, Nick

guessed she was tied into work most of her waking hours. "How many offices did you have when your grandfather turned things over to you? I thought there was only one."

"One is correct," she replied. "Good memory, Nick. I've been very lucky and have some great people who work for me."

"I imagine luck is only a part of it. Congratulations. I'm impressed," he said, meaning it. "You have to be a busy woman."

"I am busy. And I've got a full day tomorrow. I'm flying home at six in the morning. Have to be at the airport at four because I'm not one to run out there at the last minute."

"I'll take you to the airport."

She laughed, her eyes suddenly twinkling, stirring another flash of desire as he remembered the fun he once had with her. "Thanks, Nick, but that's beyond the call of 'for old times' sake.' I already have a limo reserved. Thanks, anyway. That's very nice of you."

"If you change your mind, the offer stands."

The number ended and a fast one started. As they danced and he watched her hips move, he was assailed by memories once again. He couldn't help remembering making love with her. He couldn't help wanting her now, which shocked him again. He had a reaction to Claire that he hadn't had to any other woman since Karen. Maybe it was time for him to come back into the world. Yet, even as he thought that, he knew he didn't want to get involved with any woman at this time in his life. Definitely not Claire. He'd been there and done that and gotten hurt badly.

Trying to stop watching Claire so closely and shutting down the erotic images in his memory, he was grateful when the song ended. "Ready to sit one out? I'd like a sip of wine." They returned to the table.

They talked through their dinners—steak for him and

salmon for her, which he noticed she barely ate. She had to be worried about something at home, her family or business, because she seemed preoccupied. He felt a wall between them, but he didn't particularly care. After a polite goodbye, he wouldn't see her again, so it didn't matter.

If she had said she was seeing someone, he would have not been surprised. The invisible barrier between them kept her restrained, as if she had accepted his invitation tonight to be polite and she would be glad to tell him goodbye. Two or three times he had caught her looking at him with an intensity that startled him. Was she still thinking about their last angry moments together? Each time she had quickly looked away, her face had flushed. So there was something disturbing her, keeping a wall up…

Was it him? But that was impossible, unless she was still hurting from their breakup. But he couldn't imagine that she hadn't gone on with her life. Or was it—

No. He had to stop attempting to figure out what she might be thinking. Soon she would be out of his life again, this time probably for good.

She may have been thinking the same thing, because she put down her coffee cup and said, "Nick, it's been interesting to see you and I know it's not late, but I have an early flight."

"Sure," he said, picking up on her need to leave. He signed for the check and led her out, telling himself it was for the best. But he couldn't help the disappointment that he never would know the reason for those intense looks.

As Nick drove her back to the hotel, Claire rehearsed asking him to come in for a few minutes. She knew that, being the gentleman he was, he would see her to her door. Once there, it would be so simple to invite him in. But there would be nothing simple about confessing to him she had given birth to his son. Informing him that he had a three-year-old son was not the sort of thing to tell him over dinner in a public place. She had to be alone with him and her last opportunity was approaching.

At the hotel, he gave his car to the valet, saying he'd be right back.

She shivered as they walked into the lobby, blaming the chilly evening air. As they rode up in the elevator and walked to her door, her stomach was in knots and she dreaded breaking the news to him. Nick still seemed wrapped in mourning for his wife, but the fact that he had lost his unborn child made it imperative to inform him of his son.

She couldn't look back and wish she had told him long ago because that was over and done. Maybe she should take a few days to think things through before she told him about Cody. She hadn't had time to really consider how the situation was going to change her life and Cody's life permanently. Not to mention Nick's life, too.

"Claire, is something wrong?"

His voice cut into her reverie and she started, realizing she was still standing in front of her hotel room door, the key card in her hand.

He'd given her the perfect opening...except the words wouldn't come. Even though she was freezing, perspiration broke out on her forehead and her palms grew damp.

Tell him. Tell him now.

But she couldn't.

"No, I just got to thinking about something that has become a problem in my life," she said.

"Maybe you're working too hard," Nick said quietly, running his finger along her cheek.

She looked up into those deep blue eyes with thick lashes, into Nick's handsome face. Nick was a good person, intelligent, sophisticated, reasonable, charming. She should just tell him about his son. At the same time, she recalled the bitter accusations they had flung at each other when they had parted—she'd called him a selfish rich guy who always got what he wanted, while he'd accused her of not having a life of her own.

If she told him about his son, what hurtful things would they say to each other tonight? She didn't want to go through that kind of stormy battle with Nick again.

"Nick—" She paused. The moment she told him, Cody would no longer belong to her side of the family only. She would have to share him and let him stay with Nick. Or worse. Would Nick try to take Cody from her?

"Yes?" Nick prompted, curiosity in his expression.

"I had a really good time tonight," she said softly, barely able to get out the words.

He tilted his head to look intently at her again. "I'm glad. I wasn't sure you were having that much fun. It was a good evening for me. How about a kiss for old times' sake?" he said and leaned down to place his mouth lightly on hers while his arm circled her waist.

The moment his mouth touched hers, she felt the sparks she always had with Nick. His arm tightened around her waist and his mouth pressed against hers more firmly, opening her lips as he really kissed her, a deep, sexy kiss that for a few minutes stopped her worrying and fears, and shut off memories of their past and the big problem facing her.

Her heart pounding, she clung to Nick and kissed him in return, knowing it was folly, but unable to stop. She was swept back in time, into memories of Nick's steamy, passionate kisses that had stolen her heart so quickly. She ignored the voice in her head that warned her she couldn't let that happen again.

She clung to his broad shoulders, too aware of the hard,

muscled body pressed against hers. Desire seemed to explode from his scalding kiss. It had been so long since she had been held by a man and kissed with such intensity.

When they moved apart, he was breathing as hard as she and he looked startled. His kiss had shaken her, igniting desire that burned through worry and made her stop thinking for a few minutes. But now, as she faced him again, she saw his blue eyes were filled with curiosity. Nick was an intelligent man and he had already picked up on something worrying her.

She couldn't tell him. The words wouldn't come to invite him in. She could take a few days to think about what she intended to do and to consult her family lawyer. She smiled at him, trying to pull herself together. "Thank you for the wonderful dinner, Nick. It was good to see you again. I am so sorry about your wife and baby."

"You're saying all the right things, Claire, but why do I have a feeling there is something else you want to say?" he asked, studying her as if he hadn't ever seen her before.

"No, Nick. I'm just overworked at home." Nervous, wanting to get away from him, swamped in guilt at the same time, she inserted her card into the door with such a shaky hand, she couldn't get it to work.

Nick's hand closed over hers and he opened the door for her. Even in her upset condition, she noticed the physical contact, the warmth of his fingers that sent an electric charge up her arm with his touch. "If you ever want to talk, I'm an old friend, Claire," he said quietly.

She felt as if she had fallen into ice water. "Thank you. Good night, Nick," she said, stepping inside and holding the door, turning to look at him. "I'll keep that in mind."

He nodded, giving her one more searching look before walking to the elevator.

She started to close the door and guilt swamped her.

Could she live with her conscience if she flew home to Houston and didn't tell Nick?

Closing her eyes, she opened the door just as the elevator doors opened. Nick glanced over his shoulder, saw her watching him and frowned.

"Nick, can you come in for a little while?"

He turned, once again giving her one of his probing looks that filled her with dread. Nick could be formidable. He had power, wealth and a state-wide network of cronies with influence. What would he do when he found out about Cody?

"Claire, I'll be happy to help with a problem," he said in a gentle voice, but it did nothing to ease her fear.

"Come in and let's get a drink," she said, leading him into the living area of her suite, which overlooked the sparkling lights of the city from the twenty-fourth floor. She switched on one small lamp that gave a soft glow in the quiet room. "I'm trying to think things through before I start talking. Just give me a minute," she said. "What would you like?"

"Let's see if there's any beer in that fridge you have," he said. Looking in the small refrigerator, he held up a bottle of white wine. "Would you like this?"

"Yes, thank you," she said.

"I'll pour your wine. You go ahead and think so we can talk. I'm in no hurry, Claire."

She nodded and he went to pour her wine, but as she watched him walk away, she knew she couldn't think this through in just minutes. She got her phone out of her purse, still half wanting to tell him to forget it and talk to him later, by phone from Houston. Each time she had thoughts like that, guilt chased them away. She couldn't fly home without telling Nick that he had a child.

Perching on the edge of an ottoman, she watched him

stroll back into the room. She couldn't have chosen better for the father of her child. Nick had so many good qualities. She hoped forgiveness was one of them.

He handed her a glass of white wine. When his fingers brushed hers, he frowned slightly. "You're freezing," he said, his hand covering hers. His hand was warm and in other circumstances would have been reassuring. But not now. He knelt in front of her. "What's wrong? It can't be money with the successful business you have. Are you not well?"

She shook her head, unable to say anything.

"How can I help?" he asked gently.

"I want to talk to you. Have a seat, Nick. This may take a while."

His probing gaze searched hers again before he rose, pulled a straight-back chair close and sat. She sipped her wine and set the glass on an end table. When she did, he took her hand, holding it between his two warm hands.

"Do you want me to get you a blanket?"

"No, I'll be all right." They gazed at each other and she realized he was being quiet to give her a chance to think and to let her talk when she was ready.

"Nick, the night you proposed…we had a terrible fight and you said goodbye. You walked out and we didn't see each other again. It wasn't many months until you were engaged to someone else and headed for a political career. I'm sure you remember."

"Of course I do. We couldn't work things out." He took a swallow of his beer, as if to wash away the memory of their breakup. "Karen and I had known each other for years and we'd dated in college and at one point had talked about marriage. When she came to work in DC she called me and I started seeing her. She was from Dallas, had no ties that would interfere with the two of us. My family pushed me to marry and start a family. You had already turned me down. That last time you and I were together…it was terrible. I imagine you were as hurt as I was. It was clear that it was over between us."

She nodded her head, giving him the affirmation he was looking for. Then he continued.

"I proposed to Karen and she accepted. I know it was fast and I know I should have called to let you know so you heard it from me, but…well, I didn't think you'd want to hear from me at all."

"I heard you were dating and then I heard you were engaged. I was shocked, but I understood that we couldn't work out our problems. You had your life in politics and in DC at the time, working at that well-known law firm. It was obvious you would be successful and you were ambitious. The hurtful words we had finally ended it between us. I let you go out of my life and I knew eventually you would have your own life, your wife, your family."

"That's what I planned," he said quietly, looking down at the beer in his hand and then taking a drink before he lowered it to look at her and wait for her to speak.

"We had really gone our separate ways and you were starting a new life."

"What you want to tell me—does it have something to do with me?" he asked, sounding puzzled.

She nodded. "I just want you to remember that you had your own life planned, a new career, a future in politics, a new wife. You lived in your world."

She could see she had his full attention and she was certain he was trying to figure out how anything in her life could involve him. She took a deep breath and hoped she wasn't making the biggest mistake of her life.

"Nick, at that time I was pregnant with your son."

Three

Stunned, Nick could only stare at her as he tried to register her words. "That was almost four years ago," he whispered, talking more to himself than to her. She couldn't have had his baby. He gazed into her big, dark-brown eyes that still hid secrets and saw her wring her hands. She looked pale, afraid, her shoulders slightly hunched. She was telling him the truth. Four years ago he had gotten her pregnant. Nine months later, she had given birth to his baby and hadn't told him.

He had a son. He would have to be three now. Nick was so stunned he couldn't breathe. He couldn't believe that he was a dad. Gulping for breath, he stood and walked to the window. Like shock waves that kept hitting him, the realization rocked him again that he was a dad, he had a son, a child of his own. He turned to look at Claire.

"Dammit, Claire. I have a child and you didn't tell me," he said, clenching his fists and shaking, anger and shock jolting him. "How could you not tell me? Dammit," he snapped, without giving her time to answer.

He could only stare at her and think back. He had been in love with her, had proposed to her and wanted to marry her. And then they'd fought. On the rebound he had married Karen. He hadn't talked to Claire again and she hadn't talked to him—a natural outcome of the last hours of arguing, flinging accusations, letting a wall of anger and hurt come between them.

And now to learn that he had a son and Claire had never told him shocked and angered him all over again. He placed his hands on his hips without thinking what he was doing. "You never intended to tell me. The only reason you did is because we saw each other today," he said, fury beginning to boil.

She stood and faced him. "When you told me you had lost your wife and unborn baby, I realized you had to be told. Before, an out-of-wedlock baby would have hurt or ruined your political aspirations and you know it. You wouldn't have wanted to hear from me. When you married, I always thought you would have your family with your wife and you really would never be that interested in a child I carried."

"My son? Of course, I would be interested. I have a son," he said, feeling awe. "Claire, that is the most fantastic news I could possibly hear. How in hell could you think I wouldn't be interested?"

"I just told you—news that I had given birth to your son just after your marriage would have killed your political career. You married within months after our breakup. I wondered if you had been seeing her while you were seeing me. Your new wife certainly would not have wanted to hear that I had your baby." Claire closed her eyes and swayed, and he frowned, wondering whether she was about to faint. "Nick, can't you see that I felt you shut me out of your life? Without telling me anything you became engaged. You should have let me know."

"I should have done that, I agree."

"Recriminations aren't going to help. I'm just trying to explain my actions."

"You can't ever explain not letting me know," he said.

"I just did. Would you have wanted to tell your fiancée you had recently gotten me pregnant? You married and occasionally I saw pictures in the news of you with your wife and you looked happy. Why would I think you would want my baby just when you married Karen?"

Knowing she was right, he didn't care. The knowledge that he had a son was far more important.

"I've missed all his first years. I missed his babyhood. He doesn't know me. He doesn't even know I exist, does he?"

"No, he's little."

"Dammit, Claire, I've missed too much."

"Hindsight is always better," she replied, looking pained. "I've told you why I did what I did. It's that simple. But I will say this. This son is not going to help your political life, I promise you."

"I don't give a damn about that. It's far more important that I know my son."

"You say that now, but you don't really mean it. Your adult life has revolved around politics and rising to the next office," she said.

"I mean it, Claire. My son is my future, not a job. You can't keep me from getting to know him."

"I don't plan to, Nick. That's why I've told you about him." She glanced away. "But your family will not be happy, especially your father. You know he would not have been happy to hear about a child—not then and not now."

Nick inhaled and clenched his fists, trying to hang on to his temper. "You took those years from me, and I can never get them back."

She wiped the tears from her eyes. "I regret that now."

"I've been through hell the past two years. I lost my wife and baby. I could have filled part of that void and helped the hurt by knowing my son. I can't believe you did this to me."

She looked at him. "Nick, I'm so sorry for your loss and if I had known—" She bit off her words and wrung her hands. "I wish I could undo the past few years, but I can't. We'll have to pick up from here."

"Dammit, Claire," he said, clenching his fists and closing his eyes. Hurting, he thought of all the empty moments. He'd hurt badly after the breakup with Claire. Two years ago, he'd hurt after losing Karen and the baby. Now he had another deep hurt and this one could have been so easily avoided. He tried to hang on to his temper and to avoid saying hurtful things to Claire because it really didn't help to pour out his fury on her.

"Would you like to see his picture?" she asked after a few minutes.

Nick jerked his head up. His anger melted as fast as it had come and awe filled him. He suddenly knew how he would have felt if he had been present at the birth of his son. "You have his picture? Of course I'd like to see it."

She walked back to the ottoman to pick up her phone. Nick came to stand beside her. "I named him Cody Nicholas Prentiss."

"You named him Nicholas?" he asked, pleasure filling him.

"Yes. I named him for you," she said, looking up at him. "I felt I should do that."

Nick looked at her phone and she opened it, handing it

to him. His hands shook and he was overwhelmed as he looked at a child that resembled his own pictures when he was small.

"Oh, my word, there's no doubt about his heritage. He looks just like me at that age," Nick said, the feeling of awe swamping him. "My family will love him beyond words. Thank you for naming him Nicholas."

"He looks like you. He's a sweet, happy little boy who loves people. Even as a baby, he smiled constantly when someone talked to him."

"That's great," Nick said, still staring at Cody's picture.

"My grandmother watches him a couple of days a week, and I have a nanny the rest of the time to help relieve Grandma. For his first seven months I took maternity leave. Grandpa was around until the past six months, so there was a man in the house."

Looking at his son, Nick felt the sting of tears of joy, forgetting his anger and the empty years. Getting a grip on his emotions, he wiped his eyes. "I have a son," he said, his voice filled with awe. "This is the most wonderful news. Claire, he's perfect. Was your family with you when he was born?" he asked, staring at Cody's picture.

"Oh, yes. Mom was alive then, and all of them were thrilled. When he was a baby, one of us rocked him to sleep every night. Grandpa read to him when he was so tiny he couldn't possibly understand a word, but it made him happy."

"Can you send this picture to me?"

"Yes. I have more on my iPad. I'll go get it. I'll send all of them to you," she said.

Nick watched her leave the room, his gaze sweeping down to notice her tiny waist, the slightest sway to her walk, her long legs. What if they had married? What if he had tried harder to work things out with her? He had been so in love with her, but their breakup had been final. Then Karen had come along and she seemed to be the answer to his problems. In their marriage they'd each gotten what they'd wanted. But even as he had walked down the aisle, his heart had ached. He'd tried to remind himself that Claire didn't want to marry him, but that hadn't stopped the hurt that had torn him up for a long time.

If he had known about her pregnancy—

Instantly he stopped that thought. There was no undoing the past and he wasn't going to dwell on what might have been.

As Claire left the room, he stared at the empty doorway. Fury still simmered in him because of the years he had missed with his son. At the same time, awe and joy were stronger. This couldn't bring back the baby he had lost, but Cody would fill a painful void in his life.

Staring at the picture, memorizing it, he held her phone in his hands. It was incredibly awesome to look at the picture and see a child who looked just like he had when he was that age. How long would it take to get used to Claire's revelation?

"Cody Nicholas," he whispered, running his fingers over the picture.

She came back into the room with her iPad in hand and motioned to the sofa. Again, he watched her cross the room. Her attention was on her tablet and his gaze ran from her head to her toes. His pulse raced as he looked at her. She was stunning, even better looking than she had been four years ago. Today she had been poised, self-assured, handling the business matters with ease and he'd admired her. Tonight he had seen the sexy side of her and he'd still responded to her. Now he discovered she was the mother of his baby and he was shocked.

Each time he thought about this discovery, joy, awe and

gratitude outweighed anger. He should do something to show her how happy he was and he should try to forgive her. The latter would take some time, but Claire was the mother of his child and he needed to keep that in mind.

"Come sit and I'll show you his pictures," she said, still focused on the iPad in her hands, but she sounded more like herself. "I have baby pictures on here."

"Thank heavens for that," he said. He caught her before she sat and grasped her gently by the shoulders.

Wide-eyed, she looked up. "What?"

"You're the mother of my child, Claire. We have a tie now for the rest of our lives. Even though I can't help being angry, I'm far more thrilled and grateful. I'm sorry I wasn't there for you, but that was your choosing. One thing is important for me to say. Thank you. Even though it's completely inadequate."

Wrapping his arms around her, he hugged her to him. "Thank you," he said again, his words muffled this time. She was warm, soft in his arms. It was suddenly so good to hold her. "Thank you," he repeated, a knot in his throat. They stood in silence a moment until he felt tears on his neck and leaned away.

He stroked the moisture away with his fingers. "Why are you crying?"

"Don't take him from me, Nick," she whispered, her eyes shut tightly as she wiped at her cheeks. "I know you'll want him in your life. Your parents will, too, after they meet him."

Nick folded her into his embrace again and held her close. He wasn't making any promises because he didn't know what demands she would have. He framed her face with his hands. "I don't know what we'll work out, but I will never take him totally away from you. That would be harming my own child."

Nodding, she moved away, turning her back to dry her eyes, and he wondered whether she even believed what he said.

"Let's see his pictures," Nick said. He sat beside her on the sofa and she gave him the iPad. He pulled up photos and she tapped one.

"We'll start when he was a tiny baby. This is in the hospital."

"Send these to me, all of them. Oh, hell, why didn't you let me know?" he asked, hurting as he looked at a sleeping newborn with a blue cap on his head.

"I've already given you all my reasons. But let me ask you this. Would you have felt the same about Cody then?"

He gazed into her dark eyes and thought about what she'd asked. "I might not have felt this way right after getting married, and you're right. Karen probably would not have taken the news well, but I still think you should have told me. I missed this. Especially after losing Karen and the baby. I missed these years," he said, looking down at the date Claire had written on a picture of her and Cody as they left the hospital.

"Claire, this date—" He frowned. "I wasn't engaged when you found out you were pregnant. Not if you carried Cody nine months."

She raised her chin, gazing at him with a defiant expression. "I was shocked when I found out I was pregnant. I needed time to figure out my future and adjust to the realization I was going to have a baby. I had to tell my family. I was trying to plan what I would do when I heard you were engaged."

"It was early enough I might not have married Karen," he said, wondering what he would have done.

Claire rubbed her forehead. "We had already had that

terrible breakup. I don't see how we could have gotten back together."

"True," he said, staring into space, thinking about that time in his life. He glanced at the iPad on his knee. "Let's get back to the pictures," he said, turning to the next one, another of her leaving the hospital, carrying a small bundle in her arms. Cody was so wrapped in blankets he was not visible. In the next picture the blankets were peeled back so his face showed. He was sleeping and looked wonderful to Nick. "I've been cheated of having these years together with two of my babies," he said, anger surfacing again.

Nick looked at pictures of Cody in a baby bed, of him being held in Claire's arms and then being held by each member of her family. He looked at his son's nursery room with Winnie-the-Pooh characters painted on the wall.

"You weren't ever going to tell me about him, were you?" Even though he kept his voice quiet, Nick's anger escalated, wondering if he could ever be with her again without feeling anger over keeping his son from him. Would he ever trust her in anything?

"I knew I had to eventually. Cody would get bigger and want to know about his dad. I couldn't avoid it forever, but as time passed, it just got easier to let it go," she said quietly.

Nick held back an angry reply and looked at the next group of pictures as Cody grew and had his first birthday. Nick felt another pang of longing. "Where was his first birthday?"

"At my grandparents'. Now they live in my house. I had a home built and moved Grandma in with me."

They bent over each picture with Claire telling him about the incident when the picture was taken. He laughed as he looked at a picture of Cody with chocolate cake all over his small hands and across his face.

"This is great," Nick said, more to himself than her. "He looks as if he loves the cake and is having a wonderful time."

"He did. That was the first time he ever tasted chocolate. He still doesn't get any candy."

Nick turned to look at her. "With you and your grandparents hovering over him, and your mother, too, this first year, he was probably a very well cared for baby and a very happy one."

He turned his attention back to the pictures. In the next one Claire was in a swimsuit, holding Cody's hands as he waded in the shallow end of a large swimming pool.

"Whose pool is this?"

"A friend's. I don't want a pool while Cody is little, although he does actually know how to paddle across the pool and climb out, which is an enormous relief. It doesn't mean I don't watch him, but it's good to know that he can swim out if he falls in."

Nick's attention shifted from Cody to Claire's picture in a deep blue one-piece suit. "You don't look as if you've had a baby," he said, thinking she looked great. His gaze ran over the picture as he looked at her long, shapely legs, her tiny waist and full, luscious curves. He felt it again. Desire. Claire was making him come alive again, reminding him what it felt like to know lust. He glanced her way and suddenly felt the heat emanating from her body as she sat so close beside him. He wanted to hold her. But he knew he couldn't. Not now. With an effort he kept his hands to himself and focused again on the pictures.

She thanked him for the compliment. "I used to hit the gym three days a week. Now I have an exercise room at home."

"You're bound to go out with someone, Claire."

She shook her head. "I'm so busy, and when I do have

time, I spend it with Cody. I'd much rather be doing something with him. I take at least one day a week to work from home. Of course, that may change when he starts school, but it works for right now."

"I'm glad." Nick never had any doubt she'd be a good mother for his son, though he had to admit he was surprised that no man had snatched her up yet. Successful, beautiful and single—that should draw men easily. He suspected she must be sending them on their way, which gave him a stab of satisfaction that he dismissed as ridiculous.

"Was he an easy baby or difficult?"

"Oh, so easy, but remember—there were four adults living with him, three to care for him. Mom really couldn't, but she could talk to him and read to him and do things like that with him. We'd help her hold him. Anyway, that made his care easy and everyone was relaxed, so he probably relaxed. He's a sweetie."

"I want to meet him as soon as possible."

"We'll arrange it, Nick." As she looked at him, he gazed into the eyes that always hid what she felt. Big, beautiful brown eyes that made him want to slide his hand behind her head and draw her closer. "Nick, let me take your picture so I can show it to Cody when I get home and tell him about you."

He nodded. "Why don't we take a selfie and then we'll be in it together. I'd feel better about him seeing me with you."

She nodded.

Nick placed his arm around her. "I have longer arms—why don't I take the picture?"

"Go ahead," she said, and from the somber sound of her voice he wondered whether she would even smile. She sounded as if she was headed for disaster instead of just taking a picture with him. He held out the iPad. "Try to look happy, Claire. Think about Cody." Nick took their picture.

He pulled up the picture and smiled. "Thanks, Claire. That looks good."

"He'll want to see what you look like."

"That hasn't ever come up? He hasn't asked about a dad?"

"No. We don't talk about you and he isn't in school yet, so he isn't with other kids a lot."

"Doesn't he have any little friends?"

"Oh, sure, but they play. There isn't a lot of discussion. He's three, Nick. Besides, kids take things as they come."

Nick continued looking at pictures of Cody, of Claire or her family with Cody as he went from being a baby to a toddler.

"I can't wait to meet him," he said. "I can fly to Houston Friday, so can we spend time together this weekend?"

She ran her hand across her forehead. "I didn't even think this through when I told you tonight. I was so shocked today to learn about your loss that right then and there I decided I had to tell you about Cody. But I—I need time. I'll have to break the news to Cody."

"A child accepts life as it comes. You just said that. So he'll accept meeting me. Would you prefer to bring him to Dallas? I just want to meet him as soon as possible."

"It's a complete upheaval in all of our lives, including yours," she whispered, wringing her hands.

He nodded. "Not just meeting him."

She looked stricken and he tried to hang on to his patience. His request wasn't unreasonable in his opinion. Why couldn't she see that?

"All right. Do you want to come Friday night?"

He opened his phone, checked his calendar and nodded.

"Yes. After we meet, would he like it if I take everyone to dinner? This includes your grandmother, of course."

"That's nice, Nick." But as much as her words were gracious, he could hear her trepidation in her voice and see it in her eyes. She gazed up at him solemnly, with a touch of fear in their depths. He knew she was worried that she would have to give up her child permanently, yet he couldn't feel much sympathy for her since she had kept knowledge of his baby from him all this time.

Verifying his interpretation, she took a deep breath and said, "Nick, my grandma is elderly and frail now. Since Mom died, Cody and I and Grandpa are her whole world. She's older and vulnerable. Please, think of her before you take any action. She doesn't have that many years left."

"I will, Claire. I won't spring anything on you without discussing it." He paused a few minutes and silence fell. Finally, he asked, "Does Cody have a favorite place to eat?"

"We really don't get out a lot, but there's one place he loves—a restaurant made to look like a rainforest. He thinks it's very special and a lot of fun."

"I'll make reservations."

"He'll love it." She smiled. She'd been so worried, so tearful in the last while that her smile caught him off guard. He took a moment to look at her. She really was a beautiful woman, with her smooth skin and big, dark eyes fringed with thick lashes.

"Does he resemble you at all?"

"Not in looks, as you saw. Actually, probably not much in temperament, either. He has a ready smile the way you used to, and he's a little charmer and very social. If I take him to the office, he's all over the place talking to everyone and they talk to him."

Nick smiled. "I don't know that I was all that charming as a kid. I remember Wyatt and Madison constantly telling me to be still. I don't believe I charmed them." His older brother and sister had avoided him at all costs, just the way he did his younger brother Tony.

She gave him a faint smile. "Siblings are different."

He glanced at his watch. "You're not going to have much time to sleep before leaving for the airport."

"I wouldn't have slept anyway."

He nodded, suspecting he wasn't going to sleep in the hours he had left, either. "Claire, cancel your flight. I have a family plane and a pilot. I'll get him to fly you to Houston whenever you want. This way you won't have to wait for the commercial flight and maybe you'll have a little more time to yourself before going to the office."

She stared at him a moment and then nodded. "Thanks, Nick. I can't wait to see Cody."

"Neither can I, Claire," he said. She looked startled and drew a deep breath as if he had suggested something dreadful. There was no doubt that she regretted telling him. If his client hadn't asked him to the closing, would he ever have known about his son? That question persisted and each time stirred his anger because he wondered how old Cody would have been before she told him.

"I'll make arrangements for you to fly home. What time do you want to leave?"

"As soon as I can get to the airport," she replied.

He nodded. "I'll call my pilot while you cancel your flight."

By the time she returned he had made all the arrangements. "I have a limo picking us up in an hour," he told her. "If you need to pack, go ahead. In the meantime I'll look at Cody's pictures and send copies to myself. I can't seem to look enough. I just want to sit and stare at some of these pictures. He looks like the most adorable child I have ever seen in my entire life."

She gave him a fleeting smile. "I know exactly how you feel. He is a very handsome little boy, Nick."

"What does he like? He's too little to read."

"He knows his alphabet. My grandmother plays all kinds of letter games with him. He's a smart little boy. You'll be proud of him."

"I already love him with all my heart and I haven't even seen him," Nick said, looking up at her and seeing a wistful expression on her face that startled him. Was she wondering what it might have been like if they had been together? When she met his gaze, her expression changed, a shuttered look coming across her eyes that locked him out.

"Whatever we work out and whatever happens in the future, you've made me a very happy man tonight," he said.

Her dark gaze was unfathomable as she nodded. "I'm glad, Nick. It'll be good for Cody to know you. He has a very good man for a father."

"I hope I'm a good dad. I've had a good dad, although one who liked to run everything and goes too far sometimes. I'm in politics because of him, yet at the same time, he's been a big help to me. When the dust settles, they'll all be happy about Cody."

"Nick, take a moment to think before you announce that you have a son. You have such high political ambitions, and you have a career as a politician. Judge Milan is not going to be pleased. None of your close circle of supporters will be happy. An out-of-wedlock baby so close to your marriage isn't going to be good news to any of them. Your political career means everything to you, so you should give some thought to what you're about to do."

He nodded. "I'm not shutting my son out of my life because of politics. Right now, I get sympathy because of being a widower. That will help cushion this announcement. I want this senate seat and I think I can win. I told you when we dated that I want to be President someday, Claire. There are people already working on that in the background."

She stared at him. "A scandal could make that extremely difficult, unless we marry and that's over between us."

"If Cody kills my chances, so be it. At this point in my life I'm aeons away from the White House. I have to win the senate seat first."

"Your dad is going to push you to marry me. The kind of political career he wants you to have takes a lot of background work. He's already put a lot into your career."

He put up a hand to stop her argument. "Claire, we're not going to make any big decisions tonight. And right now I only want to talk about my son. What can I bring Cody that he would really like?"

"He likes his books. I'll text you a list to choose from. And he likes to build things. He likes electronic gadgets and he knows how to find some of his games on the computer." He could see how her eyes lit up again as she talked about her son. "I can't wait to see him. I've got to go pack. Look at his pictures and I'll get ready to go home."

She left the room and he continued sending himself each picture of Cody. In a short time Claire appeared with her carry-on, a briefcase and her purse. She had changed and wore the tailored navy skirt and the matching silk blouse she had worn to the closing. Once again he thought how good-looking she was, even more than she had been years ago, and he thought of his earlier kiss, which had rocked him and stirred desire.

"You look nice. You also travel lightly."

"It was just an overnight."

"The limo is downstairs if you're ready," he said, handing her iPad back, which she slipped into her purse.

"Yes. I'm checked out and ready to go," she said. Nick

shouldered her carry-on and picked up her briefcase while she slid her purse strap over her shoulder. They were ready to leave her hotel room, and for one brief moment, he wished he could pull her into his arms and kiss her again. Controlling the urge, he held the door for her, catching a whiff of her perfume as she walked out. It was the same scent she'd worn years ago, and as he inhaled it he was transported back in time.

He remembered his third flight to Houston to see her for the weekend. She had moved back home to help with her family, and her grandmother had ushered him inside. As he'd walked in, Claire came down the stairs. She had taken his breath away that night in a bright-red crepe dress that ended above her knees. Her thick hair swung loosely across her shoulders as she descended the steps and he could only stare, not hearing what her grandmother said.

Nick was so caught up in the memory that he didn't realize they had reached the airport until the limo slowed near the plane.

At the waiting private jet, the limo driver put her carry-on and briefcase on board the plane. Claire stood with a light wind whipping her skirt around her legs as she turned to Nick, who had just introduced her to the pilot and a flight attendant. As the two men walked toward the plane and left her with Nick, she turned to him. "I'll see you Friday night in Houston about half-past six."

Nick nodded. "I can't wait. Claire, I know that any anger and hard feelings will pass. I'm thrilled beyond anything I can possibly say to you."

"I'm glad, Nick. I think you'll love Cody the moment you meet him."

They gazed into each other's eyes and he was suddenly swamped with gratitude that she had given him a son. On impulse, he stepped closer to wrap his arms around her and kiss her.

He caught her by surprise, but then she slipped her arms around him and returned his kiss, a kiss that made him remember old times with her, that made him want to be with her longer and take the kiss deeper. His reaction was even stronger than it had been to their earlier kiss. Because of Claire, his life was suddenly filled with uncertainties and one of the biggest ones was how he was going to deal with her. For just a moment, he forgot the past, the present, the problems they'd have in the future. He wanted her.

Hot with desire, he tightened his arm around her slender waist as he parted her lips and his tongue mated with hers. Running his hand down her back and over her bottom, he wanted nothing more than to peel away the barriers of clothing between them. His heart pounded in his chest, so hard he thought it would burst. He trailed kisses to her throat as she leaned back to give him access to the slender column of her neck.

From somewhere deep in his mind came the warning to stop. If he didn't, he knew he'd take her right there on the tarmac.

Reluctantly he released her. He didn't want to fall in love again because he would be hurt all over again. Perhaps a deeper hurt this time. The problems between them now were bigger than ever. Not only was she still tethered to Houston and her family, they had a bigger issue to deal with. Their son. Nick told himself he couldn't get entangled again. As much as she tempted him, he had to resist kissing her when they were together. She was a huge threat to his happiness and his future in too many ways.

On a cerebral level he knew that. All too well. But on a physical level…how was he going to cope with this intense attraction he had to her?

Four

While her heart pounded, Claire looked into his blue eyes that had darkened with passion. She felt it in his hard body pressed close to hers, in his tongue that tangled with hers, in the arms that held her tight. And she responded in kind. Desire surged through her and stirred old memories she didn't want coming alive. Memories of making love to Nick long into the night, of waking in his arms the next day, only to repeat their heart-pounding performance. She tried to shut her mind to those remembrances, to his kisses, so that she could cool down and get her thoughts back where they needed to be. Back to thinking about the coming weekend.

It was going to be one of the most important weekends of her life. And certainly her son's life.

When she stepped back and under the lights on the tarmac, she could see his face clearly. On the ride over she'd given it some thought and now she wanted to tell him her plan. "Nick," she started, "you're welcome to stay with us.

I've got plenty of room in the house. I think it'd be best for Cody to get to know you with us around."

"Thanks," Nick said. "That sounds ideal, Claire. I'll take you up on that offer because staying there would let him get more accustomed to me in surroundings that are familiar to him."

"Actually, Nick, if all goes well, you might as well stay Saturday night, also. We can see how it goes on Friday. If I don't think you should stay, I'll tell you."

He smiled. "Fair enough. You know your son."

"Our son," she corrected, but she couldn't smile. She was hurt and she was frightened because Nick had had a bigger reaction than she had anticipated.

Glancing at the plane, she looked up at Nick. "I better board. They seem to be waiting."

"They are," he said, giving her a heavy-lidded look that stirred desire again. She stepped back, knowing she needed to avoid another kiss that would make her want things she couldn't have. Nick's kisses could always melt her. She had to keep a barrier around her heart because he was a heartbreaker.

"I'll see you Friday night. C'mon. I'll walk with you." He took her arm and they walked to the foot of the steps to the plane.

"See you, Nick," she said as she boarded. Taking a seat by a window she looked out at him and watched him as the plane taxied away. He stood there, the wind blowing locks of his dark brown hair. Hair so like Cody's. Maybe it was seeing that resemblance, maybe it was everything she'd been through this night. But the reality hit her hard, knocking her back into her seat. Cody really had a dad—a dad who wanted to know him.

What kind of dad would he be? What kind of rapport would he have with Cody? Questions bombarded her, not only about his relationship with Cody but with her. What would their future hold? Was he going to push for marriage, a paper marriage to satisfy the public so he could win his political race and become a United States Senator?

His political ambitions were daunting. Nick wanted to run for President of the United States. His dad had pushed for it and laid the groundwork years earlier. Nick and his father, the judge, embodied power, clout, wealth and success, and had built a network of cronies of the same type. Nick had stayed with the prestigious DC law firm just long enough to make lasting ties with some powerful people and then he had returned to his roots in Texas to build a strong support base.

She had known him long enough to know how he made friends with influential people who could help him. Some of Nick's socializing seemed to come as naturally to him as smiling. At the same time, there was the part of him that loved his ranch and cowboy life, who could soak that up as if it was necessary to restart his engines. Nick had always claimed ranching as his first love. What would he have done if his family, particularly his dad, hadn't pushed so hard for law and politics? If left to his own decisions as he had grown up, would Nick now be a rancher? She wondered how much of his current life was due to pleasing his family instead of doing what he wanted.

She recalled that he'd seemed the happiest when she had gone home with him to his ranch. He claimed he loved living and working on his ranch the most, but that wasn't what dominated his life now. But Nick wasn't the only one with contradictory aspects to his personality. She had them too. On the one hand she didn't want to think about Nick's kisses that still set her ablaze. She didn't want a marriage of convenience that made the most sense for Nick and would aid his political pursuits. One in which love would not be part of the union.

Yet, on the other hand, she couldn't let herself fall in love with Nick, or him with her. She knew that would only end up one way. With heartbreak. And she'd already lived through that agony once.

Life was truly complicated and had just gotten more so. Because they had a child.

Nick was moving up politically, while she had a big business to run and her son and grandparents to care for. Whatever they did, she did not want to fall in love with Nick again. There had been no other man in her life because she had been busy with Cody, her family and running the business. Nick's kisses set her on fire and it was exciting to be with him, to have his arms around her, but that was lust, purely physical. It was not love. She'd remind herself of that time and time again, until she remembered it.

Sighing, she laid her head back on the seat as the plane reached cruising altitude. While she was grateful for the private flight that would get her home earlier, there was a part of her that actually dreaded going home. She'd have to break the news to her grandmother and then tell Cody. Cody would be happy, but her grandmother... Claire could almost script that conversation, and it wouldn't be good.

When she entered her house, she tiptoed into Cody's room and stood beside his bed. She wanted to hold him, to get him as close to her heart as possible. Tears threatened when she thought about having to share him with Nick now. She pulled a light blanket higher over him carefully while love for him enveloped her.

She didn't know how long she stood beside his bed watching him sleep. Finally, she went to her suite to shower and dress for the day.

By the time her gray-haired grandmother, Verna Prentiss, walked into the kitchen, Claire had made oatmeal, washed and sliced berries, and had everything set and ready. She gave her grandmother a light hug and kiss.

"I'm glad you're home and I'm glad it went well," Verna said. "Can you take today off, or even the morning before you go to the office?"

"I need to get to the office. I'll take off early this afternoon."

"Good. I'm glad. I'll see your grandfather today and take Cody with me. I'll tell him you'll see him tomorrow."

"Mom!" Cody exclaimed as he ran into the kitchen to hug her. She caught him, holding him lightly. Thin and wiry, he was still in pajamas. She kissed his cheek and then reluctantly let him go, fighting for control of her emotions.

As they ate breakfast, she listened to Cody tell her about building a spaceship out of boxes his great-grandmother had given him. As Cody and Verna talked, part of Claire's thoughts were on Nick and how he would see Cody. She was certain Nick would love his son wholeheartedly and want to be with him as much as possible.

After breakfast she said she would clear, but Verna shook her head. "I know you want to spend some time with Cody. Go ahead. This will give me something to do."

Laughing, Claire turned to Cody who was waiting and smiling. "Thanks," Claire said, and left with Cody who took her hand to show her his spaceship.

She sat on the floor playing with him, praising his spaceship. It was patched and pasted, but she knew he thought it was grand.

It was after nine when she told him she had to go to the office.

Brushing his brown hair off his forehead, she smiled at

him. "I'll take this afternoon off and we'll do something fun together. How's that?"

"Good," he said. "Can we take my spaceship outside and paint it?"

"That's a good idea. Let's go look in the garage and see what colors we have. If we don't have any paint, I'll get some while I'm out."

By the time she stood at the front door with Verna and Cody to tell them goodbye, it was approaching ten in the morning. "Kiss me goodbye." When he kissed her cheek, she wrapped her arms around him. Cody stepped back and his great-grandmother placed her hand on his shoulder.

"We'll see you this afternoon," her grandmother said, following her to the door to hold it open and wave goodbye as Claire hurried to her car. Before the front door closed, she had one last glimpse of Cody turning to run out of sight. Love for him swamped her again and she wished yesterday had never happened.

That night she read Cody his favorite bedtime story. Sitting beside him on his twin bed, which he'd dubbed his "big boy bed," she cuddled him close as she read about the caterpillar that ate a hole in everything. Her son giggled as he turned the pages, eager for what he knew was coming. He loved bugs and she'd read him this story about a hundred times. Each time was like the first time he heard it.

She cherished this time together. All day at work she looked forward to the hours they got to spend together each night. As she looked down at him now in the dim light, there was a part of her that wished she could keep him from Nick, that she could keep him to herself. But that was impossible. Now that Nick knew about his son, there was no going back.

But first she had to tell her grandmother about Nick.

She'd hold off on telling Cody until nearer to the time for Nick's visit because Cody would be too excited to wait. When she finally kissed him good-night and tiptoed from the room, she returned to the family room to rejoin her grandmother.

"Grandma, I want to tell you about the closing."

Pushing her bifocals higher on her nose, Verna looked up from her sewing. "Did everything go as you hoped?"

"Yes, except for one surprise," Claire replied, dreading breaking the news because it would forever change their lives, but putting off talking about it wouldn't change anything. "Grandma, the buyer's attorney was Nick Milan."

"Oh, my word," Verna said, putting down her needle. "I'm sure that was a surprise. Does he have children now?"

"No, he doesn't. His pregnant wife was killed two years ago in a car crash."

"Oh, no," Verna said, shaking her head. "He lost his wife and unborn baby? He's single and doesn't have any family?" Her empathy shone in her eyes.

"That's right." Claire took a deep breath and let the words flow. "Grandma, I had to tell him about Cody."

"Claire," she said, looking stricken. Tears filled her eyes and though she didn't say anything for a moment, Claire could feel her grandmother's concern wrap around her. Finally she gathered herself and added, "I'm sure he'll be here soon to meet Cody."

"That's right. He's flying in Friday to meet his son and take us out to dinner. You're invited for dinner too. He'll be here for the weekend and leave Sunday."

"No, that should be just you and Cody. I'll call my sister. Becky will pick me up." She paused a moment, emotion choking off her words. "Claire, I—"

She could see the tears in her grandmother's eyes and knew exactly how she felt. She was worried for Claire, worried how things would fall once Nick met his son. Claire felt it, too. But she needed to reassure her grandmother, not bask in her self-pity. "We'll work things out, so please don't worry about it. Nick is a nice person."

"I'll try not to, but I can't keep from worrying and I know you're worried. Go ahead and tell Grandpa tomorrow when you see him. It'll give him something to think about and pray over."

"I'll tell him if the opportunity arises. If he's with his cronies, I'll do it another day."

Her grandmother nodded. "I suppose Nick was terribly shocked. I know you felt you had to tell him. Was he angry you hadn't told him earlier?"

"Yes, he was at first, but it didn't last," Claire answered.

"He may want Cody the majority of the time."

"I don't think that will happen. We'll just work out a way to share Cody. I think Nick will be a good dad."

Her grandmother started crying and Claire, hurting for her, crossed the room to hug her. "Don't cry. We don't know how much we'll see of Nick and he has clearly said he will not take Cody from me."

"We can't fight the Milans. They're powerful people."

"We won't have to," Claire said, hoping her words proved true. "Please don't cry," Claire repeated, taking her grandmother in her arms again and noticing how much more frail and thin she was.

Her grandmother wiped her eyes as she sat back. "I'm all right and don't you worry. We'll just take each day as it comes. I'll pray for the best."

Claire nodded. "We all will. I wanted to tell you before I tell Cody. I expect him to be very happy about the news because he'll never think of the downside to this. I know he'll be eager and excited," she said, hoping that's what Cody would feel.

* * *

Claire took the day off Friday. Her grandmother had already gone for the weekend. During the afternoon Claire sat with Cody on her lap.

"Cody, I want to tell you something." His big blue eyes looked up at her and she smiled, hugging him lightly. He wore a superhero T-shirt, jeans and his tennis shoes, and she knew he wanted to run and play. "I saw your daddy this weekend. Here is a picture of me with him. His name is Nicholas Milan."

"He's my daddy?"

"Yes. And he is coming to see you tonight."

"This is my daddy and he's coming here?" Cody asked, grinning, his eyes sparkling and looking as if he had just been given a trip to Disneyland. From that moment on until it was time for Nick's arrival, Cody was giddy with excitement.

She gave Cody new Legos and left him building while she got dressed, thinking that one plus to Cody's exhilaration was she didn't have time to grow steadily more nervous about seeing Nick.

Finally, she made one last check of herself, her gaze roaming over her black hair, which fell to her shoulders. She wore a dark red cotton dress with a V neckline, a straight skirt that ended at her knees and matching high-heeled shoes. In spite of butterflies in her stomach, icy hands and a sense of dread, she felt a streak of excitement to see Nick again. An excitement she tried to ignore.

When the bell rang, she hurried to open the door, aware of Cody following her instructions and waiting in the family room. Her heartbeat spiked as she looked into Nick's blue eyes. His smile quickened her breathing. In his navy suit and matching tie, he was handsome. Too handsome, too irresistible. Taking another deep breath, she opened the storm door. "Come in, Nick. Cody is excited and there's no calming him."

"I'm excited, too," Nick said, his gaze sweeping over her. "You look beautiful, Claire," he said, his voice taking on a husky note. He glanced over her head. "Where's your grandmother?"

"She thought we should be alone for this momentous occasion, so she's gone to her sister's house for the weekend."

"That was perceptive of her," he said. "It will be good to have just the three of us. I'll thank her for understanding."

Claire glanced beyond him and noticed a white limo parked on the drive. "You came in a limo? Is the driver just going to sit in the car and wait until we go to dinner? I can drive to dinner and you can send him on his way now."

"I made arrangements for the limo through dinner and afterward, when we get back here, I'll send him away for the night. He's leaving now and I'll call him to come get us when we're ready to go. I thought Cody might like a limo ride. Has he ever ridden in one?"

"No, he hasn't and he will probably love it. He's curious."

Nick set his things down inside the door. "I brought champagne for us later, to celebrate," he said, handing her an insulated box. She was aware of the brush of his warm fingers as she took the box.

"I have presents for Cody, too, but I'd like to leave those until after I've met him."

"You might as well, because right now he is more curious about you and he won't pay attention to presents until he's met you. I told him to wait in the family room and I'd bring you in." She glanced toward the room where Cody awaited. "Let's go meet your son," she said.

She linked her arm in Nick's to take him inside, knowing that her life, as well as Nick's, was about to change forever.

Five

Nick couldn't recall a time he had felt so unprepared to meet someone, even though he wanted this more than anything else in life. He would love Cody on sight, but he didn't know how to deal with meeting his son.

Since telling Claire goodbye, he had spent the past couple of days getting ready for this moment. They entered the family room and all Nick's qualms melted away as he looked at a small boy who bore enough Milan family resemblance that there could never be a doubt about his heritage. Cody's blue eyes were large and he smiled as he watched Nick approach.

"Cody, come here," Claire said in a sweet voice. The boy ran to her. Setting the box with the champagne on a table, she placed her hand on his shoulder. "I want to introduce you to somebody," she said, "and then I'll just go into the kitchen for a few minutes. Okay?"

He looked up at her. "Yes, ma'am," he said, his curious gaze returning to Nick.

"Cody, this is your dad, Nick Milan. Nick, here's your son, Cody," she said. Then she stepped away and Nick didn't see her pick up the champagne and leave because his attention was on the small boy staring at him.

With a lump in his throat, Nick smiled and walked to Cody. He hunkered down in front of him to get closer to Cody's level. "You're my son, Cody, and I love you," Nick said in a husky voice.

"Yes, sir," Cody said quietly.

Nick's insides clutched. "Cody, can I hug you?" he asked, thinking that was the first time in his life he could recall asking permission for a hug.

Cody nodded. "Yes, sir."

With a pounding heart filled with joy and trepidation, Nick hugged him lightly. "You're my son, Cody," Nick repeated. "You'll never know how wonderful that is for me." He released the little boy. "You can think about what you want to call me—Dad or Daddy. I hope one of those will be what you'd like best. What do you think?"

Cody stared at him a few minutes that made Nick tense. What if Cody didn't want to call him either? He waited, feeling as if he couldn't catch his breath.

"Dad," he said with a nod of his head. "Okay?"

"It's more than okay. It's great. I can't tell you how wonderful it will be to hear you call me that. It means you're my little boy. Let's find your mom and get her to join us. She doesn't need to stay away. You want to go get her?"

"Yes, sir," Cody replied, nodding and running out of the room.

As Nick watched Cody go, he was overwhelmed by emotion. He'd loved Cody the first moment he saw him. He felt he couldn't get enough of seeing or being with him. Now that he knew of his existence, he wanted to be with Cody every day.

He thought about what Claire had said the other day, how his father would push for a marriage of convenience. Claire had been cool on the subject, and Nick hadn't given it much thought, but now he realized it would solve a lot of problems. Though, he had to admit, far more for him than for her. All the same problems faced them, plus more. If they married and it didn't work out, a split would mean a divorce and even more bitterness than their previous breakup. If they had a marriage of convenience, could he keep from falling in love with her and getting hurt all over again? No, he couldn't see a marriage of convenience working, or Claire ever agreeing.

Nick walked to the front entry to pick up an armload of wrapped presents and returned to the family room. He had been so taken with Cody, he hadn't really looked at the tall Christmas tree in a corner of the room. Decorations included a lot of children's ornaments and a paper chain probably made by Cody. There were already presents scattered around the base. Usually Christmas was a painful, lonely time for Nick, but he looked forward to it this year, with Cody in it. That is, if he could work it out with Claire.

In minutes Cody appeared, holding Claire's hand. "Cody said you sent him to tell me to join you."

"You might as well. Getting to know each other will take time. Cody, I brought you some presents. They're all in this sack. You can get them out and open them now."

"Nick, let's have a seat while we watch him open his presents," Claire said, sitting and crossing the long legs that he couldn't keep from noticing. She had the best legs of any woman he had ever known.

Cody sent him a questioning look and then turned to Claire, who nodded. "Go ahead and open your presents."

The first one was a book that Cody opened carefully,

but when he saw what it was, he smiled and held it up for Claire to see. "Mama, look at this."

"One of your favorites that you've been wanting," she said, smiling at Nick who was relieved that the first gift had been something Cody really wanted. Claire had sent him a list, but he still had felt uncertain.

Cody turned to him. "Thank you."

"You're welcome, Cody."

Cody set aside the book and pulled another bigger package out of the sack and tore it open to show Claire a box of Legos. "I don't have this one. Thank you," he said to Nick, smiling at him and looking at the box. "Can I do this now, Mama?"

"Open all your presents and then you may play with whatever you want," Claire said. "Let's see what else you have in the sack."

With each gift Cody ripped the paper away faster and with more enthusiasm. He pulled out one that had a stuffed monkey on a spring that he could send flying across the room. He put it on the spring and pulled the lever and the monkey shot into the air, startling Claire and sending the boy into peals of laughter.

"Cody," Claire said. "Not in the house."

"Yeah," Nick agreed. "Maybe we should try that one in the backyard, Cody."

"Yes, sir," Cody said, giggling and getting another present.

"Is this more of the same?" Claire asked, eyeing the odd shape of the next gift.

"Close, but it stays on the floor," Nick replied, looking at Cody laugh with his blue eyes sparkling and thinking he had the most adorable son possible. Cody pulled a long furry toy with black eyes and a smiling mouth. When he pushed the switch the fuzzy toy rolled around on the floor while it growled, which made Cody laugh out loud. He flopped down on the floor beside it to watch.

Charmed by Cody, Nick glanced at Claire and she looked back while she laughed and shook her head. For an instant he felt a bond with her. They had a son, and for the moment they seemed like a family. Gratitude to Claire filled him. Nick had felt grateful to her before, but it was magnified a thousandfold now that he was with both of them.

Cody opened another present. "Mama, look," he cried, jumping up to take a box to her.

"A child's computer just for you, Cody. You'll have such fun with that," she said, smiling at him as he tried to open the box. While she peeled away tape, he turned to Nick.

"Thank you for my present," he said, smiling at Nick. Cody pulled out the last box and ripped away paper to hold up a bug collecting kit that included a net.

"Super," he said. "Look, I can catch some bugs," he said, taking the kit to Claire.

"You did well, Nick. These are all perfect little-boy gifts. And he loves them all."

"Thanks. I had help from a long-time friend who has a three-year-old son." He'd have to remember to thank his close friend Mike Calhoun for the suggestions the next time he saw him.

"Looks like you asked an expert," she said, smiling at him.

"Can we build this now?" Cody asked, pulling the Lego box out from beneath his other presents and holding it out to Nick.

"Claire, what's the schedule? Can we start on this?"

"We'll go to dinner whenever you two are ready. I'm in no hurry."

Nick turned to the boy. "Okay, Cody, let's give it thirty

minutes and then I'll take you and your mother to dinner. How's that?"

"Super," Cody said, starting out of the room.

"I guess I'm supposed to follow," Nick said to Claire, who nodded.

"He's headed to the kitchen table. He's used to playing with his grandmother. She doesn't sit on the floor."

"Come join us."

"Oh, no, this is male bonding time," she said. When he didn't move right away she added, "If you don't get in there, he'll be through."

Nick stood up to leave, but stopped. "Claire, he's wonderful. He has to be the cutest kid on the whole Earth."

"Thanks. I think so too. And I can tell he's very happy to have a dad," she said. Despite her fleeting smile, she looked as if there was something worrying her and he wondered if she was unhappy that Cody knew about him. On the other hand, Nick was so overwhelmed with gratitude he wanted to cross the room, hug and reassure her so she wouldn't worry. But she had thrown up a wall between them, which was what he should also do. They were both in a vulnerable state right now and they had to be careful. With Claire, a simple kiss might lead to falling in love. And that could end in more hurt.

He left her, and when he joined his son in the kitchen, even though she had warned him, it startled him how much Cody had done by himself. He'd followed the diagrams and was working away with success.

As Nick pulled a chair beside him, Cody tossed him a smile and returned to fitting the next block into place.

Nick helped, talking with Cody, finding him easy to be with and as happy as Claire had indicated. She had done a great job raising him. What an incredible woman she was, a woman who—

He pulled the plug on that thought as he felt his heart skip a beat. He couldn't keep thinking about her as a desirable woman, wanting to touch her, to kiss her. He had to listen to common sense. It warned him to avoid falling in love again because it would be futile, another giant heartbreak he had to avoid.

After almost half an hour, Cody showed Nick his room and other creations he had built. Claire appeared, standing in the doorway. "I hate to interrupt, but before you know it, bedtime will come for Cody. We should go to dinner unless you'd like to eat here."

"No," Nick answered. "Cody, let's go to dinner. We'll look at this later or next time," he said.

"Yes, sir," Cody said as Nick's phone buzzed. He pulled it from his pocket to look at it and walked away from them to take a business call.

"You wash your hands before we go," Claire said to Cody, and he ran out of the room. Nick finished his call, returning to join Claire in the family room. She stood at the window with her back to him and his gaze ran over her again, causing desire to flare. He couldn't stop his response to her any more than he could stop breathing. She heard him and turned, her dark eyes riveting, making him draw a deep breath. He had to fight the urge to take her into his arms, stopping himself within a few feet of her.

"He's the happiest kid ever. You've done a wonderful job, Claire," Nick said, feeling another rush of gratitude to her for having Cody, for raising him to be such a polite, happy little boy, for telling him about Cody. It frightened Nick to think that she could have gone home without telling him and he might not have known about his son for years longer, if ever.

"Thank you, but I don't think I can take credit for his

disposition. I think he may have inherited it." She winked at him. "But who knows?"

When Cody returned, they donned their coats, and as they walked to the front door, Nick picked up Cody, carrying him easily. "Have you ever ridden in a limousine?"

"No, sir," he said, his eyes widening as he glanced toward the front door.

"Well, you're going to now."

Cody turned quickly to grin at Claire who had to laugh. "I think that grin means he's enthused."

"Good. Let's go see," Nick said, opening the front door and swinging Cody down to stand him on his feet.

"Wow," Cody said, standing stock-still and staring agape at the limo.

Nick was delighted with Cody's reaction and they took time, before they left Claire's house, for Cody to look at everything in the interior of the limo. Nick showed him the phone and the bar, the sliding glass divider, and all the hidden gadgets. He introduced the chauffeur and finally they buckled up and left.

From that moment until they reached the restaurant, Cody didn't say a word. He spent the whole time looking intently at everything Nick had shown him, causing Nick to chuckle. "I'm not sure he knows we're riding with him," he told Claire. "I had no idea this would be so fascinating to him."

"My guess is you've been in limos so much of your life, you don't remember the first time you rode in one."

"You're right and if it was with my dad, I wasn't investigating everything in sight. I promise you that."

As they smiled at each other, he recalled old times with her when they had shared so much laughter. Nick remembered when he had taken her to the family ranch after his parents had moved to Dallas. He and Claire had gone horseback riding at sunrise and the morning had been one of his happiest memories. They had ridden to one of his favorite places, where he had gone as a boy when he wanted to be alone. When they rode into the small clearing near the creek, a skunk had been stretched on a boulder, enjoying the morning. Nick had laughed with Claire as they rode away and left the skunk to enjoy the hideaway.

As the limo slowed to a stop at the restaurant and the valet opened their door, Nick's attention returned to the present.

They entered the restaurant that had a jungle ambience, thunder rumbling and lightning flashing, the staged animals roaring. Cody seemed lost in his own world through dinner.

As soon as they finished, they returned to the limo, and an overexcited Cody snuggled up to Claire and in minutes he crashed, falling into a deep sleep.

When the limo wound up her drive, Nick took a moment to look at the large home that he hadn't really noticed when he'd arrived earlier. The rambling two-story house was set back on a perfectly landscaped lawn with tall trees that now twinkled with Christmas lights. "You have a beautiful home, Claire. You've done well."

"Thanks. I've had a lot of luck in business, I guess. I started as a kid helping at Grandpa's office so when I finished college and came into the business, I had all sorts of wonderful contacts through him."

"You had to do a lot yourself. Wonderful contacts from your grandfather are a fine background, but you've gone way beyond what success he had."

"Fortunately, people who've been happy working with me tell their friends, so my network builds. I love my work and in spite of a 24/7 business, I get a lot of hours with Cody."

"That's good," Nick said.

When the limo stopped, Claire looked down at her sleeping son. "It's past his bedtime and he has been so excited all day. Give me a minute to wake him and he'll walk in."

"No. He's a featherweight. I'll carry him." Nick picked him up easily, and in his sleep Cody wrapped his arm around Nick's neck.

Nick paused to make arrangements with the driver to come back Saturday night in time to take them to dinner. Then he entered the front door Claire held open and carried Cody up to his room and placed him on the bed.

Claire stepped forward to get him ready for bed. "Want some help?" he asked her.

She shook her head. "No, but thanks. I'll just get his shoes and socks off and leave him alone. I'm sure he's worn out."

Nick stepped away, strolling around Cody's room, looking at shelves of family pictures of the boy with his great-grandparents, with his grandmother and with Claire. Through one doorway Nick could see an attached bathroom, but he went through the other door into an adjoining playroom filled with toys, bookshelves and a large fish tank that seemed to take center stage. Cody had a large rocking horse, plastic superheroes on the shelves and a life-size mural of Winnie-the-Pooh characters on one wall.

A door was open to an adjoining bedroom and he realized it was Claire's suite. She had a four-poster bed with a canopy, and as his gaze ran over the bed and mound of pillows, he could picture her sprawled there. He remembered how she had looked in bed, recalling her black hair spread over the pillow beside him. His insides tightened as the memories ignited desire.

Nick turned to look at her as she leaned over Cody and his gaze ran down her backside, the straight skirt of her dress fitting her hips snugly and the long legs that peeked from under her dress as she leaned over. He could feel his body heat up as he looked at her. She could still cause a reaction in him on a physical level, something no other women he had dated had done since his loss of Karen. And he'd bet Claire still had a physical response to him, too.

Logically, he could enumerate each and every reason to avoid her, but nothing could stop his body from responding to her, from desiring her. She was a sexy, beautiful woman who took his breath away. He turned abruptly, knowing he had to get her out of his thoughts. That wouldn't happen as long as he stood there staring at her long legs and remembering how they felt wrapped around his waist as they made love.

When he looked back, she had stepped away from Cody's bed. His gaze shifted to Cody, who was sleeping soundly, his dark hair falling over his forehead. Nick wanted his son in his life. He would try to cooperate with Claire, but he had to be part of Cody's life. He'd loved Cody from the first moment he saw him this afternoon.

Claire stepped toward him. "Let's go downstairs," she said softly.

When they walked into the hall, she touched his sleeve lightly to get his attention. "You can have the suite across the hall from us for the weekend," she said, stopping to switch on the lights in the room she pointed out. He poked his head in and saw a large living area done in deep blues with hardwood floors and area rugs.

"There's an adjoining bath and bedroom, giving you

your own suite," she explained. "Down the hall are two more bedroom suites and I have an office on this floor, too."

"Claire, this is a splendid house. Very luxurious, but comfortable and practical at the same time."

"I know a lot of builders, so I tried to get the best."

He smiled and ran his finger along her smooth cheek. "Good businesswoman."

"I try to be."

For whatever reason, seeing her there, backlit by the lamp in the suite, in her element in her own home that she'd built with her successful career, he was more drawn to her than ever. More than anything he wanted to lean down and kiss her. He stepped closer, unable to resist her allure, but before he could make his move, Claire stepped back. She was keeping a wall between them. She was polite, friendly, cooperative in a lot of ways about Cody, but Nick felt that, beneath the surface, she wished he would pack and go back to Dallas and get out of her life.

"Come on," she said. "Let's go downstairs. I have a monitor for Cody so I can hear if he wakes. I have an alarm that lets me know if he gets out of his bed and walks around his room. I also can see him on my iPad, so I know when he's sleeping peacefully."

"You've covered all your bases to keep him safe, I see." He followed her down the hall.

"You were very good with Cody," she said as they reached the ground floor.

"He's an easy, wonderful kid. I'm in awe, Claire. He's perfect. I know I've got a prejudiced view, but I can't think of one thing about him that isn't really great."

She laughed. "You sound just like a new dad. But you're right—he's easy, likeable and a smart little boy. And he's glad to have his dad in his life," she said. "You had the perfect gifts and the limo was the crowning touch."

"Mike suggested the limo."

"Mike sounds like a good dad. Would you like a drink?"

"It's time to break out the champagne so we can celebrate." His fingers closed on her arm to stop her and she turned to look up at him. His heart beat faster as he looked down at her. "I want you to celebrate, Claire. I don't want this to be an unhappy or difficult event to bring me into Cody's life. I know it means you have to share him, but I'll try every way I can to make that a plus for you and for Cody." Her brown eyes were wide and dark and mysterious. He couldn't read them. Nor could he keep from letting his gaze drift to her mouth that was enticing, bow-shaped with full lips that were so soft, yet fiery. He felt caught in her gaze and she must have felt the same because her eyes widened slightly and then her gaze lowered to his mouth and his heart pounded.

They were only a foot apart and it would be easy to close that gap and give into the temptation that clawed at him. So easy to touch his lips to hers and taste the sweetness that was Claire. If only…

No, he couldn't. He had to fight the temptation. It was for his own good. Reluctantly he stepped away. "Where's the champagne?" he asked, his voice far deeper and hoarse.

She gave him a searching look and finally spoke. "In the bar," she whispered, turning abruptly. "I'll get it." She went behind the bar in the far corner of the family room. He trailed behind her and stood in the entrance, watching her. She looked lost, as if she had never been in the place before, as she glanced around. Shaking her shoulders, she reached for a glass and her hand trembled.

Grasping her slender wrist lightly, Nick steadied her hand and reached beyond her to get two crystal flutes. He turned her to face him. He ached to kiss her and he fought an inner battle, wondering if her own inner battle was causing her to look upset and shaky.

"Go sit and I'll pour the champagne," he said, starting to open the bottle while trying to resist reaching for her. She nodded and stepped away, moving out of the bar to sit on a high stool.

He let out his breath. How was he going to keep from falling in love again? Usually he recalled their parting, the anger and hurt that always cooled his desire for her, but it wasn't working tonight. He set two empty flutes in front of her, popped the cork and poured the pale, bubbly champagne.

He walked around to face her, leaving a yard of space between them so he wouldn't be tempted. He raised his flute. "Here's to you, Claire, a beautiful woman."

She gave him a tight smile. "Thank you. That isn't what I thought you'd say."

He touched her flute with his. Watching her, he sipped his champagne. He wanted to set his flute down, take hers from her and pull her into his arms. That was the way to pain and he wasn't going to do it, but his inner battle was tearing him up.

"Here's to our son, a beautiful child."

"I'll drink to that one," she said, smiling broadly and looking as if she'd relaxed slightly.

"That's better."

Only one lamp was on in the large room, spilling a soft glow, and she had switched on classical music in the background.

"This next toast is to celebrate the night I met my son." He held out his glass again.

"Whatever happens, Nick, I know you'll be a good dad."

They tapped glasses and then he sipped the bubbly champagne. Too bad he couldn't cool his desire or his reactions to her as easily as the champagne quenched his thirst. She sat on the barstool, her fabulous legs crossed. He ought to stop looking, but she was too beautiful, too easy to look at.

Nick set aside his glass and crossed the room to the briefcase that he'd brought with him. He opened it and removed two small boxes.

He returned to hand her a long, flat box and place the smaller box on a table. "This is for you. I wasn't with you when you had Cody. I should have been, but we can't undo the past. I wish I could have given you this when he was born. It's a small token of gratitude."

"Nick, you didn't need to get me something," she said, shaking her head.

"Go ahead. It's your gift for being Cody's mother. Cody got his presents. Now I want you to have your gifts—what I would have given you if I had been present at his birth."

"That's sweet, Nick." She carefully untied the ribbon and paper, opening the box with a gasp. "Oh, Nick, this is beautiful," she said. He moved closer to take out the gold chain with a diamond heart pendant made with three heart-shaped rows of diamonds and a larger diamond in the center. The pendant glittered in the subdued light.

"Can I put it on you?"

"Of course," she said, smiling at him. "It's stunning."

"You're stunning, Claire," he said quietly. "More now than four years ago." As she lifted her hair out of his way, Nick stepped behind her to fasten the necklace.

She turned to face him. Her big, dark eyes held him and memories hit him with almost physical force as he recalled how much he had loved her once. "Claire, my heart has been broken twice—first with you and then when I lost my baby and my wife. I can't go through heartbreak again."

"We were both hurt," she whispered. "We can't undo the past. Don't try."

"I'm not trying to undo the past, Claire. And for this weekend, let's put aside trying to work out our future. Let's just get reacquainted and let me get to know my son. I want to make the most of each moment and not worry about how we'll move forward. Can we do that?"

"Of course. That sounds best to me." She gave him a slight smile. She fingered the diamond. "Can I go look in the mirror at my new necklace? It's beautiful. Thank you."

"You have another present. Go ahead and open it."

She carefully opened a smaller box to find a gold charm bracelet with a one-carat diamond imbedded in the gold between each charm. One charm was a baby in a small crib and inscribed on the crib were the tiny numbers of Cody's birthday. Another charm was a birthday cake with one candle followed by a charm in the shape of a small boy, then three figures, a man and a woman with a small boy between them. She smiled as she touched it. "That's special, Nick. Thank you."

"I'll add a charm each year until Nick is eighteen, but you can pick out what you want for the charms."

She turned the bracelet in her hand. "You're committing yourself for the coming years. You don't know what you'll be doing." She looked up at him. "Let's sit down," she said, moving to a chair. He sat close beside her, a table between them where they set their drinks.

"Nick, are there any grandchildren in the Milan family yet, besides Cody?"

"No. Cody is the first grandchild."

"Oh, my word," she said, rubbing her arms as if she were freezing. "Then for sure your father is going to push you to marry me. He won't want you to take no for an answer."

Nick frowned. "I'm sure you're right. You're out of his

reach, although he might contact you. My dad interfered a lot in my sister's life when she fell in love with her husband, Jake, but Dad's older now, more mellow, less energetic."

Sighing, Claire shook her head. "I don't want to deal with your father. I can if I have to, and I'm not going to marry you because your dad wants us to, but if Cody is the only grandchild and you're headed for a big political life, you know that's what's coming."

"I'm a grown man and I can make my own decisions."

"You've always pleased him. You told me that. You're very close."

"We are, but I have to live my life. I'm not going through hell to please my dad. I don't want another broken heart and I know you're deeply involved in your life, as I am in mine—even more than we were four years ago. Besides, I'll work out a way for them to see their grandson and they'll settle down eventually."

"I don't think so, Nick. There's more than seeing a grandson. There's your political career at stake."

"Stop worrying until it gets to be a problem," he said. "Right now, Dad doesn't know Cody exists."

She shook her head. "Why do I feel like I'm headed for disaster?"

"It'll be all right, Claire," he said to reassure her. But deep inside he wondered if they were, indeed, headed for disaster. She was right on target about his dad. Nick just had to head off his dad trying to contact her or, worse, bribe her, which would only anger Claire more and cause worse feelings.

He had to change the subject before she read his own fears on his face. "Now, tell me more about your life and Cody's."

"I think you mean, tell you more about Cody," she said,

smiling at him. She settled back to talk about an incident when Cody was a baby and from that on to other moments in his life. Nick listened intently, but he watched her, remembering, taken back to times before. They had seldom spent hours just talking like this because they kissed as much as possible, which always led to making love.

Something he shouldn't be thinking about, he chided himself. It conjured up steamy memories that made him want to pull her into his arms and kiss her until he could carry her to his bed. How could she still have this intense physical effect on him? Was it because he'd been without a woman in his life for the last two years? Or was it because it was Claire?

He reined in his errant thoughts and focused on formulating a full picture of his son's first three years of life as Claire regaled him with stories, some funny, some touching. Eventually, she stood.

"Nick, it's one o'clock in the morning and this day has been long and emotional. It's time to call it a night."

"Today has been nerve-racking for all adults concerned," he said, standing beside her. "Cody was the happy one, thank heavens. It worked out better than I hoped." They left the room and Claire switched off the light.

He gathered his carry-on and briefcase, turning to join her at the foot of the stairs.

"I'll switch on the alarm down here. Want anything before I do?"

"No. Not at all," he said, watching her punch buttons on her phone. When he started upstairs with her, it seemed natural to drape his free arm across her slender shoulders. The moment he touched her, he realized his mistake and pulled back.

At her door he set his things on the floor. As if he hadn't just chastised himself for touching her, he placed his hands on her shoulders. "Thanks again, Claire," he said, aware of her warm shoulders beneath her blouse. Her mouth was rosy, too tempting. It amazed him how much he wanted to kiss her and hold her close. He wanted to out of gratitude, and even more, he wanted to because she was an appealing, gorgeous, sexy woman and he could remember how her kisses had pleasured him.

"Nick, thank you for the necklace," she said, touching it briefly. "It's beautiful."

He looked at the necklace, knowing what it represented and knowing he would have showered her with more if he had been present at the time of Cody's birth. He had to stop looking back, but it was difficult when he had learned about Cody only days earlier.

"He's absolutely wonderful. Think about taking a week off and bringing him to Dallas so we can get to know each other better. We can stay several days on the ranch if you think he'd like that."

"He'd love it," Claire said. "What little boy wouldn't love it on a ranch? Especially with you doting on him."

"Then think about spending the whole time there. He'll have a wonderful time and I know you used to like being on the ranch."

"I did," she answered.

"So do I. Now more than ever."

"You were a success tonight, Nick. I think he's going to love having you for a dad."

He smiled. "We did all right tonight, didn't we?"

She returned his grin briefly, but the worry didn't leave her expression. "I suppose we did. The tough decisions are still ahead, though."

He nodded and she tilted her head toward her door. "Nick, it's late." When he stepped back, she said, "I'm an early riser. You can go downstairs and the coffee will be brewed by six. Is that early enough because I can go down an hour sooner if you'd like?"

"Six is perfect. Thank you for tonight. You did all you could to make this easy for me." Nick brushed a kiss on her forehead and looked into her eyes. Moments like this reminded him of what he'd missed, but he was doing better at putting the past behind him. "The more time I have with Cody, the sooner I'll stop longing for what might have been. Tomorrow I'll invite him to the ranch."

She nodded. "Good night, Nick," she said and stepped into her room.

He picked up his things and crossed the hall, shutting himself into his suite and letting out his breath. He couldn't spend a lot of time around her. Each time with her he had to fight the temptation to kiss her. And it was getting more and more difficult.

"Dammit," he whispered, finally giving vent to feelings that had threatened him during the evening. Claire had him tied in knots. He would take them to his ranch, which stirred memories of the week he had taken Claire to the family ranch when they had been so wildly in love. He thought about the hours they had made love there and he ached, wanting her and wondering how he was going to keep from being hurt worse than ever.

Nick raked his fingers through his hair. What did she feel? Right now, was she locked in as much turmoil over him as he was over her?

As worry filled her, Claire covered her face with her hands. Nick was appealing, sexy and he was being good to her. How was she going to avoid falling deeply in love again? And hurt even worse than before?

She was still attracted physically to Nick. Every touch had been sizzling; the light, impersonal kisses that were so meaningless to Nick had made her breathless. She didn't want to respond to him, didn't want to have her life tied in with his constantly. She couldn't forget his political ambitions. Cody's birth so close to Nick's marriage would hurt him in politics, and he'd need to marry her to smooth things over for the political races he faced. He said politics didn't matter, but she didn't believe him. Whatever Nick felt, his father was going to push Nick to marry her.

Nick wanted her to take a week and go to Dallas, to his ranch. Could she cope with being under the same roof with Nick for a week? She stood in the middle of her room, staring into space, remembering being on the ranch with Nick and how in love they had been. Memories would be intense and make it even more difficult to resist him.

Finally she began to get ready for bed, barely thinking about what she was doing because her thoughts were on Nick and how to deal with him. She turned back her bed and returned to the sitting room to switch off the light. Before she did, she saw the glitter of the heart-shaped pendant on her dresser and she crossed the room to pick it up. It had cost Nick a lot, she thought as she looked at the sparkling diamonds catching the light. Turning off the light, she carried the necklace and placed it on her night table before she got into bed. Nick was too appealing in too many ways. She couldn't see how she could avoid loving him…and that was the problem.

Six

Claire had coffee brewing when Nick walked through the kitchen door the next morning. In jeans, boots and a plaid, cotton shirt, he looked more approachable and still as handsome as ever. "You don't wear jeans often."

He crossed the kitchen to her. "I don't recall seeing you in jeans a lot of times, either. I have to say, they look infinitely better on you."

"I beg to differ, but thanks," she said, smiling at him, glad to see him relaxed and more at ease than yesterday.

"I have tickets reserved for all of us at the aquarium. If you don't think Cody would like that, I'll cancel and we'll do something else."

"Cody will love it. I've meant to take him, but just haven't done it. He's sleeping late. I guess he was worn out last night."

"So how did his mama sleep?" Nick asked, getting himself a cup of coffee and standing close.

"Fair. There's no way to turn off worries," she said quietly.

Setting down his coffee mug, he placed his hands on the counter on either side of her, hemming her in so he had her full attention. As her heartbeat accelerated, he leaned down to look directly into her eyes.

"Let's get back to the cheerful morning. You and I can be friends. We were once. There's no rush here. I can take my time getting to know Cody. I'm not pushing you and I have no deadlines where Cody is concerned. As much as we can, let's put the past behind us," he said, giving her a crooked smile.

"I'll try." Inside she was hurting more than ever, because he was so understanding, which only made him more appealing. She felt on track for a giant wreck to her heart. He stood too close, only inches away. She couldn't keep from looking at his mouth, thinking about his kisses. She drew a deep breath and looked up to find him watching her with desire blatant in his expression.

"This is life altering and I'm trying to get accustomed to the change of having you in our lives," she said, looking into his sexy, thickly lashed blue eyes, which had always captivated her. Why was she so susceptible to Nick? Her heart started racing the moment he stepped into the room and sped up again when he moved close.

"Okay, but keep in mind, I'm not pushing. We don't have to rush to make changes."

"Thank you for that concession." She could barely get out the words, yet she didn't want to ask him to move away and make more of an issue of her reaction to him.

He wrapped his arms around her lightly. "We'll work something out we can both live with."

She didn't answer. It was easy to say they would work things out, but it was going to be difficult to actually do it. Nick had hurt her badly years ago and she couldn't bear another big heartbreak. "I should get breakfast, Nick."

She moved away to stir the oatmeal she'd put on the stove.

Nick still held the appeal he once had and there was no way to stop her reactions to him. Each response would be a deeper hurt when they couldn't work out being together. She still couldn't leave Houston and Nick wouldn't leave Dallas, Washington, DC, or Austin now or in years to come if he was elected—and he would be. With a child between them life would be more complicated than ever. Not only could she be hurt, so could Cody.

Cody skipped into the room with his stuffed tiger beneath one arm. He wore his pajamas and had the bug net Nick had given him in his other hand.

"Good morning," Claire said, hugging him and wanting to keep holding him, but she let him go. He turned to look at Nick who picked him up.

"I have tickets to the aquarium today. How does that sound?"

Cody looked expectantly at Claire. "It's where they have big tanks," she explained. "Way bigger than the one you have and they hold fish bigger than you."

He turned to grin at Nick. "I'd like that. I have little fish."

"I saw your fish, and after breakfast you can show me your fish tank and tell me about your fish. Do you know what kind you have?"

"Yes, sir, I do," Cody said.

Nick set him on his feet and Cody put the net and his tiger on one chair as he climbed into his booster seat. Then Nick pushed him under the table. "I'm going to need to get one of these chairs at my house. Probably at the ranch, too."

Startled, she glanced at the booster seat. She hadn't

thought about Nick having to get equipment and toys for Cody, but she supposed he would if he planned to have him part of the time. For an instant it made the change seem more real and imminent. Nick glanced at her and she turned away quickly, but in seconds, he was beside her, taking the spoon from her hand. "I'll stir the oatmeal now. You play with Cody or do whatever you would like to do."

"Thanks, Nick," she said, certain he had guessed she was upset.

As Nick helped her get breakfast, he turned to her. "I called the limo driver I have for the weekend and he'll take us to the aquarium today."

"We're going in the limo?" she asked, and before Nick could answer, Cody asked the same question.

He looked so hopeful she had to smile as Nick nodded. "Yes, we are, Cody."

Cody beamed with pleasure while she shook her head. "Next week may be very dull around here."

"Then make arrangements and come to Dallas next week. You own the company, so get someone else to run it."

"You know it isn't that easy when I have appointments, closings and things to do. I'll check my calendar after breakfast."

"Give me the word and I'll arrange my schedule so I can be off and we can go to the ranch. Cody, would you like to spend a few days on my ranch?"

"Yes, sir," he replied, his eyes widening. "Are there horses and cows?"

"Yes, there are. And I'll let you ride a horse with me if your mama says it's okay."

Cody looked hopefully at her and she nodded. "If you're with your dad," she said with only the tiniest hesitation before she said "dad." How odd it seemed to say that and mean Nick, even though it was an accurate description.

As she worked beside him, she couldn't keep from having a sharp awareness of Nick, or having fun with him and Cody. But every moment of fun with Nick fanned the fiery attraction between them and made heartache loom more threateningly. How could she protect her heart from Nick's appeal and charm when she was tied to him forever by their son?

It was midmorning when they left in the limo for the aquarium. As they walked through the building and took a train that passed between large tanks of fish, her gaze ran across Nick's broad shoulders, his narrow waist and long legs. His boots gave him height that he didn't need, and just looking at him she felt her pulse jump. Only her squealing son deflected her attention.

At one point Nick stepped close to Claire while she stood with Cody and watched fish swim past on the other side of the glass. "I've made reservations to take you both out to eat tonight. Seven o'clock. If it's too late for Cody, I can change the time."

"No, that will be fine."

She still had the afternoon to get through at the aquarium, and now dinner. How would she make it through the day without giving in to the temptation that was Nick Milan?

That evening Nick and Cody waited downstairs. Cody played with his new laptop and Nick helped him until he heard Claire's heels in the hallway. He stood and walked toward the doorway as she entered. She'd changed into a scarlet crepe dress with a scoop neckline, and her hair fell to her shoulders and was caught up slightly on each side by a tortoiseshell comb. The only jewelry she wore was the diamond necklace he had given her and the gold charm bracelet.

"You look gorgeous, Claire," Nick said in a husky drawl.

His insides knotted and he had to struggle to stop staring at her.

"Thank you. Both the men in my life look oh, so handsome," she said, smiling at Cody who wore a white dress shirt tucked neatly into black slacks.

"Thank you," Cody said dutifully.

"Thank you, also," Nick said, barely aware of his answer because Claire took all his attention. How could he get through the evening without flirting with her, touching her, kissing her?

Nick picked up Cody. "Let's go eat dinner. The limo is waiting."

Through dinner Cody was fascinated by the sparkling city lights out the window. Nick just wanted to look at Claire. In spite of the dangers to his heart, he couldn't take his attention from her. Her smooth skin looked soft, beautiful, her dark eyes wide, luminous, her sensual mouth an invitation for erotic thoughts. He nearly groaned each time his eyes lit on her. He turned, trying to focus on his son as Cody enjoyed his macaroni and cheese.

After they'd eaten their lobster dinners, Claire told him, "I looked at my calendar this afternoon, talked to my secretary and to Grandma. Cody and I can come see you next week, Nick. I think Wednesday would be good. I don't want to overstay our welcome and I need to make plane reservations. I don't want to drive."

"You don't have to drive or make plane reservations. You can fly in the Milan plane. Come on Monday, if you possibly can, and give us a whole week. We can go to the ranch and if that begins to wear thin with him, then we can all go to Dallas."

"We'll come Tuesday. I'll need to go into the office Monday and make sure things are all set for the week."

"I'll look forward to Tuesday, then."

* * *

It was nine by the time they returned home, and by ten Cody was in bed asleep.

"He likes you—which doesn't surprise me," Claire said as she walked with Nick to the family room. Nick shed his coat and tie, unbuttoning the top buttons of his shirt, making her remember the endless nights of making love with him. Beneath his tailor-made clothes was a fit, muscular male body that she could remember far too well.

She feared sitting here with him, alone. There was no telling how traitorous her own body could be. Instead, she had an idea. "C'mon, I'll give you the deluxe tour downstairs." She grabbed her iPad. "We can hear Cody on the monitor anywhere in the house."

She started the tour in the hall. "We have two suites in that wing downstairs and there's an elevator for my grandparents even though they've already moved downstairs. My grandmother still goes upstairs, but she sleeps downstairs." Claire was aware of Nick close at her side as they strolled through the downstairs. They looked at one wing and then moved to another to enter a large gym.

"Someday I'll have a pool outside, but until then, this is where I get my exercise."

"Great," Nick said, looking at the polished wood floor. "Do you have any music in here? It would be fun to move around a bit. We can dance."

For a moment she was tempted to refuse. Dancing with Nick had always been sexy. She gazed up at him, looking into blue eyes that melted her resistance.

"I have music I exercise with," she replied.

Aware of Nick standing and watching her, she turned on a tape. "Here's a good dance tape—a bit of everything."

"First, let's change something here," he said, walking to her and reaching up to take the combs out of her hair so it fell freely around her face. "That's the way I like your hair best." He dropped the combs into his pocket.

She still reacted to him as much as she had years earlier. Was it Nick, or was it simply because there hadn't been men in her life in the years in between?

"You shouldn't take down my hair, Nick," she whispered, looking at his mouth and then back to see desire flare in his blue eyes. "And we shouldn't dance."

As he inhaled deeply, he shook his head. "It's a fast song and we'll move around, which will help blow off steam," he said, but his voice was deeper and the look in his eyes clearly indicated he wanted to kiss her. Even though she knew she shouldn't, she wanted Nick's kiss.

He stepped farther back from her and began to dance to the fast beat. As they danced, she was aware of his gaze steadily on her, moving over her body and back up to hold her gaze. Dancing didn't blow off steam as he had predicted. In fact, watching his sexy moves only stirred her desire.

Still, she gave herself over to the moment. Moving with the pounding rhythm, she finally felt some of the tension ease.

It had been a good weekend, but they had put off the decisions and the discussions that would cause problems between them. For a moment they were in a dangerous limbo—getting reacquainted as he got to know his son, deliberately avoiding decisions.

The next number was a polka. Smiling, Nick took her hands to whirl around the spacious room. She hadn't danced a polka with anyone in years and she felt as if her feet barely touched the floor while she flew around the room with Nick, laughing. A ballad followed and Nick took her hand to dance, keeping a distance between them.

He grinned as they danced slowly. "Who put this playlist together?"

"I did. I like music when I exercise and I've got eclectic taste."

"I haven't danced a polka since college and that's getting to be a long time ago."

"Oh, sure. Aeons ago," she said, smiling at him.

"That's better. It's good to see you smile," he said.

"When this one is over, let's go sit and have a cool drink. I'm ready for some quiet," she said, thinking they should stop dancing and touching each other. Every contact added to her awareness of him, building the risks to her heart.

"We can go now." They stopped dancing and he waited while she turned off the music and then hit the light switch as they left the room.

"I love your home," he said. "And you've done so well with Cody. When you come to Dallas, I'd like to have my family out so they can meet him."

"That's fine, Nick. How is your family? Is Madison still painting? I met her when she had an exhibit in Houston."

"My family is fine. Madison married Jake Calhoun and she doesn't travel as much. She has the family ranch now, but lives on Jake's ranch. Wyatt is county sheriff, of all things. Friends talked him into taking the office, but he's retiring to his ranch after this term. Tony is ranching and the busy bachelor. We see each other fairly often. My folks are in Dallas and Dad is retired."

"You should break the news about Cody to your parents first. Your father will no doubt have things he wants you to do."

"Most of my life I've gotten along with Dad and I've done what he wanted. Even more than Wyatt, who never gave Dad trouble. Madison and Tony—well, that's a different story. Particularly Tony. Frankly, I don't think he was right in the way Dad dealt with Madison, but that's over and she's married to Jake Calhoun now." He shrugged. "I think Dad will cooperate with me just because we've always gotten along."

"You mean you've always done what your dad wanted."

"Yes, I have. I don't think he's been unreasonable," he said. "Dad has helped me in my career and in politics. I owe nearly everything to him. He seems to have endless contacts."

Those *endless contacts* worried her. Judge Milan was a powerful man. While Claire had never even met his parents, she suspected they didn't want Nick marrying a woman with obligations far from DC, as well as someone who would not put Nick's career first. She could understand their concern for their son's future and his happiness, but it didn't help her feelings when she had been so in love with Nick and he had seemed to be with her.

"I'll talk to my dad. Don't worry about my family," he said as they headed to her kitchen. "This is their grandson, and right now their only grandson, so they're going to welcome him and love him. I'll admit that since he's a good kid and he looks like a Milan, they will really be happy about him."

"And want you to have him all the time."

He stopped and held her back. "I promise I will not take Cody from you," he said solemnly, looking directly at her.

While she nodded, she couldn't imagine how they were going to work out sharing their son if Nick moved to Washington.

They continued to walk and within minutes they sat in the family room.

Nick turned his chair to face her, pulling it close in front of hers and to one side so he had room for his long legs. He took her hand in his. "Claire, Cody is wonderful and

I'm so happy about him. I want you to be happy to have me in his life. I know it'll be difficult for you to share him when you've been accustomed to having him all the time. As long as I can see him some, I promise we'll go slowly."

"Thank you," she said, certain that his intentions were good, but soon he would have his family pressuring him to get Cody into the Milan family. Even as she thought over their dilemma, she was aware of her hand in his as it rested on his knee.

He sat too close and his gaze was too intense, but she didn't care to tell him and let him know that his touch or his nearness had that much of an impact on her.

"We can have his name changed to Milan without a marriage. Would you be opposed to that?"

"I'll think about it. I can't give you an answer instantly," she said, withdrawing her hand from his and sipping her drink.

"All I ask on anything I suggest is that you just think about it. We're exploring possibilities, that's all. Monday I'll open a trust fund for him and a savings account. I want to be part of his life in every way I can. You've done well and it's obvious you don't need my help, but I want to share in the costs for him."

"That's fine, Nick. We don't need to go back to things I've already paid. I've been able to take care of him. But we'll share costs as we move ahead."

"Good."

He picked up a long lock of her hair and let it fall through his fingers. "Whatever we work out, it's good to be with you again," he said.

She gave him a fleeting smile, unable to say the same thing back to him. Part of her wondered whether he really meant what he said, because every moment together moved them closer to another confrontation.

Now came the part she'd been dreading. "Sooner or later," she said, "we're going to have to work out a time for him to be with you and a time for him to be with me. I'd rather work it out between us and not involve lawyers. That is, except you."

"That's fine with me. Since I am a lawyer, if you change your mind and want one, that's acceptable. I just want you and Cody happy."

"He's never been away from home at night," she said, hating that she was about to lose control.

Nick leaned closer, placing his hand over hers, holding hers lightly. "Claire, I don't want to hurt you or Cody. I meant it when I said I promise I'll work with you. I just want to share my son's life and know him."

"There are moments I can't handle looking into the future. I've had him with me constantly since he was born."

"If I do something you don't like, tell me. Promise you will and I'll promise you that I'll try to work it out. How's that?"

Nodding, she began to breathe deeply and get control.

When Nick's gaze went to her mouth, her heart missed a beat. She didn't want this reaction to him, but she couldn't keep it from happening. Physically, she responded to every look, each touch. In too many ways, she liked being with Nick, and so far he was not pressuring her about Cody, but she expected that to come.

"This has been a good weekend," he said, his voice lower than usual, as it always was when his thoughts turned to sex. "Thank you for it, Claire." Leaning close, his hands on the arms of her chair, he brushed her lips lightly, an impersonal, casual kiss, but when his lips touched hers, the moment changed.

His arm tightened around her and he looked into her eyes. As she looked at his mouth, she couldn't catch her breath. Even knowing it was folly that could only cause her trouble, she wanted his kiss. That brief contact of his lips on hers stirred desire, a longing for a kiss, for a bonding, maybe even reassurance.

"Claire," he whispered, winding his fingers in her hair behind her head as he lifted her to his lap, drew her to him for a deep, passionate kiss. His arms tightened around her, pressing her against him, and she turned, slipping her arms around his shoulders, kissing him in return while longing enveloped her. How long had it been since she'd been kissed like this? How was she going to resist him?

She kissed him, wanting him, wanting the problems gone between them and wanting to make love, to get lost in passion once again.

Thought ceased as she spiraled away in his kiss, a kiss that made her hot and shaking with desire. She clung to him, wanting him to disappear and at the same time trying to bind him to her so he would never leave her.

He shifted, turning her to cradle her against his shoulder while she held him tightly.

Finally, through the haze of desire, that nagging voice of reason spoke up and she came to her senses. She realized how kissing him was going to have her tumbling into a bigger disaster. She did not want to fall in love with him again and set herself up for another heartbreak because Nick wasn't going to change and he wouldn't give up his ambitions or his career. Not for her or for Cody. As she thought of that, she shifted away from him and moved off his lap.

"This isn't going to solve anything," she whispered, standing to walk away from him.

She glanced back to find him staring at her with a shocked look that she couldn't fathom. Had their kisses touched him on some emotional level? She doubted it and she didn't want to be taken in by Nick's smooth talk.

He was a politician, accustomed to charming people and getting what he wanted out of them. He expected to win their friendship and trust. She had been all through that and it had been heartbreak that she didn't like to recall.

"Or it might solve everything," he said gruffly, as he sat up and placed his elbows on his knees.

"I'm tied to a business here and my family. You're tied to your career in Dallas, Austin and later in DC. That isn't changing, Nick, and marriage won't make any of it go away. Any personal relationship between us will complicate our lives as it did before."

He stood and crossed the room to her. "Kisses are like dancing—sexy and great fun. No harm done."

"And on that note, we'll call it a night."

"Sure," he said, falling into step beside her as they went upstairs together and stopped at her door.

"I'm going to church in the morning," she said, gazing into his blue eyes while knowing she should walk away. "Can I leave Cody with you? I'll have his breakfast ready."

"Absolutely. Leave him with me. Good night, Claire."

"Night, Nick."

She closed her door and ran her hand across her forehead. The day had been filled with ups and downs, moments when she forgot the circumstances and just had fun. There were moments in Nick's arms when years fell away and for a few minutes she was with a sexy, desirable man who dazzled her.

But, like the flip of a coin, moments could reverse. There had been times that reminded her of the problems that loomed: dividing Cody's time between them, remembering how she had felt when she had learned of his engagement and she was pregnant with his child, and the terrible breakup that had been the worst time of all.

She got ready for bed automatically, lost in her thoughts about Nick.

Unless she guarded her heart constantly, Nick was a threat to her happiness.

Then again…she glanced at the door, thinking about him in bed across the hall. Unwanted images came of lying in his arms when he was sprawled in bed, his virile male body so breathtaking. It was impossible to keep him out of her thoughts when she was sleeping only a hall away.

She couldn't stay away from him. She couldn't be with him. What was she to do? The time was coming when she'd have to make a choice.

She knew the wrong choice could blow her future happiness.

Seven

Sunday morning Claire heard Nick just before he stepped into the kitchen. Dressed in a dark brown knit shirt and chinos, he radiated vitality as he swept into the room. He had always commanded attention wherever he went and that hadn't changed.

"Good morning," he said, smiling at her. "Good morning, Cody."

Cody smiled at him. Still wearing his blue pajamas, Cody sat eating his breakfast. The woolly toy Nick had given him was in a nearby chair along with the fuzzy monkey.

"Have you named these?" Nick asked, picking up the woolly toy.

"Monster and Mr. Monkey," Cody answered.

"Good names."

She was pleased to see Nick's smile and how easily he dealt with her son. Their son, she corrected herself.

She checked the clock. "Nick, I need to leave. If you

have any questions, Cody can probably answer them and if you need me, I have my phone."

She crossed the room to kiss Cody on the forehead. "Be good for your dad. I'll be home after church."

"Yes, ma'am," Cody said, eating another bite of oatmeal.

"Can I leave him long enough to go to the door with you?" Nick asked her.

"I'm going out the back way and yes, you can," she said.

Nick walked beside her. "Don't worry about us, Claire."

"I won't. He's got a bright dad who can handle mostly all problems and Cody is a bright little kid, so you two will be fine. I'll see you after church."

"Seems like I should kiss you goodbye," he said, startling her, and then she saw his smile and knew he teased her.

"We're both better off if you don't," she said as she left.

Nick stayed the afternoon and the three played games. He was enjoying his time with them so much that it was five o'clock by the time he had his things in the limo and turned to tell them goodbye. He picked up Cody.

"You're a wonderful boy. I love you."

"I love you, Dad," Cody said as Nick hugged him.

Claire saw the look that crossed Nick's face when the boy told him he loved him and called him "dad," and her heart felt squeezed. Nick was going to pour out his love on his son. She hoped whatever she and Nick decided, it would be a good solution for Cody.

She saw Nick give her a quick glance and then look down, but she had seen the tears in his eyes and for just an instant felt a bond with him over the love they shared for their son.

After a moment he turned to Claire. "I can't wait until

the two of you get to Dallas. This has been a wonderful weekend. Thank you."

"We'll see you Tuesday," she said, thinking that if he had kept in touch with her or even told her he was getting engaged, she would have told him about her pregnancy. For a moment the old anger she sometimes felt surfaced and she stepped away from him. She didn't want to kiss him goodbye. Now that Nick wanted her in his life again, he was pouring on the charm, but she had to remember that this was the same man who had so easily dropped her for another woman and become engaged without even letting her know. There were flashes when she regretted telling him about Cody at all and wished she had just come home to Houston without Nick knowing about his son.

As quickly as those thoughts came, she tried to shut off her resentment. Nick had lost his baby. He'd gone through hell. She wasn't heartless; she'd needed to tell him about Cody, and she knew he was going to be a wonderful dad for their son. And she couldn't deprive Cody of the right to know his father. If the Milans didn't try to take Cody or monopolize him, then they could work together. She hoped Nick's dad stayed out of it and let them work things out in their own way. Meanwhile, she had to keep her heart intact. The only way to do that was to stay out of Nick's arms…and out of his bed.

Nick settled in the limo and looked at Claire and Cody standing on the curving front walk. Claire held Cody with one hand and with the other she pushed back her hair, which swirled across her cheek in the wind.

Cody waved and Nick's heart lurched as he waved back. Cody's declaration of love, his simple, *I love you, Dad*, had wrapped around his heart and he would never forget the moment. Cody was so small, his thin arms had been around Nick's neck. He loved his son beyond measure.

I love you, Dad. Those plain words had been the greatest gift. Briefly, he thought about Claire, wishing they didn't have all the problems between them because they both loved Cody. She had given him a wonderful son. Nick tried to stop wishful thinking. The limo pulled away, driving slowly down her street. He couldn't look continually at what might have been, but it was a struggle to avoid doing so. For an instant he questioned his future. Was a political career worth losing Claire's love and missing out on becoming a husband with a loving, caring family?

He gave his head a shake, as if trying to get rid of such thoughts. Being with Claire again, he'd been caught up in desire for her that muddled his thinking.

He already missed being with both of them. Could he keep from falling in love with her and demolishing all his future plans? Could he risk another broken heart? Their problems were bigger now and chances of working them out far less likely than before.

Everything was different now. Because of Cody.

He had never dreamed how much he would love his son. Cody was a wonderful child. A lot of credit for that went to Claire and her family. He felt another big rush of gratitude and made a mental note to order flowers for her when he got home.

He couldn't wait to take Cody to the ranch on Tuesday. In the meantime, when he got home, he had to break the news to his parents first and then let his siblings know. He had to tell Karen's family at some point, too, and they weren't going to be overjoyed to learn that he had a son who was born months after he had married their late daughter.

He sent his dad a text, asking about stopping by to see

him. In minutes he received an answer to come by as soon as he returned home to Dallas. Better to face the lion in his den right away, he told himself.

Nick walked into the study, greeted his mother with a hug and crossed the room to shake hands with his dad. With their small dog jumping around his feet, Nick sat and chatted with them, talking about the weather, the basketball season.

"Evelyn," his dad said, "I need to talk to Nick for a short time. A legal matter."

She held up her hand and smiled. "No need for me to sit through a tedious discussion. I'm gone. Peter, call me when you finish," she told her husband as she walked out with the dog trotting behind her.

As soon as they were alone and the doors were closed, Nick turned to his dad. "I have something to discuss with you when you're finished."

"I don't have anything. That was just an excuse to get your mother to leave. I guessed that you came by for a reason."

"You know me pretty well," Nick said, dreading the next few minutes, knowing he and his father had different views on a lot of basic things and this was going to be one of the biggest.

Nick stood, walking to the mantel to turn and face his dad. "Dad, you remember before I got engaged to Karen, I proposed to Claire Prentiss from Houston, but she turned me down."

"I remember. Mr. Prentiss, the grandfather, had a thriving real estate business in Houston. They handled many big homes. The young woman helped her grandfather in the business."

"That's right." Nick's dread increased. He wondered

how he'd find the words to tell his father what he knew would start a fight. Then again, he told himself that once his father knew about Cody, he'd accept him.

He took a deep breath and continued. "Let's jump ahead to last week when a client asked me to go to a real estate closing with him. The seller was hospitalized and unable to attend, but they had the real estate agent fill in for her. It was Claire Prentiss. She runs her grandfather's agency now."

"I don't think you came to tell me you're dating her again."

"No, I didn't. She didn't know I had lost Karen and our baby." He could see he had his dad's full attention now. "If you recall, I broke up with Claire because we couldn't work out how we would live. She had family responsibilities and I had started a new career. Then I began dating Karen, and you and mom pushed me to marry her."

"Which I still think was good. We just couldn't foresee the drunk driver."

"I didn't tell Claire that I was engaged, but she learned about it."

His father shrugged. "Well, we're in local magazines and papers, and so is Karen's family."

"I have something I bought for you and Mom. Let me get it."

"Nick, just tell me what it is. I don't need to see it."

"You'll want to see this. Trust me." Nick crossed the room to his briefcase and removed two iPads. He remembered how all his anger had vanished when he'd seen Cody's picture. He was counting on Cody's picture having the same effect on his father.

"This iPad is for you." He put it on a table. "But for now I want to show you something on mine." He carried the tablet back to his dad, pulled a chair close and sat. "Get ready for a shock," he said, gazing into his father's eyes.

"Well, now I am curious," he said as he pushed his bifocals up.

Nick held the iPad out and his dad grasped it. "Dad, this is Cody Nicholas Prentiss. When I married Karen, Claire was pregnant with my son."

"Oh, damn, Nick." For a moment his father looked stricken and all color left his face. "You got her pregnant and then you got engaged to Karen? She didn't tell you?" he asked, looking at Nick.

"No, sir. Remember, I didn't tell her I was engaged and marrying another woman," Nick said, as his father looked down at the iPad in his hands.

He pulled the tablet and stared intently. "Damn, Nick, this child is the image of you. He's you all over again," he said in an awestruck voice. Nick let out his breath because he had a feeling that Cody had just been accepted into his father's world.

Judge Milan looked at his son. "Are you going to marry Claire?"

Nick shook his head. "I just learned about Cody last week and I just spent the weekend with her in Houston getting to know him. This family is going to love him. He is smart, happy, a great kid. He's three years old and yes, he does look like my pictures when I was that age. He's a Milan, there's no mistaking it."

His father barely looked up, still studying Cody's picture.

"Dad, I have more pictures." Nick swiped the screen and scrolled through other pictures of Cody laughing at the camera.

"Nick, we've got to break this gently to your mother, but she is going to want this little boy in her life in the worst way." His dad looked up. "This is our first and only grandchild, Nick. And he couldn't look more like a Milan."

Nick was so relieved, but at the same time, he knew his dad's acceptance meant his parents were going to fight to get Cody into the family. Nick glanced around the room, remembering being in the same room while his dad had argued and pressured him to marry Karen and forget Claire. Nick made a silent vow to himself that when Cody was grown, he'd never interfere in his life the way his dad had interfered in his own.

"I've invited Claire to bring Cody to Dallas this week. She'll be here Tuesday and I'm taking them out to my ranch. One night while they're here I thought I'd have the family over to meet him."

"You've got to marry her, Nick. The sooner the better."

"At this point she isn't interested in marrying me. Her grandfather isn't well. Her mother has passed away and her grandmother is getting older. Claire has control of the real estate business totally and she's been very successful and built it up. She has three offices and seventy employees in Houston, and she doesn't want to leave there. She's built a big, fine mansion in an exclusive area, and Cody and her grandmother live with her. Her grandfather is in assisted living, but she hopes to bring him home. She told me there have been no other men in her life because she hasn't had time for a social life, and I can see that." The words rushed out, like an eruption. But he wanted to lay everything out on the table right away.

He wondered whether his father even heard him; he was still going through the pictures. He reminded himself that his dad could do two things at once and not miss a word of conversation around him.

Finally his father looked up. "Go get your mother. You can tell her when you get in here where she can see his picture. I know why you showed it to me first. Nick, can you print a couple of these out for us, so we can keep some?"

"I asked Claire to print a few out, so I have some for you. But, Dad, that's why I'm giving you an iPad. I've already loaded all those pictures on it for you and Mom to look at."

"That's dandy, Nick. That's just fine. Thank you," his father said, his gaze returning to Cody's picture. "Our first grandchild," he said with awe in his voice. "Three years—damn, if only we had known."

"You know why we didn't." Nick couldn't keep from saying and his father waved his hand at him without looking up. "Go get your mother. She is going to be so happy over this. Nick, we've never even met Claire."

"No, Dad, you haven't, but you will this week." Clinging to his patience he bit back pointing out that they hadn't wanted to meet Claire. "I'll get Mom."

His mother looked puzzled when she returned and Judge Milan motioned her to come sit beside him. He took her hand. "Nick has some good news that will surprise you as well as shock you."

Nick went through telling her in the same way he had told his father.

"Oh, my word, you fathered a child out of wedlock!" his mother said, frowning and sounding devastated. Then, before he could respond, her eyes grew soft. "We have a grandchild." Then she stared at the iPad.

He gave her a moment to digest it all.

"Oh, my word, Nick. This is a picture of you."

"No, it's my son and Claire is his mother," Nick said. "His name is Cody Nicholas."

"She gave him your name." Evelyn didn't look up from the pictures as she spoke. "He's definitely your son. We're grandparents and we get to meet him this week?" His mother's voice filled with excitement. She looked up at Nick. "I'm a grandmother. Oh, Nick, I'm so thrilled."

"I'm glad, Mom," he said.

It was another hour before he was ready to leave. He left the iPad with pictures of Cody with them and said he would arrange for a family dinner on whatever night they could get the most members of the family together. As he kissed his mother's cheek and started out of the room, his dad got up.

"I'll walk you to the car, Nick," he said, catching up with Nick.

Nick wasn't surprised. He knew his father had a purpose in walking him to the car.

As soon as they were out of the house, his dad cleared his throat. "Nick, think about asking Claire to marry you. She may be wealthy, comfortable, successful, but she doesn't have the wealth our family does. You can give her a sum that would win the cooperation of most any woman and you can set up a trust fund for Cody, plus give him the Milan name. That will be difficult for her to turn down."

"Dad, I hurt her badly once. I don't want to do it again. If I'd done what I should have in the first place, I would have known about Cody. But that's in the past now. I'm not going to coerce her into marriage."

"It isn't coercion to offer what I'm talking about. It's a fabulous, life-altering gift. Be smart about this, Nick. You have the highest political ambitions and we're getting a lot of powerful people lined up to support you. Don't blow this now. That little boy is a Milan, our grandchild. I can't tell you how thrilled your mother and I both are."

"I'm glad for that. You're going to be more thrilled when you meet him. He's adorable."

"Nick, if she would marry you, it would kill any breath

of scandal attached to Cody. Think about it," his dad urged, giving him one of his patented looks.

"Sure. I will," Nick answered. "I'll let my siblings know about him as soon as I get home. I'm going to let Karen's parents know too. Mom is probably already on the phone talking to Madison."

"She won't talk to any of the family until she's talked to me again." They stopped beside Nick's car and his father looked up at him. "Just think about what I said. It would help your political chances to be married with a family."

"I will." Nick climbed behind the wheel. "Night, Dad. I'll be in touch."

"Thanks for the iPad. This is an exciting night in our lives. We have a grandson. That's marvelous, Nick. I'm looking forward to meeting him and his mother."

Nodding, Nick felt a pang. He had gotten his life into a muddle, cutting Claire out of it, then losing Karen and the baby. And now it was even more mixed-up.

He drove to his Dallas home and went inside. He called Wyatt first, telling him about Cody and sending a picture. He did the same with Madison and then Tony.

Feeling Karen's parents should know, he called and talked to her dad briefly. To his relief, her father seemed happy for Nick to have a child. He realized a lot of despair over his loss was fading.

Then he called Claire. She was putting Cody to bed, but Nick got to talk to him for ten minutes. Just hearing his voice nearly brought tears to his eyes; he missed his son so much already. He could hardly wait till Tuesday. Claire promised to call Nick after she was finished with Cody.

He wondered what she thought. She kept everything bottled up and put a barrier between them. He understood why she did, and he knew he should, too, for the same reasons.

Was the career he had planned really better than having Claire's love and Cody in his life?

Somehow over the weekend, politics had lost a bit of its luster.

Giving up political office was a thought that had never crossed his mind before, and he couldn't imagine changing his whole way of life and giving up his ranch to move to Houston. He would never be happy. That thought was followed by memories of this weekend, which had been one of the happiest times of his life. How much would becoming a father change his life? And change his feelings for Claire?

He got out his iPad and looked at all of Cody's pictures again. He'd already received text messages from his siblings, congratulating him and telling him how much Cody looked like Nick and like the Milans, and responding to his invitation to meet Claire and Cody.

By consensus it'd be Saturday night when he'd host the party at his Dallas home. He could hardly wait.

Tuesday Nick went to the airport to meet Claire and Cody. He had taken little time off for two years and his office was accustomed to being able to get in contact with him during all hours. That was going to have to change and it would be a big adjustment in his life.

He was eager to see them, surprised how the anticipation had kept him awake all night. They'd been in his thoughts constantly from yesterday until now. His life had not been empty—or, at least, he hadn't thought it was—but excitement gripped him now as he watched the plane land. It was an excitement he hadn't ever felt. Not even with his late wife. In his own way, he'd loved Karen, but he realized now that what they'd had was more like a marriage of convenience. She had done what she wanted and he had been free to pursue his career for hours on end. Setting those thoughts aside to be examined at a later time, he focused on Claire and their son.

When they emerged from the plane, his heart skipped a beat as he looked at Claire. Wearing a black knee-length coat with a thick fur collar and cuffs, black slacks and black heels, she looked like a model. A cold December wind blew, causing her hair to swirl across her cheek. She still could set his pulse racing and capture his attention far too easily for his own good. Cody was almost bouncing with each step and Nick suspected the boy was wound up with excitement. Wearing a bright blue parka and khakis, he held his tiger under one arm and the monkey under the other.

Nick walked out to meet them and picked up Cody and gave him a hug. "I'm so glad to see you," he said, carrying him and smiling at him. Cody grinned in return, wrapping one thin arm around Nick's shoulder.

"I've been counting the minutes," Nick said lightly.

"So has he. The plane was as big a hit as the limo," she said, smiling up at Nick. "He's so excited. This is all new to him. We don't travel. That's one thing about the real estate business—it's better business if I stay home."

"That I know. You look great, Claire."

"Thanks. Grandma said to thank you again. She really appreciated your call and asking her yourself to come with us. Thanks also from me."

"I'd be happy to have her here to meet my family."

"I take it your dad adjusted."

Laughing, Nick nodded. "I took a lesson from you and put Cody's picture in front of him as I told him. My parents are overcome with delight at being grandparents. To them, Cody looks just like me at that age and they are ecstatic. I haven't seen them like this many times in my life. They can't wait to meet you, too."

She nodded but her smile never reached her eyes. He knew she was worried and wished there was something he could do to alleviate her concern.

"They can't wait to see Cody. If it's acceptable with you, we'll stop by for just a few minutes. I promise we won't stay."

"That's fine. We're here for your family to get to know Cody, so see any of them you want. They're his grandparents, Nick."

"Thanks," he said, wondering how he truly felt toward all of them. "They're all happy to learn about Cody and they all think he looks like me, which of course, I like to hear." When they climbed into the limo, they both focused on Cody, who seemed as interested in the interior as he'd been on the first ride.

At his parents' home, the driver slowed to park at the front door on the wide circular drive. Wearing their coats, his parents waited on the porch and came forward to greet them.

"Claire, meet my parents, Judge Peter Milan and Evelyn Milan. Mom and Dad, this is Claire Prentiss and this is our son and your grandson, Cody Nicholas Prentiss."

Cody shyly said hello and put his hand out to shake hands with Judge Milan. Nick knew his father would be impressed.

His mom hugged Claire lightly. "This is the most special moment," she said, dabbing at her eyes, and Nick wondered how Claire felt. Too many times he could not read her expression and this was another one of those times because she had that cool, shuttered look, as if she had locked away her feelings and was going through the motions.

"It's nice for Cody to know his family," Claire said.

"You can't imagine how much he looks like Nick did at that age," Evelyn said.

"Welcome to the family," Peter Milan said, extending his hand to Claire.

"Thank you, Judge Milan," Claire said, smiling at him, another cool smile that kept up a barrier, but Nick doubted if his father realized it. "It's Cody whom I hope you'll welcome into the family."

"We're thrilled beyond anything you can imagine," he said easily. "And what a fine boy he is. Hard to realize he's just three years old because he acts older."

"He's with adults all the time," Claire answered.

"Come inside. I hear you've built up that business your grandfather had to an impressive size," Judge Milan said to her.

Nick knew his dad could pour on the charm when he wanted. With a twinge of amusement he wondered how happily his parents would have accepted a rowdy little boy who looked like Claire and bore no resemblance to the Milans. He suspected it might have made very little difference, because they were almost deliriously happy to have a grandchild. He knew his mother had been devastated by Karen's death, but now he realized a lot of her grief had included the tiny baby Nick had lost.

They sat in the less formal family room and Nick was certain it was for Cody's benefit because this room had always been childproof. His father sat close to Claire, and Nick was certain that his dad was determined to win her friendship.

"Cody," Nick's mother said, "we have a present for you." From one side of her chair she picked up a big box that was wrapped and tied in a huge red bow.

Cody's eyes sparkled, but before he moved he glanced

at Claire, who nodded, and only then did he cross the room to open his present.

"Mama, look," Cody said, holding up a magic kit. He removed the big, black top hat and put it on his head. He smiled at Evelyn Milan. "Thank you very much."

"You're welcome, Cody."

He turned to the judge. "Thank you, sir."

"Cody, come here," Judge Milan said. When Cody walked over, he leaned forward and gave him a level look. "I'd like you to think about what you want to call us, and talk to your mama and daddy about it. We're your grandparents, so we need to get the right name."

"Yes, sir," Cody said, looking at Nick.

"We'll figure that one out later, Cody. Now, come look at your magic box," Nick said.

Cody ran back to the box to rummage in it and pull out the cape, which he put on.

Evelyn clapped. "Excellent, Cody. You look like a magician. You need your magic wand," she said.

They spent an hour with his parents before Nick asked Cody to put away his magic kit because they needed to go.

As they drove away, his parents stood waving and Claire and Cody waved in return. "I think they matched my own family's enthusiasm for Cody," Claire said.

"Believe me, it's sincere. It's beyond anything I dreamed. Whatever we work out in the future, you and Cody have instantly become members of the family, so I hope you like the Milans."

"I've met Madison. I haven't met Tony or Wyatt."

"The whole world likes Wyatt. He's quiet, but not as quiet as he used to be before he married. You'll like Tony, too. They all want to meet Cody. Just now with my folks, Cody was a hit, which I knew he would be. Mom would have loved him no matter what, unless he had been a hellion, but my dad was impressed and so pleased. I know how to read the signs."

"The magic kit is a hit, that's for sure. You can teach him the tricks."

"Claire, I've been counting the minutes. I'm glad you're here. We'll go by my house, eat lunch there and then fly to the ranch in Verity. We can do a little shopping before we leave Verity—get Cody some cowboy clothes. He doesn't have any boots, does he?"

"No, he doesn't and he'll be thrilled. You're doing all the right things."

"I want to do all the right things for his mom, too," Nick said.

"You're doing pretty good at that, too," she said, but her voice sounded somber, as if she wished he wouldn't bother trying to please her. Was she still angry with him? Or was she just trying to avoid getting friendly enough to fall in love again? He had no idea what Claire's thoughts were. She had a big part of herself locked away, causing him to worry about their dealings. He knew his dad was going to push him to marry Claire. Now he just had to keep his dad from trying to push Claire, because that would only make matters worse.

They went to Nick's house and when they arrived he gave them a tour. The house was only slightly larger than Claire's, set back on a lot with tall trees, fountains in front of the house, a spacious patio and a fenced area with a swimming pool in the back. "Claire, I've had an alarm installed in the pool and it already had a fence. If anything over a few pounds goes into the pool, the alarm will sound. So there's no way Cody can wander out there and fall in without us knowing."

She stared at the pool that was surrounded by a high, iron fence. She turned to him.

"Thanks, Nick, I feel much better about that because he'll be with you sometimes when I'm not and that's one worry I won't have."

"I don't want you to have any worries about Cody being with me," Nick said, glancing at his son who was digging through his box of magic tricks as they stood in an informal sitting room that overlooked the patio.

"I have a staff, but I've given them the rest of this week off since we're going to the ranch—at least, they're off until Saturday when we return. My cook and the head of my cleaning staff are at the ranch today. There should be lunch left here for us," he said. "I'll get it on, and after we eat we'll fly to Verity."

"I'll help. Cody is happy with his present."

As soon as they stepped into his kitchen she stopped. "Nick, when did you get the booster seat for Cody?"

"I called my secretary and told her what I needed and she ordered it for me. It'll do, won't it?"

"Of course, it'll do," Claire said, smiling, and Nick couldn't resist moving closer.

"At least it got a smile out of you and that makes it worth the expense and trouble. Claire, I want this to be good from your viewpoint, too."

Her smile disappeared as she gazed intently at him. "I'm trying to cooperate and I know we have to work something out between us. You've been good, and believe me, I appreciate it."

He hugged her lightly, trying to give her an impersonal, casual hug of reassurance that he meant what he said and he hoped to avoid hurting her. But the moment she was in his arms, he became aware of her soft curves pressed against him, of the exotic perfume she wore that was the faintest of scents, yet enticing. Locks of her silky hair touched his cheek. Desire swept him, sudden and unexpected, shaking him to his core. He stood still, trying to keep control. He thought back on how they used to flirt, tease each other and have fun together. That was gone. Now he intended to keep her from worrying and to be friendly with her. And "friendly" meant no kissing.

He stepped away. "Okay?"

"Sure, Nick."

"I mean, am I okay? I'm trying to do what you'd like."

"You're fine," she said, giving him a smile that made him feel better.

"Let's get lunch on before a hungry kid shows up."

"With that magic kit he won't think about food for another hour. Food comes way down on his list of fascinating things in life."

After holding her close, wanting to kiss her, Nick was acutely aware of her moving around him, brushing past him, their hands meeting as she handed him a dish. This week would be wonderful in so many ways, but tense and difficult in others. He needed to remember to resist Claire, as well as guard his heart. Could he do that when he would be with her constantly?

Eight

Claire looked out the plane window at the rolling land spread below. Mesquite trees, some brown, some still a dull, winter green, were bent by the prevailing south winds coming across Texas from the Gulf of Mexico. It was a view different from the area around Houston.

She glanced at Nick, who was poring over the magic book with Cody while Cody held a string of brightly colored scarves tied together and tried to stuff them into the hat. She never dreamed how much his family would like Cody and like being grandparents.

It was also easy to see that Judge Milan wanted her to marry Nick and wanted it badly. She could imagine he saw her as the perfect wife now for Nick. Marrying would smooth away any scandal about Cody's birth and help Nick in his career. She suspected Judge Milan would start his campaign to sway her as soon as possible.

But for Claire, the most worrisome thing was her intense physical reaction to Nick. When he had taken her into his arms for just a casual hug, her heart thudded and her breath caught. Seduction would only add to their problems and she intended to guard against it, even though it seemed to grow more difficult each hour she spent with Nick.

"Here's Verity," Nick said when the plane banked and she saw a town below.

She gazed out the window at this town she had heard about, but had only been through without stopping when Nick had taken her to his family's ranch years earlier. At that time he didn't have his own ranch, but the family ranch had been vacant the weekend they went, so they had it to themselves and Nick had been far more relaxed than any other time she had been with him.

Shortly, they rode in Nick's car down a wide street. In downtown Verity Christmas lights and wreaths were strung on lampposts and it seemed as if the whole town was decorated for the holidays. Nick parked at the back of the sheriff's office and they went inside where a small, lighted Christmas tree stood in the lobby.

They waited until the sheriff came to the front, and the minute she saw the man's blue eyes and brown hair, so like Nick's and Cody's, she knew he had to be a Milan. This was Wyatt, she realized. His features were far more rugged than Nick's, who had the appealing looks of a handsome movie star.

Wyatt's ready smile was as inviting as his brother's. "It's really good to meet you, Claire. I've heard about you and now about Cody. I'm an uncle. Wow." He turned to shake hands with Cody, who looked awed by Wyatt's uniform.

"This is your Uncle Wyatt, Cody," Nick said. "He's the sheriff."

"Cody, would you like to look around?" Wyatt asked. "Want to see the jail?"

Cody nodded, and Claire smiled because for one of the rare moments in his life, her son was suddenly shy. Nick took Cody's hand. "C'mon, we'll look at the jail."

"As thrilling as that is going to be," Claire said, "I'll leave the males to tour and I'll go shopping. Nick, I have my phone and you have my number. Wyatt, where's a good store for jeans?"

"Try The Plaza. I'm not the best to ask about women's jeans." He turned to one of his officers seated behind a desk. "Dwight?"

"The Plaza is a good one. So is Dorothy's."

"There you go," Wyatt said, and smiled. "Dwight will give you directions. When you're through, meet us at the drugstore across the street next door to the hotel. I'll get Cody a soda if he wants one and if that's all right?"

"Yes, it is with me. You can ask him if he wants one."

She left as she heard Cody say, "Yes, sir."

All the time she tried on jeans, she was aware she would be wearing them around Nick. On impulse, she bought a shirt to match.

It was over an hour later when she entered the drugstore to find the men and Cody seated at a round table in old-fashioned ice-cream-parlor chairs. A fire burned in a potbellied stove in the center of the big room and a lighted Christmas tree stood in the window. As she walked to them, she was aware of Nick's steady gaze on her. He came to his feet along with Wyatt.

"Please be seated," she said. "Looks as if everyone's had a soda."

"Best in the West," Nick said, smiling. "Love these sodas. Can I get you one?"

"I'll pass, but thank you. Cody, are they really the best?"

"Yes, ma'am," he said, licking his lips and everyone laughed. "Mama, Uncle Wyatt gave me a badge." Cody turned in his chair and she leaned down to look at a gold star that resembled Wyatt's badge and said Verity Junior Sheriff.

"That's great. I hope you thanked him."

"I did," Cody said as he shot a big grin Wyatt's way.

She smiled at Wyatt, too. "Uncle Wyatt, you're already on his favorite relative list, I'm sure."

"I hope so," Wyatt answered easily.

"Dad bought me boots and a hat," Cody said.

"Well, you will be all fixed up with your boots and junior sheriff badge and hat," she said, certain Cody would love every minute of this trip. Even though Cody's reasons would be far more simple, was she going to be pressured by her son to marry Nick?

They sat and talked for another half hour until Nick pushed back his chair. "I think we'll head to the ranch now, Wyatt."

They walked back to the sheriff's office and in minutes Nick was driving south out of Verity.

As Nick wound up the drive to the sprawling ranch house, she wondered about his life. "Do you ever stay out here, Nick?"

"Not much. I don't have time to, but someday I hope to retire early and live here because I love it. Ranching is ingrained in our family. You can't pry my youngest brother Tony off his ranch. Wyatt loves it and will go back to living on his ranch when his term as sheriff ends. He took on that job as a favor to a lot of people, but that's not his deal. Madison lives on a ranch now with her husband, Jake Calhoun, but before she married Jake, she lived on the family ranch a good part of the year and painted there. We all love the cowboy life."

"I'd think you'd arrange a little more time for it, then. If you can't work this into your life, how are you going to fit Cody in?" she asked, wondering whether Nick was actually going to want much time with Cody when they got right down to figuring out a schedule.

With a quick glance, Nick gave her a startled look. "I'll try to give Cody top priority," Nick answered. His voice was quiet, his tone somber. Was he just facing reality about how much time his political career would take away from a family?

She looked at his profile, his firm jaw, prominent cheekbones, handsome features, thickly lashed eyes. Nick was the best-looking Milan of all those she had met. Probably the best-looking man she had ever met at all. Or was she biased because of personal feelings? She couldn't answer her own question.

In the warm car she had opened her coat. Now she touched the heart pendant Nick had given her. "My necklace is beautiful," she said. "Thank you again."

"It's just a token thank-you for Cody. You should have had more."

"Nick, this has over twenty-four big diamonds. It's more than a token," she said, wondering whether he had given it to her out of gratitude or guilt.

"I promise you, that's a token for what I feel I should give you. Here we are," he said, stopping the car near the back door of a sprawling ranch house with an inviting porch. They each carried bags inside and Cody brought his toys. "C'mon, and I'll show you where your rooms will be," Nick said. "I can bring in the rest of the stuff later."

They walked into a spacious kitchen with stainless steel state-of-the-art equipment. Nick had dark fruitwood cabinets and woodwork with pale yellow walls and floor to ceiling windows overlooking the lawn along one wall and the patio on the other. Standing at the sink was a tall white-haired man who turned to smile at them.

"Claire, meet Douglas Giroux, my cook, who's worked

for me a long time now. Zelda, his wife, heads my cleaning staff," Nick said. "Douglas works for me in Dallas, but he agreed to come out here for these few days. Douglas, this is Miss Prentiss and my son, Cody."

"Welcome to the ranch," Douglas said. "I hope you enjoy your stay."

"Something you're cooking smells inviting," Nick said.

"That's a casserole to freeze. Tonight we'll have creamed pheasant, baked potatoes, asparagus and rolls."

"Sounds wonderful," Claire said, as Nick took her arm to walk down the hall. The casual touch sent a tingling current down her spine. No matter how much she decided to avoid responding to him, her body couldn't get the message. She struggled to focus on the house instead of the tall man at her side.

He led her to her bedroom for the week, done in bright colors with white furniture. Cody's room adjoined it and held a junior bed and a big white stuffed bear that Cody ran to hug the minute he walked into the room.

"That's for you, Cody," Nick said, smiling at his son.

"Thank you," Cody said, beaming as he hugged the bear again.

"My room is at the end of the hall," Nick said. "You're welcome to come see it."

"Thanks. I'll unpack instead," she said. She needed some time away from this man, to regroup.

Through dinner and playing with Cody afterward, Nick was far more aware of Claire than before. Being together at the ranch had brought memories tumbling back, making love to her, holding her naked in his arms, kissing her for hours. Grief was leaving him along with the numbness. Without wanting to, she stirred memories and desire. He wanted to kiss her, to dance with her, to make love with her.

The past weekend and this week were so totally unlike his life—all business appointments put off, his calendar cleared to meet Cody and be with him. He had turned off his cell phone, knowing his family could get him through the ranch number or his foreman. The ranch was a world of its own and insulated from the outside world. He expected his life to shift back into its usual groove when he returned to work, but this was a reprieve that he would relish. He hadn't spent enough time here over the last couple of years, and certainly not during the last year of his marriage to Karen. She had never cared for the ranch. She was meant for a social life, just as his mother preferred Dallas, and that had fit with his schedule. He had forgotten just how much he loved this place. Life would be ideal here with Claire and Cody.

The idea startled him. He had a busy, important career, a career that was vital to his family and could grow more demanding in the coming years. The ranch was an idyll, he reminded himself, and there was no way he could move to the ranch now, nor would Claire ever come with him. She would not leave the big business she had built and she wouldn't leave her family. He'd best remember that.

After putting Cody to bed, Claire returned to the family room to sit with him. Her red slacks and red sweater, which clung to tempting curves, rekindled longing, making him want to untie the scarf that held her hair and let it fall loose about her shoulders, but he resisted.

"Cody's asleep. It's been an exciting day for him, Nick. His first plane ride, his first pair of boots and his first cowboy hat. His first meeting with a real sheriff. He has met new grandparents. So many things that he's dazzled by them."

Despite his good intentions, Nick took her hand, running his thumb lightly over the back of her hand. "Now I think it's time for his mom to be dazzled."

What did he mean by that? Claire wondered as she felt her pulse race.

"You've been good about all this, Claire," he said, his voice suddenly huskier. "When you get home, go out with me. Whatever works out between us, hopefully, we're going to be friends. Let me take you out for dinner—a 'just friends' thing."

She forced a smile. "I'm tempted, Nick, but I think we should avoid that kind of evening. We've been in limbo, getting you and Cody acquainted. There have been no problems, no tomorrows. We're headed for some major decisions and major upheavals in my life, Cody's life and my family's lives. Cody will be all right with what we do, but you and I won't. There is no way to work out a wonderful, happy solution to sharing him between Washington, DC and Houston. It's an upheaval for me to share him at all."

"We might fall in love if you'd give us half a chance."

The hurt she felt stabbed deeper. "You'll be so busy with your career, I think that's impossible. I'm busy with my career and my family. All I see is more heartbreak, so I don't think dinners out together will help unless it's something we need to do involving Cody. After this week, you've broken the ice and we can move on and begin to make decisions. I think the less you and I see of each other, the better we'll each be."

Aware Nick was unaccustomed to defeat of any kind, she gazed into his penetrating blue eyes. She couldn't read his reaction or even guess what he was thinking, except that she was certain he was not happy about her answer.

"If that's what you want," he finally said. "Neither of us wants another heartbreak. I can't deal with another one, but I didn't see dinner leading to that. I've been so happy this past week that everything looks rosy."

"I'm glad, Nick, but we have a lot to work out between us."

He nodded. "If we don't go to dinner, I still would like to spend some time next week with Cody. I want to see him again. Pick a time. I can stay in Houston at a hotel and keep him there with me or just come see him each day and take him out."

"That would probably work best at this point. Eventually, I know we'll have to work out a regular arrangement, but please, not this soon."

He nodded. "I'll come Tuesday and stay at a hotel and you'll barely see me."

"I think that's best," she said, hurting all over and knowing even bigger hurts were coming.

"Want something to drink before we eat? I'm having a beer."

"Just ice water."

When he got up to get the drinks, she looked around, seeing some family pictures in a frame. Her eyes were drawn to one in particular—a shot of Nick and his brothers and their father. She remembered what he'd told her about the men in his family. "Nick, you've told me about the Milan family legend that each male had to go into the field of law or his family faced disaster."

"It was never clear what kind of disaster, and I don't think we were all pushed toward law because of the legend as much as Dad wanting us in that field since he loved it. The legend goes back too far for anyone to have heard about a time it didn't exist or how it got started."

"You sort of made light of it, but your dad, your brothers and you all studied law. If I remember correctly, your youngest brother was a practicing lawyer."

He walked over with their drinks. "Tony? Yeah, for about ten minutes. He got a law degree, graduated, went to work for a law firm for one year, quit and moved back to his ranch and there he is and he will always be." He shrugged. "It's an old legend, but I don't give it much credence. I don't think any Milan really does any longer. Madison was always talented in art and no one has ever pushed any of the females into law."

"That's good to hear. I wondered whether you would be pushing Cody someday to go to law school."

"Never. Cody can do what he wants. My dad wanted us to be lawyers, but it wasn't because of that legend." Nick squeezed her hand lightly and smiled at her. "Don't give that another thought. I promise, no pushing from me to get Cody to study law because of a legend or any other reason."

"That makes me feel better. You're his dad and you're in his life now, so I'm glad to hear your views on it."

"We've had some family legends that have come true. I guess some are based on fact, but no one knows the history of this Milan legend. Probably originated by a Calhoun to cause trouble."

Knowing he was joking, she smiled. "The old feud ought to be dying."

"For some of us, that Milan-Calhoun feud is out of date and should end. Madison has married a Calhoun and so has Wyatt. Wyatt's wife is from another branch of the Calhoun family. You'll meet Milans and Calhouns at the family gathering Saturday night. If anyone keeps the feud alive, it's Tony, who fights with his Calhoun neighbor."

"I'm looking forward to Saturday night. Wyatt was a hit today with Cody. He wanted to wear his badge to bed, but I was afraid it would stick him. He thought Uncle Wyatt was super."

"What kid wouldn't? He's a sheriff. Much more exciting than my profession."

"I have to agree with you on that one."

Nick grinned at her. "I walked into that, didn't I?"

She laughed. "Even in the winter it's beautiful out here, Nick. The sunset was gorgeous. Now I know why you love to come to the ranch."

"I do," he said. "I just don't have time for it." He turned to look at her, and the look he gave her told her she was in trouble.

He couldn't resist her any longer. He'd been trying to rein himself in all day, but he was losing the battle. "Claire." He turned his chair and moved closer, reaching over to pick her up and place her on his lap. "This has been such a good day. I want to hold you," he said in a deep voice.

He heard her intake of breath. "Nick, you're borrowing trouble," she whispered, placing her hands against his chest as if she intended to push him away, but she applied no pressure.

He slipped his arm around her waist and drew her closer, his gaze going to her mouth. As he took her hand he could feel her pulse race and his jumped. He leaned closer and gave in to the temptation. He kissed her.

Her hands slipped up his chest and around his neck. She clung to him and kissed him back, and he leaned over her, kissing her hard, letting go pent-up longings, kissing her as he had wanted to since she had stepped off the plane.

He could feel her heart pounding now. He shifted to cradle her against his shoulder and poured himself into kissing her, wanting to feel alive, to make her respond the way she used to respond to him.

Her soft moan set him ablaze. She hadn't stopped him

as he thought she might. Far from it. Instead she kissed him passionately, her fingers winding in the hair at the back of his neck. Gone were her coolness, the resentment over the past. For a moment they were simply a man and woman physically drawn to each other, wanting to feel alive and good with each other once again.

He knew he was racing into disaster, but he didn't want to stop kissing her. He felt as if he could kiss her all night. He wanted to hold her, love her, seduce her. He wanted to make love to her through the night. The realization shocked him. How had she reached him? He had shut out the world, kept his attention and life focused on only business. Suddenly Claire was in his life again, turning his world upside down and making him want love in his life once more, making him want to really live again. She was burning away his grief.

They had hurt each other long ago and this might be rushing into that same hurt again, only a lot worse this time. He should stop and walk away right now, but she was soft, hot, tempting, her scalding kisses stirring a storm of longing. Life was empty without love, and the thought startled him because his life was busy every waking moment. Since when had it become empty to him? The question left him as he tightened his arms around her and continued kissing her.

Their past couldn't be undone, but they could pick up and go on with life. And it could be good again. So good.

Nick shifted her against him, wanting to carry her to a bedroom but afraid she would stop him. As he kissed her, he ran his hand lightly along her throat, caressing her, taking his time, and then his fingers drifted lower, following her luscious curves, over the softness of her breast. He twisted open a button and then another, sliding his hand beneath her blouse to touch her warm silken skin, to caress her breast, feeling the taut bud. He was aroused, ready and aching for her. He unfastened the clasp of her bra, slipping his hand below the lace to stroke her breasts with feathery touches.

She moaned, shifting her hips and moving against him, setting him on fire with wanting her.

"Nick," she whispered, sitting up. He pushed open her blouse and leaned down to touch her breast with his tongue.

She gasped and for a moment didn't stop him while he kissed and caressed her. He felt her fingers run through his hair as she moaned softly with pleasure.

"Nick, wait. A few more minutes and I won't be able to stop," she said, her words breathless. "This isn't what I planned and I don't think it's what you intended."

Reluctantly, he straightened. "Claire, I want you," he whispered, caressing her nape. He didn't want to stop touching her. "Do you remember our times together? They were better than anything. Remember?" he asked, framing her face with his hands and staring at her.

"Yes, I remember," she replied, "but we're not going there tonight. We have all the complications in our lives we need. We have to stop this." She wiggled to stand and he helped her, doing what she wanted because he wanted her happy.

He stood, looking at her while she pulled her blouse together. "I want to make love to you all night long. Making love is good between us. I know you remember. One time wouldn't hurt. We won't fall in love."

"One time wouldn't hurt," she repeated. "You're saying that to convince yourself as well as me. We hurt each other terribly before and we can't do that again."

They stood staring at each other and he wanted her desperately. He wound his hands in the thick, black hair on either side of her head, turning her head up slightly so he could get to her mouth as he leaned down to kiss her.

The minute their lips and tongues met, he wrapped his arm around her waist, pulled her tightly against him and kissed her passionately, once again letting her feel the pent-up hunger he felt. "Claire, damn, I want you," he whispered and kissed away any answer she might have had.

Moaning, she clung to him. How long they kissed, he didn't know, but finally, she pushed against him, so he released her and she stepped away. Her blouse was still unbuttoned, revealing her tempting curves, and he ached to draw her back into his embrace.

Both of them were breathing deeply and she took another step back. "Nick, we need to call it a night now. That shouldn't have even happened."

"No one was harmed. No promises made, nothing changed," he said. But his whole world had changed. He wanted her and he felt headed for more hurt than ever. He couldn't survive a marriage of convenience, which she didn't want anyway. "Claire, don't have regrets. You've brought me out of grief. For the first time in far too long, I feel alive. Don't have regrets about kissing me tonight."

"I should go to my room. That will be better for both of us."

"Sit and talk. I'll sit across the room if it'll make you happier," he said, crossing to the other side of the room.

He looked at her, his eyes pleading with her not to walk away.

Shaking her head in surrender, she acquiesced. She sat a safe distance away and he took it as a good sign that she hadn't run to her room.

For the next hour or so he forced his libido back into hiding and he gave her what she wanted—time together to talk. They talked about their families, their lives over the past few years, and Nick kept the conversation lively so he wouldn't recall how much he wanted her. He was charming, personable, trying to please her. And he succeeded.

Time slipped away until she finally stood. "I have to get to bed. I'm exhausted. Good night."

"I'll go upstairs, too," he said, crossing the room and walking with her to her door where he turned to face her.

"I'm glad you're here," he said, toying with a lock of her hair. "Both of you. Today has been really great."

"Let's hope things stay that way," she said.

Stepping closer, Nick wrapped his arms around her to kiss again, another passionate kiss that she returned. Her response was instant, intense, and it made him think she wanted him almost as much as he wanted her.

She finally looked up at him. "We're going to say goodnight, Nick. I'll see you in the morning."

"This has been a very special day. Thanks for letting it happen. I'll see you and Cody early in the morning."

Nick went to his room. As he undressed, he wondered whether he would get any sleep at all this night. He lay in the dark and knew he wouldn't. Every time he closed his eyes he remembered what it was like to kiss her.

Nine

Claire gave up on sleep. She was on fire still from Nick's kisses and his caresses. She wanted to be in his arms, while at the same time she wished she hadn't let any of it happen because kisses could only complicate their relationship. They were getting over the past, building a relationship in the present. They didn't need lust complicating their lives.

She should have stopped Nick much sooner tonight, but she couldn't. Even though she knew she shouldn't, she had wanted his touch, wanted to hold him. Now sleep was gone, and once again their relationship had changed. No matter how either of them tried to deny it, the spark between them was still there, had never been extinguished. They could no longer deny the passion that shadowed every moment they would spend together. Everything would be different between them now.

How was she going to get through this time with Nick? Could she manage to just see him when she had to?

How would she get through this long night without him?

* * *

Wednesday morning after her shower she dressed in jeans, a black knit shirt and tennis shoes. Cody was still curled in bed asleep.

When she entered the kitchen, Nick was cooking and the tempting aroma of hot coffee and hot bread filled the air.

Her heart jumped as she looked at him. A blue plaid long-sleeved shirt covered his broad shoulders and was tucked into tight jeans that emphasized his long legs. A hand-tooled leather belt circled his narrow waist. Just like that, he had turned into the sexy rancher.

"Good morning," she said.

He turned to smile at her, moved a skillet and crossed the room to her. "Good morning," he said in a husky voice. "You look pretty." He hugged her lightly and paused to look into her eyes while his arm still circled her waist. Desire was obvious in his blue eyes and she needed to move away, but for an instant she was immobile, caught and held, wanting him to lean down and kiss her.

With an effort, she stepped away.

"I want to take Cody to look at the horses today and let him ride with me. Want to go with us?"

"Sure. I wouldn't miss Cody's first ride. I'll take pictures. Right now, he's still sleeping soundly."

"We're just hanging out at the ranch and I'm not joining the guys to do any work while we're here, so if you want to go into town or do something, let me know. This is a very quiet place."

"Frankly, a very quiet place sounds wonderful. Cody's going to have a great time. I know you'll look out for him and I'll be in charge of pictures. This will be special for him."

"It's special for me in a lot of ways," Nick said, touching a lock of her hair. "I forget how much I love it out here and I want both of you to like it, too. I've hardly been here in the past couple of years."

"You're too busy. Nick, you've got to slow down and smell the roses."

He smiled at her. "There are some other things I'd rather slow down to do," he said in a husky voice.

"And just what would you like to do?" she asked in a breathless voice, knowing she might as well toy with sticks of dynamite, but it had been aeons since she had flirted with anyone.

She caught the brief startled look as his eyes widened, and then Nick stepped closer. "Kiss you good morning," he said, taking her into his arms.

She had opened her mouth to say something, but words were lost when his mouth covered hers and he held her tightly to kiss her.

After the first startled moment, she wrapped her arms around him and kissed him in return, her heart pounding, knowing that she was going up in flames and encouraging him in every way. Guarding her heart had gone away days ago.

She finally ended the kiss and stepped away from him, fanning herself with her hand. "That starts the day with fireworks."

"That starts the day in one of the best possible ways."

She turned to find him watching her intently. "I'm not asking what the other possible ways are. I think I'll cool down with some orange juice."

"Coward," he said softly, but there was no bite in his words.

He walked back to get her a glass of juice. "I'll cook you an omelet. Tell me what you'd like."

"I can cook my own, Nick."

"I know you can, but I'll do it. Look at all the ingredients I have." She walked closer and saw little dishes of chopped mushrooms, onions, sweet peppers, jalapeño peppers, garlic, asparagus, basil leaves, spinach leaves. She looked up in surprise. "How early did you get up?"

"Early, but I can't take credit. Douglas had all this ready. He left it for us."

"Mercy, what a spread. Very tempting," she said, looking at the ingredients again and glancing at Nick to find him watching her with another intent look.

"What? Is something wrong?"

"Far, far from wrong," he said, his voice dropping lower, stirring more sizzles in her. "What's tempting in this kitchen isn't the chopped veggies."

Smiling, her heart beating faster, she moved away from him to sip her orange juice. "I'll have a bit of everything in my omelet. How's that? Can you cram it all in and still have a small omelet?"

"Just watch," he said, turning his attention to his cooking.

Was he flirting to see if he still held appeal or was he flirting for the fun of it? She wondered if she would always suspect his motives.

It was midmorning before they were on horseback. Claire took pictures of Cody, whose eyes sparkled. In his parka, Western hat, jeans and boots, he looked like a little cowboy and he sat on the big horse in front of Nick looking as if he had been given the world.

In addition to appearing almost as happy as his son, Nick was handsome, sexy and appealing in his black broad-brimmed hat, tight jeans that hugged his muscled legs and his boots. Would he kiss her again tonight? With the question came the realization that she wanted him to.

The more time she spent with him, the more she wanted to be with him and wanted to be in his arms, which was not going to help her in dealing with him.

"Well, you've cinched your place in his heart," she told Nick, looking up at him. "I imagine you can do no wrong in his eyes and there is no man on this earth who could possibly be a more wonderful dad."

"I hope you're right," Nick said. "That's awesome, but I love it. We can come out to the corral tonight after dinner when the guys spend a couple of hours riding and it'll be an eye-opener. I don't think he realizes what this animal can do. Has he ever been to a rodeo?"

She gave Nick a look.

"Well, we'll remedy that soon, maybe tomorrow night if I can find one somewhere we can get to."

"That will be the crowning touch."

Their busy schedules were not going to allow many more weeks like this one and the past weekend, when they had both cleared their calendars, so things would change soon. In the meantime, Claire was going to enjoy every moment.

All day she trailed after them, mostly to take pictures of Cody. And that night she sat down to another delicious meal with them, courtesy of Douglas and his wife who served them.

After dinner Claire passed on going to the corral to watch the cowboys with the horses.

When Nick and Cody returned, Cody ran to tell her about the bucking horses and the cowboys. He jabbered and waved his hands and she got out her iPad to take a video to show her grandmother. Cody didn't seem to notice the iPad. When he told her about his dad riding a bucking horse, she glanced at Nick in surprise. He grinned and she realized again that Nick loved ranch life, even the more rugged moments. If he hadn't been born a Milan with their legend and traditions, would his life and his choices have been different?

"Cody, I think it's time to call Grandma and go to bed so you'll be able to do things tomorrow."

"Yes, ma'am," he said as she got out her phone.

As he got ready for bed, Cody tugged on her wrist, and when she looked at him he continued telling her about the bucking horses. Nick joined them while she read to Cody and minutes after he climbed into bed he was asleep.

"Let's go look at the pictures you took today. I would like some copies." Nick draped his arm across her shoulders and they went to the sitting room to sit on the sofa together.

"I think you had another hit this evening. To say he was impressed is an understatement."

"I've told him he doesn't go around the horses unless I'm with him or Mr. Macklin, my foreman. Dusty Macklin has raised five boys and he knows kids. I would trust him with Cody, but nearly all the time Cody will be with me if he's on the ranch."

"I'm glad to hear that. You have a bull or two somewhere on the place, horses and rattlesnakes. Heaven knows what else, so I hope he's always with you."

"Don't ever worry about him here," Nick said, his blue eyes clear and direct. "Let's see the pics."

Together they went through the pictures, laughing over them. At one point Nick paused. "Claire, there's something I was thinking about even before this week. Christmas is coming. I know you have Christmas with your grandparents, and I don't want to interfere, but I want Cody around and my family will, too. Would you and Cody come back during Christmas week to have a Christmas together here at the ranch or in Dallas and include my parents? Your grandmother would be invited, and if I can possibly fly your grandfather here, he would be, too."

She hadn't wanted to think that Nick might want Cody with him at Christmastime, but now she had to make a decision. Once again her life was getting tied to Nick's and she felt on course for another giant hurt.

"If I can have Christmas morning at home with my grandparents, then we could come that afternoon, providing the weather is good enough to travel. If Grandpa can't travel, you can always join us in Houston. We'd be happy to have you."

"Thanks. I'll watch the weather. If it's good, I might have everyone here on the ranch. If not, we'll have Christmas in Dallas. We'll work it out however you agree, but that's great. What about putting a tree up while you're here? I don't want to do it all alone. We can cut a cedar here on the ranch and there are some decorations in the attic."

"Sure. Cody would love to decorate a tree," she said, wondering how much Nick was going to change her life.

"That's great. Thanks," he said, smiling.

She realized Nick was relaxed, happier and more lighthearted since they had arrived at the ranch. "It's so obvious how much you like it here, Nick. You ought to try to come more often."

"This ranch is my first love. Sometimes I envy Tony. But I can't do that to Dad. He's been good to me, helped me, and I have a good career and a good life because of him. A very good career, but I still love this life more."

"You're going to spend your life doing something you don't really love, just to please your father?"

"You've gone into a family business. Would you have chosen real estate if it hadn't been something you were raised to do?"

Taken aback by his question, she thought about her

answer as she looked into his blue eyes. "I thought about interior design, being a decorator. I like that. Even now, sometimes I can help a customer with staging a house before it's put on the market to sell."

"There, see? You're not so different."

"Not really. I don't have a whole different personality when I get involved with interior decorating. You do when you're on the ranch. You're far more laid-back and seem happier here. You're not attached to your cell phone out here."

"I turn it off. Right now it's in the kitchen." He shrugged. "I'll live here when I retire."

"Nick, you will have lived most of your life by then," she said.

"Worried about me?" he asked, his tone changing as he picked her up and placed her on his lap. Before she could answer, he kissed her and she was lost in his kisses then, wanting him more than she had before.

Need was more intense, and this time when his hands slipped beneath her knit shirt, she didn't want him to stop. Memories of making love with him bombarded her while longing spurred her to let go and love him.

Her fingers twisted free the buttons of his shirt and she ran her hands across his muscled chest, pushing away his shirt. Still kissing her, Nick shook off his shirt and tugged hers over her head to toss it away.

"Nick—" she started to protest, but his mouth covered hers and ended her words as he pulled her closer against his shoulder and kissed her passionately. Unfastening her bra, he slipped it off, his hands drifting lightly over her breasts. He caressed and teased, creating more need as she clung to him. A scarf held her hair behind her head. He unfastened it and combed his fingers through the long, luxurious strands.

Common sense cautioned her to stop. Each caress, each kiss complicated the situation and also moved her closer to another broken heart. But desire burned away caution.

Standing, he picked her up as he kissed her and carried her into his bedroom. He never broke contact, placing her down on her feet. She was so wrapped up in his lips on hers, his hands on her body, that she stopped worrying about their situation. More than even her next breath she wanted to just give herself over to the moment, over to Nick. She could no longer deny—to him or to herself—that she wanted him with an intensity that set her ablaze.

She let herself explore him, indulging for a moment the fantasies that had played out in her mind so many nights over the last four years. She ran her hands down his smooth back, slipping around his narrow waist to unbuckle his belt and tug it away. She could feel his erection pressing against her and wanted to free him, to get the barriers of clothing tossed aside.

Yet, at the same time, that niggling voice of reason echoed in her mind, telling her to stop and think about what she was doing. What kind of commitment was she about to make?

When Nick unfastened her jeans and his fingers moved beneath her clothing to caress and stroke her, she silenced that voice and let herself bask in the sensation, until she gasped with need and held him tightly.

He cupped one soft breast, his tongue swirling over and teasing the nipple. Clinging to his shoulders, she gasped with pleasure. He shifted one leg between hers, granting his hand more access to the source of pleasure between her thighs. His intimate strokes caused her to cry out again.

Just as she reached the point of no return, common sense slammed into her again and she stilled his hand. "Nick, we can't do this," she said. "There are so many reasons, not the least of which is I'm not protected." She looked up at him. Dark locks of his hair fell over his forehead. Tinged with desire, his blue eyes had darkened to the color of stormy seas. His mouth was red from their kisses. His male body was muscled, virile, perfect. She had to drag her eyes away.

"I've got protection," he said as he moved over her on the bed, still keeping all his weight from coming down on her. He held her as he showered kisses on her neck and throat. "I want you, Claire," he said between kisses. "I want you with all my being. You've given me back life and laughter and hope. The sex was always fantastic and that's real living."

"You have solutions and answers for everything. It's the politician in you." She didn't recognize her own voice; it was deep and husky with desire. She wanted him too, so badly it was nearly killing her to resist him. "But we are going to complicate our lives, Nick."

"We've already complicated the hell out of our lives." He pulled back to look at her, his lidded eyes irresistible. "Tell me you don't want this. Tell me when to stop." Even as he said those words, his one hand caressed her breast while the other hand stroked her inner thighs slowly, so lightly she ached to rise up and feel the full power of his touch.

She moaned, unable to dredge up the words to stop even though she knew she should. She wanted his mouth and hands on her. She wanted him inside her. She loved him and longed for him to make love to her again, all night long.

"I should tell you to stop," she whispered, her hand sliding over him, taking his thick rod in her hand to caress him.

"No, you shouldn't and you don't really want to," he murmured as he showered kisses on her breasts and drifted lower. His tongue trailed over her stomach, down between her thighs that she parted for him.

"Nick," she whispered, sitting up to kiss and stroke him, to try to build desire in him to the height he had in her. She wanted to kiss him from head to toe, to make love as she had longed to do so many times in so many empty nights. Now Nick was here in her arms and she was already beyond the point of stopping. This had been a dream of hers for years; now she was about to make it a reality. She pushed him down on the bed and caressed his hard body with her eyes before she followed with her hands, relishing the feel of him, wanting to build need in him until he wouldn't ever want to let her go. She was running headlong into heartbreak and disaster and she didn't care. She wanted him too desperately.

She moved over him, her hands fluttering, titillating him while she showered him with wet kisses. She trailed her tongue down his chest, and lower, lavishing kisses along his inner thighs. With a groan he grabbed her arms to roll her over, but she pushed him back down on the bed. "Wait, Nick. Just wait and let me love you."

She did, and the more she touched him, the more she wanted him. Memories taunted her, longing filled her, making her shake with need.

This time when he shifted she let him move her onto her back. He paused only long enough to look at her. "I want you," he whispered and then kissed away any answer she might have had.

He reached out to open a drawer and get a condom. She watched him, her gaze raking over his lean, muscled body, his strong shoulders and flat stomach. He was aroused, ready to love her. She wanted him and she was probably falling more in love with him than ever, something she'd feared would happen this week.

As he moved over her again, she opened wide for him, wanting him, thinking of all the nights she had dreamed of this moment when she hadn't thought it would ever happen again.

He entered her slowly, filling her, hot and hard, and she stopped thinking then, just moving, wanting him and crying out with need. He began to move slowly, driving her wild with wanting him, tension coiling tightly in her.

She clung to him, relishing that it was Nick in her arms, the man she loved and the man whose love she wanted in return. She ran her hands over his back, down over his buttocks, as they moved in perfect synchrony.

Passion swept her up, higher and higher, until she reached the apex of her desire, and with a throaty gasp leaped into ecstasy. Only then did she feel Nick lose his iron control. He pumped wildly as she kept with him. Release burst over her, shattering her, in a climax unlike any other.

His weight came down and he held her, turning his head as he kissed her cheek. They both gasped for breath while he held her close.

"You've given me so much, Claire," he whispered.

She combed locks of his hair back from his damp forehead.

He was quiet, just holding her close, and she held him, remaining just as silent, deep in her thoughts. After a while he rolled onto his side but he continued to hold her close. "I want you with me all night," he said.

"I can't do that, Nick." It pained her, but she couldn't stay the night in his bed. "I'll go in a while."

"You're a tough woman sometimes," he whispered, caressing her cheek.

"So, you think I've been tough the past hour?" she teased.

His arm circled her waist and he pulled her closer even

though he was almost covering her with his body. "Not tough. Sexy beyond my wildest dreams." His eyes darkened again and she wondered if he was feeling desire again so soon. "I admire you, Claire. You know what you want and you stick to it." He gave her a quick grin. "But you do know there's such a thing as compromise?"

"Compromise is for politicians. I have to do what I think is best for Cody, for me and for my family. Maybe I made the wrong choices by not telling you about my pregnancy and not telling you about his birth, but I thought I was doing what was best for all of us—Cody, me and my family. Actually, after a certain point, I thought it was what was best for you, too."

"Stop worrying about all that. It's done and over. Let me just hold you close."

They were quiet again as he held her and stroked her back. "This is good, Claire."

She didn't answer him, certain they hadn't made anything easier tonight.

"I don't want to let you go," he said.

"You'll have to soon," she answered, even though she wished he'd never let her go. But there was no way with their circumstances.

Finally she rolled away, starting to get up, but Nick's arm tightened around her waist and he drew her back. "Don't go."

"Nick, I'm not staying here all night."

He released her and she stepped out of bed. He lay there and watched her as she gathered her clothes. "Good night, Claire," he said before she reached the door.

She turned to look at him. He sat back in his big bed with his hands propped behind his head and a sheet across his lap. Her mouth went dry and she wanted to be back in his arms, to stay the rest of the night with him.

Tonight hadn't brought them any closer to a solution, but had simply complicated her life and made Nick far more difficult to resist. She wouldn't make it any worse by giving into the temptation and staying with him. Steeling herself, she turned away and hurried to her room.

Thursday morning after breakfast, Nick had a pickup parked at the back gate. It was a blustery day with wind gusts that carried a winter chill, and after breakfast, when Nick announced they would go select a tree, she gave Cody his parka and gloves. She pulled on her heavy coat, turning the fur collar up to protect her neck.

"You need some boots out here, Claire."

"I have socks and sneakers," she said, watching him pull on a warm shearling-lined leather jacket. He had black leather gloves and his broad-brimmed black Stetson, which made him look just as good with his clothes on as he had naked last night. She stopped that thought before it made her hot and uncomfortable in her coat. She was grateful that Cody was almost dancing with excitement beside her and needed her attention. She helped him put on his little gloves.

Nick carried Cody to the truck. Gusts of wind whipped against them as they climbed into the warm truck with the motor already running.

They drove to an isolated area that held a scattering of tall cedars.

Nick and Cody selected a tree while she took more pictures. She watched Nick work to chop down the tree, her gaze drifting across his broad shoulders and strong back as he wielded the heavy ax. Nick looked as happy as Cody and she thought he missed a lot of this ranch life locked into working so hard at a career that wasn't his first love.

It wasn't for the money; she knew that much about him. He had to be doing it to please his dad.

A light snow began to fall, sending Cody into gales of excitement as he danced around. "It's snowing," he cried, waving his arms and catching flakes.

"Doesn't take much to please him, does it?" Nick remarked, laughing.

"Everything out here dazzles him and this snow is just one more added touch. We don't see much snow in Houston. You know, he may love the ranch even more than his dad."

Nick looked startled, turning to her and then looking at Cody with a slight frown, and she wondered what he was thinking. He turned to finish his task of chopping down the big cedar. As soon as he'd loaded the felled tree into the truck, they headed home.

By the time they reached the back door and Nick hauled the tree inside, a blizzard was raging. Cody was torn between watching Nick set up the tree and rubbing circles in the frosty glass to look at the snow.

After dinner Nick brought boxes of ornaments from his attic. "Next year we'll get ornaments in Verity or Dallas or Houston, so we have our own. These are some from Mom that I grew up with and some that I bought in haste and then never even opened because I had to go back to Dallas. The ones Karen and I had are in the attic in Dallas," he said. Then he added, "I thought you'd wonder about them."

"It doesn't matter. They're all new to Cody," she said. "I'll let you take the lead with decorating and I'll continue to take more pictures."

Nick smiled as he opened a box. "Cody, let me get the lights strung on first and then you can start decorating."

Claire helped Nick with the lights, brushing against him, aware of him moving close beside her, once looking into his eyes to see his expression change. For a moment she was lost in his gaze, seeing desire flare in the depths of blue. Her heart skipped and she remembered last night in his arms. Taking a deep breath, she turned away.

Finally, they had the tree done, the top portion sparsely decorated and most ornaments on the lower half where Cody could reach.

Nick turned off all but the tree lights. On the other side of the tree, through the window, they could see the blowing snow still falling, the ground now covered. They all stood back to look at the tree, Nick in the middle with his arms around Cody and her. "That is a splendid Christmas tree," Nick said.

She was aware of Nick's arm across her shoulders as she stood pressed against his side. Cody reached over to slip his small hand into hers and she looked at her son, who looked dazzled and happy with a huge smile on his face as he stared at the tree.

A pang tore at her heart. They weren't a family and it hurt. She glanced up at Nick to find him looking down at her with a somber expression and she wondered what he was thinking. Did he realize what obstacles they faced?

"It's the best Christmas tree," Cody said in his child's voice, which caused another ache in her heart.

"I think it's beautiful," she remarked, thinking it was and knowing she would always remember this night and this moment, holding her son's hand and standing in the circle of Nick's arm. It was all a reminder of what she was lacking—a family of her own, a loving husband.

"It's a real tree that you cut down," Cody said in awe. "I like it best," he added, and she felt a twist to her heart. She would have to always share Cody at Christmas now with Nick. She was thankful that Nick would be a wonderful father for their son, but there were going to be some tough moments ahead, when Cody would have times in his life to do things with his dad and she would be no part of them.

Trying to avoid thinking about the rough moments, she moved away.

"Cody, it's way past your bedtime. Let's get you ready and then your dad can read his books to you." In the attic, when he'd gone to get the ornaments, Nick had found two old Christmas books he'd had as a child. He wanted to share them with Cody.

As Cody nodded, Nick swung him up on his shoulders and carried him from the room. She looked at them both and knew that, despite all the walls of defense that she'd erected, she was sinking more in love than ever with Nick.

Getting her iPad, Claire sent all the latest pictures to Nick, thinking about last night and wondering whether he expected a repeat tonight. Soon they would be back in Dallas, and then they'd go home on Sunday, and she felt her heart clutch.

She realized she had put herself at risk again by falling for someone who could easily walk out of her life as he had before.

How was she going to be able to work out shuffling Cody back and forth to DC? She ran her hand over her forehead, knowing problems loomed and they hadn't come one bit closer to a solution.

She looked down at the iPad at a picture of Nick and Cody on horseback. A handsome dad and an adorable son. She didn't dare give her thoughts to any "what-ifs."

She put down the iPad and went to her son's temporary room. Nick was turning out the light after having read the stories, and Cody was asleep, the covers tucked up under his chin.

When he entered the hall, Nick took her hand. "Come

here, Claire," he said, heading toward his room. As soon as they entered his sitting room, he closed the door.

"I've been waiting for this moment since last night," he said, wrapping his arms around her and leaning down to kiss her.

Warmth filled her as she wrapped her arms around him to kiss him in return. Even though she knew the folly of kissing him, she wanted to love him until he never wanted to let her go.

Ten

In the throes of an erotic dream, she realized she was getting poked in the arm by a small finger.

She opened her eyes to look at Cody. "Get up, Mama. It's morning. Dad said it's time for everyone to get up."

Smiling, she hugged Cody. "I'll get up and have a little talk with your dad. And where is your dad?"

"In the kitchen cooking. He said I could wake you, that you're a sleepyhead."

"Is that so? I'll be right there. You can go eat your breakfast while I get dressed."

As he ran out of the room, she got up to close the door. She realized then it was no erotic dream she'd been having. Instead she'd been reliving last night with Nick. Her thighs still throbbed deliciously from a night of lovemaking. They'd made love, showered together, and made love again, twice, before she'd come to her room. Sated and well loved, she'd slept like a baby.

Knowing her son awaited her, she showered and dressed

in jeans and a long-sleeved red T-shirt, and hurried to the kitchen.

"Miss Sleepyhead has arrived," she said, walking into the kitchen. Dressed in a black T-shirt and jeans, Nick was seated at the table across from Cody. Nick came to his feet when she entered and smiled at her as his gaze raked over her, sending fiery currents in its wake.

"I can think of a lot of other names that would be more appropriate," he said.

"You better not say them now," she threatened, smiling at him. "Thanks for feeding Cody."

"I'm getting the hang of it."

"Dad said we're going to build a snowman if the snow is wet enough. We'll go out after breakfast."

"And you are more than welcome to join us," Nick told her.

"Maybe for about ten minutes to take pictures." She laughed. "I'm going home with five thousand more pictures."

As Nick smiled, his gaze skimmed over her and her breath caught at the look in his eyes. She felt as if his fingers had drifted over her instead of just his eyes. She was susceptible to every glance, every touch from him, too aware of him. This had to stop or she'd never make it through the day.

"My images are in here," he said, tapping his head, his voice dropping a notch.

She knew what images he was referring to. Ones that would never be shared on Instagram. "And they better stay there and we hear no more about them," she said, and he grinned.

"This morning, with your permission, I'd like to take Cody out with me and let him see the men working. They'll break ice on the ponds and tanks so the animals can drink and put out hay for them. We'll be in the truck. I'll take good care of him."

"Do you want to go?" she asked Cody, knowing what he would answer.

"Yes, ma'am," he said, looking at Nick.

"Fine. I'll definitely pass on that one, though."

"I figured you would."

After breakfast she had fun with Nick and Cody as they made a snowman, and then she watched them as they left to go out onto the ranch. A tall cowboy holding the hand of his small son. When they returned she heard about their day in great detail and Nick showed her pictures of Cody he'd taken with his phone. Her son looked ecstatic out there with the cowboys.

After dinner that night Nick played games with Cody, lying on the floor with him and letting his son climb on him. She watched them and wondered whether Nick seemed so happy and relaxed because they were at the ranch or because he had Cody with him. Either way, his appeal heightened. There was no denying it. He was a marvelous dad for Cody.

But what kind of man was he for her?

She wanted to love someone who returned that love. What Nick felt for her was lust. He was sexy, virile, filled with energy, and he desired her and lusted after her, but he wasn't in love with her. He could walk away tomorrow, run for the US Senate, live in DC and seldom see her without it tearing him up.

He would miss her for sex, certainly, and maybe for how she could be at his side to help him in his career.

Not that that was going to happen, she told herself. Her grandfather was going through physical therapy in hopes he could return in a limited capacity to his office. She didn't want to get someone to run it and walk away, marry Nick and abandon the business and her grandparents.

Nick's deep laugh broke into her thoughts. Once more

she remarked on how much more she had heard Nick laugh, whistle and hum since he had been on the ranch. She wondered why he pursued the life he did if he was so much happier being a cowboy. Nick rolled away, stretched out a long arm and his hand closed around her ankle lightly, startling her and getting her attention.

"Why so solemn?" he asked as his fingers lightly caressed her ankle.

"I was wondering how I'm going to get him quiet enough to ever go to bed."

"I'll take care of him. Don't give it another thought." He rolled away and sat up. "Cody, it's bath time and then story time. Come get on my shoulders and I'll carry you."

Cody laughed and got on Nick's shoulders, winding his fingers in Nick's thick hair. Nick stood, smiled at her and trotted off like a horse, making Cody laugh harder.

She glanced at the clock. She would give them thirty minutes and then go kiss Cody good-night.

When she walked into the bedroom later, Nick was leaning down to brush Cody's forehead with a kiss. He crossed the room to place his arm around her shoulders.

"He couldn't last to hear the end of the story."

"Good job, Dad. Thank you very much," she said, aware of Nick close at her side. She felt his fingers toying with her hair.

In the hall he turned toward his room and stopped. "I have plans for us."

"I'm sure you do," she said, amused, but her smile vanished as she looked up at him. Desire was blatant in his blue eyes. He ran his hands lightly across her shoulders, up to caress her nape, to untie the ribbon that held her hair. He leaned down to brush her lips lightly with his.

He stroked her mouth with another kiss and then his

mouth covered hers and his tongue touched hers. As he kissed her, his arm tightened around her.

Breathless, she wanted him in return. Wrapping her arms around his neck, she pressed against him and kissed him back with fervor.

Nick picked her up and she knew without looking that he carried her to his suite. She heard the door close behind him and in seconds he'd laid her on the bed and joined her.

It was eight the next morning when she woke in her own room, then showered and dressed to go get breakfast and see where Cody and Nick were.

The family dinner was tonight, at Nick's house in Dallas. Briefly she felt butterflies at the thought and then remembered how friendly Wyatt had been and how super friendly Nick's parents had been. They made it obvious how badly they wanted Cody in the family and the butterflies left her. She joined Nick and Cody at the breakfast table, where they were eating bowls of oatmeal and berries.

"The temperature should climb today and the roads are clear," Nick said. "We're off to Dallas after breakfast and tonight should be fun. I can't wait for my family to get to know Cody."

"The only grandson—he should be very welcome," she said, smiling but feeling a pang in her heart. She would spend time with his family, but she'd never be a part of it.

By late morning they were back in Dallas at Nick's mansion. Two members of his staff were present and his cook was already there.

Cody sat at a game table in the family room, coloring, and Nick took her arm to pull her aside, walking into the hall.

"My folks will be here tonight. Can you talk to Cody—and I think it should be you—about what he would like to call them? Granddad, Grandma—whatever he comes up with will be wonderful to them. They'll be thrilled and it would be nice to start now. They are his grandparents, after all."

"Of course. I should have thought of that. I'll ask him and then we'll get your approval."

"I think I can give approval right now," he said, smiling at her and brushing her cheek with a kiss. He looked into her eyes and the moment changed. He pulled her to him, to wrap his arms around her and really kiss her until she made him stop.

"Whoa, Nick. Your house has staff and Cody's running around. The hall isn't private."

"My bedroom will be tonight, and I can't wait."

"You'll have to," she said. "I'm going to talk to Cody," she added and left him. She had stopped him, but her heart still raced and she couldn't stop that as easily.

Luckily the rest of the afternoon was taken up with party preparations, so she was too busy to get waylaid by tempting kisses.

Late in the afternoon Nick offered to get Cody ready for the party, so she handed over his clothes and left the two of them while she went to dress. It was a dinner party, and the first time she would meet some of his family—and she barely knew his parents. She'd chosen to wear a deep scarlet, long-sleeved dress with a round neck and matching high-heeled pumps.

Brushing her hair, she let it fall around her face. She fastened both the necklace from Nick and the bracelet, looking at the charm of the man and the woman holding a child's hands. She shook her head. That would not be her with Cody and Nick. She suspected when she went home this time, other than Christmas, she would see little of Nick except to work out arrangements for Cody, something she dreaded more each day.

When she walked into the family room and Nick's gaze flashed over her, she saw the approval in his eyes. "You look great."

She turned to her son first. "Cody, you look very nice," she said, her gaze going over his blue sweater and navy slacks. The gold Junior Sheriff badge was pinned to his sweater.

"And so do you, Dad," she said, taking in his navy sport jacket over a long-sleeved pale blue shirt and navy slacks. He would be the best-looking Milan in the room.

Promptly at six the doorbell rang, and in minutes Nick's parents entered. They had another gift in their hands and she was certain it was for Cody.

He dutifully shook hands with Peter again and let Evelyn hug him. "Cody, we brought you a present," she said, as her husband held out the box.

"Thank you," he answered politely, glancing at Claire and she nodded.

"Open your present, Cody."

He tore off the paper and opened the box to pull out a stuffed hippo. Grinning, Cody clutched the hippo in his arms. "Thank you, Grandmother," he said and turned to Judge Milan. "Thank you, Granddad."

"You're very welcome," Peter said, smiling broadly. Judge Milan sat on a chair and leaned forward toward Cody. "Cody, we're so happy to have you call us Granddad and Grandmother. That's very, very nice."

"Yes, sir."

"You have raised the sweetest little boy who is so well-mannered," Evelyn said. She dabbed at her eyes, which surprised Claire. "I love him already and thank you for any time you share him with us. He's a wonderful child."

"Thank you. And thank you for the hippo for him. He'll love it."

The doorbell rang and in minutes Jake and Madison Calhoun entered. Nick crossed the room, taking Cody with him. "Claire, this is my sister Madison and her husband, Jake Calhoun. Meet Claire and my son, Cody," Nick said.

"We've met at an art gallery in Houston and it's nice to see you again, Claire," Madison said. "And you, too, Cody. What do you have in your arms?"

"My hippo. My grandmother and my granddad gave it to me."

"Referring to Mom and Dad," Nick said.

"I figured that much," Madison said, laughing. "Mom is beside herself with joy about Cody," she said. "I can see why. Nick, your son looks exactly like you."

"I think so," Nick said smiling. "Here come Wyatt and Destiny."

Wyatt greeted Claire with a big smile. "I hope you had a good time at the ranch."

"Cody has never had so much fun."

In short order she met Wyatt's wife, Destiny, a beautiful woman in a dramatic black dress with red trim. Then Nick's younger brother, Tony crouched down to talk to Cody. He took his nephew's hand after a moment and they walked away with Tony talking to him.

"He's a Pied Piper with kids and animals," Nick said. "Maybe he gets on their level, I don't know. He's single and he doesn't know beans about kids, but they love him."

She smiled, watching Cody with Tony as Cody laughed.

In a short time she began to feel she knew Nick's family better. She realized he had good relationships with his siblings and they saw each other fairly often. She also saw he was very close to his dad, who could be charming. Nick, in his way, was as close to his family as she was to hers.

He had never had to take care of any of his, or be responsible for them, so he saw that differently.

Everyone was interested in Cody, who seemed to be having a good time with all the adult attention.

With Douglas serving, they ate in Nick's spacious dining room. During dinner, Jake clinked his glass for quiet and everyone became silent as Madison spoke. "I want to take this time to make one announcement that I hope does not in any way detract from the joy of meeting Claire and Cody—Jake and I are expecting. I'm due next July."

Everyone clapped and cheered as she sat down and then dinner continued. Again, Claire couldn't keep from comparing how the Milan family was enthused over the expected baby and how there had not been a word from any of them during her pregnancy. Basically, it had been her fault for not telling Nick about the baby, but if they had known, at that time there would not have been applause and cheers. She glanced at Nick and was surprised to see him looking at her. She wondered if he shared her thoughts.

The party was fun because Nick's siblings enjoyed each other. Once during the evening she looked over to see Cody sitting in Judge Milan's lap as the judge showed Cody a trick. The impact wasn't lost on her. Changes were already taking place in her life, she realized. But at the same time she was pleased that his grandparents liked her son and glad he liked them, as well.

When Nick's parents left at nine, Evelyn hugged Claire. "Thank you for telling us we can come visit Cody in Houston."

"I meant what I said. We'd love to have you, and you're more than welcome to stay at my house. I have a big home and that would make Cody happy."

"That is so sweet, Claire. We'll take you up on the offer soon."

As his mother headed toward the door, Claire looked beyond her to see Nick watching her with a solemn expression. As she closed the door behind his parents, Nick stepped close. "So, they get to visit and stay at your house and I don't."

"It isn't quite the same, but you can stay. I may not be there, but Grandma will be happy to have you."

"That isn't quite the same, either," he said. After a moment he shook his head. "Anyway, thanks for being so gracious to my parents."

"They're my son's grandparents and I think he's going to love them," she said, turning to walk away. She let Cody stay up until ten, but then she put him to bed and rejoined the others.

By the time the last couple left it was almost midnight. As Nick watched them drive away, he draped his arm across her shoulders. "Everyone loved Cody and each one was happy to see you. It was a great night. Now, let's go in. Finally I get to be alone with you," he said, closing the door and heading to his suite. "Claire, you were wonderful tonight and so was Cody. Both of you charmed my family. My parents are shocking in their reaction to Cody, because I never expected them to be this way. You know, when I mentioned to them that when I live in Austin they won't see Cody, they both looked unhappy."

Surprised, she stared at Nick. "Your dad, too?"

"Even my dad," he replied with a nod of his head. "The other thing is, I hadn't really noticed age changing them until tonight. Dad is more mellow, less energetic, but he's changed, and now with Cody I think they're both changing more."

Continuing to stare at Nick, she wondered how much their reactions would influence Nick. "Nick, if your dad is unhappy about you living in Austin when the legislature is in session, that's a huge change."

"You and Cody have turned my world, and maybe theirs, upside down. Upside down for the good," Nick said, looking intently at her. Her heart missed a beat. Was there any chance of Nick changing his political ambitions? Had the time spent at the ranch with Cody caused him to look at his life differently? A bigger question loomed in her mind. Was there a chance of Nick falling in love?

Before she could pursue a response, Nick closed the door to his suite and turned to her. "Now, let's forget family, the evening, everything except you and me. I've been waiting all day for this moment," he said, leaning down to kiss her. Held in his crushing embrace, she forgot everything else except Nick as she returned his kisses.

Long after Nick had fallen asleep, she remained awake, thinking about this past week and their future. She was in love with Nick, and his thoughtfulness, his growing love for Cody, his lovemaking, everything between them was making that love stronger and she couldn't deal with another hurt that would be bigger than when they had parted before he married.

She had to put distance between them or risk a giant hurt—a hurt that would involve Cody this time.

She needed to distance herself from Nick. Lust was not the same as love and there was no future in it.

Nick had his future mapped out, and it did not include marriage to her any more now than it had four years ago.

As difficult as it was going to be, she had to stop what was superficial and meaningless between them because she couldn't be intimate with Nick without losing her heart, but he could easily be enveloped in lust and not have his heart involved.

Tears burned her eyes and rolled down her cheeks. She

wiped them away and tried to get a grip on her emotions. She already loved him and she already hurt, but it could get worse and maybe she could save herself a bigger hurt. She should put an end to seeing him every time Cody did.

It was four in the morning when she pulled on a robe and faced Nick as she stood beside the bed. "I'm going to my room. You think about how we can work out sharing Cody. Your family will want to know him and you'll want time with him. You come up with a plan and we'll go from there."

Nick pulled the sheet around his waist and got up, walking around the bed to place his hands on her shoulders. She stood looking up at him, trying to focus while she was aware of his bare, muscled chest, his broad shoulders, only the sheet low on his hips as they faced each other. She had to resist him, but it was growing more difficult by the day.

"I'll do that. I'm not in a rush and I know it will take time to work things out. He's too little to come see me without you unless I come get him."

She shook her head. "I'm not coming to see you along with him, and I don't think you'd want that either. You think about what you want. This can't keep on. My emotions get caught up in intimacy, so in a way, this is goodbye between us. I'll still see you with Cody and family around, but that's all, Nick. Your life is set and so is mine and they don't fit together. We have to stop before we both get hurt badly again."

"What you're saying makes sense, but I don't want to say goodbye, Claire."

"We don't have a future—you and I—and I'm not going to continue to sleep with you occasionally when we're together. I get my emotions entangled. This is a private goodbye to intimacy, to moments alone or dinners out or dates. We'll just get hurt again otherwise." She turned and walked away to go to her own room.

Sunday after Nick put them on the plane he waved as it taxied away. Claire and Cody were at the window and both waved. He hated to see them go, feeling as if part of his heart was being ripped away. It startled him how empty he felt with Claire and Cody gone. He had learned to live alone the past two years, but now life loomed like one big void and he wanted Claire with him. Her goodbye had hurt. The thought of her going out of his life again—except for brief moments—seemed unbearable. The realization startled him. How deep did his feelings for her run?

As he drove home, he thought about his parents and their plans to visit Claire in Houston. They'd never been interested in getting to know her before. He thought, too, about their unhappy looks when he mentioned living in Austin. For the first time, Nick wondered if his dad would rather he didn't pursue a political career.

Claire's question echoed in his mind. Had he pursued politics for himself or for his dad?

Nick watched the road and turned into the drive, stopping before going through the gates. He felt as if his life had been built on shifting sand and he wasn't certain where he stood any longer. How deep were his feelings for Claire? Had he been consumed by lust or did he really want her as a part of his life outside his bedroom?

He didn't know the answers. He only knew he'd better figure it out soon.

As soon as he arrived home, he got out his cell phone to catch up on all the calls he had missed and pour himself into work. He tried to get back into his regular routine, but he couldn't keep his mind on work and he finally shoved it aside to think about how they would share Cody.

DC wouldn't come up for several years, but he would be in Austin most of the time from January until June, when his term was over. He thought about Claire's family and the care she continued to give them, plus the company she ran now with three offices in the Houston area. He sat thinking about her ties and his own, comparing them, and in minutes he was lost, remembering this past week on the ranch and the fun they'd had, the joy he'd felt watching Cody.

Maybe it was just because he had told Claire and Cody goodbye this morning that he was unhappy and missed them so much.

He thought Monday would be better, when he was back at work and busy.

But as he dressed for work the next morning, he was lost again in memories of Claire. Nick missed her. He walked to his bedroom to stare at his bed and remembered Claire in his arms. How right and good it had felt. He couldn't fathom not making love to her again. He missed her each time he had said goodbye to her, but the past two times, before she came to the ranch, he knew he would be with her again within days. Now he faced a future in which he would just see her briefly as he picked up Cody or took him home. And maybe not even then. He might just see her grandmother or the nanny.

What were his feelings for her now?

Life had been great on the ranch with Claire and Cody there. Now he felt empty without her, hopeless, hurt beyond words. He'd tried to guard his heart against falling for Claire, even telling himself it was impossible to fall in love with her a second time. He'd let himself have fun with her, allowed himself to bed her, thinking his heart had been secure.

But he'd been wrong.

To hurt this badly over her goodbye, he realized, he

had to be in love with her. And he might be losing the best possible life and the best possible woman for reasons that wouldn't ever bring him real happiness.

He was in love, and he'd better do something about it.

He pulled out his phone to call her, but when he heard a recorded message he put away his phone. "Claire." He whispered her name, wanting her, missing her and wishing he could conjure her up before him. He didn't want to lose her this time. But how could they work out getting together now when they couldn't do it four years ago?

Would Claire yield on any part of her life to try to be together, or did she even care? What could he change to make her happy? There had to be a way to work things out, but this time he'd better be certain about what he really wanted in life and what he could give up.

Would a political career be worth losing her? Even if he wanted to be a rancher, the only way to get Claire in his life was to move to Houston.

Was there any way to move Claire and keep her happy about the move? He crossed to his desk to make a list of all the things in Houston that were important to her. He stared blankly at the paper, sorting through all kinds of possibilities. There had to be a way...

Monday, Claire called in to say she would be late to the office. She didn't feel like concentrating on work. She missed Nick, and it surprised her how much. She missed his flirting and his companionship, and she missed the hours of passion. She loved him more than she had when she was younger. She had thought she was over the heart-break when he came back into her life. Instead, she was more drawn to him than ever, while it was less likely they could ever get together as a couple. Yet she would have to see him because of their son.

She was going to have to discuss sharing Cody, but she'd told Nick to get a plan. He was the one who wanted changes, so he could come up with something and she would have to try to work with him.

She could not leave Houston or her family obligations, which were now greater than ever. She would not abandon her grandparents or shut down the agency that meant so much to her grandfather and that they had both worked so hard to build.

One thing had changed, though—Nick's parents. She had seen the looks on their faces when he had mentioned they would not see Cody when he was in Austin. If they didn't see Cody when Nick was in Austin, they definitely would not if Nick lived in DC, and his parents were smart enough to realize that.

She never guessed his parents would care about Cody because they hadn't even bothered to try to meet her when their son had hoped to marry her. It had been a shock to find out how badly they wanted a grandchild and how much they loved Cody from the first moment. When they asked if they could visit, she had agreed and meant it. That was a giant change—would it have any influence on Nick and his decisions?

Her thoughts turned to Nick again and the wonderful week with him on the ranch that had been paradise. She missed him and it had taken all her willpower not to answer his call moments ago. She loved him and she missed him. She couldn't see any way to work out a future sharing Cody with him, but she had to.

She was alone in her room and she gave in to tears, for just a moment letting go and hurting, wondering how she would cope with seeing Nick only for minutes at a time. Or worse, watching him once again marry someone else.

It was going to hurt watching him take Cody for days

at a time, but she would never deny him that right or hurt her son. He was good for Cody, a wonderful dad, and Cody already loved him. In a lot of ways she was thankful that Nick was in Cody's life, filling a void that needed to be filled. Too bad he could never be part of *her* life.

She heard her phone and saw that it was Nick again. She didn't take the call. She couldn't talk to him yet. She didn't want to burst into tears while they were on the phone. In minutes she received a brief text: Have a plan to discuss about Cody. Can you go to dinner next Thursday and we'll talk about it? I can pick you up at 7. Would like to come at 6 so I can see Cody.

She typed her reply. She would go, wondering what Nick had in mind and if the evening would dissolve in sharp words the way it had so long ago, the night he had proposed.

Later that morning her grandmother left, taking Cody for a haircut and errands. As Claire nibbled at a late breakfast, the doorbell rang. She answered to find a deliveryman on her porch holding a giant arrangement of red roses, white orchids, red anthurium and white gladioli. A box wrapped in blue paper and tied with a big blue bow was delivered with the flowers.

As soon as she closed the door, she removed a card from the flowers that read: *To Claire: Thank you for the joy you have brought us with our grandson. Love, Peter and Evelyn.*

Startled, she looked at the flowers again. She would never know, but she wondered…if she had told Nick about her pregnancy, would things have worked out differently? It was a question that couldn't be answered. Back then, even though it was only four years ago, Nick's dad was still deeply intent on having his son move up in politics. It was obvious, now that Cody was here and the Milans were older, that that wasn't what the judge wanted for his son. He wanted his grandson in his life and in Evelyn's.

Claire removed a card from the box and saw it was to Cody from them. She smiled. Cody had four doting grandparents now. If only she and Nick—

Claire stopped instantly. She was not going to live on wishes. She would have to pick up and go on, work out something with Nick and try to live with it. She'd have to live with the hurt.

She was still telling herself that on Thursday as she dressed for the evening with Nick.

Cody stayed downstairs, playing in the family room while her grandmother was nearby. Claire was running a few minutes late, and when she heard the door chimes, she knew Cody and Grandma would both enjoy talking to Nick.

When Claire was finally ready, she assessed her image in the mirror. She smoothed her navy long-sleeved dress with a straight skirt and fingered the diamond pendant and charm bracelet. Then she picked up her small black purse and went downstairs, hoping against hope that she had her emotions under control.

Nick heard Claire seconds before she walked into the room. He stood immediately while his heart thudded. She looked stunning. He felt hot, dazzled and had to make an effort to avoid staring at her. He longed to cross the room to take her into his arms.

She smiled, her full, red lips curving and tugging on his senses. He wanted to be alone with her, back in his suite where nothing could disturb them.

"Have a seat, Nick. I'm sure Grandma and Cody are enjoying talking to you."

"Nick said he got a present for me, but the last time

he was here, I was gone, so he brought it tonight," Verna said, holding out a box. Claire crossed the room to look at a beautiful gold locket on a thin golden chain with her grandmother's initials carved into the face of the locket. She opened it and inside the locket were two pictures, one of Claire and Cody and another of Cody.

"Nick, that's lovely," Claire said, smiling at him and then looking at her grandmother. "I know you'll love it. Turn around and I'll put it on you," she said.

Her grandmother shifted in her chair and Claire fastened the locket around her neck. Verna turned back around and looked down at it. "That's beautiful, Nick. I'll treasure it. Thank you."

"I'm glad you like it."

"I got a present, too," Cody said, holding out a book.

Claire took it in her hands. "Great, Cody. Another new book, and I'll bet you and Grandma can read it at bedtime," she said, smiling at Nick.

Cody looked at his grandmother who nodded. "Of course, we will," she said.

They spent the next thirty minutes talking until Claire stood. "I'm guessing Nick has some dinner reservations somewhere."

Nick came to his feet and picked up Cody. "Be a good kid tonight and I'll see you in the morning."

Cody hugged him and kissed Nick's cheek. "Thank you for the book."

"You're very welcome. We'll read it in the morning." Nick hugged him and kissed his cheek. He carried him to the door to hug him one more time before setting him down.

Nick escorted Claire to the passenger side of his car, then got in and drove out of her neighborhood.

"You look gorgeous. I didn't tell you back there, but

that's what I was thinking," he said, keeping his attention on the road, but remembering clearly the impact she'd had when she stepped into the doorway. She had always dazzled him, from the first moment at the cocktail party where he met her, but she seemed to have more of an effect on him now that she was several years older.

"Thank you," she said. "You look very handsome yourself. I suspect you'll win most of the female votes the next time you run."

He smiled. "I hope my looks aren't the basis of votes," he said.

Nick drove to a tall hotel with sparkling Christmas lights strung over the wide entrance. He stopped in the drive to let the engine idle while he turned to her. "This is my hotel. How about dinner in my room where we can be free to talk about possibilities and what we can do to share Cody? I don't want to be in a restaurant. This could get emotional, Claire."

She had to agree, but reluctance filled her because her life was going to change again.

Eleven

Claire's heart beat faster as she nodded. "As long as it's just dinner and conversation, Nick. Nothing else. I can't keep…" She couldn't bring herself to say the words *making love*, not when they conjured hot images of a naked Nick. "I just want to hear your suggestions, see what we can work out for Cody and then go home."

"I've ordered dinner from a restaurant and they should have it in about half an hour. I got lobster for you, steak for me—how's that?"

"Excellent choices," she said, wondering if tonight would be another heartbreak. She was going to have to share Cody with Nick and she dreaded what he might propose.

Driving to the door, Nick gave the valet his keys and took Claire's arm to enter the hotel and take an elevator to his suite on the top floor. "I got you a little Christmas present," he said, unlocking the door. Barely aware of her elegant surroundings as Nick took her coat and slipped his off, she saw a small rosemary plant decorated as a Christmas tree in the center of a glass table by the sofa. One present was tucked into the branches, a small box wrapped in shiny red paper and tied with silver ribbon.

"The Christmas tree is mine, not the hotel's. The present is for you, but before you open it, let's talk," he said while she looked into his thickly lashed blue eyes, which could make her heartbeat quicken with just a glance. Her gaze drifted to his mouth and she drew a deep breath. Could she get through this evening without succumbing to his kisses? Or without getting emotional and crying?

He cleared his throat before he began, and for a moment she thought he looked nervous. "First, I've had time to think about us. The week with you and Cody at the ranch was special." He stepped closer to place his hands on her waist. She could have sworn he was trembling. Then he said the words she thought she'd never hear him speak again. The words she dreaded now.

"Claire, I love you."

She closed her eyes and took a deep breath, hurt rippling inside. "Even though I've tried to get over you, I think I've always loved you," she said, opening her eyes and looking up at him. "But that just compounds the problems between us without solving any of them."

But Nick wouldn't be stopped. "I want to be with you and Cody. I want to share my life with you," he said.

She frowned. He knew all the impossible obstacles. Surely this wasn't going to be a second round of the fight they'd had when they split four years earlier.

"You've made me stop and think, Claire. That week on the ranch was the best week of my life. Maybe I'm missing really living, having love and a family in my life. I've thought about what you want and need, and what I want and need—what I can give up to make you happy."

She stared at him intently, suddenly afraid to breathe. She had never heard those words from him before.

"Now I want you to hear what I have to say and then we'll talk."

She nodded, wondering what he had planned, remembering that Nick was a politician, so accustomed to saying what he thought people wanted to hear, able to talk people into seeing things his way. Yet there was a tiny part of her that was hanging on his every word because he had never offered to give up one thing for her happiness before.

"You want to stay in Houston, I know. I made a list of what you need and want—take care of your grandparents and continue running the three offices of the real estate business. Right?"

"Yes," she whispered, wondering what he would suggest.

"I'll tell you what I want. I've thought about my political career, my legal career in Dallas and the ranch. I love being a rancher and you made me stop and think. Why am I pursuing the others when ranching is what I love? But I can move to Houston and practice law there, and if I have to live in Houston to make you happy, I will."

She stared at him, barely able to breathe and wondering if she had heard him correctly. "You'd give up your political career?" she whispered.

"Absolutely. I'll do what I need to if it means you and Cody would be in my life. But now here is what I'm thinking—see if you would want this at all. I can move your grandparents with us to the ranch and get full-time care for your grandfather with as many nurses as you want. I can afford it. If it's not satisfactory to live on the ranch, we could live in Dallas where I can practice law. Your grandparents can live in our house."

She blinked as another shock hit her...*our house*...was that a convoluted proposal? "You're forget—"

"Shh. Wait until I'm through," he said, touching her lips lightly with his finger. "You can hire someone to run your business in Houston and you can open another one in Dallas. Between all the members of my family, we'll have more contacts than your grandfather did, so you'll not lack for customers. We know builders, too."

He stepped closer. "How am I doing so far?"

Dazed, she stared at him. "Pretty good. You covered my grandparents, my business, the ranch, your career—you left out one thing, Nick. Us. Me and Cody."

"I just wanted you to know what I'm willing to do before I get to us," he said. "Claire, I can't tell you how empty my life has been without you and Cody. I don't want to live that way." His hands slipped to her waist and he drew her closer.

"I love you, Claire. I love you with all my heart. I'll do whatever I need to do to make you happy."

Her heart thudded and her breath left her. "Nick," she gasped, wrapping her arms around his neck, fighting back tears. "You're really willing to do all of that?"

"If it gets me you and Cody, your love, yes, I am. You don't need to ask twice. I'll do what you want. I'm not losing you again. Will you marry me?"

"Nick," she said, her heart pounding with joy as she stood on tiptoe to kiss him.

His arms banded her and he held her tightly, leaning over her to kiss her. She couldn't stop tears of joy, of relief, thinking how much she had hurt just thinking of the empty nights ahead. Instead, Nick was willing to do whatever would make her happy so they could be together.

"Hey, darlin', you're crying. Don't cry. That's the last thing I intended. I don't want to hurt you ever again, Claire.

I promise. You tell me what you want. I love you. Will you marry me?" he repeated.

"Yes," she answered, smiling and still crying. "Nick, I've hurt so badly and wanted you so much. Yes, I'll marry you." She kissed him then.

When his words had had a moment to sink in, she asked him, "You really mean you're giving up politics after you finish this term of office?"

"I'm already finished. I resigned. It'll be in the news tomorrow, I'm sure."

Staring at him, she was stunned. "You resigned as a Texas State Representative?"

"Yes, I did. I thought we could work things out better if I gave that up right now."

"I'm stunned. You did that for me?"

"I want you to know that I mean all this. I love you, Claire, and I'm not losing you again."

"Have you told your dad?"

"Yes, I have, and he was delighted because he thinks now he'll get to see more of Cody, and Mom is even happier about it. Mom said she regrets that they didn't meet you when I was dating you."

"This is a day of one shock right after another," she said, looking at Nick. She kissed him, trying to convey the love she felt for him, love that she no longer tried to crush or ignore or deny. Stepping back, she gazed into the blue eyes that she loved. He'd taken a huge step, given up something important to him, just for her. Now it was her turn.

"Nick, I might want to commute and open a Dallas office after we get my grandparents settled, but if you want to be a rancher, I'll move to Verity. The ranch would be a wonderful place for Cody to grow up."

Nick leaned close to kiss her, drawing her tightly against him. She closed her eyes, kissing him with joy and love.

Happiness filled her as he leaned over her and kissed her passionately, and she held him tightly, thrilled that she had his love and they would be together, a family for Cody.

In minutes, she leaned back to look up at him. "You would really have moved to Houston for me?"

"Yes, ma'am, I would have. Whatever it takes to make you happy. I thought a lot about it and decided that all that was really important was the woman I love, my child, my family. That's true happiness for me."

"I'm amazed. I love you, Nick," she said before he kissed her.

When he released her, she gazed up at him. "Cody will be hyper when he finds out he's going to live on a ranch." She giggled then, feeling like an excited child herself. Then she realized she'd been remiss. "Nick, I need to ask my grandmother if they'll be willing to move. I want to ask my grandfather, too."

"Fine. You talk to them first, but then I will. I can afford to get whatever medical help we need for your grandfather. Think I should ask your grandfather for your hand in marriage?"

She laughed. "I don't think you need to, since we have a three-year-old son."

"Remember, you have an early Christmas present on the tree. You can open it now."

She looked at the small box tucked between the branches of rosemary. She pulled it out, carefully untying the ribbon while Nick showered light kisses on her temple, her ear, her throat. As she unwrapped the paper, he turned to watch when she raised the lid. A small black box was inside. She glanced at him and then pulled it out to open it. She gasped as she looked at the sparkling ring with one huge diamond surrounded by a circle of smaller stones.

"Oh, Nick. It's beautiful."

Nick took it from her, taking her hand. "I love you, Claire, with all my heart."

"I love you," she repeated, more tears of happiness falling.

She hugged him and he kissed her, picking her up tightly in his arms to carry her to bed.

Later, as she lay cradled against him, she ran her finger along his jaw, feeling the tiny stubble. "Nick, I love you so. There's never been another man since we first met. Not ever." She kissed away his answer, holding him tightly, feeling giddy with happiness.

"I'm going to spend a lifetime trying to make up to you for the breakup and the harsh words. I—"

She placed her fingers on his lips. "Shh. That's over and in the past, and we've moved on. Let it go, Nick, and I will, too. We're together now and that's what is important."

She rose slightly to look down at him. "Christmas is next week. What are your plans?"

"This year the whole family is going to Mom and Dad's for dinner on Christmas Eve. Christmas Day everyone is on their own. I'll be with you and your family that afternoon. Then everyone's invited to Wyatt's for dinner Christmas night."

"If you'd like, come Christmas Eve and join us. You'll miss dinner at your parents' house, but we'll be happy to have you."

"I accept," he said, kissing her briefly.

She rolled off the bed to gather her clothes. "Nick, I need to go home. I'm not spending the night here."

"Home, it is," he said.

She loved the sound of that word on his lips.

As Nick drove her home, she placed her hand on his knee. "Nick, we've never talked about children. We've lost some time. Cody is already three. I'd like Cody to have a sibling or two."

Nick smiled. "I think that's a marvelous idea. I agree. As soon as you want."

"I might want to just retire to the ranch with you and raise a family."

"That would suit me fine," he said.

She laughed. "Cody is going to be impossible to calm down. If he thinks he is moving to the ranch, he won't sleep for a week."

"So maybe we ought to both take the rest of the time until Christmas and go to the ranch. I can fly your grandmother and grandfather there, also his nurse and a caregiver, whoever you need to hire for him."

"I'll ask if they want to do that," she said, watching him drive and bubbling with happiness over the changes in her life. "I love you so much, Nick. You'll never ever know, even though I'm going to try to show you. Even though I've held out for things, I love you with all my heart."

"Tomorrow I'll come by and let's tell Cody the news." He snagged a quick kiss. "Get your camera ready."

Twelve

In a white silk dress with a square neckline, short sleeves and a narrow skirt that ended at her knees, Claire stood in the vestibule of her church in Houston. Her great-uncle stood beside her with her arm linked in his as they watched Cody walk down the aisle with the wedding ring.

In the front, on the aisle, sat her grandma. Next to her was Grandpa and beside him a nurse. A wheelchair was set out of the way temporarily.

When it was her turn to walk down the aisle, her gaze honed in on Nick, who had never looked more handsome in his black suit.

As Nick took her hand, he stepped close beside her to repeat their vows. Near them, Cody stood with a big smile. She glanced up at Nick who squeezed her hand.

As soon as they were pronounced man and wife, Nick picked up Cody and the three of them walked up the aisle to the vestibule where Nick turned so they could hug.

"I love you both with all my heart," Nick said gruffly.

Cody smiled. "I love you, too, you and Mama," he said, smiling at her.

"This is going to be good, Claire," Nick said. "I'll do my best to see that it is."

"I think it's going to be difficult to see who's the happiest—Cody or me," she answered.

"Let's get this reception over."

While the wedding had been small, the reception was large, filled with relatives and friends from all over Texas. The January party was held at a Houston country club. As the band played, Claire and Nick mingled with guests. At one point they stood in a Milan family gathering.

"You've been the miracle worker," Tony said, "getting my brother to finally take up ranching. If anyone had challenged me, I would have bet my spread that wouldn't ever happen."

Nick merely grinned and kept his arm around Claire's waist.

"I'm betting you never have a second's regret," Madison said, smiling at them.

"Well, my term as sheriff will be up before you know it, so if you need a political office, I can throw your hat—"

"Brother, stop right there," Nick said, grinning. "You can forget that one. Wait until Cody is old enough. I can't get him to stop wearing that little badge."

Wyatt smiled. "He can visit anytime he wants."

"We still need to get that kid to a rodeo," Tony stated.

"That's on my agenda," Nick said. "Once he sees one, he'll want to go all the time."

They stood laughing and talking, and at one point Madison took Claire's arm to walk away and leave the brothers. "I thought you might need a break from horse talk. Seriously, Claire, I've never seen Nick look as happy. Frankly, he didn't at his wedding to Karen. You and Cody are so good for him. He's way more laid-back now."

"I'm glad. I hope he doesn't have regrets. He gave up a lot."

"I don't think there's the slightest chance of that happening. These boys had a grandfather who caused them to all love being cowboys. It doesn't matter what kind of fortune the Milans have, those guys are happiest on the back of a horse or riding across the ranch in a pickup. You'll see. Nick will never look back. That was something our Dad wanted him to do—law and politics. Now, because of you, Nick's married his first love."

"Thanks, Madison. You make me feel good," Claire said, smiling.

"And here he comes, looking like a man ready to escape a party," Madison said, laughing and walking away.

Nick joined her. "I suppose I just ran Madison off."

"She didn't mind."

"I'm ready to bow out of this. They've already taken your grandfather home. Your grandmother and Irene are waiting with Cody for us to tell them goodbye and there's a limo to take them home. Can I get you to leave now?"

"Of course," she said, taking his hand. They walked out of the room and outside the club, where Grandma and Cody stood in the sunshine beside a white limousine. The tall gray-haired nanny stood nearby and smiled at Claire.

Claire stopped to speak briefly with Irene and then moved to Cody and her grandmother.

Claire picked up her son. "We'll be back at the end of the week. I promise to call you every night, and you tell Grandma if you want to call me. All right?"

"Yes, ma'am."

"I love you," she said, hugging him and loving the feel of his thin arms around her neck. She handed him over to Nick, who also gave him a big hug.

"We'll be back in a week," he said, setting Cody on his feet. Verna reached out to take his hand.

Claire hugged and kissed her grandmother and then climbed into the limo. Nick followed and the chauffeur closed the door behind him. They waved as they drove away, and then Nick pulled her into his arms.

"Mrs. Nick Milan. I've waited a long time for this, Claire. I love you," he said as he pulled her close again to kiss her.

"I love you, Nick," she whispered. Claire clung to him tightly while she kissed him. Joy filled her and she hoped they could give Cody a little brother and a little sister. She squeezed Nick tightly, still astounded that she was married to the man she had always loved. Like the diamonds on her finger, happiness held a glittering promise of her future with Nick and Cody. Her family.

* * * * *

"Interesting seeing you again, Ryan," Jaci said in a catch-a-clue voice.

A puzzled frown pulled his brows together. "Maybe we should have coffee, catch up."

"Honey, you don't even know who I am, so what, exactly, would be the point? Goodbye, Ryan."

"Okay, busted. So who are you?" Ryan roughly demanded. "I know that I know you. . ."

"You'll work it out," Jaci told him and heard him utter a low curse as she walked away. But she wasn't sure if he would connect her with the long-ago teenager who'd hung on his every word. She doubted it. There was no hint of the insecure girl she used to be. . .on the outside anyway. Besides it would be fun to see his face when he realized that she was Neil's sister, the woman Neil wanted him to help navigate the "perils" of New York City.

"Then how about another kiss to jog my memory?" Ryan called out just as she was about to walk into the ballroom.

She turned around slowly and tipped her head to the side. "Let me think about that for a minute. . . mmm. . .no."

But hot damn, Jaci thought as she walked off, she was tempted.

TAKING THE
BOSS TO BED

BY
JOSS WOOD

Published in Great Britain 2015
by Mills & Boon, an imprint of Harlequin (UK) Limited,
Eton House, 18-24 Paradise Road, Richmond, Surrey, TW9 1SR

© 2015 Joss Wood

ISBN: 978-0-263-25290-3

51-1215

Harlequin (UK) Limited's policy is to use papers that are natural, renewable and recyclable products and made from wood grown in sustainable forests. The logging and manufacturing processes conform to the legal environmental regulations of the country of origin.

Printed and bound in Spain
by CPI, Barcelona

Joss Wood wrote her first book at the age of eight and has never really stopped writing. Her passion for putting letters on a blank screen is matched only by her love of books and traveling—especially to the wild places of Southern Africa—and possibly by her hatred of ironing and making school lunches.

Fueled by coffee, when she's not writing or being a hands-on mum, Joss—with her background in business and marketing—works for a nonprofit organization to promote the local economic development and collective business interests of the area where she resides. Happily and chaotically surrounded by books, family and friends, she lives in KwaZulu-Natal, South Africa, with her husband, children and their many pets.

One

Jaci Brookes-Lyon walked across the art deco, ridiculously ornate lobby of the iconic Forrester-Grantham Hotel on Park Avenue to the bank of elevators flanked by life-size statues of 1930s cabaret dancers striking dance poses. She stopped next to one, touching the smooth, cool shoulder with her fingertips.

Sighing through pursed lips, she looked at the dark-eyed blonde staring back at her in the supershiny surface of the elevator doors in front of her. Short, layered hair in a modern pixie cut, classic, fitted cocktail dress, perfect makeup, elegant heels. She looked good, Jaci admitted. Sophisticated, assured and confident. Maybe a tad sedate but that could be easily changed.

What was important was that the mask was in place. She looked like the better, stronger, New York version of herself, the person she wanted to be. She appeared to be someone who knew where she was going and how she was going to get there. Pity, Jaci thought, as she pushed her long bangs out of a smoky eye, that the image was still as substantial as a hologram.

Jaci left the elevator and took a deep breath as she walked across the foyer to the imposing double doors of the ballroom. *Here goes*, she thought. Stepping into the room packed with designer-dressed men and women, she reminded herself to put a smile on her face and to keep her spine straight. Nobody had to know that she'd rather stroll around Piccadilly Circus naked than walk into a room filled with people she didn't know. Her colleagues from Starfish were here somewhere. She'd sat with them earlier through the interminably long awards ceremony. Her new friends, Wes and Shona, fellow writers employed by Starfish, had promised to keep her company at her first film industry after-party, and once she found them she'd be fine. Between now and then, she just had to look as if she was having fun or, at the very least, happy to be surrounded by handsome men and supersophisticated women. Dear Lord, was that Candice Bloom, the multiple Best Actress award winner? Was it unkind to think that she looked older and, dare she even think it, fatter in real life?

Jaci took a glass of champagne from a tray that wafted past her and raised the glass for a taste. Then she clutched it to her chest and retreated to the side of the room, keeping an eye out for her coworkers. If she hadn't found them in twenty minutes she was out of there. She spent her entire life being a wallflower at her parents' soirees, balls and dinner parties, and had no intention of repeating the past.

"That ring looks like an excellent example of Georgian craftsmanship."

Jaci turned at the voice at her elbow and looked down into the sludge-brown eyes of the man who'd stepped up to her side. Jaci blinked at his emerald tuxedo and thought that he looked like a frog in a shiny suit. His thin black hair was pulled back off his forehead and was gathered at his neck in an oily tail, and he sported a silly soul patch under his thin, cruel mouth.

Jaci Brookes-Lyon, magnet for creepy guys, she thought.

He picked up her hand to look at her ring. Jaci tried to tug it away but his grip was, for an amphibian, surprisingly strong. "Ah, as I thought. It's an oval-faceted amethyst, foiled and claw-set with, I imagine, a closed back. The amethyst is pink and lilac. Exquisite. The two diamonds are old, mid-eighteenth century."

She didn't need this dodgy man to tell her about her ring, and she pulled her hand away, resisting the urge to wipe it on her cinnamon-shaded cocktail dress. Ugh. Creep factor: ten thousand.

"Where did you get the ring?" he demanded, and she caught a flash of dirty, yellow teeth.

"It's a family heirloom," Jaci answered, society manners too deeply ingrained just to walk off and leave him standing there.

"Are you from England? I love your accent."

"Yes."

"I have a mansion in the Cotswolds. In the village Arlingham. Do you know it?"

She did, but she wouldn't tell him that. She'd never manage to get rid of him then. "Sorry, I don't. Would you exc—"

"I have a particularly fine yellow diamond pendant that would look amazing in your cleavage. I can just imagine you wearing that and a pair of gold high heels."

Jaci shuddered and ruthlessly held down a heave as he ran his tongue over his lips. Seriously? Did that pickup line ever work? She picked his hand off her hip and quickly dropped it.

She wished she could let rip and tell him to take a hike and not give a damn. But the Brookes-Lyon children had been raised on a diet of diplomacy and were masters of the art of telling someone to go to hell in such a way that they immediately started planning the best route to get there. Well, Neil and Meredith were. She normally just stood there with a mouth full of teeth.

Jaci wrinkled her nose; some things never changed.

If she wasn't going to rip Mr. Rich-but-Creepy a new one—and she wasn't because she had the confrontational skills of a wet noodle—then she should remove herself, she decided.

"If you leave, I'll follow you."

Dear God, now he was reading her mind? "Please don't. I'm really not interested."

"But I haven't told you that I'm going to finance a film or that I own a castle in Germany, or that I own a former winner of the Kentucky Derby," he whined, and Jaci quickly suppressed her eye roll.

And I will never *tell you that my childhood home is a seventeenth-century manor that's been in my family for over four hundred years. That my mother is a third cousin to the queen and that I am, distantly, related to most of the royal families in Europe. They don't impress me, so you, with your pretentious attitude, haven't a chance.*

And, just a suggestion, use some of that money you

say you have to buy a decent suit, some shampoo and to get your teeth cleaned.

"Excuse me," Jaci murmured as she ducked around him and headed for the ballroom doors.

As she approached the elevators, congratulating herself on her getaway, she heard someone ordering an elderly couple to get out of the way and she winced as she recognized Toad's nasally voice. Glancing upward at the numbers above the elevator, she realized that if she waited for it he'd catch up to her and then she'd be caught in that steel box with him, up close and personal. There was no way he'd keep his hands or even—gack!—his tongue to himself. Thanks, but she'd rather lick a lamppost. Tucking her clutch bag under her arm, she glanced left and saw an emergency exit sign on a door and quickly changed direction. She'd run down the stairs; he surely wouldn't follow.

Stairs, lobby, taxi, home and a glass of wine in a bubble bath. Oh, yes, that sounded like heaven.

"My limousine is just outside the door."

The voice to her right made her yelp and she whirled around, slapping her hand to her chest. Those sludgy eyes looked feral, as if he were enjoying the thrill of the chase, and his disgusting soul patch jiggled as his wet lips pulled up into a smarmy smile. Dear God, he'd been right behind her and she hadn't even sensed him. Street smarts, she had none.

Jaci stepped to the side and looked past him to the empty reception area. Jeez, this was a nightmare... If she took the stairs she would be alone with him, ditto the elevators. Her only option was to go back to the ballroom where there were people. Across the room, the elevator doors opened on a discreet chime and Jaci watched as a tall man, hands in the pockets of his tuxedo pants, walked out toward the ballroom. Broad shoulders, trim waist, long legs. His dark hair was tapered, with the top styled into a tousled mess. He had bright, light eyes under dark brows and what she imagined was a three-day-old beard. She knew that profile, that face. Ryan?

Neil's Ryan? Jaci craned her neck for a better look.

God, it *was* the grown-up version—and an even more gorgeous version—of that young man she'd known so long ago. Hard, tough, sexy, powerful; a man in every sense of the word. Jaci felt her stomach roll over and her throat tighten as tiny flickers of electricity danced across her skin.

Instant lust, immediate attraction. And he hadn't even noticed her yet.

And she *really* needed him to notice her. She called out his name and he abruptly stopped and looked around.

"Limo, outside, waiting."

Jaci blinked at Mr. Toad and was amazed at his persistence. He simply wasn't going to give up until he got her into his car, into his apartment and naked. She'd rather have acid-coated twigs shoved up her nose. Seeing Ryan standing there, head cocked, she thought that there was maybe one more thing she could do to de-barnacle herself.

And, hopefully, Ryan wouldn't object.

"Ryan! Darling!"

Jaci stepped to her right and walked as fast as she possibly could across the Italian marble floor, and as she approached Ryan, she lifted her arms and wound them around his neck. She saw his eyes widen in surprise and felt his hands come to rest on her hips, but before he could speak, she slapped her mouth on his and hoped to dear Lord that he wouldn't push her away.

His lips were warm and firm beneath hers and she felt his fingers dig into her hips, their heat burning through the fabric of her dress to warm her skin. Her fingers touched the back of his neck, above the collar of his shirt, and she felt tension roll through his body.

Ryan yanked his head back and those penetrating eyes met hers, flashing with an emotion she couldn't identify. She expected him to push her away, to ask her what the hell she thought she was doing, but instead he yanked her closer and his mouth covered hers again. His tongue licked the seam between her lips and, without hesitation, she opened up, allowing him to taste her, to know her. A strong arm around her waist pulled her flush against him and then her breasts were flat against his chest, her stomach resting against his—*hello, Nelly!*—erection.

Their kiss might have lasted seconds, minutes, months or years, Jaci had no idea. When Ryan finally pulled his mouth away, strong arms still holding her against him, all she was capable of doing was resting her forehead on his collarbone while she tried to get her bearings. She felt as if she'd stepped away from reality, from time, from the ornate lobby in one of the most renowned hotels in the world and into another dimension. That had never happened to her before. She'd never been so swept away by passion that she felt as if she'd had an out-of-body experience. That it had happened with someone who was little more than a stranger totally threw her.

"Leroy, it's good to see you," Ryan said, somewhere above her head. Judging by his even voice, he was very used to being kissed by virtual strangers in fancy hotels. *Huh.*

"I was hoping that you would be here. I was on my way to find you," Ryan blithely continued.

"Ryan," Leroy replied.

Knowing she couldn't stay pressed against Ryan forever—sadly, because she felt as if she belonged there—Jaci lifted her head and tried to wiggle out of his grip. She was surprised when, instead of letting her go, he kept her plastered to his side.

"I see you've met my girl."

Jaci's head snapped back and she narrowed her eyes as she looked up into Ryan's urbane face. His girl?

His.

Girl?

Her mouth fell open. Bats-from-hell, he didn't remember her name! He had no idea who she was.

Mr. Toad pulled a thin cheroot from the inside pocket of his jacket and jammed it into the side of his mouth. He narrowed his eyes at Jaci. "You two together?"

Jaci knew that she often pulled on her Feisty Girl mask, but she'd never owned an invisibility cloak. Jaci opened her mouth to tell them to stop talking about her as if she wasn't there, but Ryan pinched her side and her mouth snapped shut. Mostly from indignant surprise. "She's my girlfriend. As you know, I've been out of town and I haven't seen her for a couple of weeks."

Weeks, years… Who was counting?

Leroy didn't look convinced. "I thought that she was leaving."

"We agreed to meet in the lobby," Ryan stated, his voice calm. He brushed his chin across the top of her head and Jaci shivered. "You obviously didn't get my message that I was on my way up, honey."

Honey? Yep, he definitely didn't have a clue who she

was. But the guy lied with calm efficiency and absolute conviction. "Let's go back inside." Ryan gestured to the ballroom.

Leroy shook his head. "I'm going to head out."

Thank God and all his angels and archangels for small mercies! Ryan, still not turning her loose, held out his right hand for Leroy to shake. "Nice to see you, Leroy, and I look forward to meeting with you soon to finalize our discussions. When can we get together?"

Leroy ignored his outstretched hand and gave Jaci another up-and-down look. "Oh, I'm having second thoughts about the project."

Project? What project? Why was Ryan doing business with Leroy? That was a bit of a silly question since she had no idea what business Ryan, or the amphib, was in. Jaci sent her brand-new boyfriend an uncertain glance. He looked as inscrutable as ever, but she sensed that beneath his calm facade, his temper was bubbling.

"I'm surprised to hear that. I thought it was a done deal," Ryan said, his tone almost bored.

Leroy's smile was nasty. "I'm not sure that I'm ready to hand that much money to a man I don't know all that well. I didn't even know you had a girlfriend."

"I didn't think that our *business* deal required that level of familiarity," Ryan responded.

"You're asking me to invest a lot of money. I want to be certain that you know what you are doing."

"I thought that my track record would reassure you that I do."

Jaci looked from one stubborn face to the other.

"The thing is… I have what you want so I suggest that if I say jump, you say how high."

Jaci sucked in breath, aghast. But Ryan, to his credit,

didn't dignify that ridiculous statement with a response. Jaci suspected that Leroy didn't have a clue that Ryan thought he was a maggot, that he was fighting the urge to either punch Leroy or walk away. She knew this because his fingers were squeezing her hand so hard that she'd lost all feeling in her digits.

"Come now, Ryan, let's not bicker. You're asking for a lot of money and I feel I need more reassurances. So I definitely want to spend some more time with you—" Leroy's eyes traveled up and down her body and Jaci felt as if she'd been licked by a lizard "—and with your lovely girlfriend, as well. And, in a more businesslike vein, I'd also like to meet some of your key people in your organization." Leroy rolled his cheroot from one side of his mouth to the other. "My people will call you."

Leroy walked toward the elevators and jabbed a finger on the down button. When the doors whispered open, he turned and sent them an oily smile.

"I look forward to seeing you both soon," he said before he disappeared inside the luxurious interior. When the doors closed, Jaci tugged her hand from Ryan's, noting his thunderous face as he watched the numbers change on the board above the elevator.

"Dammittohellandback," Ryan said, finally dropping her hand and running his through his short, stylishly messy hair. "The manipulative cretin."

Jaci took two steps backward and pushed her bangs out of her eye. "Look, seeing you again has been…well, odd, to say the least, but you do realize that I can't do this?"

"Be my girlfriend?"

"Yes."

Ryan nodded tersely. "Of course you can't, it would never work."

One of the reasons being that he'd then have to ask her who she was...

Besides, Ryan, as she'd heard from Neil, dated supermodels and actresses, singers and dancers. His old friend's little sister, neither actress-y nor supermodel-ly, wasn't his type, so she shrugged and tried to ignore her rising indignation. But, judging by the party in his pants while he was kissing her, maybe she was his type...just a little.

Ryan flicked her a cool look. "He's just annoyed that you rebuffed him. He'll forget about you and his demands in a day or two. I'll just tell him that we had a massive fight and that we split up."

Huh. He had it all figured out. Good for him.

"He's your connection, it's your deal, so whatever works for you," she said, her voice tart. "So...'bye."

Ryan shoved his hand through his hair. "It's been interesting. Why don't you give him ten minutes to leave then use the elevators around the corner? You'd then exit at the east doors."

She was being dismissed and she didn't like it. Especially when it was by a man who couldn't remember her name. Arrogant sod! Pride had her changing her mind. "Oh, I'm not quite ready to leave." She looked toward the ballroom. "I think I'll go back in."

Jaci saw surprise flicker in his gorgeous eyes. He wanted to get rid of her, she realized, maybe because he was embarrassed that he couldn't recall who she was. Not that he looked embarrassed. But still...

"Interesting seeing you *again*, Ryan," she said in a catch-a-clue voice.

A puzzled frown pulled his brows together. "Maybe we should have coffee, catch up."

Jaci shook her head and handed him a condescending smile. "*Honey*, you don't even know who I am so what, exactly, would be the point? Goodbye, Ryan."

"Okay, busted. So who are you?" Ryan roughly demanded. "I know that I know you…"

"You'll work it out," Jaci told him and heard him mutter a low curse as she walked away. But she wasn't sure if he would connect her with the long-ago teenager who'd hung on his every word. She doubted it. Her mask was intact and impenetrable. There was no hint of the insecure girl she used to be…on the outside, anyway. Besides, it would be fun to see his face when he realized that she was Neil's sister, the woman Neil, she assumed, wanted him to help navigate the "perils" of New York City.

Well, she was an adult and she didn't need her brother or Ryan or any other stupid man doing her any favors. She could, and would, navigate New York on her own.

And if she couldn't, her brother and his old friend would be the last people whom she'd allow to witness her failure.

"Then how about another kiss to jog my memory?" Ryan called out just as she was about to walk into the ballroom.

She turned around slowly and tipped her head to the side. "Let me think about that for a minute… Mmm…no."

But hot damn, Jaci thought as she walked off, she was tempted.

Two

Jaci slipped into the crowd and placed her fist into her sternum and tried to regulate her heart rate and her breathing. She felt as if she'd just experienced a wild gorge ride on a rickety swing and she was still trying to work out which way was up. She so wanted to kiss him again, to taste him again, to feel the way his lips moved over hers. He'd melted all her usual defenses and it felt as if he was kissing her, the *real* her. It was as if he'd reached inside her and grabbed her heart and squeezed…

That had to be a hormone-induced insanity because stuff like that didn't happen and especially not to her. She was letting her writer's imagination run away with her; this was real life, not a romantic comedy. Ryan was hot and sexy and tough, but that was what he looked like, wasn't what he was. *As you do, everybody wears masks to conceal who and what lies beneath*, she reminded herself. Sometimes what was concealed was harmless—she didn't think that her lack of confidence hurt anybody but herself—and occasionally people, including her ex-fiancé, concealed secrets that were devastating.

Clive and his secrets… Hadn't those blown up in their faces? It was a small consolation that Clive had fooled her clever family, too. They'd been so thrilled that, instead of the impoverished artists and musicians she normally brought home to meet her family, she'd snagged an intellectual, a success. A *politician*. In hindsight, she'd been so enamored by the attention she'd received by being Clive's girlfriend—not only from her family but from friends and acquaintances and the press—that she'd been prepared to put up with his controlling behavior, his lack of respect, his inattention. After years of being in the shadows, she'd loved the spotlight and the new sparky and sassy personality she'd developed to deal with the press attention she received. Sassy Jaci was the brave one; she was the one who'd moved to New York, who walked into crowded ballrooms, who planted her lips on the sexiest man in the room. Sassy Jaci was who she was going to be in New York, but this time she'd fly solo. No more men and definitely no more fading into the background…

Jaci turned as her name was called and she saw her friends standing next to a large ornamental tree. Relieved, she pushed past people to get to them. Her fellow scriptwriters greeted her warmly and Shona handed her a champagne glass. "Drink up, darling, you're way behind."

Jaci wrinkled her nose. "I don't like champagne." But she did like alcohol and it was exactly what she needed, so she took a healthy sip.

"Isn't champagne what all posh UK It girls drink?" Shona asked cheerfully and with such geniality that Jaci immediately realized that there was no malice behind her words.

"I'm not an It girl," Jaci protested.

"You were engaged to a rising star in politics, you attended the same social events with the Windsor boys, you are from a very prominent British family."

Well, if you looked at it like that. Could she still be classified as an It girl if she'd hated every second of said socializing?

"You did an internet search on me," Jaci stated, resigned.

"Of course we did," Shona replied. "Your ex-fiancé looks a bit like a horse."

Jaci giggled. Clive did look a bit equine.

"Did you know about his…ah…how do I put this? Outside interests?" Shona demanded.

"No," Jaci answered, her tone clipped. She hadn't even discussed Clive's extramural activities with her family—they were determined to ignore the crotchless-panty-wearing elephant in the room—so there was no way she would dissect her ex–love life with strangers.

"How did you get the job?" Shona asked.

"My agent sold a script to Starfish over a year ago. Six weeks ago Thom called and said that they wanted to develop the story further and asked me to work on that, and to collaborate on other projects. So I'm here, on a six-month contract."

"And you write under the pen name of JC Brookes? Is that because of the press attention you received?" Wes asked.

"Partly." Jaci looked at the bubbles in her glass. It was easier to write under a pen name when your parent, writing under her *own* name, was regarded as one of the most detailed and compelling writers of historical fiction in the world.

Wes smiled at her. "When we heard that we were getting another scriptwriter, we all thought you were a guy. Shona and I were looking forward to someone new to flirt with."

Jaci grinned at his teasing, relieved that the subject had moved on. "Sorry to disappoint." She placed her glass on a tall table next to her elbow. "So, tell me about Starfish. I know that Thom is a producer but that's about all I know. When is he due back? I'd actually like to meet the man who hired me."

"He and Jax—the big boss and owner—are here tonight, but they socialize with the movers and shakers. We're too far down the food chain for them," Shona cheerfully answered, snagging a tiny spring roll off a passing tray and popping it into her mouth.

Jaci frowned, confused. "Thom's not the owner?"

Wes shook his head. "Nah, he's Jax's second in command. Jax stays out of the spotlight but is very hands-on. Actors and directors like to work for him, but because they both have a low threshold for Hollywood drama, they are selective in whom they choose to work with."

"Chad Bradshaw being one of the actors they won't work with." Shona used her glass to gesture to a handsome older man walking past them.

Chad Bradshaw, legendary Hollywood actor. So that was why Ryan was here, Jaci thought. Chad had received an award earlier and it made sense that Ryan would be here to support his father. Like Chad, Ryan was tall and their eyes were the same; they could be either a light blue or gray, depending on his mood. Ryan might not remember her but she recalled in Technicolor detail the young man Neil had met at the London School of Economics. In between fantasizing about Ryan and writing stories with him as her hero inspiration, she'd watched the interaction between Ryan and her family. It had amused her that her academic parents and siblings had been fascinated by the fact that Ryan lived in Hollywood and that he was the younger brother of Ben Bradshaw, the young darling of Hollywood who was on his way to becoming a screen legend himself. Like the rest of the world, they'd all been shocked at Ben's death in a car accident, and his passing and funeral had garnered worldwide, and Brookes-Lyon, attention. But at the time they knew him, many years before Ben's death, it seemed as if Ryan was from another world, one far removed from the one the Brookes-Lyon clan occupied, and he'd been a breath of fresh air.

Ryan and Neil had been good friends and Ryan hadn't been intimidated by the cocky and cerebral Brookes-Lyon clan. He'd come to London to get a business degree, she remembered, and dimly recalled a dinner conversation with him saying something about wanting to get out of LA and doing something completely different from his father and brother. He visited Lyon House every couple of months for nearly a year but then he left the prestigious college. She hadn't seen him since. Until he kissed the hell out of her ten minutes ago.

Jaci pursed her lips in irritation and wondered how he kissed women whose names he *did* know. If he kissed them with only a smidgeon more skill than he had her, then the man was capable of melting polar ice caps.

He was *that* good and what was really, really bad was that she kept thinking that he had lips and that she had lips and that hers should be under his…*all the damn time*.

Phew. Problematic, Jaci thought.

* * *

Ryan "Jax" Jackson nursed his glass of whiskey and wished that he was in his apartment stretched out on his eight-foot-long couch and watching his favorite sports channel on the huge flat-screen that dominated one wall of his living room. He glanced at his watch, grateful to see that the night was nearly over. He'd had a run-in with Leroy, kissed the hell out of a sexy woman and now he was stuck in a ballroom kissing ass. He'd much rather be kissing the blonde's delectable ass… Dammit, who the hell was she? Ryan discarded the idea of flicking through his mental black book of past women. He knew that he hadn't kissed that mouth before. He would've remembered that heat, that spice, the make-him-crazy need to have her. So *who* was she?

He looked around the room in the hope of seeing her again and scowled when he couldn't locate her. Before the evening ended, he decided, he'd make the connection or he'd find her and demand some answers. He wouldn't sleep tonight if he didn't. He caught a flash of a blond head and felt his pants tighten. It wasn't her but if the thought of seeing her again had him springing up to half-mast, then he was in trouble. Trouble that he didn't need.

Time to do a mental switch, he decided, and deliberately changed the direction of his thoughts. What was Leroy's problem tonight? He'd agreed, in principle, to back the film and now he needed more assurances? *Why?* God, he was tired of the games the very rich boys played; his biggest dream was to find an investor who'd just hand over a boatload of money, no questions asked.

And that would be the day that gorgeous aliens abducted him to be a sex slave.

Still, he was relieved that Leroy had left; having his

difficult investor and his DNA donor in the room at the same time was enough to make his head explode. He hadn't seen Chad yet but knew that all he needed to do was find the prettiest woman in the room and he could guarantee that his father—or Leroy, if he were here—would be chatting her up. Neither could keep his, as Neil used to say, pecker in his pants despite having a wife at home.

What was the point of being married if you were a serial cheater? Ryan wondered for the millionth time.

Ryan felt an elbow in his ribs and turned to look into his best friend's open face. "Hey."

"Hey, you are looking grim. What's up?" Thom asked.

"Tired. Done with this day and this party," Ryan told him.

"And you're avoiding your father."

Well, yeah. "Where is the old man?"

Thom lifted his champagne glass to his right. "He's at your nine o'clock, talking to the sexy redhead. He cornered me and asked me to talk to you, to intercede on his behalf. He wants to *reconnect.* His word, not mine."

"So his incessant calls and emails over the past years have suggested," Ryan said, his expression turning cynical. "Except that I am not naive to believe that it's because he suddenly wants to play happy families. It's only because we have something he wants." As in a meaty part in their new movie.

"He would be great as Tompkins."

Ryan didn't give a rat's ass. "We don't always get what we want."

"He's your father," Thom said, evenly.

That was stretching the truth. Chad had been his guardian, his landlord and an absent presence in his life.

Ryan knew that he still resented the fact that he'd had to take responsibility for the child he created with his second or third or fifteenth mistress. To Chad, his mother's death when he was fourteen had been wildly inconvenient. He was already raising one son and didn't need the burden of another.

Not that Chad had ever been actively involved in his, or Ben's, life. Chad was always away on a shoot and he and Ben, with the help of a housekeeper, raised themselves. Ben, just sixteen months older than him, had seen him through those dark and dismal teenage years. He'd idolized Ben and Ben had welcomed him into his home and life with open arms. So close in age, they'd become best buds within weeks and he'd thought that there was nothing that could destroy their friendship, that they had each other's backs, that Ben was the one person who would never let him down.

Yeah, funny how wrong he could be.

Ben. God, he still got a lump in his throat just thinking about him. He probably always would. When it came to Ben he was a cocktail of emotions. Betrayal always accompanied the grief. Hurt, loss and anger also hung around whenever he thought of his best friend and brother. God, would it ever end?

The crowds in front of him parted and Ryan caught his breath. There she was… He'd kissed that wide mouth earlier, but between the kiss and dealing with Leroy he hadn't really had time to study the compact blonde. Short, layered hair, a peaches-and-cream complexion and eyes that fell somewhere between deep brown and black.

Those eyes… He knew those eyes, he thought, as a memory tugged. He frowned, immediately thinking of his time in London and the Brookes-Lyon family. Neil had mentioned in a quick email last week that his baby sister was moving to New York… What was her name again? Josie? Jackie… Close but still wrong… Jay-cee! Was that her? He narrowed his eyes, thinking it through. God, it had been nearly twelve years since he'd last seen her, and he struggled to remember the details of Neil's shy sibling. Her hair was the same white-blond color, but back then it hung in a long fall to her waist. Her body, now lean, had still been caught in that puppy-fat stage, but those eyes… He couldn't forget those eyes. Rich, deep brown, almost black Audrey Hepburn eyes, he thought. Then and now.

Jesus. He'd kissed his oldest friend's baby sister.

Ryan rubbed his forehead with his thumb and index finger. With everything else going on in his life, he'd completely forgotten that she was moving here and that Neil had asked him to make contact with her. He'd intended to once his schedule lightened but he never expected her to be at this post-awards function. And he certainly hadn't expected the shy teenager to have morphed into this stunningly beautiful, incredibly sexy woman; a woman who had his nerve endings buzzing. On the big screen in his head he could see them in their own private movie. She'd be naked and up against a wall, her legs around his waist and her head tipped back as he feasted on that soft spot where her neck and shoulders met…

Ryan blew out a breath. He was a movie producer, had dabbled in directing and he often envisioned scenes in his head, but never had one been so sexual, so sensual. And one starring his best and oldest friend's kid sister? That was just plain weird.

Sexy.

But still weird.

As if she could feel his eyes on her, Jaci turned her head and looked directly at him. The challenging lift of her eyebrow suggested that she'd realized that he'd connected the dots and that she was wondering what he intended to do about it.

Nothing, he decided, breaking their long, sexually charged stare. He was going to do jack about it because his sudden and very unwelcome attraction to Jaci was something he didn't have time to deal with, something he didn't *want* to deal with. His life was complicated enough without adding another level of crazy to it.

Frankly, he'd had enough crazy to last a lifetime.

Jaci stumbled through the doors to Starfish Films at five past nine the next morning, juggling her tote bag, her mobile, two scripts and a mega-latte, and decided that she couldn't function on less than three hours of sleep anymore. If someone looked up the definition of *cranky* in the dictionary, her picture next to the word would explain it all.

It hadn't helped that she'd spent most of the night reluctantly reliving that most excellent kiss, recalling the strength of that masculine, muscular body, the fresh, sexy smell of Ryan's skin. It had been a long time since she'd lost any sleep over a man—even during the worst of their troubles she'd never sacrificed any REMs for Clive—and she didn't like it. Ryan was sex on a side plate but she wasn't going to see him again. Ever. Besides, she hadn't relocated cities to dally with hot men, or any men. This job was what was important, the only thing that was important.

This was her opportunity to carve out a space for herself in the film industry, to find her little light to shine in. It might not be as bold or as bright as her mother's but it would be hers.

Frowning at the empty offices, she stepped up to her desk and dropped the scripts to the seat of her chair. This was the right choice to make, she told herself. She could've stayed in London; it was familiar and she knew how to tread water. Except that she felt the deep urge to swim…to do more and be more. She had been given an opportunity to change her life and, although she was soul-deep scared, she was going to run with it. She was going to prove, to herself and to her family, that she wasn't as rudderless, as directionless—as useless—as they thought she was.

This time, this job, was her one chance to try something different, something totally out of her comfort zone. This was her time, her life, her dream, and nothing would distract her from her goal of writing the best damn scripts she could.

Especially not a man with blue-gray eyes and a body that made her hormones hum.

Shona peeked into their office and jerked her head. "Not the best day to be late, sunshine. A meeting has started in the conference room and I suggest you get there."

"Meeting?" Jaci yelped. She was a writer. She didn't do meetings.

"The boss men are back and they want to touch base," Shona explained, tapping a rolled-up newspaper against her thigh. "Let's go."

A few minutes later, Shona pushed through the door at the top of the stairs and turned right down the identical hallway to the floor below. Corporate office buildings were all the same, Jaci thought, though she did like the framed movie posters from the 1940s and 1950s that broke up the relentless white walls.

Shona sighed and covered her mouth as she yawned. "We're all, including the boss men, a little tired and a lot hungover. Why we have to have a meeting first thing in the morning is beyond me. Jax should know better. Expect a lot of barking."

Jaci shrugged, not particularly perturbed. She'd lived with volatile people her entire life and had learned how to fly under the radar. Shona stopped in front of an open door, placed her hand between Jaci's shoulder blades and pushed her into the room. Jaci stumbled forward and knocked the arm of a man walking past. His coffee cup flew out of his hand toward his chest, and his cream dress shirt, sleeves rolled up past his elbows, bloomed with patches of espresso.

He dropped a couple of blue curses. "This is all I freakin' need."

Jaci froze to the floor as her eyes traveled up his coffee-soaked chest, past that stubborn, stubble-covered chin to that sensual mouth she'd kissed last night. She stopped at his scowling eyes, heavy brows pulled together. Oh, jeez...*no*.

Just no.

"Jaci?" Coffee droplets fell from his wrist and hand to the floor. "What the hell?"

"Jax, this is JC Brookes, our new scriptwriter," Thom said from across the room, his feet on the boardroom table and a cup of coffee resting on his flat stomach. "Jaci, Ryan 'Jax' Jackson."

He needed a box of aspirin, to clean up—the paper napkins Shona handed him weren't any match for a full cup of coffee—and to climb out of the rabbit hole he'd climbed into. He'd spent most of last night tossing and turning, thinking about that slim body under his hands, the scent of her light, refreshing perfume still in his nose, the dazzling heat and spice of her mouth.

He'd finally dozed off, irritated and frustrated, hours after he climbed into bed, and his few hours of sleep, starring a naked Jaci, hadn't been restful at all. As a result, he didn't feel as if he had the mental stamina to deal with the fact that the woman starring in his pornographic dreams last night was not only his friend's younger sister but also the screenwriter for his latest project.

Seriously? Why was life jerking his chain?

His mind working at warp speed, he flicked Jaci a narrowed-eyed look. "JC Brookes? You're him? Her?"

Jaci folded her arms across her chest and tapped one booted foot. How could she look so sexy in the city's uniform of basic black? Black turtleneck and black wide-leg pants… It would be boring as hell but she'd wrapped an aqua cotton scarf around her neck, and blue-shaded bracelets covered half her arm. He shouldn't be thinking about her clothes—or what they covered—right now, but he couldn't help himself. She looked, despite the shadows under those hypnotically brown eyes, as hot as hell. Simply fantastic. Ryan swallowed, remembering how feminine she felt in his arms, her warm, silky mouth, the way she melted into him.

Focus, Jackson.

"What the hell? You're a scriptwriter?" Ryan demanded, trying to make all the pieces of the puzzle fit. "I didn't know that you write!"

Jaci frowned. "Why should you? We haven't seen each other for twelve years."

"Neil didn't tell me." Ryan, still holding his head, kneaded his temples with his thumb and index finger. "He should've told me."

Now he sounded like a whining child. Freakin' perfect.

"He doesn't know about the scriptwriting," Jaci muttered, and Ryan, despite his fuzzy shock, heard the tinge of hurt in her voice. "I just told him and the rest of my family that I was relocating to New York for a bit."

Ryan pulled his sticky shirt off his chest and looked at Thom again. "And she got the job how?"

Thom sent him a what-the-hell look. "Her agent submitted her script, our freelance reader read it, then Wes, then me, then you read the script. We all liked it but you fell in love with it! Light coming on yet?"

Ryan looked toward the window, unable to refute Thom's words. He'd loved Jaci's script, had read it over and over, feeling that tingle of excitement every time. It was an action comedy but one with heart; it felt familiar and fresh, funny and emotional.

And Jaci, his old friend's little sister, the woman he'd kissed the hell out of last night, was—thanks to fate screwing with him—the creator of his latest, and most expensive, project to date.

And his biggest and only investor, Leroy Banks, had hit on her and now thought that she was his girlfriend.

Oh, and just for kicks and giggles, he really wanted to do her six ways to Sunday.

"Could this situation be any more messed up?" Ryan grabbed the back of the closest chair and dropped his head, ignoring the puddles of coffee on the floor. He groaned aloud. Banks thought that his pseudo girlfriend was the hottest thing on two legs. Ryan understood why. He also thought she was as sexy as hell.

She was also now the girlfriend he couldn't break up with because she was his damned scriptwriter, one of—how had Banks put it?—his key people!

"I have no idea why you are foaming at the mouth, dude," Thom complained, dropping his feet to the floor. He shrugged. "You and Jaci knew each other way back when, so what? She was employed by us on her merits, with none of us knowing of her connection to you. End of story. So can we just get on with this damn meeting so that I can go back to my office and get horizontal on my couch?"

"Uh…no, I suggest you wait until after I've dropped the next bombshell." Shona tossed the open newspaper onto the boardroom table and it slid across the polished top. As it passed, Ryan slapped his hand on it to stop its flight. His heart stumbled, stopped, and when it resumed its beat was erratic.

In bold color and filling half the page was a picture taken last night in the reception area outside the ballroom of the Forrester-Graham. One of his hands cradled a bright blond head, the other palmed a very excellent butt. Jaci's arms were tight around his neck, her mouth was under his, and her long lashes were smudges on her cheek.

The headline screamed Passion for Award-Winning Producer!

Someone had snapped them? When? And why hadn't he noticed? Ryan moved his hand to read the small amount of text below the picture.

Ryan Jackson, award-winning producer of *Stand Alone*—the sci-fi box office hit that is enthralling audiences across the country—celebrates in the arms of JC Brookes at the Television and Film Awards after-party last night. JC Brookes is a scriptwriter employed by Starfish Films and is very well-known in England as the younger daughter of Fleet Street editor Archie Brookes-Lyon and his multi-award-winning author wife, Priscilla. She recently broke off her longstanding engagement to Clive Egglestone, projected to be a future prime minister of England, after he was implicated in a series of sexual scandals.

What engagement? What sexual scandals? More news that his ever-neglectful friend had failed to share. Jaci had been engaged to a politician? Ryan just couldn't see it. But that wasn't important now.

Ryan pushed the newspaper down the table to Thom. When his friend lifted his eyes to meet his again, his worry and horror were reflected in Thom's expression. "Well, hell," he said.

Ryan looked around the room at the nosy faces of his most trusted staff before pulling a chair away from the table and dropping into it. It wasn't in his nature to explain himself but this one time he supposed, very reluctantly, that it was necessary. "Jaci and I know each other. She's an old friend's younger sister. We are not in a relationship."

"Doesn't explain the kiss," Thom laconically stated.

"Jaci, on impulse, kissed me because Leroy was hitting on her and she needed an escape plan."

That explained her first kiss. It certainly didn't explain why he went back for a second, and hotter, taste. But neither Thom nor his staff needed to know that little piece of information. *Ever.*

"I told him that she was my girlfriend and that we hadn't seen each other for a while." Ryan kept his attention on Thom. "I had it all planned. When next we met and if Leroy asked about her, I was going to tell him that we'd had a fight and that she'd packed her bags and returned to the UK. I did not consider the possibility that my five-minute girlfriend would also be my new scriptwriter."

Thom shrugged. "This isn't a big deal. Tell him that you fought and that she left. How is he going to know?"

Ryan pulled in a deep breath. "Oh, maybe because he told me, last night, that he wants to meet the key staff involved in the project, and that includes the damned scriptwriter."

Thom groaned. "Oh, God."

"Not sure how much help he is going to be." Ryan turned around and looked at a rather bewildered Jaci, who had yet to move away from the door. "My office. Now."

Well, hell, he thought as he marched down the hallway to his office. It seemed that his morning could, after all, slide further downhill than he'd expected.

Three

Jaci waited in the doorway to Ryan's office, unsure whether she should step into his chaotic space—desks and chairs were covered in folders, scripts and stacks of papers—or whether she should she just stay where she was. He was in his private bathroom and she could hear a tap running and, more worrying, the steady stream of inventive cursing.

Okay, crazy, crazy morning and she had no idea what had just happened. It felt as if everyone in that office had been speaking in subtext and that she was the only one who did not know the language. All she knew for sure was that Jax was Ryan and Ryan was Neil's friend—and her new boss—and that he was superpissed.

And judging by their collective horror, she also knew that Banks's clumsy pass and her kissing Ryan had consequences bigger than she'd imagined.

Ryan walked out of the bathroom, shirtless and holding another dress shirt, pale green this time, in his right hand. He was coffee-free and that torso, Jaci thought on an appreciative, silent sigh, could grace the cover of any male fitness magazine. His shoulders were broad and strongly muscled as were his biceps and his pecs. And that stomach, sinuously ridged, was a work of art. Jaci felt that low buzz in her stomach, the tingling spreading across her skin, and wondered why it had taken her nearly twenty-eight years to feel true attraction, pure lust. Ryan Jackson just had to breathe to make her quiver…

"You used to be Ryan Bradshaw. Why Jackson?" Jaci blurted. It was all she could think of to say apart from "Kiss me like you did last night." Since she was already in trouble, she decided to utter the only other thought she had to break the tense, sexually saturated silence.

Ryan blinked, frowned and then shook his shirt out, pulling the fabric over one arm. "You heard that Chad was my father, that Ben was my brother, and you assumed that I used the same surname. I don't," Ryan said in a cool voice.

She stepped inside and shut the door. "Why not?"

"I met Chad for the first time when I was fourteen, when the court appointed me to live with him after my mother's death. He dumped my mother two seconds after she told him she was pregnant and her name appeared on my birth certificate. I'd just lost her, and I wasn't about to lose her name, as well." Ryan machine-gunned his words and Jaci tried to keep up.

Ryan rubbed his hand over his face. "God, what does that have to do with anything? Moving rapidly on…"

Pity, Jaci thought. She would've liked to hear more about his childhood, about his relationship with his famous brother and father, which was, judging by his pain-filled and frustrated eyes, not a happy story.

"Getting back to the here and now, how the hell am I going to fix this?" Ryan demanded, and Jaci wasn't sure whether he was asking the question of her or himself.

"Look, I'm really sorry that I caused trouble for you by kissing you. It was an impulsive action to get away from Frog Man."

Ryan shoved his other arm into his sleeve and pulled the edges of his shirt together, found the buttons and their corresponding holes without dropping his eyes from her face.

"He was persistent. And slimy. And he wouldn't take the hint!" Jaci continued. "I'm sorry that the kiss was captured on camera. I know what an invasion of your privacy that can be."

Ryan glanced at the paper that he'd dropped onto his desk. "You seem to know what you're talking about." Ryan tipped his head. "Sexual scandals? Engaged?"

"All that and more." Jaci tossed her head in defiance and held his eyes. "You can find it all online if you want some spicy bedtime reading."

"I don't read trash."

"Well, I'm not going to tell you what happened," Jaci stated, her tone not encouraging any argument.

"Did I ask you to?"

Hell, he hadn't, Jaci realized, as a red tide crept up her neck. *Jeez, catch a clue. The guy kissed you. That doesn't mean he's interested in your history.*

Time to retreat. What had they been talking about? Ah, their kiss. "Look, if you need me to apologize to your girlfriend or wife, then I will." She thought about adding

"I won't even tell her that you initiated the second kiss" but decided not to fan the flames.

"I'm not involved with anyone, which is about the only silver lining there is."

Jaci pushed her long bangs to one side. "Then I really don't understand what the drama is all about. We're both single, we kissed. Yeah, it landed up in the papers, but who cares?"

"Banks does and I told him that you're my girlfriend."

Jaci lifted her hands in confusion. This still wasn't any clearer. "So?"

Ryan started to roll up his sleeves, his expression devoid of all emotion. But his eyes were now a blistering blue, radiating frustration and a healthy dose of anxiety. "In order to produce *Blown Away*, to get the story you conceived and wrote onto the big screen, to do it justice, I need a budget of a hundred and seventy million dollars. I don't like taking on investors, I prefer to work solo, but the one hundred million I have is tied up at the moment. Besides, with such a big budget, I'd also prefer to risk someone else's money and not my own. Right now, Banks is the only thing that decides whether *Blown Away* sees the light of day or gets skipped over for a smaller-budget film.

"I thought that we were on the point of signing the damn contract but now he just wants to jerk my chain," Ryan continued.

"But why?"

"Because he knows that I caught him hitting on my girlfriend and he's embarrassed. He wants to remind me who's in control."

Okay, now she got it, but she wished she hadn't. She'd

put a hundred-million deal in jeopardy? With a kiss? When she messed up, she did a spectacular job of it.

Jaci groaned. "And I'm your screenwriter." She shoved her fingers into her hair. "One of the project's key people."

"Yep." Ryan sat down on the edge of his desk and picked up a glass paperweight and tossed it from hand to hand. "We can't tell him that you only threw yourself into my arms because you found him repulsive… If you do that, we'll definitely wave goodbye to the money."

"Why can't I just stay in the background?" Jaci asked. She didn't want to—it wasn't what she'd come to the city to do—but she would if it meant getting the film produced. "He doesn't know that I wrote the script."

Ryan carefully replaced the paperweight, folded his arms and gave her a hard stare. After a long, charged minute he shook his head. "That's problematic for me. Firstly, you did write that script and you should take the credit for it. Secondly, I don't like any forms of lying. It always comes back to bite me on the ass."

Wow, an honest guy. She thought that the species was long extinct.

Jaci dropped into the nearest chair, sat on top of a pile of scripts, placed her elbows on her knees and rested her chin in the palm of her hand. "So what do we do?"

"I need you as a scriptwriter and I need him to fund the movie, so we do the only thing we can."

"Which is?"

"We become what Leroy and the world thinks we are, a couple. Until I have the money in the bank, and then we can quietly split, citing irreconcilable differences."

Jaci shook her head. She didn't think she could do it. She'd just come out of a relationship, and she didn't

think she could be in another one, fake or not. She was
determined to fly solo. "Uh…no, that's not going to work
for me."

"You got me into this situation by throwing yourself
into my arms, and you're going to damn well help me
get out of it," Ryan growled.

"Seriously, Ryan—"

Ryan narrowed his eyes. "If I recall, your contract
hasn't be signed…"

It took twenty seconds for his words to sink in. "Are
you saying that you won't formalize my contract if I
don't do this?"

"I've already bought the rights for the script. It's mine
to do what I want with it. I did want some changes and
I would prefer it if you write those, but I could ask Wes,
or Shona, to do it."

"You're blackmailing me!" Jaci shouted, instantly in-
furiated. She glanced at the paperweight on his desk and
wondered if she could grab it and launch it toward his
head. He might not lie but he wasn't above using manip-
ulation, the dipstick!

Ryan sighed and placed the paperweight on top of a
pile of folders. "Look, you started all this trouble, and
you need to figure out how to end it. Consider it as part
of your job description."

"Don't blame this on me!"

Ryan lifted an eyebrow in disbelief and Jaci scowled.
"At least not all of it! The first kiss was supposed to be
a peck, but you turned it into a hot-as-hell kiss!" Jaci
shouted, her hands gripping the arms of the chair.

"What the hell was I supposed to do? You plastered
yourself against me and slapped your mouth on mine!"
Ryan responded with as much, maybe even more, heat.

"Do you routinely shove your tongue into a stranger's mouth?"

"I knew that I'd met you, dammit!" Ryan roared. He sprang to his feet and stormed over to his window and stared down at the tiny matchbox cars on the street below. Jaci watched as he pulled in a couple of deep breaths, amazed that she was able to fight with this man, shout at him, yet she felt nothing but exhilaration. No feelings of inadequacy or guilt or failure.

That was new. Maybe New York, with or without this crazy situation, was going to be good for her.

"So what are we going to do?" Jaci asked after a little while. It was obvious that they had to do something because walking away from her dream job was not an option. She was not going to go back to London without giving this opportunity her very best shot. Giving up now was simply not an option. She had to prove herself and she'd do it here in New York City, the toughest place around. Nobody would doubt her then.

"Do you want to see this film produced? Do you want to see your name in the credits?" Ryan asked without turning around.

Well, duh. "Of course I do," she softly replied. This was her big break, her opportunity to be noticed, to get more than her foot through the door. She'd been treading water for so long, she couldn't miss this opportunity to ride the wave to the beach.

"Then I need Banks's money."

"Is he the only investor around? Surely not."

"Firstly, they don't grow on trees. I've also spent nearly eighteen months thrashing out the agreement. I can't waste any more time on him and I can't let that effort be for nothing."

There was no way out of this. "And to get his money we have to become a couple."

"A fake couple," Ryan hastily corrected her. "I don't want or need a real relationship."

Jeez, chill. She didn't want a relationship, either.

"So I can see some garden parties in the Hamptons in our future. Maybe theater or opera tickets, dinners at upscale restaurants because Banks will want to show me how important he is and he'll want to show you what you missed out on."

"Oh, joy."

Ryan shoved his hands in his hair and tugged. "We don't have a choice here and we have to make this count."

Jaci rubbed her hands over her face. Who would've thought that an impulsive kiss could lead to such a tangle? She didn't have a choice but to go along with Ryan's plan, to be his temporary girlfriend. If she didn't, months of work—Ryan's, hers, Thom's—would evaporate, and she doubted that Ryan and Thom would consider working with her again if she was the one responsible for ruining their deal with Banks.

She slumped in her chair. "Okay, then. It's not like we—I—have much of a choice anyway."

Ryan turned and gripped the sill behind him, his broad back to the window. He sighed and rubbed his temple with the tips of his fingers, his action telling her that he had a headache on board. Lucky she hadn't clobbered him with that paperweight; his headache would now be a migraine.

"For all we know, Leroy might change his mind about socializing and we'll be off the hook," Ryan said, rolling his head from side to side.

"What do you think are the chances of that happening?" Jaci asked.

"Not good. He doesn't like the fact that I have you. He'll make me jump through hoops."

"Because you're everything he isn't," Jaci murmured.

"What do you mean?"

You're tall, hot and sexy. Charming when you want to be. You're successful, an acclaimed producer and businessman. You're respected. Leroy, as far as she knew, just had oily hair and enough money to keep a third-world economy buoyant. Jaci stared at her hands. She couldn't tell Ryan any of that; she had no intention of complimenting her blackmailer. Even if he could kiss to world-class standards.

"Don't worry about it." Jaci waved her words away and prayed that he wouldn't pursue the topic.

Thankfully he didn't. Instead he reached for the bottle of water on his desk and took a long sip. "So, as soon as I hear from Banks I'll let you know."

"Fine." Jaci pushed herself to her feet, wishing she could go back to bed and pull the covers over her head for a week or two.

"Jaci?"

Jaci lifted her eyes off her boots to his. "Yes?"

"We'll keep it completely professional at work. You're the employee and I'm the boss," Ryan stated. That would make complete sense except for the sexual tension, as bright and hot as a lightning arc, zapping between them. Judging by his hard tone and inscrutable face, Ryan was ignoring that sexual storm in the room. She supposed it would be a good idea if she did the same.

Except that her feet were urging her to get closer to

him, her lips needed to feel his again, her… God, this was madness.

"Fine. I'll just get back to work then?"

"Yeah. I think that would be a very good idea."

When Jaci finally left his office, Ryan dropped into his leather chair and rolled his head from side to side, trying to release the tension in his neck and shoulders. In the space of ten hours, he'd acquired a girlfriend and the biggest deal of his life was placed in jeopardy if he and Jaci didn't manage to pull off their romance. He hadn't been exaggerating when he told Jaci that Leroy would be furious if he realized that Jaci was just using him as an excuse to put some distance between her and his wandering hands…but hell, talk about being in the wrong place at the wrong time!

It was the kiss—that fantastic, hot, sexy meeting of their mouths—that caused the complications. And, dammit, she was right. The first kiss, initiated by her, had been tentative and lightweight and he was the one who'd taken it deeper, hotter, wetter. Oh, she hadn't protested and had quickly joined him on the ride. A ride he wouldn't mind taking to its logical conclusion.

Concentrate, moron. Sex should have been low on his priority list. It wasn't but it should have been.

When he'd come back down to earth and seen Banks's petulant face—pouty mouth and narrowed eyes—he'd realized that he'd made a grave miscalculation. Then he'd added fuel to the fire when he'd informed him that Jaci was his girlfriend. Banks wanted Jaci and didn't like the fact that Ryan had her, and because of that, Ryan would be put through a wringer to get access to Banks's cash.

Like his father, Banks was the original playground

bully; he instantly wanted what he couldn't and didn't have. Ryan understood that, as attractive as he found Jaci—and he did think that she was incredibly sexy—for Leroy his pursuit of her had little to do with Jaci but, as she'd hinted at earlier, everything to do with him. With the fact that she was with him, that he had her…along with a six-two frame, a reasonable body and an okay face.

This was about wielding power, playing games, and what should've been a tedious, long but relatively simple process would now take a few more weeks and a lot more effort. He knew Leroy's type—his father's type. He was a man who very infrequently heard the word *no*, and when he did, he didn't much care for it. In the best-case scenario, they'd go on a couple of dinners and hopefully Leroy would be distracted by another gorgeous woman and transfer his attention to her.

The worst-case scenario would be Leroy digging his heels in, stringing him along and then saying no to funding the movie. Ryan banged his head against the back of his chair, feeling the thump of the headache move to the back of his skull.

The thought that his father had access to the money he needed jumped into his brain.

Except that he'd rather drill a screwdriver into his skull than ask Chad for anything. In one of his many recent emails he'd skimmed over, his father had told him that he, and some cronies, had up to two hundred million to invest in any of his films if there was a part in one of his movies for him. It seemed that Chad had conveniently forgotten that their final fight, the one that had decimated their fragile relationship, had been about the industry, about money, about a part in a film.

After Ben's death, his legions of friends and his fans,

wanting to honor his memory, had taken to social media and the press to "encourage" him—as a then-indie filmmaker and Ben's adoring younger brother—to produce a documentary on Ben's life. Profits from the film could be donated to a charity in Ben's name. It would be a fitting memorial. The idea snowballed and soon he was inundated with requests to do the film, complete with suggestions that his father narrate the nonexistent script.

He'd lost the two people he'd loved best in that accident, the same two people who'd betrayed him in the worst way possible. While he tried to deal with his grief—and anger and shock—the idea of a documentary gained traction and he found himself being swept into the project, unenthusiastic but unable to say no without explaining why he'd rather swim with great whites in chum-speckled water. So he'd agreed. One of Ben's friends produced a script he could live with and his father agreed to narrate the film, but at the last minute Chad told him that he wanted a fee for lending his voice to the documentary.

And it hadn't been a small fee. Chad had wanted ten million dollars and, at the time, Ryan, as the producer, hadn't had the money. Chad—Hollywood's worst father of the year—refused to do it without a financial reward, and in doing so he'd scuttled the project. He was relieved at being off the hook, felt betrayed by Ben, heartbroken over Kelly, but he was rabidly angry that Chad, their father, had tried to capitalize on his son's death. Their argument was vicious and ferocious and he'd torn into Chad as he'd wanted to do for years.

Too much had been said, and after that blowout he realized how truly alone he really was. After a while he started to like the freedom his solitary state afforded him and really, it was just easier and safer to be alone. He liked his busy, busy life. He had the occasional affair and never dated a woman for more than six weeks at a time. He had friends, good friends he enjoyed, but he kept his own counsel. He worked and he made excellent films. He had a good, busy, productive life. And if he sometimes yearned for more—a partner, a family— he ruthlessly stomped on those rogue thoughts. He was perfectly content.

Or he would be if he didn't suddenly have a fake girlfriend who made him rock-hard by just breathing, a manipulative investor and a father who wouldn't give up.

Four

Jaci, sitting cross-legged on her couch, cursed when she heard the insistent chime telling her that she had a visitor. She glanced at her watch. At twenty past nine it was a bit late for social visits. She was subletting this swanky, furnished apartment and few people had the address, so whoever was downstairs probably had the wrong apartment number.

She frowned and padded over to her front door and pressed the button. "Yes?"

"It's Ryan."

Ryan? Of all the people she expected to be at her door at twenty past nine—she squinted at her watch, no, that was twenty past ten!—Ryan Jackson was not on the list. Since leaving his office four days before, she hadn't exchanged a word with him and she'd hoped that his ridiculous idea of her acting as his girlfriend had evaporated.

"Can I come up?" Ryan's terse question interrupted her musings.

Jaci looked down at her fuzzy kangaroo slippers—a gag Christmas gift from her best friend, Bella—and winced. Her yoga pants had a rip in the knee and her sweatshirt was two sizes too big, as it was one of Clive's that she'd forgotten to return. Her hair was probably spiky from pushing her fingers into it and she'd washed off her makeup when she'd showered after her run through Central Park after work.

"Can this wait until the morning? It's late and I'm dressed for bed."

She knew it was ridiculous but she couldn't help hoping that Ryan would assume that she was wearing a sexy negligee and not clothes a bag lady would think twice about.

"Jaci, I don't care what you're wearing so open the damn door. We need to talk."

That sounded ominous. And Ryan sounded determined enough, and arrogant enough, to keep leaning on her doorbell if he thought that was what it would take to get her to open up. Besides, she needed to hear what he had to say, didn't she?

But, dammit, the main reason why her finger hit the button to open the lobby door was because she wanted to see him. She wanted to hear his deep, growly voice, inhale his cedar scent—deodorant or cologne? Did it matter?—have an opportunity to ogle that very fine body.

Jaci placed her forehead on her door and tried to regulate her heart rate. Having Ryan in her space, being alone with him, was dangerous. This apartment wasn't big—this was Manhattan, after all—and her bedroom was a hop, skip and a jump away from where she was standing right now.

You cannot possibly be thinking about taking your boss to bed, Jacqueline! Seriously! Slap some sense into yourself immediately!

Ryan's sharp knock on the door had her jerking her head back. Because her father had made her promise that she wouldn't open the door without checking first—apparently the London she'd lived in for the past eight years was free of robbers and rapists—she peered through the peephole before flipping the lock and the dead bolt on the door.

And there he was, dressed in a pair of faded jeans and a long-sleeved, collarless black T-shirt. He held a leather jacket by his thumb over his shoulder and, with the strips of black under his eyes and his three-day beard, he looked tired but tough.

Ryan leaned his shoulder into the door frame and kept his eyes on her face, which Jaci appreciated. "Hey."

Soooo sexy. "Hello. What are you doing here? It's pretty late," she said, hoping that he missed the wobble in her voice.

"Leroy Banks finally returned my call. Can I come in?"

Jaci nodded and stepped back so that he could walk into the room. Ryan immediately dropped his jacket onto the back of a bucket chair and looked around the room, taking in the minimalist furniture and the abstract art. "Not exactly Lyon House," he commented.

"Nothing is," Jaci agreed. Her childhood home was old and stately but her parents had made it a home. It had never been a showpiece; it was filled with antiques and paintings passed down through the generations but also packed with books and dog leashes, coffee cups and magazines.

"Did your mother ever get that broken stair fixed? I remember her nagging your father to get it repaired. She said it had been driving her mad for twenty years."

Did she hear longing in his voice or was that her imagination? Ryan had always been hard to read, and her ability to see behind the inscrutable mask he wore had not improved with age. And she was too tired to even try. "Nope, the stair is still cracked. It will never be fixed. She just likes to tease my father about his lack of handyman skills. Do you want something to drink? Coffee? Tea? Wine?"

"Black coffee would be great. Black coffee with a shot of whiskey would be even better."

She could do that. Jaci suggested that Ryan take a seat but instead he followed her to the tiny galley kitchen, his frame blocking the doorway. "So, how are you enjoying work?"

Jaci flashed him a quick smile at his unexpected question. "I'm loving it. I'm working on the romcom at the moment. You said that you want changes done to *Blown Away* but I need to spend some time with you and Thom to find out exactly what you want and, according to your PA, your schedules are booked solid."

"I'll try to carve out some time for you soon, I promise."

Jaci went up onto her toes to reach the bottle of whiskey on the top shelf. Then Ryan's body was flush up against hers, his chest to her back, and with his extra height he easily took the bottle off the shelf. Jaci expected him to immediately move away but she felt his nose in her hair, felt the brush of his fingers on her hip.

She waited with bated breath to see if he'd turn her to face him, wondered whether he'd place those broad hands on her breasts, lower that amazing mouth to hers…

"Here you go."

The snap of the whiskey bottle hitting the counter jerked her out of her reverie, and then the warmth of his body disappeared. With a dry mouth and a shaking hand, Jaci unscrewed the cap to the bottle and dumped a healthy amount of whiskey into their cups.

Hoo, boy! And down, girl!

"It's a hell of a coincidence that you, the sister of my old friend, had a script accepted by me, by us," Ryan said, lifting his arms up so that he gripped the top of the door frame. The action made his T-shirt ride up, showing a strip of tanned, muscled abdomen and a hint of fabulous oblique muscles. Jaci had to bite her tongue to stop her whimper.

"Actually, I'm not at all surprised that you like the script. After all, *Blown Away* was your idea."

"Mine?" Ryan looked confused.

Jaci poured hot coffee into the cups and picked them up. She couldn't breathe in the small kitchen—too much distracting testosterone—and she needed some space between her and this sexy man. "Shall we sit?"

Ryan took his cup, walked back to the living room and slumped into the corner of her couch. Jaci took the single chair opposite him and immediately put her feet up onto the metal-and-glass coffee table.

Ryan took a sip of his coffee and raised his eyebrows. "Explain."

Jaci blew air across the hot liquid before answering him. "You came down to Lyon House shortly before you dropped out of uni—"

"I didn't drop out, I graduated."

Jaci shook her head. "But you're the same age as Neil and he was in his first year."

Ryan shrugged, looking uncomfortable. "Accelerated classes. School was easy."

"Lucky you," Jaci murmured. Unlike her siblings, she'd needed to work a lot harder to be accepted into university, which she'd flunked out of halfway through her second year. She thought that she and Ryan had that in common, but it turned out that he was an intellectual like her sister. And brother. And her parents. She was, yet again, the least cerebral person in the room.

Lucky she'd had a lot of practice at being that.

"So, the script?" Ryan prompted.

"Oh! Well, you came home with Neil and the two of you were playing chess. It was raining cats and dogs. I was reading." Well, she'd been watching him, mooning over him, but he didn't need to know that! Ever. "You were talking about your careers and Neil asked you if you were going into the movie business like your father."

Jaci looked down into her cup. "You said that your dad and Ben had that covered, that you wanted your own light to shine in." His words had resonated with her because she understood them so well. She'd wanted exactly the same thing. "You also said that you were going to go into business management and that you were going to stay very far away from the film industry."

"As you can see, that worked out well," Ryan said, his comment bone-dry and deeply sarcastic.

"Neil said that you were fooling yourself, that it was as much in your blood as it was theirs." Jaci quirked an eyebrow. "He called that one correctly."

"Your brother is a smart man."

As if she'd never noticed.

"Anyway, Neil started to goad you. He tossed out plots and they were all dreadful. You thought his ideas were ridiculous and started plotting your own movie about a burnt-out cop and his feisty female newbie partner who were trying to stop a computer-hacking serial bomber from taking a megacity hostage. I was writing, even then, mostly romances but I took some of the ideas you tossed out, wrote them down and filed them. About eighteen months ago I found that file and the idea called to me, so I sat down and wrote the script." Jaci sipped her coffee. "I'm not surprised that you liked the script but I am surprised that you own a production company and that I'm now working for you."

Ryan's eyes pinned her to her chair. "Me, too." He pushed his hand through his hair. "Talking of non-scriptwriting work—"

Jaci sighed. "Toad of Toad Hall—"

"—has issued his first demand." Jaci groaned but Ryan ignored her. "He's invited us to join him at the premiere of the New York City Ballet Company's new production of *Swan Lake*."

Jaci groaned again but more loudly and dramatically this time.

"You don't like ballet? I thought all girls like ballet," he said, puzzled. "And didn't your family have season tickets to the Royal Opera House to watch both ballet and opera?"

"They did. They dragged me along to torture me." Jaci pulled a face. "I much prefer a rock concert to either."

"But you'll do it?"

Jaci wrinkled her nose. "I suppose I have to. When is it?"

"Tomorrow evening. Black tie for me, which means a ball gown, or something similar, for you." His eyes focused on the rip in her pants before he lifted amused eyes to hers. "Think you can manage that?"

Jaci looked horrified. "You're kidding me right? Tomorrow?"

"Evening. I'll pick you up at six."

Jaci leaned back in her chair and placed her arm over her eyes. "I don't have anything to wear. That one cocktail dress I brought over was it."

Ryan took a sip from his cup and shrugged. "Last time I checked, there are about a million clothes stores in Manhattan."

She'd made a promise to herself that, now that she was free of Clive and free of having her outfits picked apart by the fashion police in the tabloids, she could go back to wearing clothes that made her feel happy, more like herself. Less staid, more edgy. When she left London with the least offensive of the clothes that had been carefully selected by the stylist Clive employed to shop for her, she'd promised herself that she would overhaul her wardrobe. She'd find the vintage shops and the cutting-edge designers and she would wear clothes that were a little avant-garde, more edgy. And she wouldn't wear another ball gown unless someone put a gun to her head.

Unfortunately, risking so many millions wasn't a gun, it was a freaking cannon...

She'd thought she was done with playing it safe.

"You're still frowning," Ryan said. "This is not a big deal, Jaci. How difficult can shopping be?"

"Only a man would say that," Jaci replied, bouncing to her feet. She slapped her hands onto her hips and jerked her head. "What do you want me to wear?"

Ryan shrugged and looked confused. "Why the hell should I care?"

"It's your party, Ryan, your deal. Give me a clue... regal, flamboyant, supersexy?"

"What the hell are you talking about?" Ryan demanded. "Put a dress on, show up, smile. That's it. Just haul something out of your closet and wear it. You must have something you can wear."

He really didn't get it. "Come with me," she ordered.

Ryan, still holding his coffee, followed her down the supershort hallway to the main bedroom. Jaci stomped over to the walk-in closet and flung the doors open. She stepped inside and gestured to the mostly empty room. Except for the umber cocktail dress she'd worn the other night, nearly every single item hanging off the rod and on the shelves was a shade of black.

Ryan lifted an eyebrow. "Do you belong to a coven or something? Or did the boring stuff get left behind when they robbed you?"

"I have enough clothes to stock my own store," Jaci told him with frost in her voice. "Unfortunately they aren't on this continent."

Ryan looked at her empty shelves again. "I can see that. Why not?"

Jaci pushed her hair behind her ears. "They are in storage, as I wasn't intending to wear them anymore."

"I can't believe that I am having a conversation about clothes but...and again...why not?"

Jaci stared at the floor and folded her arms across her chest. After a long silence, Ryan put his finger under her chin and lifted her eyes to his. "Why not, Jace?"

"I only brought a few outfits with me to the city. I was going to trawl the vintage shops and edgy boutiques to find clothes that were me…clothes that I liked, that I wanted to wear, clothes that made me feel happy. Now I have to buy a staid and boring ball gown that I'll probably never wear again."

Ryan narrowed his eyes. "Why does it have to be staid and boring?"

"You're in the public eye, Ryan. And there's a lot riding on this deal," Jaci pointed out. "It's important that I look the part."

The corners of Ryan's mouth twitched. "If our deal rests on what you are wearing then I'm in bigger trouble than I thought. You're making too big a deal of this, Jace. Wear whatever the hell you want, wherever and whenever. Trust me, I'm more interested in what's under the clothes anyway."

He really wasn't taking this seriously. "Ryan, impressions matter."

"Maybe if you're a politician who has a stick up his ass," Ryan retorted, looking impatient.

He didn't understand; he hadn't been crucified in the press for, among other things, his clothes. He hadn't been found wanting. She'd had enough of that in the United Kingdom. She didn't want to experience it on two continents. That was why she was trying to stay out of the public eye, why she was avoiding functions exactly like the one Ryan was dragging her to. And if she had to go, and it seemed as if she had little choice in the matter, she'd wear something that didn't attract attention, that would let her fly under the radar.

She waved her hand in the air in an attempt to dismiss the subject. "I'll sort something out."

Ryan sent her a hot look. "I don't trust you… You'll

probably end up buying something black and boring. Something safe."

Well, yes. That was the plan.

Ryan put his hands on his hips. "You want vintage and edgy?"

Where was he going with this? "For my day-to-day wardrobe, yes."

"And for the ball gown?" Jaci's shrug was his answer. "I'm taking you shopping," Ryan told her with a stubborn look on his face.

Ryan...shopping? With her? For a ball gown? Jaci couldn't picture it. "I don't think... I'm not sure."

"You need a dress, and I am going to get you into one that isn't suitable for a corpse," Ryan promised her, his face a mask of determination. "Tomorrow."

"It would be a lot easier if you just excused me from the ballet," Jaci pointed out.

"Not going to happen," Ryan said as his eyes flicked from her face to the bed and back again. And, just like that, her insecurities about her clothes—okay, about herself— faded away, replaced by hot, flaming lust. She saw his eyes deepen and darken and she knew what he was thinking because, well, she was thinking it, too. How would it feel to be on that bed together, naked, limbs tangled, mouths fused, creating that exquisite friction that was older than time?

"Jaci?"

"Mmm?" Jaci blinked, trying to get her eyes to focus. When they did she saw the passion blazing in Ryan's eyes. If that wasn't a big enough clue as to what he wanted to do then there was also the impressive ridge in his pants. "The only real interest I have in your clothes is how to get you out of them. I really want to peel off that ridiculous shirt and those ratty pants to see what you're wearing underneath."

Nothing—she wasn't wearing a damn thing. Jaci touched the top of her lip with her tongue and Ryan groaned.

"I'm desperate to do what we're both thinking," Ryan said, his voice even huskier coated with lust. "But that would complicate this already crazy situation. It would be better if I just left."

Better for whom? Not for her aching, demanding libido, that was for sure. Jaci was glad that she didn't utter those words out loud. She just stood there as Ryan brushed past her. At the entrance of her room, he stopped and turned to look back at her. "There's a coffee shop around the corner from here. Laney's?"

"Yes."

"I'll meet you there at nine to go shopping."

Jaci nodded. "Okay."

Ryan's smile was slow and oh so sexy. "And, Jace? I value authenticity above conventionality. Just an FYI."

Ryan left the coffee shop holding two takeout cups and looked right and then left, not seeing Jaci anywhere. The outside tables were full and he brushed past some suits to stand in a patch of spring sunshine, lifting his leg behind him to place his foot against the wall.

He had a million things to do this morning but he was taking a woman shopping. There was something very wrong with this picture. He had a couple of rules when it came to the women he dated: he never slept over, he never took the relationship past six weeks, and he never did anything that could, even vaguely, be interpreted as something a "couple" would do. Clothes shopping was right up there at the top of the list.

A hundred million dollars…

Yeah, that was a load of bull. Jaci could turn up in nipple caps and a thong and it wouldn't faze him. He didn't care jack about what Leroy, or people in general, thought. Yet Jaci seemed to be determined to hit the right note, sartorially speaking. Something about their conversation last night touched Ryan in a place that he thought was long buried. He couldn't believe that the sexy, stylish, so outwardly confident Jaci could be so insecure about what she wore and how she looked. Somebody had danced in her head, telling her that she wasn't enough exactly as she was, and that made him as mad as hell.

Maybe because it pushed a very big button of his own: the fact that, in his father's eyes, he'd never been or ever would be the son he wanted, needed, the son he lost. It was strange that he'd shared a little of his dysfunctional family life with Jaci; he'd never divulged any of his past before, mostly because it was embarrassing to recount exactly how screwed up he really was. That's what happened when you met your father and half brother for the first time at fourteen and within a day of you moving in, your father left for a six-month shoot across the country. He and Ben were left to work out how they were related, and they soon realized that they could either ignore each other—the house was cavernous enough that they could do that—or they could be friends and keep each other company. That need for company turned into what he thought was an unbreakable bond.

Ryan stared at the pavement and watched as a candy wrapper danced across the sidewalk, thinking that bonds could be broken. He had the emotional scars to prove it.

All it took was two deaths in a car crash and the subsequent revelation of an affair.

"Hi."

The voice at his elbow came out of nowhere and the cups in his hands rattled. God, he'd been so deep in thought that she'd managed to sneak up on him, something that rarely happened. Ryan looked into her face, noticed the splash of freckles across her nose that her makeup failed to hide and handed her a cup of coffee. Today she was wearing a pair of tight, fitted suit pants and a short black jacket. Too much black, Ryan thought. Too structured, too rigid.

But very New York.

"Thanks." Jaci sipped her coffee and lifted her face to the sun. "It's such a gorgeous day. I'd like to take my laptop and go to the park, find a tree and bang out a couple of scenes." She handed him a puppy-dog look. "Wouldn't you rather have me do that instead of shopping?"

"Nice try, but no go."

Ryan placed his hand on her lower back and steered her away from the wall. He could feel the warmth of her skin through the light jacket, and the curve of her bottom was just inches away. He was so damn tempted. Screw writing and shopping. His idea of how to spend a nice spring morning was to take this woman to bed.

Boss/employee, fake relationship/Leroy Banks, friend's kid sister…there were a bunch of reasons why that wasn't a viable option. But, hellfire, he really wanted to.

Ryan lifted his fingers to his mouth and let out a shrill whistle. Seconds later a taxi pulled up next to them. Ryan opened the door and gestured Jaci inside.

"Where to?"

Ryan started to give the address of his apartment then

mentally slapped himself and told the driver to take them to Lafayette Street in Soho. "If we don't find what we're looking for there, we'll head to Nolita."

He saw Jaci's frown. "Nolita?"

"North of little Italy," Ryan explained. "It's like a cousin to Soho. It also has curb-to-curb boutiques."

Her frown deepened. "I thought we were heading for Fifth Avenue and the department stores or designer stores there."

"Let's try something different," Ryan replied, eyeing her tailored jacket. The unrelenting black was giving him a headache. The plump, happy teenager he knew had loved bright colors, and he'd love to see her in those shades again. He operated in a fake world and if he had to be saddled with a girlfriend, pretend or not, then he wanted the real Jaci next to him, not the cardboard version of whom she thought she should be.

As he'd said, authenticity was a seldom-found commodity, and he wasn't sure why it was so important that he get it from her.

Ryan watched as the taxi driver maneuvered the car through the busy traffic. He was going shopping. With his fake girlfriend. Whom he wanted, desperately, to see naked.

All because a narcissistic billionaire also had the hots for her. Yes, indeed. There was something very wrong with this picture.

Five

Her previous visits to New York had always been quick ones and because of that, Jaci had never taken in the time to let the nuances of the city register. She'd visited Soho before but she'd forgotten about the elegant cast-iron architecture, the cobblestone streets, the colorful buildings and the distinct artistic vibe.

Obviously, the artists peddling their creations contributed to the ambience but she could also smell the art in the air, see it in the fabulous window displays, in the clothes of the people walking the streets. Jaci—for the first time in years—felt like the fish out of water. The old Jaci, the one she'd been before Clive and the stylist he insisted she used, dressed in battered jeans, Docs and her favorite Blondie T-shirt belonged in Soho. This Jaci in her funeral suit? Not so much.

Ryan, with his messy hair and his stubble and stunning eyes, would fit in anywhere. He wore a black-and-white plaid shirt under a black sweater, sleeves pushed up. His khaki pants and black sneakers completed his casual ensemble and he looked urban and classy. Hot.

Ryan paid the taxi driver and placed his hand on her back. He'd done that earlier and it was terrifying to admit how much she liked the gesture. His broad hand spanned the width of her back and it felt perfect, right there, just above the swell of her bottom.

Ryan gestured to the nearest boutique and Jaci sighed. Minimalistic, slick and, judging by the single black halter neck in the window, boring. But, she reluctantly admitted, it would probably be eminently suitable for an evening spent at the ballet.

Jaci followed Ryan to the shop window and he pulled the door open for her to enter. As she was about to step inside, he grabbed her arm to hold her back. "Hey, this isn't a torture session, Jace. If this isn't your type of place, then let's not waste our time."

Jaci sucked in her bottom lip. "It's the type of shop that Gail, my stylist, would take me to."

"But not your type of shop," Ryan insisted.

"Not my type of shop. Not my type of clothes. Well, not anymore," Jaci reluctantly admitted. "But I should just look around. The dress is for the ballet and I will be going with a famous producer and a billionaire."

Ryan let go of the door and pulled her back onto the pavement. He lifted his hand and brushed the arch of his thumb along her cheekbone. "I have a radical idea, Jaci. Why don't you buy something that you want to wear instead of wearing something you think you should wear?"

God, she wished she could. The thing was, her style was too rock-chick and too casual, as she explained to

Ryan. "Tight Nirvana T-shirts didn't project the correct image for a politician's SO."

"Jerk." Ryan dropped his eyes to her breasts, lingered and slowly lifted them again. Jaci's breath hitched at the heat she saw in the pale blue gray. Then his sexy mouth twitched. "There is nothing wrong, in my opinion, with a tight T-shirt." Jaci couldn't help her smile. "The thing is…you're not his fiancée anymore and you're not in London anymore. You can be anyone you want to be, dress how you wish. And that includes any function we attend as a fake couple."

He made it sound so simple… She wished it was that easy. Although she'd made up her mind to go back to dressing as she wanted to, old habits were hard to break. And sometimes Sassy Jaci wasn't as strong as she needed her to be. She still had an innate desire to please, to do what was expected of her, to act—and dress—accordingly. When she dressed and acted appropriately, her family approved. When she didn't they retreated and she felt dismissed. She was outgrowing her need for parental and sibling approval, but sometimes she simply wished that she was wired the same as them, that she could relate to them and they to her. But she was the scarlet goat in a family of sleek black sheep.

"Hey." Ryan tipped her chin up with his thumb and made her meet his startling eyes. "Come on back to me."

"Sorry."

"Just find something that you want to wear tonight. And if I think it's unsuitable then I'll tell you, okay?"

Jaci felt a kick of excitement, the first she'd felt about clothes and shopping for a long, long time. It didn't even come close to the galloping of her heart every time she laid eyes on Ryan, but it was still there.

Jaci reached up and curled her hand around his wrist, her eyes bouncing between his mouth and those long-lashed eyes. She wanted to kiss him again, wanted to feel those clever lips on her, taste him. She wanted to—

Then he did as she'd mentally begged and kissed her. God, that mouth, those lips, that strong hand on her face. Kissing him in the sunlight on a street in Soho… Perfection. Jaci placed her hands on his waist and cocked her head to change the angle and Ryan, hearing her silent request, took the kiss deeper, sliding his tongue into her mouth to tangle with hers. Slow, sweet, sexy. He tasted of coffee and mint, smelled of cedar and soap. Jaci couldn't help the step that took her into his body, flush against that long, muscled form that welcomed her. She didn't care that they were in the flow of the pedestrian traffic, that people had to duck around them. She didn't hear the sniggers, the comments, the laughter.

There was just her and Ryan, kissing on a city street in the spring sunshine.

Jaci lost all perception of time; she had no idea how long it had been when Ryan pulled back.

Don't say it, Jaci silently begged. *Please don't say you're sorry or that it was a mistake. Just don't. I couldn't bear it.*

Ryan must have seen something on her face, must have, somehow, heard her silent plea, because he stepped away and jammed his hands into his pockets.

"I really need to stop doing that," he muttered.

Why? She rather liked it.

"We need to find you a dress," he said, in that sexy growl.

Jaci nodded and, wishing that she had the guts to tell him that she'd far prefer that he find them a bed, fell into step beside him.

* * *

They left another shop empty-handed and Jaci walked straight to a bench and collapsed onto it. Her feet were on fire, she was parched and was craving a cheeseburger. They'd visited more than ten shops and Ryan wouldn't let her buy any of the many dresses she'd tried on, and Jaci was past frustrated and on her way to irritated. "I'm sick of this. I need a vodka latte with sedative sprinkles."

Ryan sat on the bench next to her, and his cough sounded suspiciously like "lightweight." Jaci narrowed her eyes at him. "I would never have taken you for a shopaholic, Jackson."

"For the record, normally you couldn't get me to do this without a gun to my head."

Because there was a hundred million on the line…

"You're the one who is drawing this out," Jaci pointed out. "The second shop we visited had that black sheath that was imminently suitable. You wouldn't let me buy it."

"You hated it." Ryan wore an expression that Jaci was coming to realize was his stubborn face. "As I said, tonight I'd like you to wear something you feel sexy in."

I'd feel sexy wearing you… Moving the hell on.

"Denim shorts, a Ramones tee and cowboy boots?" Jaci joked, but she couldn't disguise the hopeful note in her voice.

His mouth quirked up in a sexy smile that set her hormones to their buzz setting. "Not tonight but I'd like to see that combination sometime."

Jaci crossed one leg over the other and twisted her body so that she was half facing him. Sick of discussing clothes, she changed the subject to something she'd been wondering about. "When did you open Starfish and why?"

Ryan took a long time to answer and when he started to speak, Jaci thought that he would tell her to mind her own business. "Neil was right, I couldn't stay away from the industry. I landed a job as business manager at a studio and I loathed it. I kept poking my nose into places it didn't belong, production, scripts, art, even direction. After I'd driven everybody mad, the owner took me aside and suggested I open up my own company. So I did." Ryan tipped his face up to the sun. "That was about six months before Ben died."

His dark designer shades covered his eyes, but she didn't need to see them to know that, on some level, he still mourned his brother. That he always would. "I'm so sorry about Ben, Ryan."

"Yeah. Thanks."

Jaci sucked in some air and asked the questions she, and a good portion of the world, still wondered about. "Why did they crash, Ryan? What really happened?"

Ryan shrugged. "According to the toxicology screen, he wasn't stoned or drunk—not that night, anyway. He wasn't suicidal, as far as we knew. Witnesses said that he wasn't driving fast. There was no reason why his Porsche left the road and plunged down that cliff. It was ruled a freak accident."

"I'm sorry." The words sounded so small, so weak. She bit her bottom lip. "And the woman who died along with him? Had you met her? Did you know her?"

"Kelly? Yeah, I knew her," Ryan replied, his voice harsh as he glanced at his watch. Subject closed, his face and body language stated. "It's nearly lunchtime. Want to hit a few more shops? If we don't find anything, we'll go back for that black sheath."

"Let's go back for that black sheath now," Jaci said

as she stood up, pulling her bag over her shoulder. As they stepped away from the bench, she saw a young woman holding four or five dresses on a hanger, her arm stretched above her head to keep the fabrics from skimming the ground. The top dress, under its plastic cover, made her heart stumble. It was a striking, A-line floor-length dress in watermelon pink with a deep, plunging, halfway-to-her-navel neckline.

Without hesitation she crossed the pavement and tapped the young woman on her shoulder. "Hi, sorry to startle you." She gestured to the garments. "I love these. Are they your designs?"

The woman nodded. "They are part of a consignment for The Gypsy's Caravan."

Jaci reached out and touched the plastic covering the top dress. It was simple but devastatingly so, edgy but feminine. It was a rock-chick dress trying to behave, and she was in love. The corners of Ryan's mouth kicked up when she looked at him.

"What do you think?" she asked, not quite able to release the plastic covering of the dress, her dress.

"I think that you love it." Ryan flashed his sexy smile at the woman carrying the dresses and Jaci was sure that she saw her knees wobble. This didn't surprise her in the least. Her knees were always jelly-like around Ryan.

"It looks like we're going where you are," Ryan said as he reached for the dresses and took them from her grasp, then held them with one hand so that they flowed down his back. With his height they didn't even come close to the dirty sidewalk. He placed his other hand on Jaci's back.

Jaci shook her head, planting her feet. "I don't think

it's suitable. It's too sexy… I mean, I couldn't wear a bra with it!"

After looking at her chest, Ryan lifted his eyebrows. "You don't need a bra." He grabbed her hand and tugged it. "It's the first time I've seen you remotely excited about a dress all morning. You're trying it on. Let's go."

"The black sheath is more appropriate."

"The black sheath is as boring as hell," Ryan whipped back. "Jace, I'm tired and sick of this. Let's just get this done, okay?"

Well, when he put it like that… He was still—despite their hot kisses and the attraction that they were trying, and failing, to ignore—the boss.

As an excuse, it worked for her.

In the end it was just the three of them who attended the ballet, and despite the fact that Ryan did his best to keep himself between her and Leroy, Jaci knew that he couldn't be her buffer all evening and at some point she would have to deal with Leroy on her own. The time, Jaci thought as she sent Ryan's departing back an anxious look, had come. It was intermission and Ryan, along with what seemed to be the rest of the audience, was making his way toward the bar for the twelve-year-old whiskey Leroy declared that he couldn't, for one more minute, live without.

Keeping as much distance as she could from him in the crowded, overperfumed space, she fixed her eyes on Ryan's tall frame, trying to keep her genial smile in place. It faltered when a busty redhead bumped her from behind and made her wobble on her too-high heels. She gritted her teeth when she felt Leroy's clammy grip on her elbow. *Ick*. Jaci ruthlessly held back her shiver of distaste as she pulled her arm from his grasp. Strange that Ryan, with one look, could heat her up from the inside out, that he could have her shivering in anticipation from a brief scrape of his hand against any part of her, yet Leroy had exactly the opposite effect. They were two ends of the attraction spectrum and she was having a difficult time hiding her reactions, good and bad, to both of them.

One because there was a hundred million on the line; the other because she was, temporarily, done with men and a dalliance with Ryan—her boss!—would not be a smart move. She wouldn't jeopardize her career for some hot sex…as wonderful as she knew that hot sex would be. Mmm, not that she'd ever had any hot sex, but a girl could dream. She'd had hurried sex and boring sex and blah sex but nothing that would melt her panties. Judging by the two kisses they'd shared, Ryan had a PhD in melting underwear.

Yep, just the thought had the thin cord of her thong warming; if she carried on with this train of thought she'd be a hot mess. Jaci straightened her back and mentally shook herself off. She was enough of a mess as it was. She was in New York to get a handle on her crazy life, to establish her career and to find herself. She was not supposed to be looking for ways to make it more complicated!

"I have a private investigator."

Jaci tucked her clutch bag under her arm and linked her fingers together. *Be polite, friendly but distant.* She could make conversation for ten minutes or so; she wasn't a complete social idiot. A private investigator? Why would he be telling her that? "Okay. Um…what do you use him for?"

"Background checks on business associates, employees," Leroy explained. His eyes were flat and cold and Jaci felt the hair on her arms rise. "When I was considering whether to go into business with Jackson, I had him investigated."

"He wouldn't have found anything that might have given you second thoughts," Jaci quickly replied.

Leroy cocked his head. "You seem very sure of that."

"Ryan has an enormous amount of integrity. He says what he means and means what he says." Jaci heard the heat in her voice and wished that she could dial it down. Leroy hadn't said anything to warrant her defense of Ryan but something in his tone, in his body language, had her fists up and wanting to box. This was very unlike her. She wasn't a fighter.

"Strange that you should be so sure of that since you've only known him for a few weeks," Leroy replied, his words silky. Leroy ran a small, pale hand down the satin lapels of his suit in a rhythmic motion. Where was he going with this? Jaci, deciding that silence was a good option, just held his reptilian eyes.

"So tell me, Jacqueline, how involved can you be with Ryan after knowing him for just seventeen days?"

"I broke up with my ex six weeks before that and sometimes love—" she tried not to choke on the word "—happens in unexpected places and at unexpected times." Jaci allowed herself a tiny, albeit cold, smile. "You really should hire better people, Leroy, because your PI's skills are shoddy. I've known Ryan for over twelve years. He attended university with my brother, and he was a guest in my parents' home. We've been in contact for far longer than two weeks." Jaci tacked on the last lie with minimal effort.

It was time for Sassy Jaci, she thought. She needed to throw politeness out the window, so she nailed Leroy with a piercing look. "Why the interest in me? And if you have to color outside the lines, there are hundreds of gorgeous, unattached girls, interested girls, out there you can dally with."

"My pursuit of you annoys Ryan and that puts him off guard. I like him off guard. But I do find you attractive and taking you from Ryan would be an added bonus." After a minute, he finally spoke again. "I like to have control in a relationship, whether that's business or personal."

That made complete sense, Jaci thought. "And Ryan won't be controlled."

"He will if he wants my money." Leroy's smile was as malicious as a snakebite. He lifted his hand and the tip of his index finger touched her bare shoulder and drifted down the inside of her arm. "He'll toe the line. They always do. Everyone has their price."

"I don't. Neither does Ryan."

"Everyone does. You just don't know what it is yet and neither do I."

There was a relentless determination in his eyes that made her think he was being deadly serious.

"This conversation has become far too intense," Leroy calmly stated. "You do intrigue me... You're very different from what I am used to, from the women I usually meet."

"Because I'm not rich, or plastic, or crazy?" Jaci demanded.

Leroy's laugh sounded like sandpaper on glass and it was as creepy as his smile. "At first, perhaps. But mostly you fascinate me because Ryan is fascinated by you. I want to know why."

There was that one-upmanship again, Jaci thought.

What was with this guy and his need to feel superior to Ryan? The chip on his shoulder was the size of a redwood tree. Didn't he realize that few men could compete with Ryan? Ryan was a natural leader, utterly and completely masculine, and one of his most attractive traits was the fact that he didn't care what people thought about him.

Leroy had a better chance of corralling the wind than he did of controlling Ryan. Why couldn't he see that? Couldn't he see Ryan was never going to kowtow to him, that he would never buckle?

Ryan marched to the beat of his own drum.

"Everything okay here?"

Jaci whirled around at Ryan's voice and reached for the glass of wine she'd ordered. Taking a big sip, she looked at him over her glass, her expression confused and uneasy.

"Everything is fine," Leroy said.

Ryan ignored him and kept his eyes on Jaci's face. "Jace?"

Jaci drank in his strong, steady presence and nodded. He held her stare for a while longer and eventually his expression cleared. He finally handed over Leroy's glass into his waiting hand, accompanied by a hard stare. Ryan wasn't a fool. He knew that words had been exchanged and Jaci knew that he'd demand to know what they'd discussed. How serious was Leroy's need to control Ryan? Jaci wasn't as smart about these things as her siblings were, but with her career and Ryan's film on the line, she couldn't afford to shove her head in the sand and play ostrich.

The lights flickered and Ryan placed his hand on her lower back. "Time to head back in," he said.

As Ryan led her back to their seats, Jaci thought that

they had to manage the situation and, right now, she was the only pawn on the chessboard. If she removed herself, Ryan and Leroy wouldn't have anything to tussle over. But they couldn't admit to their lie about being a couple; that would have disastrous consequences. But what if they upped the stakes, what if they showed Leroy that she was, in no uncertain terms, off-limits forever? Right now, as Ryan's girlfriend, there was room for doubt… Maybe they should remove all doubt.

Not giving herself time to talk herself out of the crazy idea that popped into her head, she stopped to allow an older couple to walk into the theater in front of her and slipped her hand into Ryan's, resting her head on his shoulder. She sent Leroy a cool smile. "There is one other thing your PI didn't dig up, Leroy."

Ryan's body tensed. "PI? What PI?"

Jaci ignored him and kept her eyes on Leroy's face. She watched as his eyebrows lifted, those eyes narrowed in focus. "And what might that be?"

Here goes, Jaci thought. *In for a penny and all that, upping the stakes, throwing the curveball.* "He wouldn't know that Ryan and I are deeply in love and that we are talking about marriage." She tossed Ryan an arch look. "I expect to be engaged really soon and I can't wait to wear Ryan's ring."

Six

What.
   The.
     Hell?

Two hours and a couple of lukewarm congratulations from Leroy later, and Ryan was still reeling from Jaci's surprise announcement and "what the hell" or other variations of the theme kept bouncing around his head. Leaving the theater, back teeth grinding, he guided Jaci through the door, his hand on her back. She'd, once again and without discussion, flipped his world on its head. *Thinking about marriage?* Did she *ever* think before she acted?

On the sidewalk, Ryan saw a scruffy guy approaching them from his right, an expensive camera held loosely in his hands, and he groaned. He immediately recognized Jet Simons. He was one of the most relentless—and annoying—tabloid reporters on the circuit. Part journalist, part paparazzo, all sleaze. Ryan knew this because the guy practically stalked him in the month following Ben's death. Jet had witnessed his grief and every day Ryan would pray that Jet wouldn't capture his anger at Ben and his pain at being betrayed by his brother and Kelly. He definitely hadn't wanted Jet to capture how alone he felt, how isolated. Soul-sucking bottom-feeder.

Ryan sent a back-the-hell-off look in his direction, which, naturally, Simons ignored. Dammit, he needed him around as much he needed a punch in the kidneys. Ryan grabbed Jaci's hand, hoping to walk away before they were peppered with questions.

"Leroy Banks and Jax Jackson," Simons drawled, stepping up to them and lifting his camera, the flash searing their eyes. "How's it hanging, guys?"

"Get out of my face or I'm going to shove that camera where it hurts," Ryan growled, pushing the lens away. Unlike the actors he worked with who played a cat-and-mouse game with the press, he didn't need to make nice with the rats.

The flash went off another few times and Ryan growled. He was about to make good on his threat when Simons lowered the camera and looked over it to give Jaci a tip-to-toe look, his gaze frankly appreciative. Ryan felt another snarl rumble in his throat and reminded himself that Jaci was his pretend girlfriend and that he had no right to feel possessive over her. The acid in his stomach still threatened to eat a hole through its lining.

Just punch him, caveman Ryan said from his shoulder, *you'll feel so much better after.*

Yeah, but sitting in jail on assault charges would suck.

"So, you're Jaci Brookes-Lyon," Simons said, his eyes appreciative. "Not Jax's usual type, I'll grant you that."

Ryan squeezed Jaci's hand in a silent reminder not to respond. It was good advice, and he should listen to it, especially since he still wanted to shove that lens down Simons's throat or up his…

"Mr. Banks, how you doing? You still in bed with Jackson? Figuratively speaking, that is? Where's Mrs. Banks?" Simons machine-gunned his words. "What do you think about Jax's little sweetie here? Do you think she is another six-weeker or does she have the potential to be more?"

Ryan heard Jaci's squawk of outrage but his attention was on Leroy's face, and his slow smile made Ryan's balls pull up into his body. Dammit, he was going to dump them right in it. He knew it as he knew his own signature. Ryan's mind raced, desperate for a subject change, but before he could even try to turn the conversation Leroy spoke again. "They are talking about marriage, so maybe I suspect she does—" he waited a beat before speaking again "—have potential, that is."

Ryan let fly with a creative curse and shook his head when he realized that his outburst just added a level of authenticity to Banks's statement. He knew that a vein was threatening to pop in his neck and he released a clenched fist. Maybe he should just punch Leroy, as well, and make his jail stay worth his while.

"So you're engaged?" Simons demanded, his face alight with curiosity.

"Look, that's not exactly…" Jaci tried to explain but Ryan tightened his grip on her hand and she muttered a low "Ow."

"Stop talking," Ryan ordered in her ear before turning back to Simons and pinning him to the floor with a hard glance. "Get the hell out of my face."

Simons must have realized that he was dancing on his last nerve because he immediately took a step backward and lifted his hands in a submissive gesture. *Wuss*, Ryan internally scoffed as he watched him walk away. When Simons was out of earshot, Ryan finally settled his attention on Banks and allowed him to see how pissed he was with him, too. "I don't know what game you're playing, Banks, but it stops right now."

Leroy shrugged. "I am the one financing your film so you don't get to talk to me like that."

Wusses. He was surrounded by them tonight.

"I haven't seen any of your money so you're not in any position to demand a damn thing from me," Ryan said, keeping his voice ice cold. Cold anger, he realized a long time ago, was so much more effective than ranting and raving. "And even if we do still do business together, it'll always be my movie. You will never call the shots. Think about that and come back to me if you think those are terms you can live with."

Banks flushed under Ryan's hard stare and Ryan thought that it was a perfect time to throw in one last threat. "And this thing you have for my girlfriend stops right here. Leave her the hell alone."

"Ryan…" Jaci tried to speak as he pulled her toward a taxi sitting behind Leroy's limo and yanked the door open. He bundled her inside and when she was seated, he gripped the sides of the door and glared at her. This was all her and her big mouth's fault! What the hell had she been thinking by telling Leroy that they were talking about marriage? And how could he still be so intensely angry with her but still want to rip her clothes off? How could he want to strangle and kiss her at the same time?

He was seriously messed up. Had been since this crazy woman dropped back into his life.

"Not one damn word," he ordered before slamming the door closed and walking around the back of the cab. He slid inside and Jaci opened her mouth again.

"Ryan, I need you to understand why—"

God, she seriously wasn't listening. "What part of 'not one damn word' didn't you understand?" he growled after he tossed the address to her place to the driver up front.

"I understand that you are angry—"

"Shut. Up." Ryan felt as if a million spiders were dancing under his skin and that his temper was bubbling, looking for a way to escape. He'd spent his teenage years with a volatile father who didn't give a damn about him, and when he did pay him some attention, it was always negative. He'd learned to ignore the disparaging comments, to show no reaction and definitely no emotion. His father had fed off drama, had enjoyed baiting him, so he'd learned not to lose control, but tonight he was damn close. Engaged? Him? The man who, thanks to his brother and Kelly, rarely dated beyond six weeks? Who would believe it? And he was engaged to Jaci, who wasn't exactly his type…mostly because she wasn't like the biddable, eager-to-please women he normally dated. God, he hadn't even slept with Jaci yet and he was halfway to being hitched? On what planet in what freaking galaxy was that fair?

"I need to explain. Leroy—"

Okay, obviously she had no intention of keeping quiet, and he had two options left to him. To strip sixteen layers of skin off her or to shut her up in the only way he knew how. Deciding to opt for the second choice, he twisted, leaned over and slapped his mouth on hers. He dimly heard her yelp of surprise, and taking advantage of her open mouth, he slid his tongue inside...

His world flipped over again as he licked into her mouth, his tongue sliding over hers. She tasted of mint and champagne and heated surprise. The scent of her perfume, something light but fresh, enveloped him and his hands tightened on her hips, his fingers digging into the fabric of the dress he'd helped her choose, the dress he so desperately wanted to whip off her to discover what lay underneath. The backs of his fingers skimmed the side of her torso, bumped up and over her ribs, across the swelling of her breasts. He wanted to cup her, to feel her nipple pucker into his hand, but he was damned if he'd give the taxi driver a free show. Knowing her, discovering her, could wait until later. He needed to delay gratification, even if his erection felt as if it was being strangled by his pants. He could do it but that didn't mean he had to like it.

He wanted her. He wanted all of her...

Jaci yanked him back to the present by whipping her mouth off his and pushing herself into the corner of the cab, as far away from him as possible. "What are you doing?"

That was obvious, wasn't it? "Kissing you."

Dark eyes flashed her annoyance. "You tell me to shut up and then you kiss me? Are you crazy?"

That was highly possible.

"You wouldn't shut up," Ryan pointed out, his temper reigniting as he remembered her stupid declaration.

"You wouldn't let me explain," Jaci retorted.

"Yeah, I can't wait to see what you come up with." Ryan retreated to his corner of the cab, knowing that a muscle was jumping in his cheek. "Why would you make up such a crazy story? Are you that desperate to be engaged, to show the world that someone wants to marry you, that you would just go off half-cocked? I don't want to be engaged. God, I've been battling to wrap my head around having a fake girlfriend, and now I have a fake fiancée? And that it's you? Jesus!"

Ryan would never have believed it possible if he didn't witness her already brown-black eyes darken to coals. Anger and pride flashed but he couldn't miss the hurt, couldn't help but realize that he'd pushed one button too many, that he'd gone too far. He fumbled for words as she turned away to stare out the window, her hands in a death grip in her lap.

But God, his work was *his life* and she was screwing with it. He wanted that hundred million, he wanted to share the risk with an investor. And the one he'd had on his hook he'd just cut loose because of this woman and her way of speaking without thinking, of screwing up his life.

And it killed him to know that if she made one move to sleep with him, even kiss him, he'd be all over her like a rash. He was a reasonably smart guy, a guy who'd had more than his fair share of gorgeous women, but this one had him tied up in knots.

Not.

Cool.

Thinking that he needed separation from her before he did something stupid—not that this entire evening hadn't been anything but one long stupidity—he reached across her and pushed her door open. Jaci seemed as eager to get away from him as he was from her, and she quickly scrambled out of the cab, giving him a superexcellent flash of a long, supple leg and the white garter holding up a thigh-high stocking. He felt the rush of blood to his groin and had to physically restrain himself from bolting after her and finding out whether the rest of her lingerie was up to the fantastic standard her garters set.

Ryan banged the back of his head on the seat as he watched Jaci walk toward the doormen standing on the steps of her building. She was trying to kill him, mentally and sexually.

It was the only explanation he could come up with.

Jaci, vibrating with fury, stood outside Ryan's swanky apartment building in Lenox Hill and stormed into the lobby, startling the dozy concierge behind the desk. He blinked at her and rubbed his hand over his face before lifting his hefty bulk to his feet.

"Help you?"

Jaci forced herself to unclench her jaw so that she could speak. "Please tell Ryan Jackson that Jaci Brookes-Lyon is here to see him."

Deputy Dog Doorman looked doubtful. "It's pretty late, miss. Is he expecting you?"

Jaci's molars ground together. "Just call him. Please?"

She received another uncertain look but he reached for the phone and dialed an extension. Within twenty seconds she was told that Ryan had agreed to see her—how kind of him!—and she was directed to the top floor.

"What number?" she demanded, turning on her spiked heel, wishing that she'd changed out of the dress she'd worn to the ballet before she'd stormed out of her apartment to confront him in his.

"No number. Mr. Jackson's apartment is on the top floor, *is* the top floor." The doorman sighed at her puzzled expression. "He has the penthouse apartment, miss."

"The penthouse?"

"Mr. Jackson recently purchased one of the most sought-after residences in the city, ma'am. Ten thousand square feet, four bedrooms with a wraparound terrace. Designer finishes, with crown moldings, high ceilings and custom herringbone floors," the concierge proudly explained.

"Good for him," Jaci muttered and headed for the elevator, the doorman on her heels. At the empty elevator, the doorman keyed in a code on the control panel on the wall and gestured her inside. "The elevator opens directly into his apartment, so guests need to be authorized to go up."

Whatever, Jaci thought, as the doors started to close.

"Have a good evening, miss."

She heard the words slide between the almost closed doors and she knew that she was about to have anything but. She'd been heading up to her apartment, intending to lick her wounds, when she'd suddenly felt intensely angry. It made her skin prickle and her throat tighten. How dare Ryan treat her as if she was something he'd caught on the bottom of his shoe? He'd refused to let her speak, had ignored her pleas to allow her to explain and had acted as if she were an empty-headed bimbo who should be grateful to spend any time she could in his exalted presence. And how stupid was he to challenge Leroy like that? It was entirely possible that he'd decimated any chance of Leroy funding *Blown Away* with his harshly uttered comments… And he accused *her* of acting rashly!

Unable to enter her apartment and stay there like a good little woman, she'd headed downstairs, hailed a cab and headed for Ryan's apartment, seething the whole way.

Maybe he could afford to let *Blown Away* blow away but she couldn't! She wasn't going to allow him to lose this chance to show the world, her family—to show herself—that she could be successful, too. It was a good script and she was determined that the world would see it!

Jaci released her tightly bunched hands and flexed her fingers; for an intensely smart man, Ryan could be amazingly stupid. And Jaci was going to tell him so—no man was going to get away with dismissing her again. She didn't care if he was her boss, or her fake boyfriend or her almost, albeit fake, fiancé. There was too much at stake: the film, her career and, most important right now, her pride.

Jaci rested her forehead against the oak-paneled interior of the elevator.

Unlike in her arguments with Clive, this time she would scream and shout. She'd do anything to be heard, dammit! And Ryan, that bossy, alpha, sexy sod, was going to get it with both barrels! Jaci had barely completed that thought when the elevator doors opened and she was looking into Ryan's living room, which was filled with comfortable couches and huge artwork. He stood in front of the mantel, and despite her anger, Jaci felt the slap of attraction. How could she not since he looked so rough and tough in his white dress shirt that showed off the breadth of his shoulders, his pants perfectly tailored to show off his lean waist and hips, his long, muscled legs.

The top two buttons of the shirt were open and the ends of his bow tie lay against his chest, and she wanted her hands there, on his chest, under his shirt, feeling that warm, masculine skin.

Focus. She wasn't here to have sex with him…but,

dear God with all his angels and archangels, she wanted to. She wanted to as she wanted her heart to keep beating.

If she was a man at least she would have the excuse of thinking with the little head, but because she was a woman she was out of luck.

"What do you want, Jaci?" Ryan demanded, jamming his hands into his suit pockets.

You. I want you. So much.

Jaci shook her head to dislodge that thought. This wasn't about a tumble, this was about the way he had treated her. Her third-grade teacher, Mrs. Joliet, was correct: *Jacqueline is too easily distracted.* Nothing, it seemed, had changed.

Jaci licked her lips.

"God, will you stop doing that?" Ryan demanded, his harsh voice cutting through the dense tension between him.

"What?" Jaci demanded, not having a clue what he was talking about. Her eyes widened as he stalked toward her, all fierce determination and easy grace, his eyes on her mouth.

"Licking your lips, biting your lip! That's my job." He grabbed her arms and jerked her up onto her toes. It was such a caveman-like action, but she couldn't help the thrill she felt when her chest slammed into his and her nipples pushed into his chest. If she wasn't such a sap she would be protesting about him treating her like a ditsy heroine in a romcom movie, but right now she didn't care. She was pressed so close to him that a beam of light couldn't pass through the space between them, and his mouth was covering hers.

And, God, then her world tipped over and flipped inside out. The kisses she'd shared with him before were a pale imitation of the passion she could taste on the tongue that swept inside her mouth, that she could feel in the hand that made a possessive sweep over her back, in the appreciative, low groans that she could hear in the back of his throat. In a small, rarely used part of her brain— the only cluster of brain cells that weren't overwhelmed by this fantastically smoking-hot kiss—she was in awe of the fact that Ryan wanted her like this.

It almost seemed as if kissing her, touching her, was more important to him than breathing. Actually, Jaci agreed, breathing was highly overrated. Her hands drifted up his chest, skimmed the warm skin beneath the collar of his shirt and wound around the back of his strong neck, feeling his heat, his strength. Then his hand covered her breast and he rubbed his palm across her nipple and, together with feeling the steel pipe that was pressing into her stomach, those last few brain cells shut down.

Ryan jerked his head back and, when she met them, his light eyes glittered down at her. "So, we're engaged, right?"

Jaci half shrugged. "Probably. At least we will be, in the eyes of the world, when the news breaks in a few hours."

"Well, in that case…" Ryan bent his knees and ran his hands up the outside of her thighs, her dress billowing over his forearms. "It's a damn good excuse to do this."

Jaci gasped as he played with the lace tops of her garters, danced up and across her hip bone and slid down to cover her bare butt cheek.

"Garters and a thong. I've died and gone to heaven," Ryan muttered, sliding his fingers under that thin cord.

Ryan sucked the soft spot where her jaw and neck

met, and she whimpered in delight. "God, Ryan…is this a good idea?"

Ryan pulled his head up and frowned down at her. "Who the hell knows? But if I'm going to be bagged and tagged, then I'm going to get something out of the deal. Stop playing with my hair and put your hands on me, Jace. I'm dying here."

Jaci did as she was told and she placed her hand flat against his sex. He jumped and groaned and she wanted more. She wanted him inside her, filling her, stretching her…but she had to be sensible.

"Just sex?" she asked, unable to stop her hand from pulling down the zipper to his pants and sliding on inside. She pushed down his underwear and there he was, hot and pulsing and hard and…oh, God, his hands were between her legs and he'd found her. Found that most magical, special, make-her-crazy spot…

"Yeah, one night to get this out of our systems. You okay with that? One night, no strings, no expectations of more?"

How was she supposed to think when his fingers were pushing their way inside? Her thumb rubbed his tip and she relished the groan she pulled from him. They were still fully dressed yet she was so damn close to gushing all over his hand. If he moved his thumb back to her hot nub, she'd lose it. Right here, right now.

"I'm supposed to be fighting with you right now," Jaci wailed.

Ryan responded by covering her mouth with his. After swiping his tongue across the indents her teeth marks made, he lifted his head to speak. "We can fight later. So, are we good? If not, now is the time to say no, and you'd better do it fast."

His words and attitude were tough but she couldn't miss the tension she felt in his body, in the way his arms tightened his hold on her, as if he didn't want to let her go. She should say no; it was the clever thing to do. She couldn't form the word, so she encased him in her fist and slid her hand up and then down his shaft in a low, sensuous slide.

Ryan responded by using his free hand to twist the thin rope of her underwear. She felt it rip, felt the quick tug, and then the fabric drifted down her leg to fall onto her right foot.

"This dress is killing me," he muttered, trying to pull the long layers up so that he could get as close to her as possible, while nudging her backward to the closest wall. She wasn't this person, Jaci thought. She didn't have sex up against a wall, she didn't scream and moan and sigh. She'd never been the person to make her lovers shout and groan and curse.

But, unless she was having a brilliant, mother of a hallucination, she was being that person right now. And… yay!

"It would be a lot easier if we just stripped," Jaci suggested, feeling the cool wall against her back. She leaned forward to push Ryan's pants and underwear down his thighs.

"That'll take too long." Ryan leaned his chest into hers, gripped the back of her thighs and lifted her. With unerring accuracy, his head found her channel and he slid along her, causing her to let out a low shriek of pleasure. "I can't wait for you, I can't leave…but God, we need a condom."

Jaci banged her head against the wall as he probed

her entrance. "On the pill and I've been tested for every STD under the sun," she muttered.

"I'm clean, too." Ryan choked the words out.

"I need you now. No more talking, no more fighting, just you and…" She lifted her hips and there he was, inside her, stretching her, filling her, completing her.

Ryan's mouth met hers and his tongue mimicked the movement of his hips, sliding in and out, leaving no part of her unexplored. Jaci felt hyperaware, as if her every sense was jacked up to maximum volume. She yanked his shirt up and ran her hands over his chest, around his ribs and down his strong back, digging her nails into his buttocks when he tilted his hips and went even deeper. She cried out and he yelled, and then suddenly she was riding a white-hot wave. In that moment of magical release, she felt connected to all the feminine energy in the world and she was its conduit.

She felt powerful and uninhibited and so damn wild. When she came back to herself, back to the wall and to Ryan's face buried in her neck, his broad hands were still holding her thighs.

Jaci dropped her face into his neck and touched her tongue to the cord in his neck. "Take me to bed, Ryan. We can fight later."

"I can do that, and we most likely will," Ryan muttered as he pulled out of her and allowed her to slide down his body. He kicked off his pants and pulled her, her hair and dress and mind tangled, down the hallway to his bedroom. "But, for now, I can't wait any longer… I've got to see you naked."

Seven

Jaci pushed back the comforter and left the bed, glancing down at her naked body. Clothes would be nice and she wrinkled her nose at the pile of fabric in a heap on the floor, just on this side of the door. Pulling that on was going to be horrible, as was the walk of shame she'd be doing later as she headed back to her apartment in a wrinkled dress and with messy hair.

Then Jaci saw the T-shirt and pair of boxer shorts on Ryan's pillow. They hadn't been there earlier so Ryan must have left them for her to wear. Sweet of him, she thought, pulling the T-shirt over her head. It was enormous on her, the hem coming to midthigh. It was long enough for her to be decent without wearing underwear but there was no way that she was going commando. She couldn't even pull on the thong she wore last night since Ryan had, literally, ripped it off her. Sighing, she pulled up his boxers, rolling the waistband a couple of times until she was certain they wouldn't fall off her hips.

"Mornin'."

Jaci yelped and spun around, her mouth drying at the sight of a rumpled, unshaven Ryan standing in the doorway, dressed only in a faded pair of jeans, zipped but not buttoned. She was so used to seeing him impeccably, stylishly dressed that observing him looking like a scruffy cowboy had her womb buzzing. She started to bite her lip and abruptly stopped.

"Hi," she murmured, unable to keep the heat from flaring on her cheeks. She'd kissed those rock-hard abs, raked her fingers up those hard thighs, taken a nip of those thick biceps. And if he gave her one hint that he'd like her to do it again, she'd Flash Gordon herself to his side.

But Ryan kept his face impassive. "Coffee?"

"Yeah." Jaci made herself move toward the door and took the cup from his hand, being careful not to touch him. She took a grateful sip, sighed and met his eyes. His shoulder was against the door frame and he looked dark and serious, and she quickly realized that playtime was over. "I guess you want to talk?"

What about? Being engaged? Leroy? The script? The amazing sex they'd shared?

"Since we are the leading story in the entertainment world, I think that would be a very good idea." Ryan peeled himself from the door and walked down the hallway. Well, that answered that question. Good thing, because while she knew that she was old enough to have a one-night stand with her fake boyfriend, she doubted that she could talk about it. Jaci followed, trying but not succeeding at keeping her eyes off his tight, masculine butt.

"I have a million messages on my mobile and in my inbox, from reporters and friends, asking if it's true," Ryan said, heading across his living room to the luxurious open-plan kitchen. He grabbed the coffeepot and refilled a cup that had been sitting on the island in the center of the kitchen. Judging by the fact that the coffeepot was nearly empty, he'd been up for a while and this was his third or fourth cup.

Jaci took a sip from her own cup of coffee and wrinkled her nose at the bitter, dark taste. "What do you want to do? Deny or confirm?"

Ryan rested his bottom against the kitchen counter and pushed a hand through his hair. "I suppose that depends on your explanation on why you made such an asinine comment."

Jaci swallowed down her retort and another sip of coffee. Taking a seat on one of the stools that lined the breakfast bar, she put her cup on the granite surface and placed her chin in the palm of her hand. "I tried to explain last night."

"Last night there was only one thing I wanted from you and it wasn't an explanation." He waved his coffee cup. "Go."

Jaci rubbed her forehead with her fingertips in an effort to ease the headache that was gaining traction. Too much sex and not enough sleep. "Leroy hired a PI to investigate me, and you, by the way. He obviously found out about my broken engagement and was questioning how quickly I moved on."

Ryan's focus on her face didn't waver. "Okay. I presume that you had a very good reason for leaving the politician?"

"You still haven't done your own digging?" Jaci asked, surprised.

"I'm waiting for your version," Ryan replied. "Not important now... Go back to explaining how we got engaged."

"Right." Jaci sipped and sighed. "I asked Banks why me, what this was all about. I mean, this makes no sense to me... I'm nothing special. He said that it didn't matter why he wanted me, only that he always gets what he wants. That he's now using me to get a handle on you." Jaci ran a fingertip around the rim of her cup. "I thought that we needed to take me out of the equation, to remove me as a pawn. That can only happen if we break up or if he thinks that the relationship between us is more serious than he realized. So I thought that if I told him that we were thinking of marriage—thinking of, not that we were engaged—he'd back off."

Ryan shook his head. "Marriage, fidelity, faithfulness mean nothing to him. He's married to a sweet, sexy, lovely woman whom he treats like trash. You just handed him more ammunition to mess with me by suggesting we're that deeply involved. You poured blood into the water and the sharks are going to come and investigate."

Jaci looked bleak. "You mean the press."

"Yep. There's a reason why I keep a low profile, Jaci, and I've appeared more in the press since I've met you than in the last few years." Ryan banged his coffee cup as he placed it on the counter and rubbed the back of his neck. "They were relentless when Ben died, and I had so much else I was dealing with that the last thing I needed was to read the flat-out fiction they were printing in the papers. And the last thing I need right now is dealing with the press as I deal with Banks."

Jaci tilted her head. "And you smacked him down last night… Are you worried about the consequences? Think he might bail?"

Ryan lifted a powerful shoulder in an uneasy shrug. "We'll have to wait and see."

"Wait and see?" Jaci demanded, her face flushing. "Ryan, this is my career we're talking about, my big break. You might be able to afford to let this project go down the toilet but I can't. If I have any chance of being recognized as a serious scriptwriter, I need this film to be produced, I need it to be successful."

"I know that!" Ryan slapped his hands on his hips and scowled at her. "I don't want this project to fail, either, Jaci. I'll lose millions of my own money, money that I've paid into the development of this film. It'll take a good while for me to recover that money if I lose it."

"This is such a tangled mess," Jaci said in a low voice. She flipped him a look. "I shouldn't have kissed you. It was an impulsive gesture that has had huge consequences."

Ryan looked at her for a long time before replying. "Don't beat yourself up too much. I am also to blame. You didn't deepen that kiss, I did, and I told Leroy that you were my girlfriend."

"Okay, I'll happily let you accept most of the blame."

"*Some* of the blame. It wasn't my crazy idea to say that we were thinking of getting married." Ryan shook his head at her when she opened her mouth to argue. "Enough arguing, okay? I need sustenance."

Ryan walked over to the double-door, stainless steel fridge and yanked open a door and stared inside. "You're wrong, you know," he said, and Jaci had to strain to hear his words.

"Since I've been wrong so many times lately you're going to have to be more specific," Jaci told him.

"About not being special." Ryan slammed the door shut and turned around, slowly and unwillingly and, it had to be said, empty-handed. "You are the dream within the dream."

Jaci frowned. "Sorry?"

Ryan cleared his throat and she was amazed that this man, so confident in business and in bed, could look and sound this uneasy. "Banks has everything money can buy except he wants what money can't buy. Happiness, normality, love."

"But you've just said that he has a stunning, lovely wife—"

"Thea was a top supermodel and Banks knows that she is far too good for him." Ryan folded his arms and rocked on his heels. "Look, forget about it…"

Jaci shook her head, thinking that she needed to know where he was going with this. "Nope, your turn to spill. Are you telling me that I am more suited to Banks than his gorgeous, sweet, stunning wife?"

"Jesus, no!" Ryan looked horrified and he cursed. "But he knows that you are different from the women he normally runs into."

Oh, different, yay. Generally in her experience that meant less than. "Super," she said drily.

"Look, you're real."

"Real?" Jaci asked, confused.

"Yeah. Despite your almost aristocratic background, you seem to have your feet planted firmly on the ground. You aren't a gold digger or a slut or a party girl or a diva. You're as normal as it comes."

"Is normal higher up on the attractiveness ladder than real?" She just couldn't tell.

Ryan muttered a curse. "You are determined to misunderstand me. I'm just trying to explain why your openness, lack of bitchiness and overall genuineness is helluva attractive."

"Oh, so you *do* think that I am attractive?" Jaci muttered and heard Ryan's sharp intake of breath.

"No, of course not. I just made love to you all last night because I thought you were a troll." Ryan sent her one of those male looks that clearly stated he thought she was temporarily bat-lolly insane.

"Oh." Jaci felt heat creep across her face. She noticed him clenching and releasing his fists as if he were trying to stop himself from reaching for her. And in a flash she could feel the thump-thump-thump of her own heart, could hear the sound as clearly as she could read the desire in his eyes.

Ryan Jackson hadn't had nearly enough of her or, she had to admit, her of him. One more time, Jaci told herself, she could give herself the present of having, holding, feeling Ryan again. He wanted her, she wanted him, so what was the problem?

Career, Banks, sleeping with your boss? Jaci ignored the sensible angel on her shoulder and slid off her chair, her body heating from the inside out and her stomach and womb taking turns doing tumbles and backflips inside her body.

"One more time," she muttered as she stroked her hand up Ryan's chest to grip his neck and pull his mouth down to hers.

"Why do I suspect that's not going to be enough?" Ryan muttered, his lips a fraction from hers.

"It has to be. Shut up and kiss me," Jaci demanded, lifting herself up on her toes.

Ryan's lips curved against hers. "Just as long as we won't be married when we come up for air."

"Funny." Jaci just got the words out before Ryan took possession of her mouth, and then no words were needed.

Jaci, sitting in Ryan's office four days later, was struggling to keep her pretend-you-haven't-licked-me-there expression, especially now that their conversation had moved on from discussing the script changes he and Thom wanted. She hadn't seen Ryan since she left his apartment the morning after the ballet; he hadn't called, he hadn't texted.

And that was the way it should be, she told herself. What they'd shared was purely bedroom based. It meant nothing more than two adults succumbing to a primal desire that had driven mankind for millennia. He'd wanted her, she'd wanted—God, that was such a tame word for the need he'd aroused in her!—him and that was all it was.

Then why did she want to ask him why his eyes looked bleak? Why did she want to climb into his lap, place her face into his neck and tell him that it would all work out? She wanted to massage the knots out of his neck, smooth away the frown between his heavy brows, kiss away the bracket that appeared next to his mouth. He was off-the-charts stressed and it was all her fault.

She'd put his relationship with his investor on the line. It was amazing that she was still discussing script changes, that he hadn't fired her scrawny ass.

"Have you heard anything from Banks yet?" she demanded, pulling her gaze away from the view of the Hudson River.

Ryan looked startled at the sudden subject change. He exchanged a long look with Thom and after their silent communication, Thom stood up. "Actually..."

Thom lifted a hand and he ambled to the door. "You can explain. Later."

Jaci's eyebrows rose. "Explain what?"

Ryan tapped the nib of a pen on the pad of paper next to his laptop. "We've been invited to join a dinner on a luxury yacht tonight. The invitation came from Banks's office. Apparently Leroy's just bought himself an Ajello superyacht and this is its initial voyage. Lucky Leroy, those are only the best yachts in the world."

Jaci stood up and walked toward the floor-to-ceiling window, shoving her hands into the back pockets of her pants.

"I like your outfit," Ryan commented.

Jaci looked down at the deep brown leather leggings she'd teamed with a flowing white top and multiple strands of ethnic beads. It was nice to wear something other than black, she thought, and it made her feel warm and squirmy that Ryan approved. "I must be doing something right because a random man complimented my outfit in a coffee shop yesterday, as well."

"Honey, any man under dead would've noticed those stupendous legs under that flirty skirt." She saw the flare of heat in his eyes and looked down at her feet encased in knee-high leather boots. Damn but she really wanted to walk over to him and kiss him senseless. Her fingers tingled with the need to touch and her legs parted as if... Dear Lord, this was torture!

"I'm glad that the furor over our possible engagement

has died down," she said, trying to get her mind to stop remembering how fantastic Ryan looked naked.

"It was nothing that my PR firm couldn't handle," Ryan said, leaning back in his chair and placing his hands on his flat stomach. "As of the columns this morning, we're still seeing each other, but any talk of marriage is for the very distant future."

Jaci felt her shoulders drop and quickly pulled them up again. She had no reason to feel let down, no reason at all. She wasn't looking for a relationship, not even a pretend one. She'd been engaged, had talked incessantly about marriage—and what did she get out of that? Humiliation and hurt. Yeah, no thanks.

"As for Leroy's silence, you know what they say, no news is good news." Ryan picked up a file from his desk and flipped it open.

"Shouldn't you call him, say something, do something?" Jaci demanded, and his eyes rose at her vehement statement.

Ryan closed his file and leaned back in his chair. "It's a game, Jaci, and I'm playing it," he replied, linking his fingers on his stomach. Then his eyes narrowed. "You don't like the way I'm playing it?"

"I don't know the flipping rules!" Jaci snapped back. "And it's my future that's at stake, too. I have a lot to lose, but I can't do anything to move this along."

Ryan frowned at her outburst. "It's not the end of the world, Jace. Don't you and your siblings have a big trust fund that's at your disposal? It's not like you'll be out on the streets if this movie never gets produced. And you'll write other scripts, have other chances."

Could she tell him? Did she dare? She'd hinted at how important this was to her before, but maybe if he understood how crucial it really was, he'd understand why this situation was making her stress levels redline. And it wasn't as if he was a stranger; she had known him for years.

"This script means more to me than just a break into the industry, Ryan. It's more than that. It's more than my career or my future…" She saw him frown and wondered how she could explain the turbulent, churning emotions inside. "It's a symbol, a tipping point, a fork in the road."

She expected him to tell her to stop being melodramatic, but he just sat calmly and waited for her to continue. "You buying my script and offering me a job to work on *Blown Away* was—is—more than a career opportunity. It was the catalyst that propelled me into a whole new life." Jaci gestured to her notes on the desk. "That's all mine…my effort, my words, my script. This is something I did, without my parents' knowledge or without pulling any strings. It's the divide between who I was before and who I am now. God, I am so not explaining this well."

"Stop editing yourself and just talk, Jace."

"On one side of the divide, I was the Brookes-Lyon child who drifted from job to job, who played at writing, maybe to get her mother's attention. Then I became Clive's fiancée and an object of press attention and I had to grow a spine, fast. I couldn't have survived what I did without it. When I left London, I vowed that I wasn't going to fade into the background again."

"Yeah, you used to do that as a kid. Your family would take over and dominate a room, a conversation, yet you wouldn't contribute a thing." His mouth twitched. "Now you won't shut up."

"It's because I'm different in New York!" Jaci stated, her face animated. "I'm better here. Happier, feistier!"

"I like feisty." Ryan murmured his agreement in a low voice, heat in the long, hot glance he sent her.

It was so hard to ignore the desire in his voice. But she had to. "I don't want to go backward, Ry. If I lose this opportunity…"

Ryan frowned at her and leaned forward. "Jaci, what you do is not who you are. You can still be feisty without the job."

Could she be? She didn't think so; Sassy Jaci needed to be successful. If she wasn't then she'd just be acting. She didn't want to skate through her life anymore. She wanted to live and feel and be this new Jaci. She *liked* this new Jaci.

Ryan pinned her to the floor with his intense blue-gray stare. "Have a little faith, Jace. It will all work out."

But what if it didn't? Who would she be if she couldn't be New York Jaci? She didn't know if she could reinvent herself again. She saw Ryan looking over his desk, saw his hand moving toward the folder he'd discarded minutes before and read the silent message. It was time to go back to work, so she started for the door.

Ryan's phone rang and he lifted his finger to delay her. "Hang on a sec. We still need to talk about the yacht thing tonight."

Oh, bats, she'd forgotten about that. Jaci stopped next to his desk.

"Hey, Jax." The voice of Ryan's PA floated through the speakers of the phone. "Jaci's mother is on the phone and she sounds…determined. I think Jaci needs to take this."

"Sure, put her through."

Jaci shot up and pulled her hand across her throat in a

slashing motion. Dear Lord, the last person in the world she wanted to talk to was her mother. She still hadn't told them that she was working as a scriptwriter, that she was pseudo-dating Ryan...

"Morning, Priscilla."

Jaci glared at him and grabbed the pen out of his hand and scribbled across the writing pad in front of him. *I'm NOT here*; she underlined the *not* three times.

He cocked an eyebrow at her and quickly swung his right leg around the back of her knees to cage her between his legs. Jaci sent him her death-ray glare, knowing that she couldn't struggle without alerting her mother to her presence. As it was she was certain that Priscilla could hear her pounding heart and shaky breathing as she stood trapped between Ryan's legs.

"Ryan, darling boy." Priscilla's voice was as rich and aristocratic as ever. "How are you? It's been so long since we've seen you. I can't wait to see you at Neil's wedding next weekend."

Jaci slapped her hand against her forehead and stifled her gasp of horror. She'd forgotten all about Neil's blasted wedding. It was next weekend? Good Lord! How had that happened?

Jaci quickly drew a hanging man on the pad, complete with a bulging tongue, and she felt the rumble of laughter pass through Ryan as he exchanged genialities with her mother, quickly explaining that Jaci had just left his office. Ryan was talking about his duties as best man when she felt him grip the waistband of her pants and pull her down to sit on his hard thigh. Jaci sent him a startled look. Being this close was so damn tempting...

Oh, who was she kidding? Being in the same room as Ryan was too damn tempting. Jaci closed her eyes as his hand moved up her back and gripped the nape of her neck. His other hand briefly rested on her thigh before he pulled the pen from her hand and scribbled on the pad with his left hand. Huh, he was left-handed… She'd forgotten.

Jaci looked down at the pad, and it took a moment for her to decipher his scrawl. *Why don't you want to talk to your mother?*

"Yes, I have my suit and Neil told me, very clearly and very often, that he didn't want a stag party. He couldn't take the time away from work."

Jaci grabbed another pen from his container of stationery and scribbled her reply. *Because she doesn't know what I am doing in New York and that we're…you know.*

Why not? & what does "you know" mean? Sleeping together? Pretending to date?

Jaci kept half an ear on her mother's ramblings. After nearly thirty years of practice, she knew when she'd start slowing down, and they had at least a minute.

All of it, she replied. *She—they—just think that I'm licking my wounds. They don't take my work—*

Jaci stopped writing and stared at the page. Ryan tapped the page with the pen in a silent order for her to finish her sentence. She sent him a small smile and lifted her shoulders in an it-doesn't-matter shrug. Ryan's glare told her it did.

"Anyway, what on earth is this nonsense I'm reading in the press about you and Jaci?"

Ah, her mother was upset. Jaci, perfectly comfortable on Ryan's knee, sucked in her cheeks and stared at a point beyond Ryan's shoulder.

"What have you heard?" Ryan asked, his tone wary. The hand moved away from her neck to draw large, comforting circles on her back. Jaci felt herself relax with every pass of his hand.

"I have a list," Priscilla stated. Of course she did. Priscilla would want to make sure that she didn't forget anything. "Firstly, is she working as a scriptwriter for you?"

"She is."

"And you're paying her?" There was no missing the astonishment in her voice.

"I am." Jaci heard the bite in those two words as he drew three question marks on the pad.

Not serious writing, Jaci replied. Ryan's eyes narrowed at her response, and she felt her stomach heat at his annoyance at her statement. Nice to be appreciated.

"She's a very talented writer," Ryan added. "She must have got that from you."

Thanks, Jaci wrote as his words distracted her mother and she launched into a monologue about her latest book, set in fourteenth-century England. Jaci jumped when she felt his hand on the bare skin of her back. His fingers rubbed the bumps on her spine and Jaci felt lightning bolts dance where he touched her.

Concentrate! she wrote.

Can do two things at once. God, your skin is so soft. We're not doing this again!

And you smell so good.

"Anyway, I'm getting off the subject. Are you and Jaci engaged or not?" Priscilla demanded.

"Not," Ryan answered, his eyes on Jaci's mouth. She knew that he wanted to kiss her and, boy, it was difficult to resist the desire in his eyes, knowing the amount of pleasure he was capable of giving her.

"Good, because after that louse she was engaged to, she needs some time to regroup. *That stuffed cloak-bag*

of guts!" Ryan's eyebrows flew upward at Priscilla's ven-
omous statement. *Shakespeare*, Jaci scribbled. *Henry IV.*

"Jaci was far too good for him!" Jaci jerked her eyes
away from Ryan's to stare at the phone. Really? And why
couldn't her mother have told *her* this?

"That business with the Brazilian madam was just too
distasteful for words, and so stupid. Did he really think
he wouldn't get caught?"

Brazilian? Madam?

My ex liked a little tickle and a lot of slap.

Ryan stared down at the page before lifting his eyes
back to Jaci's rueful face. "Jesus," he muttered.

"I do hope that she got herself tested after all of that
but I can't ask her," Priscilla stated in a low voice. "We
don't have that type of relationship. And that's my fault."

Jaci's mouth fell open at that statement. Her mother
wished that they were closer? Seriously?

"And what's going on between you? Are you dating?
Is it serious? Are you sleeping together?" Priscilla demanded.

Jaci opened her mouth to tell her that it was none of
her damn business, but Ryan's hand was quicker and he
covered her mouth with his hand. She glowered at him
and tried to tug his hand away.

"It's complicated, Priscilla. I'm involved in a deal and,
bizarrely, I needed a girlfriend to help me secure it. Jaci
stepped up to the plate." Ryan kept his hand on her mouth.
"It's all pretend."

"Well, I'm looking at a photograph of the two of you
and it doesn't look like either of you are pretending to
me."

Ryan dropped his hand but not his eyes. "We're good
actors, it seems," he eventually replied.

"Huh. Well, I hope this mess gets sorted out soon," Priscilla said. "Not that I would mind if you and Jaci were involved. I have always liked you."

"Thank you," Ryan replied. "The sentiment is returned."

Such a suck-up, Jaci scribbled and gasped when his arm pulled her against his chest. Against her hip she could feel his hard erection, and she really couldn't help nestling her face into his neck and inhaling his scent. Damn, she could just drift away, right here, right now, in his arms.

"I must go. Take care of my baby, Ryan."

Ryan's arms tightened around Jaci and she sighed. "Will do, Priscilla."

"Bye, Ryan. Bye, my darling Jaci."

"Bye, Mom," Jaci replied lazily, the fingers of her left hand diving between the buttons of his dress shirt to feel his skin. Then her words sank in and she shot up and looked at Ryan in horror as the call disconnected.

"She knew that I was here. The witch!"

Ryan just laughed.

Eight

That evening, Leroy, too busy showing off his amazing yacht, ignored them, and Ryan was more than happy with that. He and Jaci stood at the back of the boat, where there was less of a crowd, and watched the city skyline transition from day to night. Dusk was a magical time of the day, Ryan thought, resting his forearms on the railing and letting his beer bottle dangle from his fingers over the Hudson River. It had the ability to soothe, to suggest that something bolder and brighter was waiting around the next corner. Or maybe that was the woman standing next to him.

Ryan stood up and looked at her. Tonight's dress was a frothy concoction with beads up top, no back and a full skirt that ended midthigh. He wanted to call it a light green but knew that if he had to ask Jaci to tell him what color it was she'd say that it was pistachio or sea foam or something ridiculous. Equally ridiculous was his desire to walk her down to one of the staterooms below deck and peel her out of it. His nights had been consumed with thoughts and dreams—awake and asleep—about her. He wanted her again, a hundred times more. He'd never—he ran his hand over his face—*craved* anyone before.

Ryan rubbed the back of his neck and was grateful that his heavy sigh was covered by the sound of the engine as it pushed the yacht and its fifty-plus guests through the water. Jaci had him tied up in every sailor knot imaginable. In his office this morning, it had taken every atom of his being to push her out of his lap so that he could get back to work. He was watching his multimillion-dollar deal swirling in the toilet bowl, Jaci's career—her big break and, crazily, her self-worth—was on the line, and all he could think about was when next he could get her into bed.

Despite wanting her as he wanted his next breath, he also wanted to go back to being the uncomplicated person he'd been before Jaci hurtled into his life. And it had been uncomplicated: he had an ongoing love–hate relationship with his dead brother, a hate–hate relationship with his father and, thanks to Kelly's lack of fidelity, a not-getting-involved attitude to women.

Simple, when you looked at it like that.

But Jaci made him feel stuff he didn't want to feel. She made him remember what his life had been like before Ben's death. He'd been so damn happy, so confident and so secure in the belief that all was right with his world. He'd accepted that his father was a hemorrhoid but that he could live with it; at the time his best mate was also his brother and he was engaged to the most beautiful girl in the world. He was starting to taste success…

And one evening it all disappeared. Without warning. And he learned that nothing lasted forever and no one stuck around for the long haul. It was just a truth of his life.

God, get a grip, Jackson. You sound like a whiny, bitchy teenager. Ryan turned his attention back to Jaci, who'd been content to stand quietly at his side, her shoulder pressed into his, her light perfume dancing on the breeze.

"So, whips and chains, huh?" It was so much easier to talk about Jaci's failures than his own.

Jaci sent him a startled look and when his words made sense, her expression turned rueful. "Well, I'm not so sure about the chains but there definitely were whips involved."

Dipstick, Ryan thought, placing his hand in the center of Jaci's back. She sent him a tentative smile but her expressive eyes told him that she'd been emotionally thrown under a bus. He nodded to a padded bench next to him and guided Jaci to it, ordering another glass of wine for Jaci and a whiskey for himself. Jaci sat down, crossed one slim leg over the other and stared at the delicate, silver high heel on her foot.

"Talk to me," Ryan gently commanded. He was incredibly surprised when she did just that.

"I was impressed by him and, I suppose, impressed by the idea that this rising-star politician—and he really was, Ryan—wanted to be with me. He's charismatic and charming and so very, very bright."

"He sounds like a lightbulb."

His quip didn't bring the smile to her face he'd hoped to see. "Did you love him?"

Jaci took a long time to answer. "I loved the fact that

he said that he loved me. That everyone seemed to adore him and, by extension, adored me. Up to and including my family."

Another of the 110 ways family can mess with your head, Ryan thought. It had been a long time since he'd interacted with the Brookes-Lyon clan but he remembered thinking that, while they were great individually, together they were a force of nature and pretty much unbearable. "My family loved him. He slid right on in. He was as smart and as driven as them, and my approval rating with them climbed a hundred points when I brought him home and then skyrocketed when I said yes to getting married."

The things we do for parental and familial approval, Ryan thought with an internal shake of his head. "But he wasn't the Prince Charming you thought he was."

Jaci lifted one shoulder in a shrug. "We got engaged and it was a big deal, the press went wild. He was a tabloid darling before but together with the fact that he was gaining political power, he became the one to watch. And they really watched him."

Ryan frowned, trying to keep up. "The press?"

"Yeah. And their doggedness paid off," Jaci said in a voice that was pitched low but threaded with embarrassment and pain. "He was photographed in a club chatting up a Brazilian blonde, looking very cozy. The photos were inappropriate but nothing that couldn't be explained away."

She pushed her bangs out of her eyes and sighed. "About two weeks after the photographs appeared, I was at his flat waiting for him to come home. I'd prepared this romantic supper, I'd really pulled out the stops. He was running late so I decided to work on some wedding plans while I waited. I needed to contact a band who'd play at the reception and I knew that Clive had the address in his contacts, so I opened up his email program."

Ryan, knowing what was coming, swore.

"Yep. There were about sixteen unread emails from a woman and every one had at least four photos attached." Jaci closed her eyes as the images danced across her brain. "They were explicit. She was known as the Mistress of Pain."

He winced.

Jaci stared across the river to the lights of Staten Island. When she spoke again, her words were rushed, as if she just wanted to tell her story and get it done. "I knew that this could blow up in our faces so I confronted Clive. We agreed that we would quietly, with as little fuss as possible, call it quits. Before we could, the story broke that he was seeing a dominatrix and the bomb blew up in our faces." Ryan lifted his eyebrows as Jaci flicked her fingers open, mimicking the action of a bomb detonating.

"Ouch."

"Luckily, a month later a crazy producer made me an offer to work in New York as a scriptwriter and I jumped at the chance to get the hell out of, well, hell."

"And you didn't tell your family that you had a job?"

"It's not like they would've heard me, and if they did, they wouldn't have taken it seriously. They'd think my writing is something I play at while I'm looking to find what I'm really going to do with the rest of my life."

Ryan heard the strains of a ballad coming from the band on the front deck and stood up. Pulling Jaci to her feet, he placed his hand on her hip and gripped her other hand and started to sway. She was in his arms, thank God. He rubbed his chin through her hair and bent his head so that his mouth was just above her ear. He thought about telling her how sorry he was that she'd been hurt, that she deserved none of it, how much he wanted to kiss her…everywhere. Instead, he gathered her closer by placing both his hands on her back and pulled her into him.

"For a bunch of highly intellectual people, your family is as dumb as a bag of ostrich feathers when it comes to you."

Jaci tipped her head and he saw appreciation shining in those deep, hypnotic eyes. "That's the nicest thing you've ever said to me."

He was definitely going to have to try harder, Ryan thought as he held her close and slowly danced her across the deck.

Leroy didn't bother to engage with them, Jaci thought, when they were back in the taxi and making their way from the luxury marina in Jersey City back to Manhattan. She wasn't sure whether that was a good or a bad thing.

She sighed, frustrated. "God, the business side of moviemaking gives me a headache."

"It gives me a freakin' migraine," Ryan muttered. "I've got about a two-week window and then I need to decide whether to pull the plug on the project or not."

Two weeks? That was all? Jaci, hearing the stress in Ryan's voice, twisted her ring around her finger. Who could magic that much money out of thin air in less than two weeks? This was all her fault; if she hadn't kissed him in that lobby, if she hadn't gone to that stupid party, if she hadn't moved to New York… It was one thing messing up her own life, but she'd caused so much trouble for Ryan, this hard-eyed and hard-bodied man who didn't deserve any of this.

"I'm so, so sorry." Jaci rested her head on the window and watched the buildings fly past. "This is all my fault."

Ryan didn't respond and Jaci felt the knife of guilt dig a little deeper, twist a little more. She thought about apologizing again and realized that repeating the sentiment didn't change the facts. She couldn't rewrite the past. All she could do was try to manage the present. But there was little—actually nothing—that she could do to unravel this convoluted mess, and she knew that Ryan would tie her to a bedpost if he thought that there was a minuscule chance of her complicating the situation any further.

Out of the corner of her eye she saw him dig his slim cell phone out of the inner pocket of his gray jacket. He squinted at the display. His long fingers flew across the keypad and she saw the corners of his mouth twitch, the hint of a smile passing across his face.

Ryan lifted his eyes to look at her. "Your brother just reamed me a new one for sleeping with you."

Jaci ignored the swoop of her stomach, pushed away the memory of the way Ryan's arms bulged as he held himself above her, the warmth of his eyes as he slid on home. "He thinks that we're sleeping together?"

"Yep," Ryan responded. "And if you check your cell, you'll probably find a couple messages from the rest of your family." Ryan placed a hand on her thigh, and her breath hitched as his fingers drew patterns on her bare skin. "Priscilla has a very big mouth."

"Oh, dear Lord God in heaven." Jaci resisted the desire to slap her mouth against his and made herself ignore the heat in his eyes, the passion that flared whenever they were breathing the same air. She grabbed her evening bag, pulled out her own phone and groaned at the five missed calls and the numerous messages on their family group chat.

Oh, this was bad, this was very bad.

Jaci touched the screen to bring up the messages.

Meredith: You have some explaining to do, sunshine.

Priscilla: Screenwriting? Really? Since when? Why don't you tell me anything?

Ryan moved up the seat so that his thigh was pressed against hers, and her shoulder jammed into his arm. She inhaled his scent and when heat dropped into her groin, she shifted in the seat. Ryan moved her phone so that he could see the screen.

Neil: Ryan? I was expecting you to have coffee with him, not an affair!

Meredith: Admittedly, anyone is better than the moron, but I don't think you should be jumping into a relationship this quickly!

Archie: Ryan? Who the hell is Ryan?

Neil: My Yank friend from uni, Dad.

Archie: The Hollywood one? The pretty boy?

Jaci rubbed her fingertips across her forehead. Damn, the Atlantic Ocean might be between them but her family still managed to exacerbate her headache. She looked at Ryan and shrugged. "Well, you *are* pretty."

Ryan dug an elbow into her side. "Your opinion on how I look is a lot more important than your father's," he said, his tone low and oozing sex.

Jaci deliberately lifted her nose in a haughty gesture, her eyes twinkling. "You'll do."

Ryan squeezed her thigh in response. "I suppose I asked for that." He nodded to the phone in her hands. "So, what are you going to tell them?"

Jaci tapped her finger against her lips. "The same

thing you told my mother—that it was a pretend thing, that we aren't in a relationship, that this isn't going anywhere." She turned her head to look out the window. "Basically the truth."

Ryan's finger and thumb gripped her chin and turned her face to look at him. Jaci stifled a sigh at his gorgeous eyes and gripped her phone with both hands to keep them from diving into his hair, from rubbing his neck, his shoulders. Her mouth wanted to touch his, her legs wanted to climb onto his lap…

Ryan looked at her mouth and she felt his fingers tighten on her chin. He was fighting the urge to kiss her, as well, she realized. His rational side was barely winning and that realization made her feel powerful and feminine and so wanted. She'd never felt this desired. No man had ever looked at her the way Ryan was looking at her right now, right here.

"Your family is thinking that we are sleeping together," Ryan stated, his thumb moving up from her chin to stroke her full bottom lip.

Well, that was obvious. She glanced at her phone in confusion. "Well, yeah."

"Not that I give a rat's ass what your family thinks, but…"

Jaci felt her breath stop somewhere on the way to her lungs. "But?"

"Screw this, we don't need to explain this or justify this or make excuses for this."

For what? Jaci frowned, confused. "What are you trying, very badly, to say, Ryan?"

"I want you. I want you in my bed. Screw the fact that you work for me and the film and all the rest of the craziness. I just want you. Come home with me, Jace. Be mine for as long as this madness continues."

Be his. Two words, two syllables, but so powerful. How was she supposed to be sensible, to back away, to resist? She wasn't an angel and she definitely wasn't a saint. Jaci quickly justified the decision she was about to make. He wanted her, she—desperately—wanted him. They were both single and this was about sex and passion and lust… No love was required. They weren't hurting anyone…

If you fall in love with him, you'll hurt yourself.

Then I won't fall in love with him, Jaci told herself. But a little part of her doubted that statement and she pulled back, wondering if she shouldn't just take a breath and get oxygen to her brain. *You've been hurt enough,* that same cautious inner voice told her. And Ryan would take what was left of her battered heart and drop-kick it to the moon.

"I can't get enough of you," Ryan muttered before slanting his mouth over hers and pushing his tongue between her parted lips. One swipe, another lick and all doubts were gone, all hesitation burned away by the heat of his mouth, the passion she tasted on her tongue. His arm pushed down between her back and the seat, and his other hand held her head in place so that he commanded the kiss. And command he did, and Jaci followed him into that special, magical place where time stood still.

Under his touch… This was where she felt alive, powerful, connected to the universe and sure of her place in it. When she kissed him she felt confident and desired and potent. Like the best version of herself. Ryan's mouth left hers and he feathered openmouthed kisses across her cheekbone, along her jaw, down her neck. Jaci shivered when he tasted the hollow of her collarbone.

"We've got to stop making out in cabs," Ryan murmured against her skin.

"We've got to stop making out, full stop," Jaci tartly replied.

"News flash, honey, that's probably not going to happen." Jaci felt Ryan's lips curve into a smile against her neck. The backs of his fingers brushed her breast as he straightened and moved away from her, his expression regretful. He looked past her and Jaci finally noticed that they were parked outside Ryan's swish apartment building.

"Come inside with me, please."

How could she resist the plea in his eyes, the smidgen of anxiety she heard in his voice? Did he really think that she was strong enough to say no, that she was wise enough to walk away from this situation, to keep this as uncomplicated as it could possibly be? Well, no chance of that. Her brain thought that she should stay in the cab and have the driver deliver her home, but the need to erase the distance between them, to feel every naked inch of him, was overpowering. She wanted Ryan, she needed him. She was going to take him and have him take her.

The morning and its problems could look after themselves. Tonight was hers. He was hers. Jaci opened the door and left the cab, teetering on her heels as she spun around and held out her hand to Ryan.

"Take me to bed, Ry."

Ryan enjoyed women; he liked their curves, their soft-feeling, smooth skin, the small, delicate sounds they made when his touch gave them pleasure. He loved the sweet-spicy taste of their skin, their pretty toes, the way their tantalizing softness complemented his hard, rougher body.

Yeah, he liked women, but he adored Jaci, he thought as he slowly pulled her panties down her hips. Naked at last. Ryan, minus his jacket and black tie, was still dressed and liking the contrast. He dropped the froth of lace to the floor and sat on the side of the bed, his hand stroking her long thigh, watching how her small nipples puckered when he looked at them. He'd had more than his share of women but none of them reacted to his look as if it was a touch. There had never been this arc of desire connecting them. He'd never felt a driving need to touch anyone the way he wanted to touch her.

It was both terrifying and amazingly wonderful.

"What are you thinking?" Jaci asked him, her voice low and sexy. Ryan usually hated that question, thought it was such an invasion of his privacy, but this time, and with this woman, he didn't mind.

"I'm thinking that you are absolutely perfect and that I'm desperate to touch you, taste you." Ryan was surprised to hear the tremble in his voice. This was just sex, he reminded himself. He was just getting caught up in the moment, imagining more than what was actually there.

Except that Jaci was naked, open to his gaze, her face soft and her eyes blazing with desire. And trust. He could do anything right now, suggest anything, and she'd probably acquiesce. She was that into him and he was that crazy about her.

Jaci sat up and placed an openmouthed kiss on his lips. He put his hand on the back of her head to hold her there as her fingers went to the buttons on his black-and-white-checked shirt, ripping one or two off in her haste to get her hands on his skin. Then her small hands, cool and clever, pushed the shirt off his shoulders and danced across his skin, over his nipples, down his chest to tug on the waistband of his pants. Her mouth lifted off his and he felt bereft, wanting—no, needing—more.

"Need you naked." Jaci tugged on his pants again.

He summoned up enough willpower to resist her, wanting to keep her naked while he explored her body. He'd had a plan and that was to torture Jaci with his tongue and hands, kissing and loving those secret places and making her scream at least twice before he slid on home...

He shrugged out of his shirt and removed his socks and shoes, but his pants were staying on because discovering Jaci, pleasing Jaci, was more important than a quick orgasm. It took all of his willpower to grab her hand and pull it from his dick. He gently gripped her wrists and pushed them behind her back, holding them there while he dropped his head to suck a nipple into his mouth. From somewhere above him Jaci whimpered and arched her back, pushing her nipple against the roof of his mouth. Releasing her hands, he pushed her back and spent some time alternating between the two, licking and blowing and sucking.

He could make her come by just doing this, he realized, slightly awed. But he wanted more for her, from her. Leaving her breasts, he trailed his mouth across her ribs, down her stomach, probed her cute belly button with his tongue. He licked the path on each side of her landing strip and, feeling her tense, dipped between her folds and touched her, tasted her, circling her little nub with the tip of his tongue.

It all happened at once. He slid his finger inside her hot

channel, Jaci screamed, his tongue swirled in response and then she was pulsing and clenching around his fingers, thrusting her hips in a silent demand for more. He sucked again, pushed again and she arched her back and hips and shattered, again and again.

Ryan pulled out and dropped a kiss on her stomach before hand-walking his way up the bed to look into her feverish eyes. "Good?" he asked, balancing himself on one hand, biceps bulging, to push her hair out of her eyes.

"So good." Jaci linked her hands around his neck, her face flushed with pleasure and...yeah, awe.

He'd made her scream, he'd pushed her to heights he was pretty sure—judging by the dazed, surprised look on her face—that she hadn't felt before. Mission so accomplished.

Jaci's hands skimmed down his neck, down his sides to grip his hips, her thumbs skating over his obliques before she clasped him in both hands. He jerked and sighed and pushed himself into her hands. "Let me in," he begged. Begged! He'd never begged in his life.

"Nah." Jaci smiled that feminine smile that told him that he was in deep, deep trouble. The best type of trouble. "My turn to drive you crazy."

He knew that he was toast when, in the middle of fantastic, mind-altering sex he realized that this wasn't just sex. It was sex on steroids and that happened to him only when he became emotionally attached. Well, that had to stop, immediately. Well, maybe after she'd driven him crazy.

Maybe then.

Nine

Sunlight danced behind the blinds in Ryan's room as Jaci forced her eyes open the next morning. She was lying, as was her habit, on her stomach, limbs sprawled across the bed. And she was naked, which was not her habit. Jaci squinted across the wide expanse that was Ryan's chest and realized that her knee was nestled up against a very delicate part of his anatomy and that her arm was lying across his hips, his happy-to-see-you morning erection pressing into her skin.

She gazed at his profile and noticed that he looked a lot younger when his face was softened by sleep and a night of spectacular sex. Spectacular sex… Jaci pulled in a breath and closed her eyes as second and third and tenth thoughts slammed into her brain.

Why was she still lying in bed with him in a tangle of limbs and postorgasmic haze? She was smart enough to know that she should've taken the many orgasms he'd given her last night, politely said thank you and high-tailed it out of his apartment with a breezy smile and a "see you around." She shouldn't have allowed him to wrap his big arm around her waist or to haul her into a spooning position, her bottom perfectly nestled in his hips. She shouldn't have allowed herself to drift, sated and secure, feeling his nose in her hair, reveling in the soft kisses he placed on her shoulders, into her neck. She shouldn't have allowed herself the pleasure of fall-ing asleep in his arms.

Straight sex, uncomplicated sex, wham-bam sex she could handle; she knew what that was and how to deal with it. It was the optional extras that sent her into a spi-ral. The hand drifting over her hip, his foot caressing her calf, his thick biceps a pillow under her head. His easy affection scared the pants off her—well, they would if she were wearing any—and generated thoughts of *what if* and *I could get used to this*.

This wouldn't do, Jaci told herself, and gently—and reluctantly—removed her limbs from his body. Nothing had changed between them. They had just shared a physi-cal experience they'd both enjoyed. She was not going to get too anal about this. She wasn't going to overthink this. This was just sex, and it had nothing to do with the fact that they were boss and employee or even that they were becoming friends.

Sex was sex. Not to be confused with affection or car-ing or emotion or, God forbid, love. She'd learned that lesson and, by God, she'd learned it well. Jaci slipped out of bed, looking around for something to wear. Un-able to bear the thought of slipping into her dress from the night before—she'd be experiencing another walk of

shame through Ryan's apartment lobby soon enough—
she picked up his shirt from the night before and pulled
it over her head, grimacing as the cuffs fell a foot over
her hands. She was such a cliché, she thought, roughly
rolling back the fabric. The good girl in the bad boy's
bedroom, wearing his shirt...

After checking that Ryan was still asleep, Jaci rolled
her shoulders and looked around Ryan's room, taking in
the details she'd missed before. The bed, with its leather
headboard, dominated the room and complemented the
other two pieces of furniture: a black wing-back chair
and four-drawer credenza with a large mirror above it.
Jaci tipped her head as she noticed that there were photograph frames on the credenza but they were all facedown
and looked as if they'd been that way for a while. Curious, she padded across the room, past the half-open door
that led to a walk-in closet, and stood in front of the credenza. Her reflection in the mirror caused her to wince.
Her hair was a mess. She had flecks of mascara on her
eyelids, and on her jaw she could see red splotches from
Ryan rubbing his stubble-covered chin across her skin.
Her eyes were baggy and her face was pale with fatigue.

The morning after the night before, she thought,
rubbing her thumb over her eyes to remove the mascara. When the mascara refused to budge, she shrugged
and turned her attention back to the frames. Silver, she
thought, and a matching set. She lifted the first one up
and her breath caught in her throat as the golden image
of Ben, bubbling with life, grinned back at her. He looked
as if he was ready to step out of the frame, handsome and
sexy and so, well, alive. Hard to believe that he was gone,
Jaci thought. And if she found it hard, then his brother
would find it impossible, and she understood why Ryan

wouldn't want to be slapped in the face with the image of Ben, who was no more real than fairy dust.

And photograph number two? Jaci lifted up the frame and turned it over, then puzzled at the image of a dark-haired, dark-eyed woman who looked vaguely familiar. Who was this and why did she warrant being in an ornate, antique silver frame? She couldn't be Ryan's mother. This was a twenty-first-century woman through and through. Was she one of Ryan's previous lovers, possibly one who got away? But Ryan, according to the press, didn't have long-term relationships and she couldn't imagine that he'd keep a photo of a woman he'd had a brief affair with. Jaci felt the acid burn of jealously and wished she could will it away. You had to care about someone to be jealous and she didn't want to care about Ryan…not like that, anyway.

Jaci replaced the frame and when she looked at her reflection in the mirror, she saw that Ryan was standing behind her and that a curtain had fallen within his fabulous eyes. Her affectionate lover was gone.

"Don't bother asking," Ryan told her in a low, determined voice. He was as naked as a jaybird but his emotions were fully concealed. He might as well have been wearing a full suit of armor, Jaci thought. She couldn't help feeling hurt at his back-off expression; she found it so easy to talk to him but he, obviously, didn't feel the same.

Maybe she'd read this situation wrong; maybe they weren't even friends. Maybe the benefits they'd shared were exactly that, just benefits. The thought made her feel a little sad. And, surprisingly, deeply annoyed. How dare he make incredible, tender-but-hot love to her all night and then freeze her out before she'd even said good-morning?

The old Jaci, Lyon House Jaci, would just put her tail between her legs, scramble into her dress and apologize for upsetting him. New York Jaci had no intention of doing the same.

"That's it?" she demanded, hands on her hips. "That's all you're going to say?"

Ryan pushed a hand through his dark hair and Jaci couldn't miss his look of frustration. "I am not starting off the morning by having a discussion about her."

"Who is she?" Jaci demanded.

Ryan narrowed his eyes at her. "What part of 'not discussing this' didn't you hear?" He reached for a pair of jeans that draped across the back of his chair and pulled them on.

Jaci matched his frown with one of her own. "So it's okay for you to get me to spill my guts about my waste-of-space ex and his infidelities but you can't even open up enough to tell me who she is and why she's on your dresser?"

"Yes."

Jaci blinked at him.

"Yes, it's okay for you to do that and me not to," Ryan retorted. "I didn't torture you into telling me. It was your choice. Not telling you is mine."

Jaci pressed the ball of her hands to her temples. How had her almost perfect night morphed into something so… She wanted to say *ugly* but that wasn't the right word. Awkward? Unsettling? Uncomfortable? She desperately wanted to argue with him, to insist that they were friends, that he owed her an explanation, but she knew that he was right; it was his choice and he owed her

nothing. He'd given her physical pleasure but there had
been no promises to give her his trust, to let her breach
his emotional walls. His past was his past, the girl in the
photograph his business.

If his reluctance to talk, to confide in her, made her
feel as if she was just another warm body for him to play
with during the night, then that was her problem, not
his. She would not be that demanding, insecure, irritat-
ing woman who'd push and pry and look to him to give
more than he wanted to.

He'd wanted sex. He'd received sex and quite a lot of
it. It had been fun, a physical release, and it was way past
time for her to leave. Jaci dropped her eyes from his hard
face, nodded quickly and managed to dredge up a cool
smile and an even cooler tone. "Of course. Excuse me, I
didn't mean to pry." She walked across the room, picked
up her dress and her shoes, and gestured to the door to
the en suite bathroom. "If I may?"

Ryan rubbed the back of his neck and sent her a hot
look. "Don't use that snotty tone of voice with me. Just
use the damn bathroom, Jace."

Hell, she just couldn't say the right thing this morning, Jaci thought. It was better if she just said nothing
at all. Jaci walked toward the bathroom without looking
at him again, silently cursing herself and calling herself
all kinds of a fool.

Stupid, stupid, stupid. She should've left last night
and avoided this morning-after-the-night-before awk-
wardness.

Lesson learned.

Stupid, stupid, stupid.

Ryan gripped the edge of the credenza with white-knuckled hands and straightened his arms, dropping his head to stare at the wooden floor beneath his bare feet. *You handled that with all the sophistication of a pot plant, moron.* She'd asked a simple question to which there was a simple answer.

Who is she?

There were many answers to that, some simple, some a great deal more complicated. *She was someone who was, once, important to me.* Or… *She was an ex-girlfriend.* Or that, *She was my fiancée.* Or, if he really wanted to stir up a hornets' nest, he could've said that she was Ben's lover.

All truth.

What a complete mess of the morning, Ryan thought, straightening. He stepped over to the window and yanked up the blind and looked down onto the greenery of Central Park in spring. It was a view he never failed to enjoy, but this morning he couldn't even do that, his thoughts too full of the woman—who was probably naked—in the next room.

Instead of slipping out of bed and getting dressed long before his lover woke up, this morning he'd opened his eyes on a cloud of contentment and had instinctively rolled over to pull her back into his arms. The empty space had been a shock to his system, a metaphorical bucket of icy water that instantly shriveled his morning erection. She'd left him, he'd thought, and the wave of disappointment that followed was even more of a shock. He did the leaving, he was in control, and the fact that he was scrambling to find his mental equilibrium floored him. He didn't like it.

At all.

He'd long ago perfected his morning-after routine, but nothing with Jaci was the same as those mindless, almost faceless encounters in his past. Last night had been the most intense sexual experience of his life to date and he hated that she'd had such an effect on him. He wanted to treat her like all those other encounters but he couldn't. She made him want things that he'd convinced himself he had no need for, things such as trust and comfort and support. She made him feel everything too intensely, made him question whether it was time to remove the barbed wire he'd wrapped his heart in.

Seeing her holding Kelly's photograph made him angry and, worse, confused. There was a damn good reason why he kept their photographs in a prominent place. Seeing them there every morning, even facedown, was like being flogged with a leather strap, but after the initial flash of pain, it was a good and solid reminder of why he chose to live his life the way he did. People couldn't be trusted; especially the people who were supposed to love you the most.

Yet a part of him insisted that Jaci was not another Kelly, that she'd never mangle his heart as she'd done, but then his common sense took over and reminded him that he couldn't take the chance. Love and trust—he'd never run the risk of having either of those emotions thrown back at him as if they meant nothing.

They meant something to him and he'd never risk them again.

It was better this way, Ryan told himself, sliding a glance toward the still-closed bathroom door. It was better that he and Jaci put some distance between them, allowed some time to dilute the crazy passion that swirled between them whenever they were alone. Because passion had a sneaky way of making you want more, tempting you to risk more than was healthy.

No, they needed that distance, and the sooner the better. Ryan walked into his closet, grabbed a T-shirt and shoved his feet into a pair of battered athletic shoes. He raked his hands through his hair, walked back into his bedroom and picked up his wallet from the credenza, in front of the now-upright photo of Ben.

"Hey, Jaci?" Ryan waited for her response before speaking again in an almost jovial voice. God, the last thing in the world he felt was jovial. He felt horny, and frustrated and a little sick, but not jovial. "I'm running out for bagels and coffee. I'll be back in ten."

He already knew how she'd respond and she didn't disappoint. "I won't be here when you get back. I've got a…thing."

She didn't have a thing any more than he wanted bagels and coffee but it was an out and he'd take it. "Okay. Later."

Later? Ryan saw that his hand was heading for the doorknob and he ruthlessly jerked it back. He was not going in there. If he saw Jaci again he'd want to take her to bed and that would lead to more confusing…well, feelings, and he didn't need this touchy-feely crap.

Keep telling yourself that, Jackson. Maybe you'll start to believe it sometime soon.

It was spring and the sprawling gardens at Lyon House, Shropshire, had never looked so beautiful with beds of daffodils and bluebells nodding in the temperate breeze. At the far edge of the lawn, behind the wedding tent, it looked as if a gardener had taken a sponge and dabbed the landscape with colored splotches of rhododendron and azalea bushes, a mishmash of brilliant color that hurt the eyes.

It was beautiful, it was home.

And she was miserable.

Sitting in the chapel that had stood for centuries adjacent to Lyon House, Jaci rolled her head to work out the kinks in her neck. If she looked out the tiny window to her left, she could see the copse of trees that separated the house from the chapel, and beyond that the enormous white designer fairy-tale tent—with its own dance floor—that occupied most of the back lawn. It was fairly close to what she'd planned for her own wedding, which had been scheduled for six weeks from now. Like the bride, she would've dressed at Lyon House, in her old room, and her mother would've bossed everyone about as she had been doing all day. The grounds would have been as spectacular, and she would've had as many guests. Like Neil, her groom would've been expectant, nervous, excited.

Her only thought about her canceled wedding was that she'd dodged a bullet. And then she'd run to the States, where she'd fallen into the flight path of a freakin' bazooka. Jaci blew her frustration out and sneaked another look at Ryan. So far she'd spent a lot of the ceremony admiring his broad shoulders, tight butt and long legs, and remembering what he looked like naked. Jaci wiggled in her seat, realizing that it was very inappropriate to be thinking of a naked man in a sixteenth-century English church. Or, come to think of it, *any* church, for that matter...

Jaci crossed her legs and thought that she should be used to seeing him in a tuxedo, but today he looked better than he had any right to. The ice-blue tie turned his eyes the same color and she noticed that he'd recently had his hair trimmed. He'd spent the week avoiding her since their—what could she call it?—*encounter* in LA, and while her brain thought that some time apart was a wonderful idea, every other organ she possessed missed him. To a ridiculous degree. She sighed and sent another longing look at his profile. So sexy, and when he snapped his head around and caught her looking, she flushed.

No phone call. No email. No text. Nothing, she reminded herself. It was horrifying to realize that if he so much as crooked his baby finger she'd kick off her shoes, scramble over the seats and, bridal couple be damned, fly into his arms.

She wanted him. She didn't want to want him.

A slim arm wrapping around her waist had her turning, and she sighed at the familiar perfume. Meredith, her big sister, with her jet-black, geometric bob, red lipstick and almost oriental eyes looked sharp and sleekly sexy in a black sheath that looked as if it had been painted on her skinny frame. Twelve-year-olds had thighs fatter than hers, Jaci thought.

Merry gave her shoulders a squeeze. "Hey, are you okay?"

Jaci lifted one shoulder. How should she answer that? *No, my life is an even bigger mess now than it was when I left. I might not have a job soon and I think I might be in love with my fake boyfriend, who has the communication skills of a clam. That's the same fake boyfriend who left New York the morning after a night of marvelous sex. The same one whom I haven't spoken to or had an email or a text or a smoke signal from.*

Not that she was sure she wanted to talk to the moronic, standoffish, distant man who used a stupid excuse to run out of his apartment as quickly as he could. As if he could fool her with that bagels-and-coffee comment.

After Clive she had a master's degree in the subject of crap-men-say.

Merry spoke in her ear. "So...you and Ryan."

"There is no me and Ryan," Jaci retorted, her voice a low whisper.

Merry looked at Ryan and licked her lips. "He is a *babe*, I have to admit. Mum thinks you're having a thing."

"The supposed relationship between us has been wildly exaggerated." Nobody could call a few hot nights a relationship, could they?

"Come on, tell me." Meredith jammed an elbow in her ribs.

The elderly aunt on her other side nudged her in the ribs. "Shh! The reverend is trying to give his sermon!"

"And I'm trying not to fall asleep." Merry yawned.

Ryan shifted his position and subtly turned so that he was practically facing her and she felt his eyes, like gentle fingers, trace her features, skim her cheekbones, her lower lips, down to her mouth. When his eyes dropped to look at her chest, her nipples responded by puckering against the fabric of her dress. The corners of Ryan's mouth lifted in response and she flamed again. Traitorous body, she silently cursed, folding her arms across her chest and narrowing her eyes.

"Some of your attention should be on your brother," Merry said out of the side of her mouth. "You know, the guy who is getting married to the girl in the white dress?"

"Can't help it, he drives me batty," Jaci replied, sotto voce. "He's arrogant and annoying and...annoying. The situation between us is...complicated."

"Complicated or not he is, holy bananas, *so* sexy."

Priscilla, on the bench in front of them, spun around in her seat and sent them her evil-mother laser glare. Her purple fascinator bounced and she slapped a feather out of her eye. Her voice, slightly quieter than a foghorn, boomed through the church. "Will you two please be quiet or must I put you outside?"

If Jaci hadn't been so embarrassed she might have been amused to see her ever-cool and unflappable world-class-journalist sister slide down in her seat and place her hand over her eyes.

Ten

The band was playing those long, slow songs that bands played for the diehard guests who couldn't tear themselves away from the free booze or the dance floor or, as was Merry's case, the company of a cousin of the bride. Her sister looked animated and excited, Jaci thought, watching them from her seat at a corner table, now deserted. She hoped that the man wasn't married or gay or a jerk. Her sister deserved to have some fun, deserved a good man in her life. Always so serious and so driven, it would be good for her to have someone in her life who provided her with some balance. And some hot sex. You couldn't go wrong with some hot sex.

Well, you could if you were on the precipice of falling in love with the man who, up to a couple of days ago, had provided you with some very excellent sex. Jaci closed her eyes and rested her temple against her fist. She couldn't be that stupid to be falling in love with Ryan, could she? Maybe she was just confusing liking with love. Maybe she was confused because he made her feel so amazing in bed.

If so, why did she miss him so intensely when he wasn't with her? Why did she think about him constantly? Why did she wish that she could provide him with the emotional support he gave to her by just standing at her side and breathing? Why did she want to make his life better, brighter, happier? She couldn't blame that on sexual attraction or even on friendship.

Nope, she was on the verge of yanking her heart out and handing it over to him. And if she did that, she knew that if he refused to take it, which he would because Ryan didn't do commitment in any shape or form, it would be forever mangled and never quite the same. She had to pull back, had to protect herself. Hadn't her heart and her confidence and her psyche endured enough of a battering lately? Why would she want to torture herself some more?

A strong, tanned hand placed a cup full of hot coffee in front of her and she looked up into Ryan's eyes. "You look like you need that," he said, taking the chair next to her and flipping it so that he faced her, his long legs stretched out in front of him.

"Thanks. I thought you were avoiding me."

"Trying to." Ryan sent her a brooding look before looking at his watch. "I managed it for six hours but I'm caving."

Jaci lifted her eyebrows. "That's eight days and six hours. I heard you went to LA."

Ryan glowered at her. "Yeah. Waste of a trip since I spent most of my time thinking of you. Naked."

Lust, desire, need swirled between them. How was she supposed to respond to that? Should she tell him that she'd spent less time writing and more time fantasizing? *He's still your boss*, she reminded herself. Maybe she should keep that to herself.

"I've spent most of the evening watching you talk to your ex." Ryan frowned.

Now, that was an exaggeration. She'd spoken to Clive, sure, but not for that long and not for the whole evening.

"You're not seriously considering giving him another chance, are you?" Ryan demanded, his eyes and voice hot.

No calls, no text messages, no emails and now stupid questions. Jaci sighed. Going back to Clive after being with Ryan would be like living in a tiny tent after occupying a mansion. In other words, completely horrible. But because he'd been such a moron lately, she was disinclined to give him the assurance his question seemed to demand. Or was she just imagining the thread of concern she heard in his voice?

That was highly possible.

"Talk to me, Jace," Ryan said when she didn't answer him.

Jaci's lips pressed together. "You're joking, right? Do you honestly think that you can sleep with me and then freeze me out when I ask a personal question? Do you really think it's okay for you not to call me, to avoid me for the best part of a week?"

Ryan released a curse and rubbed the back of his neck. "I'm sorry about that."

Jaci didn't buy his apology. "Sure you are. But I bet that if I suggest that we go back to your B and B you'd be all over that idea."

"Of course I would be. I'm a man and you're the best sex I've ever had." Jaci widened her eyes at his statement. The best sex? Ever? *Really?*

"Dammit, Jace, you tie me up in knots." Ryan tipped his head back to look at the ceiling of the tent. The main lights had been turned out and only flickering fairy lights illuminated the tent, casting dancing shadows on his tired face. What was she supposed to say to that? *Sorry that I've complicated your life? Sorry that I'm the best sex you've ever had?*

She'd apologized for too many things in her life, many of them that weren't her fault, but she would be damned if she was going to apologize to Ryan. Not about this. She liked the fact that she, at least, had some effect on the man. So Jaci just crossed her legs and didn't bother to adjust her dress when the fabric parted and exposed her knee and a good portion of her thigh. She watched Ryan's eyes drop to her legs, saw the tension that skittered through his body and the way his Adam's apple bobbed in his throat.

Another knot, she thought. Good, let him feel all crazy for a change.

Instead of touching her as she expected, Ryan sat up, took a sip of her coffee and, after putting her cup back in its saucer, tapped his finger on the white damask tablecloth. "I'm not good at sharing my thoughts, at talking."

That didn't warrant a response, so Jaci just looked at him.

"I have a messed-up relationship with my family, both dead and alive." Ryan stared off into the distance. "My mother is dead, my father is a stranger to me, someone who always put his needs above those of his kids. I'm not looking for sympathy, I'm just telling you how it was."

Ryan stopped talking and hauled in another breath. It took a moment for his words to sink in, to realize that he was talking to her. Jaci's heart stopped momentarily and then it started to pound. He was *talking* to her? For real?

"I don't talk to people because I don't want them getting that deep into my head," Ryan admitted with a lot of reluctance. He closed his eyes momentarily before speaking again. "That girl in the picture? Well, she died in the same car accident as Ben."

"Ben's fiancée? I'm sorry but I don't remember her name." And why did he have a photograph of Ben's fiancée in his bedroom? Facedown, but still…

"Kelly. Everyone thought that she was engaged to Ben because she was wearing an engagement ring," Ryan said, but something in his voice had Jaci leaning forward, trying to look into his eyes. Judging by his hard expression, and by the muscle jumping in his cheek, talking about Ben and this woman was intensely difficult for Ryan. Of course, they were talking about his brother's death. It had to be hard, but there was more to this story than she was aware of.

Ryan stared at the ground between his knees and pulled in a huge breath, and Jaci was quite sure that he wasn't aware that his hand moved across the table to link with hers. "Kelly wasn't Ben's fiancée, she was mine."

Jaci tangled her fingers in his and held on. "What?"

Ryan lifted his head and dredged up a smile but his eyes remained bleak. "Yeah, we'd got engaged two weeks earlier."

Jaci struggled to make sense of what he was saying. "But the press confirmed that they had spent a romantic weekend together." Jaci swore softly when she realized what he was trying to tell her. "She was *cheating.*

On you." She lifted her hand to her mouth, aghast. "Oh, Ryan!"

How horrible was that? Jaci felt her stomach bubble, felt the bile in the back of her throat. His fiancée and his brother were having an affair and he found out when they both died in a car crash? That was like pouring nitric acid into a throat wound. How…how…how dare they?

How did anyone deal with that, deal with losing two people you loved and finding out they were having an affair behind your back? What were you supposed to feel? Do? Act? God, no wonder Ryan had such massive trust issues.

Fury followed horror. Who slept with her fiancé's brother, who slept with their brother's fiancée? *Who did that?* She was so angry she could spit radioactive spiders. "I am so mad right now," was all she could say.

The corners of Ryan's mouth lifted and his eyes lightened a fraction. "It was a long time ago, honey." He removed his fingers from her grasp and flexed his hand. "Ow."

"Sorry, but that disloyalty, that amount of selfishness—"

Ryan placed the tips of his fingers on her mouth to stop her talking. Jaci sighed and yanked her words back. It didn't matter how angry she was on his behalf, how protective she was feeling, the last thing he needed was for her to go all psycho on him. Especially since Ben and Kelly had paid the ultimate price.

"Sorry, Ry," she muttered around his fingers.

"Yeah. Me, too." Ryan dropped his hand. "I never talk about it—nobody but me knows. Kelly wanted to keep the engagement secret—"

"Probably because she was boinking your brother."

"Thank you, I hadn't realized that myself," Ryan said, his voice bone-dry.

Jaci winced. "Sorry." It seemed as if it was her go-to phrase tonight.

"Anyway, you're the first person I've told. Ever." Ryan shoved his hand through his hair. "You asked who she was and I wanted to tell you, but I *didn't* want to tell you and it all just got too…"

Jaci waited a beat before suggesting a word. "Real?"

Ryan nodded. "Yeah. If I explained, I couldn't keep pretending that we were just…friends."

What did that mean? Were they more than friends now? Was he also feeling something deeper than passion and attraction, something that could blossom and grow into…something deeper? Jaci wished she had the guts to ask him, but a part of her didn't want to risk hearing his answer. It might not be what she was looking for or even wanting. Her heart was in her hands and she was mentally begging him to take it, to keep it. But she wanted him to keep it safe and she wasn't sure that he would.

Ryan closed his eyes and rubbed his eyelids with his thumb and forefinger. "God, I'm tired."

"Then go back to the B and B," Jaci suggested.

"Will you come with me?"

Jaci cocked her head in thought. She could but if she did she knew that she would have no more defenses against him, that she would give him everything she had, and she knew that she couldn't afford to do that. And, despite the fact that he'd opened up, he wasn't anywhere near being in love with her and he didn't want what she did. Oh, she was in love with him. He had most of her heart, but she was keeping a little piece of that organ back, and all of her soul, because she needed them to carry on, to survive when he left.

Because he would leave. This was her life, not a fairy tale.

He stood up and held out his hand. "Jace? You coming?"

"Sorry, Ry."

Ryan frowned at her and looked across the room to where Clive stood, watching them. Watching *her*. Creepy. "You've got something better to do?" Ryan demanded, his eyes dark with jealously.

"Oh, Ryan, you are such an idiot!" she murmured.

She was tempted to go with him, of course she was. Despite his opening up and letting her a little way in, they weren't in a committed relationship, and the more she slept with him the deeper in love she would fall. She had to be sensible, had to keep some distance. But she didn't want to make light of the fact that he'd confided in her and that she appreciated his gesture, so Jaci reached up and touched her lips to his cheek. Then she held her cheek against his, keeping her eyes closed as she inhaled his intoxicating smell. "Thank you for telling me, Ry."

The tips of Ryan's fingers dug into her hips. He rested his forehead on hers and sighed heavily. "You drive me nuts."

Jaci allowed a small laugh to escape. "Right back at you, bud. Are you coming to the family breakfast in the morning?"

"Yeah." Ryan kissed her nose before stepping back. He tossed a warning glance in Clive's direction. "Don't let him snow you, Jace. He's a politician and by all reports he's a good one."

"So?"

"So, don't let him con you," Ryan replied impatiently. "He cheated on you and lied to you and treated you badly. Don't get sucked back in."

Jaci looked at him, astounded. She wasn't a child and she wasn't an idiot and she knew, better than anybody, what a jerk Clive was. Did she come across that naive, that silly, that in need of protection? She was a grown woman and she knew her own mind. She wasn't the weak-willed, wafty, soft person Ryan and her family saw her as. Sometimes she wondered if anyone would ever notice that she'd grown up, that she was bigger, stronger, bolder. Would they ever see her as she was now? Would anyone ever really know her?

She didn't need a prince or a knight to run to her rescue anymore.

She'd slay her own dragons, thank you very much, and she'd look after herself while she did it.

The next morning Jaci, her mother and Merry sat on the terrace and watched as the people from the catering company dismantled the tent and cleared up the wedding detritus. When Ryan got there they would haul Archie out of his study and they'd rustle up some breakfast. The bride and groom would arrive when they did—they weren't going to wait for them—but for now she was happy to sit on the terrace in the spring sunshine.

"One down, two to go," Priscilla stated without looking up. Her mother, wearing an enormous floppy hat, sat next to her, a rough draft of her newest manuscript in her hands.

"Don't look at me," Merry categorically stated, placing her bare feet on the arm of Jaci's chair.

"It should've been my marriage next," Jaci quietly stated.

"Speaking of," Merry said, "I saw you talking to Clive last night. You looked very civilized. Why weren't you slapping his face and scratching his eyes out?"

Jaci rested her cup of coffee on her knee. "Because I don't care about him anymore. He's coming here today. I stored some things of his in my room that he needs to collect." Jaci pushed her sunglasses up her nose. "Once that's done I'll be free of him, forever."

Merry snorted her disbelief and Jaci wanted to tell her that it was true because she was in love with Ryan, but that was too new, too precious to share.

"So what did you talk about?" Merry asked. "Your relationship?"

"A little. He was very apologetic and sweet about it. He groveled a bit and that was nice."

"I don't buy it," Merry stated, her eyes narrowed. "Clive isn't the type to grovel."

Merry was so damn cynical sometimes, Jaci thought. "Look, he tried to talk me into trying again but I told him about New York, about everything that happened there and how happy I was. He eventually gave up and said that he understood. He wished me well and we parted on good terms."

"Clive doesn't like hearing the word *no*," Merry stated, her lips in a thin line. "I don't trust him. Be careful of him."

Merry really was overreacting, thought Jaci, bored with talking about her ex.

"And Ryan?" Merry asked.

Ryan? Jaci rested her head on the back of her chair. "I don't know, Merry. He has his own issues to work through.

I don't know if we will ever be anything more than just friends."

"He doesn't look at you like you're just friends," Merry said.

"That's just because we are really good in bed together," Jaci retorted, and sent her mother a guilty look. "Sorry, Mum."

"I know you had sex with him, child," Priscilla drily replied. "I'm not that much of a prude or that oblivious. I have had, and for your information, still do have, a sex life."

"God." Jaci placed her hand over her eyes and Merry groaned. "Thanks for putting that thought into my head. Eeew. Anyway, coming back to Ryan…he's a closed book in so many ways. I take one step forward with him and sixty back. I thought we took a couple of steps forward last night."

"I thought you said that things are casual between you," Merry said.

"They are." Jaci tugged at the ragged hem of her denim shorts. "Sort of. As I said, I think we turned a corner last night but, knowing me, I might be reading the situation wrong." She pulled her earlobe. "I tend to do that with men. I'm pretty stupid when it comes to relationships."

"We all are, in one way or another," Merry told her.

"Yeah, but I tend to take stupidity to new heights," Jaci replied, tipping her face up to the sun. She'd kissed Ryan impulsively, agreed to be his pretend girlfriend, slept with him and then fell in love with him. *Stupid* didn't even begin to cover it.

Well, she'd made those choices and now she had to live the consequences…

Jaci jerked when she heard the slap of paper hitting

the stone floor and she winced when the wind picked up her mother's manuscript and blew sheets across the terrace. Before her mother could get hysterical about losing her work, Jaci jumped up to retrieve the pages, but Priscilla's whip-crack voice stopped her instantly. "Sit down, Jacqueline!"

"But...your papers." Jaci protested.

"Leave them," Priscilla ordered and Jaci frowned. Who was this person and what had she done with her mother? The Priscilla Jaci knew would be having six kittens and a couple of ducks by now at the thought of losing her work.

Priscilla yanked off her hat and shoved her hand into her short cap of gray hair. She frowned at Jaci but her eyes looked sad. "I don't ever want to hear those words out of your mouth again."

Jaci quickly tried to recall what she'd said and couldn't pinpoint the source of her ire. "What words?"

"That you are stupid. I won't have it, do you understand?"

Jaci felt as if she was being sucked into a parallel universe where nothing made sense. Before she could speak, Priscilla held up her hand and shook her head. "You are not stupid, do you understand me?" Priscilla stated, her voice trembling with emotion. "You are more intelligent than the rest of us put together!"

No, she wasn't. "Mum—"

"None of us could have coped with what Clive put you through with the grace and dignity you did. We just shoved our heads in the sand and ignored him, hoping that he would go away. But you had to deal with him, with the press. The four of us deal with life by ignoring what makes us unhappy and we're selfish, horrible creatures."

"It's okay, Mum. *I'm* okay."

Jaci flicked a look at Merry, who appeared equally uncomfortable at their mother's statement. "It's not okay. It's not okay that you've spent your life believing that you are second-rate because you are not obsessive and selfish and driven and ambitious."

"But I'm not smart like you." Jaci stared at her intertwined fingers.

"No, but you're smart like you," Merry quietly said. "Instead of falling apart when Clive raked you, and your relationship, through the press, you picked yourself up, dusted yourself off and started something new. You pursued your dream and got a job and you started a new life, and that takes guts, kid. Mum's right. We ignore what we don't understand and bury ourselves, and our emotions, in our work."

Jaci let out a low, trembling laugh. "Let's not get too carried away. I'm a scriptwriter. It's not exactly *War and Peace.*"

"It's a craft," Priscilla insisted. "A craft that you seem to excel at, as I've recently realized. I'm sorry that you felt like you couldn't share that with us, that you thought that we wouldn't support you. God, I'm a terrible mother. I'm the failure, Jaci, not you. You are, by far, the best of us."

Merry reached out and squeezed her shoulder. "I'm sorry, too, Jace. I haven't exactly been there for you."

Jaci blinked away the tears in her eyes and swallowed the lump in her throat. What a weekend this had been, she thought; she'd fallen in love and she'd realized that she was a part of the Brookes-Lyon family—quite an important part, as it turned out. She was the normal one. The rest of her family were all slightly touched. Clever but a bit batty.

It was, she had to admit, a huge relief.

"And you are not stupid when it comes to men," Priscilla stated, her voice now strong and back to its normal no-nonsense tone. "Ryan is thick if he can't see how wonderful you are."

She wished she could tell them about Ben and Kelly's betrayal, but that was Ryan's story, not hers. Maybe they had made some progress last night, but how much? Jaci knew that Ryan wasn't the type to throw caution to the wind and tumble into a relationship with her; he might have told her the reasons for his wariness and reserve but he hadn't told her that he had any plans to change his mind about trusting, about loving someone new. She knew that he would still be the same guarded, restrained, unable-to-trust person he currently was, and she didn't know if she could live with that…long term. How did you prove yourself worthy of someone's trust, someone's love? And if she ignored these concerns and they fell back into bed, she'd be happy until the next time he emotionally, or physically, disappeared. And she would be hurt all over again. She could see the pattern evolving before her eyes, and she didn't want to play that game.

She wanted a relationship, she wanted love, she wanted forever.

Jaci gnawed at her bottom lip. "I don't know where I stand with him."

Priscilla sent her a steady look. "As much as I like Ryan, if you can't work that out, and if he won't tell you, then maybe it's time that you stopped standing and started walking."

Stop standing and start walking… Jaci felt the truth of her mum's words lodge in her soul. Would Ryan ever let her be, well, more? Was she willing to stand around waiting for him to make up his mind? Was she willing to try to prove herself worthy of his love? His trust?

But did she have the strength to let him go? She didn't think so. Maybe the solution was to give him a little time to get used to having someone in his life again. After all that he'd suffered, was that such a big ask? In a month— or two or three—she could reevaluate, see whether he'd made any progress in the trust department. That was fair, wasn't it?

Jaci had the niggling thought that she was conning herself, that she was delaying the inevitable, but when she heard the sound of a car pulling up outside she pushed out her doubts and jumped to her feet, a huge smile blossoming.

"He's here!" she squealed, running to the edge of the railing and leaning over to catch a glimpse of the car rolling up the drive. Her face fell when she recognized Clive's vintage Jaguar. She pouted. "Damn, it's Clive."

Merry caught Priscilla's eye. "Music to my ears," she said, sotto voce.

Priscilla smiled and nodded. "Mine, too."

Eleven

Ryan, parking his rental car in the driveway of Lyon House, felt as if he had a rope around his neck and barbed wire around his heart. He looked up at the ivy-covered, butter-colored stone house and wondered which window on the second floor was Jaci's bedroom. The one with frothy white curtains blowing in the breeze? It would have been, he thought, a lot easier if they'd spent the night having sex instead of talking. Sex, that physical connection, he knew how to deal with, but talking, exposing himself? Not so much.

If he wanted to snow himself, he supposed he could try to convince himself that he'd told her about Ben and Kelly's deception, their betrayal, as a quid pro quo for her telling him about her disastrous engagement to Horse-face. But he'd had many women bawl on his shoulder while they told him their woes and he'd never felt the need to return the favor.

Jaci, unfortunately, could not be lumped into the masses.

Ryan leaned his head against the headrest and closed his eyes. What a week. In his effort to treat her like a flash-in-the-pan affair, he'd kept his distance by putting the continent between them, but he'd just made himself miserable. He'd missed her. Intensely. His work and the drive and energy he gave it made his career his primary focus, but he'd had only half his brain on business this past week. Not clever when so much was at stake.

He had to make a decision about what to do with her, about her, soon. He knew that she wasn't the type to have a no-strings affair. Her entire nature was geared to being in a steady relationship, to being committed and cared for. She was paying lip service to the idea of a fling but sooner or later her feelings would run deeper... His might, too.

He'd put his feelings away four years ago, and he didn't like the fact that Jaci had the ability to make him feel more, be more, made him want to be the best version of himself, for her. She was becoming too important and if he was going to walk, if he was going to keep his life emotionally uncomplicated, then he had to walk away *now*. He couldn't sleep with her again because every time they had sex, every moment he had with her, with every word she spoke, she burrowed further under his skin. He had to act because his middle ground was fast disappearing.

Ryan picked up his wallet and mobile from the console and opened his door on a large sigh. It was so much easier to remain single, he thought. His life had been so uncomplicated before Jaci.

Boring, admittedly, but uncomplicated. Ryan turned to close the car door and saw Jaci's father turning the corner to walk up the steps. "Morning, Archie," he said, holding out his hand for Jaci's father to shake. "Have you seen Jaci?"

Archie, vague about anything that didn't concern his newspaper or world news, thought for a moment. "In her room, with the politician," he eventually said.

Blood roared through Ryan's head. "Say what?" he said, sounding as if he was being strangled. What the hell did that mean? Had Whips and Chains spent the night? With Jaci?

What the...

"Ryan!"

Ryan looked up as Jaci's slim figure walked out of the front door of Lyon House, her ex close on her heels. He had a duffel bag slung over his shoulder and his hand on Jaci's back, and he sent Ryan a look that screamed *Yeah, I did her and it was fantastic, dude*. Ryan clenched his fist as Jaci skipped down the stairs. He could watch her forever, he thought, as she approached him with a smile on her face that lit her from the inside out. God, she was beautiful, he thought. Funny, smart, dedicated. Confident, sexy and, finally, starting to realize who she was and her place in the world.

Clive greeted Archie as he walked back into the house, then he kissed Jaci's cheek, told her to give him a call and walked toward his car. Jaci stared at Clive's departing back for more time than Ryan was comfortable with and when she turned to look at him she was—damn, what was the word?—*glowing*. She looked—the realization felt like a fist slamming into his stomach—soft and radiant, the way she looked after they'd shared confidences, ex-

actly the way she looked after they made love. Her eyes
were a gooey brown, filled with emotion. He could read
hope there and possibilities and…love. He saw love.

Except that *they* hadn't made love. He hadn't made
love…

Jesus, no.

Maybe she *had* slept with Whips and Chains again,
Ryan thought, his mind accelerating to the red zone. It
was highly possible; three months ago she'd loved him,
was planning to marry him. Those feelings didn't just
disappear, evaporate. He was a politician and he probably talked her around and charmed her back into bed.
Had he read too much into whatever he and Jaci had?
Had it just been a sexual fling? Maybe, possibly…after
all, Jaci hadn't given him the slightest indication of her
desire to deepen this relationship, so was he rolling the
wrong credits? They'd slept together a couple of times.
For all he knew, she might just regard him as a way to
pass some time until her ex came to his senses.

Did Jaci still love Clive? The idea wasn't crazy; yeah,
the guy was a jerk-nugget, but love didn't just go away.
God, he still loved Ben despite the fact that he'd betrayed
him, and a part of him still loved Kelly, even after five
years and everything that happened.

But, God, it stung like acid to think of Jaci and Clive
in bed, that moron touching her perfect body, pulling her
back into his life. He'd shared a woman before and he
would *never* do it again. Ryan felt the bile rise up in his
throat and he ruthlessly choked it down. God, he couldn't
be sick, not now.

Feeling sideswiped, he looked down and noticed that
his mobile, set to silent, was ringing. He frowned at the
unfamiliar number on the screen. Thinking that taking

the call would give him some time to corral his crazy thoughts, he pushed the green button and lifted the phone to his ear.

"Jax? This is Jet Simons."

Ryan's frown deepened. Why would Simons, the slimiest tabloid writer around, be calling him and how the hell did he get his number? He considered disconnecting, blowing him off, but maybe there was a fire he needed to put out. "What the hell do you want? And how did you get my number?"

"I have my sources. So, I hear that you and Jaci Brookes-Lyon think that Leroy Banks is a slimy troll and that you two are pretending to be in a relationship to keep him sweet. What did you two call him, 'Toad of Toad Hall'?"

Ryan's eyes flew to Jaci's face. The harsh swear left his mouth, and only after it was out did he realize that it, in itself, was the confirmation Simons needed.

"No comment," he growled, wishing he could reach through the phone and wrap his hand around Simons's scrawny neck. Strangling Jaci was an option, too. She was the only person who used that expression. He sent her a dark look and she instinctively took a step back.

"So is that a yes?" Simons persisted.

"It's a 'no comment.' Who did you get that story from?" Ryan rested his fist against his forehead.

Simons laughed. "I had a trans-Atlantic call earlier. Tell Jaci that you can never trust a politician."

"Egglestone is your source?" Ryan demanded, and Simons's silence was enough of an answer.

Yep, it seemed that Jaci had shared quite a bit during their pillow talk. Ryan sent her another blistering look, deliberately ignoring her pleading, confused face. Ryan felt the hard, cold knot of despair and anger settle like a concrete brick in his stomach. He remembered this feeling. He'd lived with it for months, years after Ben and Kelly died. God, he wanted to punch something. Preferably Simons.

He was furiously angry and he needed to stay that way. This was why he didn't get involved in relationships; it was bad enough that his heart was in a mess and his love life was chaotic. Now it was affecting his business. Where had this gone so damn wrong?

He hated to ask Simons a damn thing, but he needed to know how much time he had before he took a trip up that creek without a paddle. "When are you running the story?"

"Can't," Simons said cheerfully. "Banks threatened to sue the hell out of my paper if we so much as mentioned his name and my editor killed it. That's why I feel nothing about giving up my source."

"You spoke to Banks?" Ryan demanded. He felt a scream starting to build inside him. This was it, this was the end. His business had been pushed backward and Jaci's career was all but blown out of the water.

"Yeah, he was…um, what's the word? *Livid*?" Ryan could hear the smile in his voice. The jackass was enjoying every second of this. "He told me to tell you to take your movie and shove it——"

"Got it." Ryan interrupted him. "So, basically, you just called me to screw with me?"

"Basically," Simons agreed.

Ryan told him to do something physically impossible and disconnected the call. He tossed his mobile through the open window of the car onto the passenger seat and linked his hands behind his neck.

"What's happened?" Jaci asked, obviously worried.

"That must have been a hell of a cozy conversation you had with Horse-face last night. It sounds like you covered a hell of a lot of ground."

Jaci frowned. "I don't understand."

"Your pillow talk torpedoed any chance of Banks funding *Blown Away*," he stated in his harshest voice.

Jaci looked puzzled. "What pillow talk? What are you talking about? Has Banks pulled his funding?" Jaci demanded, looking surprised.

"Your boyfriend called Simons and told him the whole story about how we snowed Banks, how we pretended to be a couple because he repulsed you. Nice job, kid. Thanks for that. The movie is dead and so is your career." He knew that he should shut up but he was so hurt, so angry, and he needed to hurt her, needed her to be in as much pain as he was. He just wished he was as angry at losing the funding as he was at the idea of Jaci sleeping with that slimy politician. Of losing Jaci to him.

Jaci just stood in the driveway and stared at him, her dark eyes filled with an emotion he couldn't identify. "Are you crazy?" she whispered.

"Crazy for thinking you could be trusted." Ryan tossed the statement over his shoulder as he yanked open the door to the car and climbed inside. "I should've run as hard and as fast as I could right after you kissed me. You've been nothing but a hassle. You've caused so much drama in my life I doubt I'll ever dig myself out of it. You know, you're right. You are the Brookes-Lyon screwup!"

Ryan watched as the poison-tipped words struck her soul, and he had to grab the steering wheel to keep from bailing out of the car and whisking her into his arms as she shrunk in on herself. He loved her, but he wanted to hurt her. He didn't understand it and he wasn't proud of it, but it was true. Because, unlike four years ago, this time he could fight back.

This time he could, verbally, punch and kick. He could retaliate and he wouldn't have to spend the rest of his life resenting the fact that death had robbed him of his chance to confront those who'd hurt him. He could hurt back and it felt—dammit—good!

"Why are you acting like this? Yes, I told Clive about Banks, about New York, but I never thought that he would blab to the press! I thought that we were friends again, that we had come to an understanding last night."

"Yet you still hopped into bed with that horse's ass."

"I did not sleep with Clive!" Jaci shouted.

Sure, you didn't, he mentally scoffed. Ryan started the engine of the car. He stared at the gearshift before jamming it into Reverse. He backed up quickly and pushed the button to take down the window of the passenger door. On the other side of the car stood Jaci, tears running down her face. He couldn't let her desperate, confused, emotional expression affect him. He wouldn't let anything affect him again…not when it came to her, or any other woman, either.

He didn't trust those tears, didn't trust her devastated expression. He didn't trust her. At all. "Thanks for screwing up my life, honey. I owe you one."

"Have you been fired?" Shona asked, perching her bottom on the corner of the desk Jaci was emptying.

It was Wednesday. Jaci'd been back in New York for two days and she'd sent Ryan two emails and left three voice mails asking him to talk to her and hadn't received a reply. Ryan, she concluded, was ignoring her.

She'd reached out five times and he'd ignored her five times. Yeah, she got the message.

"Resigned. I'm saving them the hassle of letting me go," Jaci said, tossing her thesaurus into her tote bag. "Without funding, *Blown Away* is dead in the water and I'm not needed."

Shona tapped her fingernails on her desk in a rat-a-tat-tat that set Jaci's teeth on edge. "I hear that Jax has been in meetings from daybreak to midnight trying to get other funding."

Jaci wasn't one to put any stock in office rumors. No, Ryan had moved on. It was that simple.

Thanks for screwing up my life, honey...

Moron man! How *dare* he think that she'd slept with Clive? Yes, she told Clive about Leroy, but only because a part of her wanted him to see that she was happy and content without him, that she had other men in her life and that she wasn't pining for him. But she'd forgotten that Clive hated to share and that he still, despite everything, considered her his. Under those genial smiles was a man who had still been hell-bent on punishing her; payback for the fact that she'd had the temerity to move on to Ryan from him. But while she knew that Clive could be petty, she'd never thought that he'd be so vengeful, so malicious as to call up a tabloid reporter and cause so much trouble for her and Ryan.

Oh, she was so mad. How dare Ryan have so little faith in her? How could he think that she would sleep with someone else, and just after they'd shared something so deep, as important as they had earlier that night? She might have a loose mouth and trust people too easily and believe that they were better than they were, but she wouldn't cheat. She'd been cheated on, so had he, and they both knew how awful it made the other person feel. How could he believe that she was capable of inflicting such pain?

She got it, she did. She understood how much it had to have hurt to be so betrayed by Ben and Kelly and she understood why he shied away from any feelings of intimacy. She understood his reluctance to trust her, but it still slayed her that Ryan didn't seem to know her at all. How could he believe that she would do that, that she would hurt him that way after everything they'd both experienced? Didn't he have the faintest inkling that she loved him? How could he be so blind?

"I'm so sorry, Jaci," Shona said and Jaci blinked at her friend's statement. She'd totally forgotten that she was there. "Are you going back to London?"

Jaci lifted her shoulders in a slow shrug. "I'm not sure."

"Sorry again." Shona squeezed her shoulder before walking back to her desk.

So was she, Jaci thought. But she couldn't make someone love her. Her feelings were her own and she couldn't project them onto Ryan. She could, maybe, forgive his verbal attack in the driveway of Lyon House, but by ignoring her he'd shown her that he regretted sharing his past with her, that he didn't trust her and, clearly, that he did not want to pursue a relationship with her. It hurt like open-heart surgery but she could deal with it, she *would* deal with it. She was never going to be the person who loved too much, who demanded too much, who gave too much, again.

When she loved again, *if* she ever loved again, it would be on her terms. She would never settle for anything less than amazing again. She wanted to be someone's sanctuary, her lover's soft place to fall. She wanted to be the keeper of his secrets and, harder, the person he confided his fears to. She wanted to be someone's everything.

Walking away from another relationship, from this situation that was rapidly turning toxic, wasn't an easy decision to make, but she knew that it was the right path. It didn't matter that it was hard, that she felt the brutal sting of loss and disappointment. She couldn't allow it to dictate her life. She was stronger and braver and more resilient than she'd ever been, and she wouldn't let this push her back into being that weak, insecure girl she'd been before.

It was time that she started protecting her heart, her feelings and her soul. It was time, as her mum had suggested, to stop standing and start walking.

Because he'd spent the past week chasing down old contacts and new leads, Ryan quickly realized that there was no money floating around to finance *Blown Away. We're in a recession, we don't have that much, it's too risky, credit is tight.* He'd heard the same excuses time and time again.

This was the end of the line. He was out of options.

Not quite true, he reluctantly admitted. He still had his father's offer to finance a movie, but he'd rather wash his face with acid than ask him. He could always come back to *Blown Away* in the future, but Jaci's career would take a hit…

Jaci… No, he wasn't going to think about her at all. It was over and she had—according to the very brief letter she'd left with his PA—released him from her contract.

She was out of his life, and that was good. But his mind kept playing the last scenes of their movie in his head. Instead of fighting the memory, as he had been doing, instead of pushing it aside, he let it run. It wasn't as if he was doing any work, and maybe if he just remembered, properly, the events of that night, he'd be able to move *on*. He *had* to get his life back to normal.

He remembered the wedding, how amazing Jaci looked in that pale pink cocktail dress with the straps that crisscrossed her back. Her eyes looked deep and mysterious and her lips had been painted a color that matched her dress. He'd kept his eyes on her all night, had followed her progress across the tented room, watched her talk to friends and acquaintances, noticed how she refused the many offers to dance. After the meal, the horse's ass had approached her and she'd looked wary and distant. They'd talked and talked and Clive kept moving closer and Jaci kept putting distance between them.

Ryan frowned. She *had* done that. He wasn't imagining that. Clive had eventually left her, looking less than happy. Then he'd joined her at that table and they'd chatted and the pinched look left her eyes. Her attention had been on him, all on him; her eyes softened when they looked at *him*. Her entire attention had been focused on him; she hadn't looked around. Clive had been forgotten when they were together.

She'd been that into me...

So how had she gone from being so into him to jumping into bed with Whips? *Did she? Are you so sure that she did?* Ryan picked up his pen and tapped it against his desk. He had no proof that Jaci had slept with Clive, just his notoriously unreliable gut instinct. And his intuition was clouded by jealously and past insecurities about being cheated on...

He wished he could talk to someone who would tell him the unvarnished, dirty truth.

Jaci's ball-breaker sister would do that. Merry had never pulled her punches. Ryan picked up his mobile and within a minute Meredith's cut-glass tones swirled around his office. "Are you there, you ridiculous excuse for a human being?"

Whoa! Someone sounded very irritated with him. That was okay because he was still massively irritated with her sister. "Did she sleep with Whips and Chains?" he demanded.

"We video chatted last night and she looked like death warmed up. I have never seen her so unhappy, so…so… so heartbroken. She cries herself to sleep every night, Ryan, did you know that?"

Ryan's heart lurched. "Did. She. Sleep. With. Him?"

There was a long, intense silence on the other end of the phone and Ryan pulled the receiver away, looked at it and spoke into it again. "Are you there?"

"Oh, dear Lord in heaven," Merry stated on a long sigh. Her voice lost about 50 percent of its tartness when she spoke again. "Ryan Jackson, why would you think that Jaci slept with Clive?"

"That morning she looked…" Ryan felt as if his head was about to explode. "… God, I don't know. She… glowed. She looked like something wonderful had happened. Your dad told me that they were in her bedroom so I presumed that they'd…reconciled."

"You are an idiot of magnificent proportions," Merry told him, exasperated. "Now, listen to me, birdbrain. Clive came to pick up some stuff of his she was storing at Lyon House. That's the only reason he was there. Yes, she told him about New York, how happy she was there.

Because she's a girl and she has her pride, she wanted Clive to know how happy and successful she was, how much she didn't need him. She told Clive about Banks, and you, because she wanted to show him that there were other men out there, rich, powerful and successful men, who wanted and desired her. She wanted him to know that she didn't need him anymore because she was now a better version of who she used to be with him."

Ryan struggled to keep up. "She told you all that?"

"Yeah. She's proud of who she is now, Ryan, proud of the fact that she picked herself up and dusted herself off. Sure, she should never have told Clive what she did but she never thought that he would talk to the press… I would've suspected him but she's not cynical like me. Or you."

"I'm not cynical," Ryan objected but he knew that he was. Of course he was.

Merry snorted. "Sure, you are. You thought Jaci slept with her ex because she looked *happy*. Anyway, Jaci blames herself for you losing the funding. She blames herself for all of it. Her dream is gone, Ryan."

He'd made a point of not thinking about that because if he did, it hurt too damn much. He rubbed his eyes with his index finger and thumb. "I know."

"But worse than that, she's shattered that you could think that she slept with Clive, that she would cheat on you. She feels annihilated because she never believed that you could think that of her."

Ryan rested his elbow on his desk and pushed the ball of his hand into his temple. He felt as if the floor had fallen out from under his feet. "Oh." It was the only word he could articulate at the moment.

"Fix this, Jackson," Merry stated in a low voice that was superscary. "Or I swear I'll hurt you."

He could do that, Ryan thought, sucking in air. He could…he could fix this. He *had* to fix this. Because Jaci had been hurt and no one, especially not him, was allowed to do that.

The fact that Merry would—actually—hurt him was just an added incentive.

There was only one person in the world whom he would do this for, Ryan thought, as the front door to Chad's house opened and his father stood in the doorway with an openly surprised look on his face.

Ryan held his father's eyes and fought the urge to leave. He reminded himself that this was for Jaci, this was to get her the big break that she so richly deserved. Shelving *Blown Away* meant postponing Jaci's dream. He couldn't do that to her. Once the world and, more important, other producers saw the quality of her writing, she'd have more work than she could cope with and she'd be in demand, and maybe then they could find a way to be together. Because, God, he missed her.

He loved her, he needed her, and there was no way that he could return to her—to beg her to take him back—without doing everything and anything he could to resurrect her dream. She'd probably tell him to go to hell, and he suspected that he had as much chance of getting her back as he did of having sex with a zombie princess, but he had to try. Writing made her happy and, above all, he wanted her happy.

With or without him.

"Are you going to stand there and stare at me or are

you going to come in?" Chad asked, that famous smile hovering around his lips.

Yeah, he supposed he should. Bombshells shouldn't be dropped on front porches, especially a porch as magnificent as this one. Ryan walked inside the hall and looked around; nothing much had changed since the last time he was here. What was different, and a massive surprise, was the large framed photograph of Ben and himself, arms draped around each other's shoulders, wearing identical grins, that stood on a hall table. Well...huh.

"Do you want to talk in the study or by the pool?" Chad asked.

Ryan pushed his hand through his hair. "Study, I guess." He followed his father down the long hallway of the sun-filled home, catching glances of the magnificent views of the California coastline through the open doors of the rooms they passed. He might not love his father, but he'd always loved this house.

Chad opened the door to the study and gestured Ryan to a chair. "Do you want a cup of coffee?"

Ryan could see that Chad expected him to refuse but he was exhausted, punch-drunk from not sleeping for too many nights. He needed caffeine so he quickly accepted. Chad called his housekeeper on the intercom, asked for coffee and sat down in a big chair across the desk from him. "So, what's this about, Ryan? Or should I call you Jax?"

"Ryan will do." Ryan pulled out a sheaf of papers from his briefcase and slapped them on the table. "According to the emails you've sent me in the past, you are part of a group prepared to invest in my films. I'd like to know whether you, and your consortium, would like to invest in *Blown Away*."

Chad looked at him for a long time before slowly nodding. "Yes," he eventually stated, quietly and without any fanfare.

"I need a hundred million."

"You could have more if you need it."

"That'll do." Ryan felt the pure, clean feeling of relief flood through him, and he slumped back in his chair, suddenly feeling energized. It had been a lot easier than he expected, he thought. He was prepared to grovel, to beg if he needed to. Asking his father for the money had stung a lot less than he expected it to. Because Jaci, and her happiness, was a lot more important to him than his pride.

It was that simple.

"That's it? Just like that?" Ryan thought he should make sure that his father didn't have anything up his sleeve, a trick that could come back and bite him on the ass.

Chad linked his hands across his flat stomach and shrugged. "An explanation would be nice but it's not a deal breaker. I know that you'd rather swallow nails than ask me for help, so it has to be a hell of a story."

Ryan jumped to his feet and walked over to the open door that led onto a small balcony and sucked in the fragrant air. He rested his shoulder against the doorjamb and looked at his father. In a few words he explained about Banks and Jaci's part in the fiasco. "But, at the end of the day, it was my fault. Who risks a hundred million dollars by having a pretend relationship with a woman?"

"Someone who desperately wanted a relationship but who was too damn scared to admit it and used any excuse he could to have one anyway?"

Bull's-eye, Father. Bull's-eye. He had been scared and stupid. But mostly scared. Scared of falling in love, of trusting someone, terrified of being happy. Then scared of being miserable. But hey, he was miserable anyway, and wasn't that a kick in the pants?

"As glad as I am that you've asked me to help, I would've thought that you'd rather take a hit on the movie than come to me," Chad commented, and Ryan, from habit, looked for the criticism in his words but found none. Huh. He was just sitting there, head cocked, offering his help and not looking for a fight. What had happened to his father?

"Why are you being so nice about this?" he demanded. "This isn't like you."

Chad flushed. With embarrassment? That was also new. "It isn't like the person I used to be. Losing Ben made me take a long, hard look at myself, and I didn't like what I saw. Since then I've been trying to talk to you to make amends."

Now, that was pushing the feasibility envelope. "And you did that by demanding ten million for narrating the documentary about Ben's life?" He shot the words out and was glad that his voice sounded harsh. Anger he could deal with, since he was used to fighting with his father.

Chad didn't retaliate and he remained calm. A knock on the door broke the tension and he turned to see Chad's housekeeper in the doorway, carrying a tray holding a carafe and mugs. She placed it on his desk, smiled when Chad politely thanked her and left the room. Chad, ignoring Ryan's outburst, poured him a cup and brought it over to him.

Ryan took the mug and immediately lifted the cup to his lips, enjoying the rich taste. He needed to get out of this room, needed to get back to business. He gestured to the contract. "There's the deal. Get it to your lawyers but tell them that they need to get cracking. I don't have a lot of time."

"All right." Chad nodded. "Let's go back a step and talk about that demand I made for payment for narrating that movie."

"We don't have to… What's done is done."

"It really isn't," Chad replied. His next question was one Ryan didn't expect. "Did you want to do that documentary? I know that Ben's friends were asking you to, that you were expected to."

God, how was he supposed to answer that? If he said yes, he'd be lying—the last thing he'd wanted at the time was to do a movie about his brother, who died on his way back from a dirty weekend with his fiancée—and if he said no then Chad would want an explanation as to why not. "I don't want to talk about this."

"Tough. I think it's time that you understood that I made that demand so that you couldn't do the movie… to give you an out."

Ryan frowned, disconcerted. Chad jammed his hands into the pockets of his shorts and looked Ryan in the eye. "I knew that Ben was fooling around with Kelly and I told him to stop. It wasn't appropriate and I didn't approve. You didn't deserve that amount of disloyalty, especially not from Ben."

Chad's words were like a fist to his stomach, and he couldn't get enough air to his brain to make sense of his statements. "What?"

"Ben told me that they were just scratching an itch and I told him to scratch it with someone else. He promised me that that weekend would be the last time, that they'd call it off when they got back. I wanted to warn you about marrying her but I knew that you wouldn't have listened to me."

"I wouldn't have," Ryan agreed. He and Chad had been at odds long before the accident.

Chad dropped his eyes. "My fault. I was a useless father and terrible role model. I played with women and didn't take them seriously. Ben followed my example." He walked back to his desk, poured coffee into his own cup and sipped. "Anyway, to come back to the documentary… I knew that asking you to make that film would've been cruel so I made damn sure that the project got scuttled."

Ryan wished he could clear the cobwebs from his head. "By asking for that ridiculous fee."

"Yeah. I knew that you didn't have the cash, that you wouldn't borrow the money to do it and that you wouldn't ask anyone else to narrate it." Chad shrugged. "That being said, I still have the script and if you ever want to take on the project, I'll narrate it, for free."

Ryan slid down the door frame to sink to his haunches. "God." He looked up. "I came to ask you for a hundred million and I end up feeling totally floored."

Chad rubbed the back of his neck. "Neither you nor your mother deserved any of the pain I put you through. I've been trying to find a way to say I'm sorry for years." His jaw set and he looked like the stubborn, selfish man whom Ryan was used to. "And if I have to spend a hundred million to do it then I will." He grabbed the stack of papers, flipped to the end page and reached for a pen. Ryan watched, astounded, as he dashed his signature across the page.

"Don't you have to talk to your partners?" Ryan asked.

"I'm the only investor," Chad said, quickly initialing the pages.

Well, okay, then. "Don't you think your lawyers should read the contract or, at the very least, that you should?" Ryan asked as he stood up, now feeling slightly bemused. He was still trying to work through the fact that his father had been trying to protect him from further hurt, that Chad seemed to want a relationship with him, that it seemed as if his father had, to some measure, changed.

"No, no lawyers. We'll settle this now and before you leave town I'll do a direct deposit into your account for half of the cash. I'll need some time to get you the other half. A week, maybe. Besides, if you take me for a hundred million then it's no less than what I deserve for being the worst father in the world."

Ryan picked his jaw up from the floor. "Chad, hell… I don't know what to say."

"Say that you'll consider me for a part in the movie… any part," Chad retorted, as quick as lightning.

Ryan had to laugh and felt strangely relieved knowing that his father hadn't undergone a total personality change.

"I'll consider it."

Chad lifted his head and flashed him a smile. "That's my boy."

Twelve

In all honesty, Jaci was proud of her heart. It had been kicked, battered, punched, stabbed and pretty much broken but it still worked…sort of, kind of. It still pumped blood around her body but, on the downside, it still craved Ryan, missed him with every beat.

This was the height of folly because his silence over the past ten days had just reinforced her belief that he'd been playing with her, possibly playing her. If he felt anything for her, apart from sex, he would've contacted her long before this, but he hadn't and that was that.

Ryan aside, she had other problems to deal with. Her career as a screenwriter was on the skids and there was absolutely nothing she could do about that. Before she'd left Starfish the office rumors had been flying, and even if she took only 5 percent of what was being said as truth, then she knew that there was more chance of the world ending this month than there was of *Blown Away* reaching the moviegoing public. And with that went her big break, her career as a screenwriter. She would have to start again with another script and see if her agent could get lucky a second time around. She wasn't holding her breath…

Being the scriptwriter for a blockbuster like *Blown Away*—and it would have been a blockbuster, of that she had no doubt—would have got her noticed and she would have been on her way to the success that she'd always craved.

She didn't crave it so much anymore. Since her conversation with her mother and Merry on the terrace at Lyon House, the desire to prove herself to her family, to herself, had dissipated. She knew that she was a good writer, and if it took another ten years for her to sell a script, she'd keep writing because this was what she was meant to do. This was what made her happy, and writing scripts was what she was determined to stick with. She'd keep on truckin' and one day, someday, her script would see the big screen.

It was wonderfully liberating to be free of that choking need to prove herself… She was Jaci and she was enough. And if that stupid, moron man couldn't see that, then he was a stupid moron man.

And who was leaning on her doorbell at eleven thirty at night? What was so important that it couldn't wait until morning?

Jaci hauled herself to her feet and walked to her door. When she pressed the intercom button and asked who was there, there was silence. Yay, now she had a creepoid pressing random doorbells. Well, they could carry on. She was going to bed, where she was determined to not think about stupid men in general and a moronic man in particular.

A hard rap had her spinning around, and she glared at her door. Frowning, she walked back to the door and looked through the peephole and gasped when she saw Ryan's distorted face on the other side. Now he wanted to talk to her? Late at night when she was just dressed in a rugby jersey of Neil's that she'd liberated a decade ago, fuzzy socks and crazy hair? Was he insane?

"Let me in, Jace."

At the sound of his voice, her traitorous heart did a long, slow, happy slide from one side of her rib cage to the other. Stupid thing. "No."

"Come on, Jaci, we need to talk." Ryan's voice floated under the door.

Jaci, forgetting that she looked like an extra in a vampire movie, jerked the door open and slapped her hands on her hips. She shot him a look that was hot and frustrated. "Go away. Go far, far away!"

Ryan pushed her back into her apartment, shut the door behind him and shrugged out of his leather jacket. Despite her anger, and her disappointment, Jaci noticed that Ryan looked exhausted. He had twin blue-black stripes under his eyes and he looked pale. So their time apart hadn't been easy on him, either, she realized, and she was human enough to feel a tiny bit vindicated about that. But she also wanted to pull him into her arms, to soothe away his pain.

She loved him, and always would. Dammit.

Jaci slapped her hands across her chest. "What do you want, Ryan?"

Ryan shoved his hands into the front pockets of his

jeans and rocked on his heels. "I came to tell you that I've secured another source of funding for *Blown Away*."

Really? Oh, goodie! Jaci realized that he couldn't hear her sarcastic thoughts, so she glared at him again. "*That's* why you're here?"

Ryan looked confused. "Well, yeah. I thought you'd be pleased."

Jaci brushed past him, yanked her door open and waved her arm to get him to walk out. When he didn't, she pushed the words through her gritted teeth. "Get out."

"The funding isn't from Banks, it's from…" he hesitated for a moment before shaking his head. "…someone else."

"I don't care if it's from the goblins under the nearest bridge."

"Jaci, what the hell? This is your big break. This is what you wanted." Ryan looked utterly confused and more than a little irate. "I've been busting my ass to sort this out, and this is your response?"

"Did I ask you to?" Jaci demanded. "Did I ask you to roar off, ignore me for days, refuse to take my calls and keep me in the dark?"

"Look, maybe I should've called—"

"Maybe?" Jaci kicked the door shut with her foot and slapped her hands on his chest, attempting and failing to push him back. "Damn right you should've called! You don't get to fall in and out of my life. I'm not a doll you can pick up and discard on a whim."

"No, you're just an enormous pain in my ass." Ryan captured her wrists with one hand and gripped her hip with his other hand, pulling her into his rock-hard erection. "You drive me mad, you're on my mind first thing in the morning and last thing at night and, annoyingly, pretty much any minute in between." He dropped his mouth onto hers and slid his tongue between her lips. Jaci felt her joints melt and tried not to sink into him. He was like the worst street drug she could imagine—one hit and she was addicted all over again.

She felt Ryan's hands slide up her waist to cover her breasts and she shuddered. One more time, one more memory. She needed it and she needed him.

One more time and then she'd kick him out. Of her apartment and her life.

"There you are," Ryan murmured against her mouth. "I needed you back in my arms."

He needed *her*? Back in his arms? Oh, God, he wasn't back because he loved her or missed her. He was back because he loved the sex and he missed it. Stiffening, she pulled her mouth from his and narrowed her eyes. "Back off," she muttered.

Ryan lifted his hands and took a half step away. He ran a hand around the back of his neck and blew air into his cheeks. "Jace, I—"

Jaci shook her head and pushed past him, thinking that she needed some distance, just a moment to get her heart and head under control. She walked into the bathroom and gripped the edge of the sink, telling herself that she had to resist temptation because she couldn't kid herself anymore; Ryan wanted to have sex and she wanted to make love. Settling for less than she wanted wasn't an option anymore. She didn't want to settle for a bouquet of flowers when she needed the whole damn florist. Jaci placed her elbows on the bathroom counter and stared at her pale reflection in the mirror.

She needed more and she had to tell him. It was that simple. And that hard. She'd tell him that she loved him and he'd walk, because he wasn't interested in anything that even hinted at permanence.

Her expiration date was up.

"You can do this, you are stronger than you think." Jaci whispered the words to herself.

"You can do what?"

Jaci stood up and slowly turned around to Ryan standing in the entrance to the bathroom, holding the top rim of the door. He looked hot and sexy and rumpled. Still tired, she thought, but so damn confident. God, she needed every bit of willpower she possessed to walk away from him, but if she didn't do it now she never would.

Jaci pulled in a deep breath. "I'm walking away... from you, from this."

Ryan tipped his head to the side and Jaci saw the corners of his mouth twitch in amusement. Ooh, that look made her want to smack him silly.

"No," he calmly stated. He dropped his hands and crossed his arms over that ocean of a chest and spread his legs, effectively blocking her path out of the bathroom.

That just made her mad. "What do you mean *no*? I am going to leave New York and I am definitely leaving you."

"No, you are not leaving New York and you are definitely not leaving me."

Jaci leaned back against the counter and thought that it was ridiculous that they were having this conversation in the bathroom. "I refuse to be your part-time plaything."

"You're not my plaything and, judging by the space you take up in my head, you're not a part-time anything."

"You run, Ryan. Every time I need you to talk to me, you run," Jaci cried.

To her surprise, he nodded his agreement. "Because you scare me. You scare the crap out of me."

"Why?" Jaci wailed, not understanding any of it.

Ryan lifted one powerful shoulder in a long shrug. "Because I'm in love with you."

No, he wasn't. He *couldn't* be. "You're not in love with me," Jaci told him, her voice shaky. "People in love don't act like you did. They don't accuse people of having affairs. They don't try to hurt the people they love!"

Horror chased pain and regret across his face. "Sorry. God, I'm so sorry that I hurt you," Ryan said in a strangled voice. "I'd just heard that you discussed us with that horse's butt and you looked all dewy, and soft, and in love. I thought that you'd gone back to him."

"Why did you think that?"

"Because it's the way you look after I make love to you!" Ryan shouted, his chest heaving. "I was jealous and scared and I didn't want to be in love with you, to expose myself to being hurt. You loved him three months ago, Jaci."

"That was before I learned that he liked S&M and that he cheated on me. It was before I grew stronger, bolder. It was before I met you. How could you think that, Ryan? How could you believe that I would hurt you like that?"

"Because I'm scared to love you, to be with you." Ryan's jaw was rock hard and his eyes were bleak. When he spoke again, his words sounded as if he was chipping them from a mound of granite. "Because all the people who I loved have let me down in some way or the other. I love you, and why would life treat me any different now?" He shrugged and he swallowed, emotion making his Adam's apple bounce in his strong throat. "But I'm willing to take the chance. You're that important."

No, he wasn't, and he couldn't be in love with her. It sounded far too good to be true.

"You don't love me," Jaci insisted, her voice shaky.

Yet she could hear, and she was sure he could, too, the note of hope in her voice.

"Yeah, I do. I am so in love with you. I didn't want to be, didn't think I ever would fall in love again, but I have. With you." He didn't touch her, he didn't try to persuade her with his body because his eyes, his fabulous eyes, radiated the truth of that statement. He loved her? Good grief. Jaci gripped the counter with her hands in an effort to keep from hurtling herself into his arms.

"But you run, every time. Every time we get close, you bolt."

"And that's something I will try to stop doing," Ryan told her, a smile starting to flirt with his eyes and mouth. He held out his broad hand to her and waited until she placed hers in it. Jaci sighed at the warmth of his fingers curling around hers. She stared down at their intertwined hands and wondered if she was dreaming. But if she was, surely she would've chosen a more romantic setting for this crazy conversation? It was a tiny bathroom in a tiny apartment... It didn't matter, she'd take it. She'd take him.

Ryan's finger under her chin lifted her face up and she gasped at the love she saw in his eyes. No, this was too good to be a dream. "I really don't want to carry on this conversation in the bathroom, but you're not getting out of here before I hear what I need to."

Jaci grinned and picked up her spare hand and ran her finger over his collarbone, down his chest, across those ridges in his abdomen, stopping very low down. "What do you want to hear? That I love your body? I do," she teased and saw his eyes darken with passion.

Ryan gripped her finger to stop it going lower. "You know what I want to hear, Jace. Tell me."

When Jaci saw the emotion in his eyes, all thoughts

of teasing him evaporated. He looked unsure and a little scared. As if he was expecting her to reject him, to reject them. Her heart, bottom lip and hands trembled from excitement, from love…

"Ryan, of course I love you. I have for a while."

Ryan rested his forehead on hers and she could feel the tension leaving his body. "Thank God."

"How could you not know that?" Jaci linked her arms around his neck and placed her face against his strong chest. "Honestly, for a smart man you can be such an idiot on occasion."

"Apparently so," Ryan agreed, his arms holding her tightly. He pulled his head back to smile at her, relief and passion and, yes, love dancing in his eyes. "Come back to bed, darling, and let me show you how much I love and adore you."

"You've just missed sex," Jaci teased him on a happy laugh.

Ryan pushed her bangs off her forehead and rubbed the pad of his thumb across her delicately arched brow. "No, sweetheart, I've just missed you." He grinned. "But hey, I'm a guy, and if you're offering…"

Jaci launched herself upward and he caught her as she wrapped her legs around his waist. "Anywhere, anyhow, anytime."

Ryan kissed her open mouth, and Jaci's body sighed and shivered in anticipation. "Can I add that to your contract?" he asked as he backed out of the bathroom into the bedroom.

Lover, friend, boss…there wasn't much she wouldn't do for him, Jaci thought as he lowered her onto the bed and covered her body with his.

Anything. Anywhere. Anytime.

* * *

Much, much later Ryan was back in his jeans and Jaci was wearing his button-down shirt and they were sitting cross-legged on her bed, digging chocolate chip ice cream from the container she'd abandoned earlier.

What an evening, Jaci thought, casting her mind back over the past few hours. She felt as if she'd ridden a crazy roller coaster of emotion, stomach churning, heart thumping adrenaline, and she'd come out the other side thrilled. Happy. Content. Dopey. Oh, they still had a lot to talk about, but they'd be fine.

Had he really said that he'd secured funding for *Blown Away*? Her spoon stopped halfway to her mouth and she didn't realize that ice cream was rolling off the utensil and dropping to her knee. "Did I hear you say that you have funding for *Blown Away*?"

Ryan leaned forward, maneuvered the spoon in her hand to his mouth and ran his thumb over the ice cream on her knee, licking his digit afterward. "Uh-huh."

"Do I have to pretend to be your girlfriend or your wife this time?" Jaci teased.

"No pretending needed this time," Ryan said, peering into the empty container. "Is that it? Damn! I'm still starving. Don't you have any real food in this house?"

"No, I was on the I-hate-men diet. Ice cream and wine only." Jaci tossed her spoon into the container and placed her elbows on her knees. "Who is your investor, Ry? Did you make nice with Banks?"

"Hell no! However, I did meet with him. I felt I owed him that."

"And?"

"He ripped into me, which I expected. Afterwards

he offered me half of the money, told me that he wanted you off the project and that he wanted creative control."

"And you said no. You'd never give him control."

Ryan sent another longing look at the empty ice cream container. "That was part of it but not having you as part of the project was the deal breaker. I need real food."

He was trying to change the subject, Jaci realized. *No chance, buddy.* "Ok, so who is this new investor that you found so quickly?"

Ryan stretched his legs out and placed them on each side of her hips. He leaned forward and dropped his head to nibble on her exposed collarbone. Jaci frowned, pushed his head away and leaned back so that she could see his face. "Stop trying to distract me, Jackson, and keep talking to me."

Ryan twisted his lips and tipped his face up so that he was looking at the ceiling. Okay, it didn't take a rocket scientist to realize that he didn't want to talk about this, but the sooner he learned that she was the one person he could talk to, the easier the process would get.

"Chad Bradshaw," he reluctantly admitted.

Jaci gasped. "What? Chad? Your father?"

"You know any other Chad Bradshaw?" Ryan muttered.

Jaci rubbed her forehead with the tips of her fingers. "Wait, hold on a second, let me catch up. Your father, the father you don't talk to, is financing your movie?"

"Yep."

Oh, right, so she was going to have to drag this out of him. Well, she would, if she had to. "Ryan, we're in a relationship, right?"

Ryan smiled and it warmed every strand of DNA in her body. "Damn straight," he replied.

"Okay, then, well, that means that we get to have spectacular sex—" Jaci glanced at her messy bed and nodded "—check that—and that we talk to each other. So talk. Now."

"I went to go see him," Ryan eventually admitted in a low voice. "I needed the money, I knew that he wanted to invest in one of my projects, so I made it happen."

That didn't explain a damn thing. "But why? You told me that if Banks bailed, you would mothball *Blown Away.*"

Ryan squeezed her hips with the insides of his calves. "My and Thom's careers would withstand the hit, but yours wouldn't."

It took a minute for her to make sense of those words, and when she did, she tumbled a little deeper and a little further into love. She hadn't thought it possible, but this was just another surprise in a night full of them. "But you hate your father."

"Well, *hate* is a strong word." He pulled his long legs up and rested his elbows on his knees. "Look, Jace, the reality is that your career is on a knife's edge. Your script is stunning but if nobody sees your work, it could be months, years before you get another shot at the big leagues. I don't want you to have to wait years for another chance, so I made it happen."

Jaci placed her hands on his strong forearms and rested her forehead on her wrists. "Oh, Ryan, you do love me."

His fingers tunneled into her hair. "Yep. An amazing amount, actually."

Jaci's heart sighed. She lifted her head and pulled back. "Did he make you grovel?"

Ryan shook his head. "He was…pretty damn cool, actually." Ryan took a deep breath and Jaci listened intently

as he explained how Chad had known about Ben's affair
with Kelly and how Chad had clumsily, Jaci thought, tried
to protect Ryan. It was so Hollywood, so messed up, but
sweet nonetheless.

"Chad tried to explain that they, Ben and Kelly and
Chad himself, looked at affairs differently than I did.
That to them sex was just sex, an itch to scratch, I think
he said. That they didn't mean to hurt me."

"It shouldn't have mattered how they felt about sex.
They knew how you felt and they should've taken that
into account," Jaci said, her voice hot. She looked at
Ryan's bemused face and reined her temper in. "Sorry,
sorry, it just makes me so angry when excuses are made."

"I've never had anyone defend me before."

"Well, just so you know, I'll always be in your corner,
fists up and prepared to fight for you," Jaci told him, ignoring the sheen of emotion in his eyes. Her big, tough
warrior-like man…emotional? He'd hate her to comment
on it so she moved the conversation along briskly. "What
else did Chad have to say?"

"That he would narrate the documentary on Ben if I
ever chose to do it. For free this time. But I don't know
if I can make that film."

"You'll know when you're ready."

Ryan's hand gripped her thigh. "It's not because I care
about their affair or care about her anymore, Jace. You
understand that, don't you? It feels like another life, another time, and I'm ready to move on, with you. It's just
that he was…"

"Your hero. Your brother, your best friend." Jaci
touched his cheek with her fingertips. "Honey, there is
no rule that you have to make a movie on him. Maybe

you should remember him like you'd like to remember him and let everyone else do the same."

Ryan placed his hand on top of hers and held it to his cheek. He closed his eyes and Jaci looked at him, her masculine, strong, flawed man. God, she loved him. She saw his Adam's apple bob and knew that he was fighting to keep his emotions from bubbling up and over.

"Don't, Ry, don't hide what you're feeling from me," she told him, her voice low. "I know talking about Ben hurts. I'm sorry."

Ryan jerked his head up and his eyes blazed with heat, and hope, and love. "I'm not thinking about him. I'm thinking about you and us and this bright new life we have in front of us. I'm so damn happy, Jace. You make me."

Jaci cocked her head. "You make me…what?"

"That's all. You just make me."

Jaci sighed as he kissed the center of her palm and placed her hand on his heart. "I never realized how alone I was until you hurtled into my life. You've put color into my world, and I promise I'll make you happy, Jace."

Jaci blinked away her happy tears. "For how long?" she whispered.

Ryan pushed her long bangs out of her eyes and tucked them behind her ear. "Forever…if you'll let me."

Jaci leaned in for a kiss and smiled against his mouth. "Oh, Ry, I think we can do better than that. Amazing love stories last longer than that."

* * * * *

MILLS & BOON®

Desire™

PASSIONATE AND DRAMATIC LOVE STORIES

A sneak peek at next month's titles...

In stores from 18th December 2015:

- **Twin Heirs to His Throne** – Olivia Gates *and*
  Nanny Makes Three – Cat Schield

- **A Baby for the Boss** – Maureen Child *and*
  Pregnant by the Rival CEO – Karen Booth

- **That Night with the Rich Rancher** – Sara Orwig *and*
  Trapped with the Tycoon – Jules Bennett

Available at WHSmith, Tesco, Asda, Eason, Amazon and Apple

Just can't wait?
Buy our books online a month before they hit the shops!
visit www.millsandboon.co.uk

These books are also available in eBook format!

MILLS & BOON®

**If you enjoyed this story,
you'll love the the full *Revenge Collection*!**

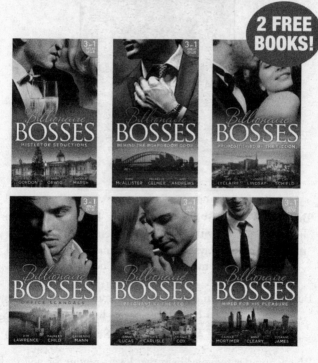

Don't miss Sarah Morgan's next Puffin Island story

Brittany Forrest has stayed away from Puffin Island since her relationship with Zach Flynn went bad. They were married for ten days and only just managed not to kill each other by the end of the honeymoon.

But, when a broken arm means she must return, Brittany moves back to her Puffin Island home. Only to discover that Zach is there as well.

Will a summer together help two lovers reunite or will their stormy relationship crash on to the rocks of Puffin Island?

'High drama and lots of laughs'
—*Fabulous* magazine

Fed up with disastrous internet dates and
conflicting advice from her friends, Ellie Rigby
decides to take matters into her own hands.
Instead of looking for a man for herself, she's
going to start a dating agency where she can
use her extensive experience in finding
Mr Wrong to help others find their Mr Right.

Well, that is until a match with one of her clients,
charming, infuriating Nick, has her questioning
everything she's ever thought about love…

MILLS & BOON®

Why shop at millsandboon.co.uk?

Each year, thousands of romance readers find their perfect read at millsandboon.co.uk. That's because we're passionate about bringing you the very best romantic fiction. Here are some of the advantages of shopping at www.millsandboon.co.uk:

* **Get new books first**—you'll be able to buy your favourite books one month before they hit the shops

* **Get exclusive discounts**—you'll also be able to buy our specially created monthly collections, with up to 50% off the RRP

* **Find your favourite authors**—latest news, interviews and new releases for all your favourite authors and series on our website, plus ideas for what to try next

* **Join in**—once you've bought your favourite books, don't forget to register with us to rate, review and join in the discussions

Visit **www.millsandboon.co.uk**
for all this and more today!